A Lotus in the Dark

Katie Masterman

A LOTUS IN THE DARK

"Like a lotus flower, we too have the ability to rise from the mud, bloom out of the darkness and radiate into the world." – Thich Nhat Hahn

KATIE MASTERMAN

Copyright © 2024, Katie Masterman. All rights reserved.
No portion of this book may be reproduced in any form
without permission from the publisher. KDP Publishing.
ISBN: 9798807344274

To Lily and Harry, forever my light in the dark.
And to Jules, always.

Acknowledgements

First and foremost, I of course would like to thank you for taking the time to read this. The fact that even one person has read my book does not feel real, but is a dream come true. Writing this book has been harder than expected, the biggest hurdle for me to overcome being the fact that I am a reader myself. Every time I finish a book I stop my own writing, because how could I ever write a book as good as others, as good as the likes of Sara J Maas, Jennifer Armentrout, Rebecca Yarros. I decided I could not physically finish this book until I stopped worrying about what other people would think. Will they cringe at my writing, what if they don't like my book, what if the genre isn't what they enjoy? Instead, I wrote this book for myself. I wrote a book inspired by the books I enjoy reading myself, and most importantly, I have loved every moment of writing this book, and if others enjoy it, that is one hell of a bonus.

To my partner Jules, thank you for supporting me through every step of the way, thank you for reading my books and keeping my bookshelves full, and thank you for keeping the kids thoroughly (albeit noisily) entertained while I write. I could not have done this without you by my side and it is because of you I am able to push myself to do these things, you make me the strongest version of myself. To Lily and Harry, the reason I strive to better myself every day, thank you for never failing to put a smile on my face. To my mother-in-law Nikki, for welcoming me into the family, always supporting me and promoting my books at every opportunity (if you happen to find any copies in charity shops here lies the culprit). To Jen, thank you for always supporting me and reading countless drafts, but most of all, thank you for encouraging the smut scenes (sorry mum!). To Cam, my best friend, I would have been lost without you these past years. Thank you for embracing my love of fantasy, for reading my drafts and being one hell of a hype woman. Thank you for believing in me so much that I began to believe in myself, life is a little easier with you by my side.

Thank you also to my thorough editors and beta readers for your helpful feedback and kind words, and to Charlotte Lucas for creating my beautiful book cover.

Most of all, to those who read late into the night until their eyes hurt, those who wish on shooting stars and fallen eyelashes, those who see dragons in the clouds and who feel most alive in fictional worlds of magic, this is for you.

Part One

Memory Is All We Are

-CHAPTER ONE-

Pain. That's all there was, consuming me like a wave of both ice and fire coursing through my veins at the same time.

It's all I could feel, all I could think about.

My eyes fluttered open, even that hurt. I shut them again immediately as the bright lights burned my corneas. I tried again with one eye this time, hoping maybe that would hurt less. It didn't, so I kept them shut as I tried to make sense of what was going on around me.

I had no *thoughts*; my mind was numb... empty. No thoughts, no feelings, no memories. Just overwhelming pain. I think I heard mumbled tones. They were hurried and forceful. I tried to speak but I couldn't even cry out in pain, I couldn't make a single sound. I felt the pressure of something pressing down onto my face, maybe an oxygen mask.

Was I in the hospital?

I tried one last time to open my eyes. This time I willed them to stay open through the burning lights. As my sight began to focus my other senses joined in and I took in my blurred surroundings. The lights, the beeping and whirring of machines, the barked orders from the silhouette standing by my head.

The silhouette bent down over me, although I couldn't make sense of any features because of the bright lights glaring from behind. All I could see was shapes.

"It's okay we've got you," said the silhouette, its voice was light and soothing. "You're safe now. The morphine will kick in soon. We just need to move you onto the bed, okay? It will be quick, I promise."

I couldn't respond. I simply closed my eyes again, squeezing them shut as I braced myself for the inevitable pain that was to follow.

"1...2...3."

I screamed as pain filled every pore of my being, and my world descended into darkness.

I didn't know how long I was unconscious for, but the pain had subsided. It was still there, lingering in the background of my senses, but it was bearable. I laid still for a few moments and then fluttered my eyes open. The lights didn't seem quite so bright this time, so I took in the room around me. I was *definitely* in the hospital.

I had a window to my left; the curtains were drawn but there was no light trying to shine through, so I assumed it nighttime. I wondered again how long I had been asleep for. I looked down at the IV in my bruised left arm.

"Hey there, can you hear me?" I heard the same soothing voice I had heard before. I could hear, but faintly, the voice muffled as though I was underwater.

I swallowed hard and then flinched as I felt something pop as my ears started to ring.

I tried to turn my head towards the voice, answering the question. I felt the pain again, although alleviated from the pain meds, but I managed to turn my head which I thought was a good sign.

The doctor looked down at me with kind, hazel eyes. The wrinkles around his eyes and lips creased as he smiled down at me reassuringly.

A Lotus in the Dark

"Hi Rose-" *Rose?* "-I'm Dr Saunders. Can you hear me alright?"

I nodded, but the panic started to build in my chest.

"Good, that's good," he smiled again. "Do you think you're able to speak aloud for me?"

I swallowed hard and then said, "Yes." My voice came out harsh and scratchy. I hadn't noticed how thirsty I was until that moment.

"What..." I attempted to clear my throat. "What happened?"

"You were in quite a serious car accident I'm afraid but you're going to be okay. You were extremely lucky. Can you tell me what happened?"

I looked away from him, focusing my eyes on my bare bloodied feet, and I stayed silent.

"Is there anyone we can call for you Rose? Family or friends?"

I remained silent again.

"Alright, I need to do a few tests, is that okay?" Dr Saunders asked gently.

I nodded but still didn't look up at him. He walked down to stand at the end of the bed by my feet and pulled a small metal stick out of his white coat pocket.

"Can you tell me if you can feel this?" he asked, and then he ran the metal stick down the middle of my left foot. I nodded, so he ran the stick down my right foot, and I nodded again.

"Can you wriggle your toes for me?" I did as he asked.

"Excellent, and your fingers?" I again did as he asked.

He walked up to stand at my side again and clicked the end of the metal stick and I realised it was a small torch.

"Can you follow the light for me," he asked. "Just with your eyes please."

I once again did as he asked, following the light to the left and then to the right.

He nodded and pulled out my chart and scribbled something down quickly. Then he walked over to the side of the room, pulled a chair up to the side of my bed and sat next to me. I looked at him and he smiled at me again. He was trying to comfort me.

"Okay, like I said, you were extremely lucky, there's no extreme head injury and there doesn't appear to be any internal damage. You have a sprained wrist and some cuts and bruises but compared to your car, you basically came out unscathed."

I frowned. That didn't make any sense. Those injuries didn't match the level of agonising pain I had felt through every fibre of my body.

"I'm going to ask you some questions, you're doing really well, just answer as best as you can, okay?"

I nodded but remained silent through all of the questions.

"Can you remember what happened?"

"Do you know where you are?"

"Can you tell me what the date is?"

I didn't answer any of them. Not because I didn't want to, not because of the mild lingering pain coursing through my body or because of the ringing in my ears, but because I didn't have the answers.

No, I didn't remember anything, and I didn't know where I was.

I didn't even know who I was.

The next few hours blurred into one as I laid in my hospital bed with no thoughts or memories to comfort me. Nurses came in and out, checking my vitals, refilling my water, offering words of solace. Dr Saunders had put my

A Lotus in the Dark

memory loss down to a concussion as a result of my head injury and said hopefully after a good few hours' sleep it would all come back to me.

I didn't know how, but I knew in my gut he was wrong. The level of amnesia I was experiencing didn't coincide with my injury, it was just a few stitches and a bit of bruising. I could understand maybe if I solely couldn't remember the accident but... I couldn't remember *anything*.

Dissociative amnesia occurs when a person blocks out certain information, usually associated with a stressful or traumatic event, leaving them unable to remember important personal information. The knowledge flooded in and I blinked, wondering how I knew that.

How could I possibly remember anything about amnesia when I couldn't even remember who I was? I didn't know my name; I didn't know if I had any friends or family... I couldn't even remember what I had looked like until I had requested a mirror. I only glanced quickly at my slim bruised face, at the stiches on my head covered by my dark, chocolate brown hair. It was like looking into a stranger's face for the first time.

Dr Saunders had a nurse bring in the personal items they had found at the scene of the accident. I didn't have much, just a key ring with three keys and a purse containing nothing but a twenty-pound note and a driving licence.

The driving licence had my photograph, although I looked younger than I was now. It had my name, Rose Montgomery. It had my date of birth, 5th May, 1996. Dr Saunders had told me it was the 26th June, 2021 which means I had just turned 25. The license also had an address. Flat 5A, Winnow Drive, Oxfordshire, but I still didn't recognise it. The doctor had said it was only ten minutes from the hospital.

I was baffled, how could I remember how to talk and communicate, understand concepts such as amnesia and hospitals, know I should have friends and family around me but... not remember *any* of it? It didn't make any sense.

I didn't even know how I felt, I didn't have any particularly strong emotions. I didn't feel upset or scared I just felt... nothing, except perhaps exhaustion. I couldn't keep my heavy eyelids open any longer so I let them close, praying I'd wake up in the morning with my memories returned.

I didn't. The next morning, after my routine checks, Dr Saunders told me the police wanted to have a conversation.

"The police? Why?" I frowned and then winced as the action pulled on the stitches on my forehead.

"Well... I will let them explain everything," he smiled his reassuring smile I'd become accustomed to and then walked over to the door to open it. Two uniformed policemen followed him into the room and positioned themselves next to each other at the end of my hospital bed. Dr Saunders closed the door silently but remained inside the room. My shoulders relaxed at his reassuring presence.

As I took in their serious expressions my pulse quickened. I swallowed hard and then painfully pushed myself into a more upright position.

"I'm Police Constable Gary Martin," said the one on the left, he looked older than his colleague and there was an air around him that gave the impression that he had seniority. "This is PC Hammond, we understand you're having trouble recovering any substantial memories but we do have a few questions for you."

I nodded silently, knowing I wouldn't be able to answer any of their questions even if I wanted to. Something about them being here made me nervous. I wondered if it was a

A Lotus in the Dark

subconscious reaction to something I couldn't remember or if it was just a natural reaction. Either way, I could feel my palms begin to sweat.

"Your name is Rose Montgomery, is that correct?" said PC Martin.

"Well, that's what my license says," I said, then realised he might have thought I was being sarcastic. "As in... I couldn't even remember my own name."

He narrowed his eyes as if he didn't quite believe me and then said, "What were you doing at the time of the accident?"

I frowned slightly, "Sorry... I don't understand the question?"

"CCTV footage shows that the accident happened at 3:47am on Stourbridge Road, just outside a block of flats. What were you doing driving at that time of the morning?" said the other policeman, I had already forgotten his name.

"I... I've told you I don't remember anything."

"Just think," he said with a smile that didn't really look like a smile, there was no kindness in his eyes.

"What's going on? Why are you asking these questions?"

My stomach tensed as I had a sudden thought.

"Was... Was someone else hurt?" I looked towards Dr Saunders. "Did I hurt someone else?"

He took a few steps towards me. "No, nobody else was hurt in the accident. It was just you at the scene, no witnesses until, luckily for you, a paramedic drove past in the middle of their nightshift and brought you in."

I swallowed hard, thank *God*. Why hadn't I thought of any of this yet? What was I doing when I crashed?

"I was obviously going *somewhere*..." I thought out loud. "I obviously have a life if I was going somewhere at nearly 4 in the morning. Why hasn't anyone come for me yet?"

"Look," PC Martin said, although his voice was stern his eyes had softened slightly. "I know you don't remember anything, and I know you've been through a rough accident but there are just some abnormalities to this case."

"Well come on then," I huffed, as I became frustrated with the dramatics. "Just tell me what the hell is going on."

He nodded and then said, "When we got to the scene, the car was a mess. A complete wreck. When I saw it, I thought we were dealing with a DOA. When they told us that you were alive and in the ambulance on the way to the hospital, I was honestly completely astounded, I thought there was no way anyone could survive that, at least not without horrendous fatal injuries. But here you are, sat up talking to me, barely a scratch."

I swallowed. This had also been on my mind. I remember the pain, my *god* the pain. It was an all-consuming, overwhelming pain that had me certain I was dying. My injuries didn't match that level of pain either.

He looked towards the doctor now and nodded. I narrowed my eyes at Dr Saunders who stepped forwards again so he was standing by my side.

"As we were all confused by the seemingly minor injuries, we did a full exam to ensure we weren't missing anything and the thing is, we did find extensive injuries... but they're not from the accident."

My pulse accelerated.

"What do you mean?" I asked.

"X-Rays and full body examinations showed a huge amount of scarring and broken bones, all healed, and we predict they're from various different dates ranging at least ten years."

A Lotus in the Dark

"Tell me," I swallowed and willed my voice to come out strong. "Tell me exactly what my injuries are, I need to know."

Dr Saunders sighed like he knew I was going to ask this, and he opened my file and began to read... and read and *read*. The list went on and with each injury the nausea built in my stomach.

"Extensive healed scarring on back from a large, predicted second-degree burn. Healed broken bones, one in left clavicle, humerus and ulna, predicted in the last six months. Healed fractures in right wrist, predicted a year ago. Healed broken bones predicted between one to ten years ago: two in left leg, one in left arm, two in right arm, left hip, both ankles and one skull fracture."

I gripped the sides of mattress tightly with my probably broken fingers as he carried on.

"Tissue scarring from various puncture wounds, in lower abdomen and upper thigh, scarring from stitches on left collar bone and elbow and various healed lacerations all over body."

He stopped and closed my file and put it down. The room was silent for a moment.

I didn't have any words; I couldn't even form a coherent thought at this point. I blinked silently, waiting for someone to say something. Explain to me where all of these wounds came from.

Instead, the damn policeman spoke again.

"I'm sorry, but there's more."

A hysterical laugh bubbled out of me, out of my control.

"Of course, there's more."

"When the hospital informed us that you had no memories, we ran a check on the vehicle's registration to see if we could help get any information. That car, the car you were driving, had already been flagged up on our system. It had been reported stolen from the scene of a crime."

He sighed and looked at the other police officer and then back at me and when he said his next few words my blood ran cold.

"The owner of that car had been murdered."

-CHAPTER TWO-

After the police dropped their bombshells, they left me alone in a state of shock. They'd informed me they would be back later as I was now part of a murder investigation. They didn't say I was a suspect, but it didn't look good.

What the hell was I doing driving some dead man's car at nearly four in the morning?

And that wasn't even half of the absolute absurdities that had been thrust upon me yesterday. The list of injuries the doctor had read was running on a continuous loop in my mind, creating endless and probably ridiculous theories.

The most credible theory I had decided on was that I had been a victim of some sort of horrendous long-term abuse. Maybe I had been held hostage and abused for all these years, it would explain the injuries and why I had nobody trying to find me.

Or maybe I was in a gang.

I rubbed my hands roughly over my eyes and then through my hair. I was going to drive myself insane. I just needed answers.

I turned on the television in the corner of the room and put a crappy daytime soap on that seemed vaguely familiar. Not that I was really paying much attention, I couldn't focus on anything with my thoughts spiralling down some pretty disturbing paths.

Katie Masterman

The doctor checked on me again in the early evening, just after I had unsuccessfully spent 20 minutes trying to salvage any sort of edible part of the lasagne they had served.

"You must try to eat something to get your strength back up," Dr Saunders said, looking down at my file. He looked back up at me and I nodded politely.

He checked my vitals and scribbled something in my chart and then smiled at me sympathetically. "The police would like to speak to you again, I'm going to send them in now, okay?"

He phrased it as though I had a choice but we both knew I didn't. He exited the room and a few short moments later the two police men from this morning entered and closed the door behind them.

PC Martin cleared his throat, "We'll just jump straight to it shall we?" He paused and looked at me and I nodded once so he continued, "Do you recognise the name Frank Rogers?"

I shook my head and had to force myself not to roll my eyes, when would they understand?

"I don't even recognise my own name."

"He was the casualty we spoke about this morning; suspicious circumstances had led our investigation team to open the case as a murder enquiry, however new information has come to light that gives us strong evidence Mr Rogers in fact committed suicide."

I shook my head, feeling guilty of the relief that swept over my body. "What suspicious circumstances? What new evidence?"

"Well, there were signs of forced entry, as well as the report of Mr Roger's stolen car." He looked at me meaningfully. The car I was driving when I crashed. "However, records show that the ownership of that car was in fact changed over to yourself on the evening of Mr Roger's passing. It would appear he sold you the car beforehand and had accidentally left his house keys inside the vehicle which

A Lotus in the Dark

were found by forensics, we believe he forced his way back into his home himself. Toxicology reports showed high levels of fluoxetine in his body and forensics found a suicide note that was somehow missed the first time. All evidence suggests suicide."

And yet, the way he was looking at me with narrowed eyes and a tight jaw, showed he didn't believe what he was saying. Even though the evidence was there, he was still suspicious of me.

I swallowed, unsure of what to say. "Right, well... That's very sad."

The only connection I had to this man was that I bought his car. I couldn't help the relief that washed over me, I hadn't really believed I'd had anything to do with his death, but I wasn't completely sure. I didn't know anything about who I was.

PC Martin nodded in agreement and then looked to his partner PC Hammond who stepped forward and said, "With the additional information about yourself, we managed to pull your file."

I frowned. "I have a file?"

"It would appear you were questioned back in May 2012, interestingly, regarding a stolen car." He smirked, not in a friendly way and it instantly got my back up.

I narrowed my eyes. "I would have only been 16 in May 2012. I was just a kid."

He held his chubby hands up in a mock defensive position. "Hey we're not here to pass judgements, we just thought you'd like to know more about yourself. You were brought in after officers found what looked to be a stolen car abandoned in some overgrown fields. When they went to inspect the car, they found you living in it."

My chest tightened suddenly. So, at 16 I was... homeless? Living out of a stolen car?

PC Martin looked at me and his eyes softened. "You were brought back to the station, questioned on how you came to be living in a stolen brand-new Range-Rover–"

"Those babies must cost about seventy grand!" PC Hammond interrupted.

PC Martin gave him a death stare and then continued, "Anyway, funnily enough, the PC that interviewed you at the time is a Detective Inspector now and–"

He was interrupted again, this time by the door swinging open.

As soon as my eyes settled on the gentleman walking through the door I was slammed with a wave of distorted images. Memories.

Torch lights shining through a car window.

Banging on the windows.

A young man looking at me, soft eyes filled with sympathy and... something else I couldn't identify.

I couldn't help the gasp that escaped my lips. "I... I recognise you." I rubbed my forehead. "I think."

He stepped forward and smiled. His soft blue eyes matched those of my memories, and I frowned. It was such a strange feeling, to know you know someone... to have memories and a life and yet not be able to remember any of it.

"I'm Detective Inspector Jones," he said, as he walked over and sat down on the chair next to my bed. He looked towards the two policemen standing by the door. "Thank you, gentlemen. I'll take it from here."

They acknowledged their dismissal with a nod each and then silently left the room.

DI Jones looked back to me. He had matured since my memory; he had additional age lines and a dark beard, but he still had the same kind blue eyes that were prominent against his dark hair.

"What can you tell me Rose, what do you remember?"

A Lotus in the Dark

I sighed. "Nothing. I haven't remembered a single thing until you walked through that door and suddenly, I had images of you finding me, I think... living in a stolen car. That's it just... torch lights and banging and... your face." I looked down. "That's all I remember about my life; I didn't even know my name. I don't know who I am, where I'm from or how I got here."

"That must be incredibly scary," he said softly. I looked up and his eyebrows were pinched together, sincere eyes looking at me intensely. He rubbed one hand across his beard and then said, "It would have been nine years ago when we found you in your car and when I heard someone mention your case at work, I instantly remembered you."

I frowned, "Why would you remember me?"

"I'm going to be completely honest here, Rose. I was a PC at the time, but throughout our entire encounter, from finding you in your car to interviewing you back at the station... I didn't believe a single word that came out of your mouth."

I blinked; I hadn't expected him to say that.

But then he smiled, and there was a twinkle in his eye as though he found it amusing.

I raised an eyebrow at him, and he continued, "When we realised you were living out of the car, we immediately thought it was stolen. Who could afford a brand-new Range-Rover but couldn't afford a place to live? So, we brought you back to the station and you said you'd found it abandoned there and thought you could stay there for a while as it was in a private area. It didn't sit right with me, a brand-new expensive car, unlocked and in pristine condition may I add, is highly unlikely to have been abandoned. We checked the reg and yet nothing came up, no reports of a stolen car... nothing at all." His eyes narrowed at me. "They were fake plates. I don't know how a young 16-year-old, came to be living in a car like that, but that's the story you were going with. We had no proof you'd stolen it and no reports so we couldn't hold you."

He sighed, my brain wasn't making much sense of anything these days so I stayed silent and let him continue. "The keys weren't in the car or on your person, you said you'd found the car unlocked and yet when we found you inside, the car heating had been on. After we'd let you go, a local garage said you'd hot-wired the engine to start for the heating. Now in my time I've not met many young ladies that can do that." He huffed out a laugh and then looked at me.

"But after all that, the main thing that made you so memorable was the way you acted. It's incredibly sad but we find more homeless kids than you'd think holed up in places they shouldn't be, trying to find some warmth. When we find them, they're sometimes scared, apologetic... sometimes they go on the defensive, start acting arrogant and overly aggressive. You however," he huffed out a laugh and shook his head. "You were completely unbothered. You acted unfazed, as if you were bored by the whole thing. Except your eyes, there was something in your eyes that told me I'd be seeing you again one day... and here we are."

I frowned. "What could you possibly have seen in my eyes that could predict this?"

"Guilt, as though we'd caught you doing something you shouldn't have been but it was mixed with relief. Relief that we hadn't caught what you were actually doing that night. We'd caught you, but not for the right thing."

I sighed; this was heavy. "Right well... I don't mean to sound rude but, what is it you actually want? Because I can't tell you anything about what I was doing that night, or any other night for that matter."

"It's just pure curiosity, Rose." He smiled but this time it didn't meet his bright blue eyes. He leaned forward, as if he was going to say something important and took a deep breath. "We tried to contact your family when you told us you'd been

A Lotus in the Dark

bouncing around different foster homes your entire life and had run away from the latest one. You didn't know anything about what happened to your real family." He paused briefly. "You'd accepted our offer to give you a lift back to the current foster home you were supposed to be staying at. When they came back from getting a coffee for the ride, you'd gone and we never saw you again."

"So, that's why nobody has come for me." I had thought even with memory loss this severe, surely, I'd remember my family, but how could I when I didn't have any?

I chewed on the inside of my lip. I didn't feel sad exactly, I guess I couldn't grieve something I never had. I just felt a deep sense of... emptiness.

DI Jones smiled softly at me, and I felt the blood rise to my cheeks. I didn't want his sympathy.

"It's been nearly ten years since then, Rose."

I hated the way he kept saying my name, it didn't sound right. It didn't sound like it belonged to me.

"I'm sure a lot has changed since then, you're an adult. You have a life, someone out there who cares about you, I'm sure of it."

I waved him off, not wanting his comfort. "Oh yeah, I've been in here for three days and look at all the people gathered round me. I'm surprised you even made it in here through the huge piles of flowers and cards."

I gave him a sarcastic smile and the corner of his mouth twitched.

If I had learned anything about myself so far it was that I used humour as a defence mechanism, to deflect the severity of a situation.

"Well... You'll find out soon enough," he said, he got the message. "I spoke with your doctor earlier he said you were okay to be discharged, they're just filling out the forms and then I'm going to take you home... to the address on your driving licence anyway."

"I..." I didn't know what to say. It was daunting to think I was going to go to a place supposed to be my home that I probably wouldn't even recognise.

I blew out a determined breath. No, this was a good thing. It was time to get my life back.

"That's very kind of you," I said genuinely. "But I'm okay, I think I'd rather go alone."

"They don't just discharge amnesiac patients to go and fend for themselves you know." He looked at me pointedly.

I frowned back at him, asking a silent question.

"Usually, you'd be assigned a liaison officer." He hesitated. "But I've volunteered to be your support system; the doctors are happy for you to leave in my care. I'm sure you're more than capable but, with your memory loss you might have some trouble getting inside the building or something. Just... let me help you."

I stared at him with wide eyes. "Why would you do that? You don't even know me."

"I can't explain it, I knew in my gut all those years ago you needed my help and it's telling me you do now too. It's either that or you stay in the hospital until someone claims you, which let's be honest, doesn't look like is going to be anytime soon."

Harsh but fair. I pursed my lips; I really didn't want to stay here any longer.

"I thought you'd have more pressing issues than a foster kid with amnesia, 'DI' Jones." I raised an eyebrow.

He smirked. "Call me James."

"Your name is James Jones?"

He rolled his eyes and nodded.

"JJ it is."

"Please don't call me JJ."

"Okay James Jones," I said mockingly and then frowned. "Why are you helping me?"

A Lotus in the Dark

He shrugged with a slight smile. "Like I said, it's pure curiosity, Rosc."

After what felt like hours of mundane paperwork that I signed without reading a word, the doctors decided they were happy for me to leave in the company of DI Jones.... *James*. All I had to do was return in three days for them to remove the stitches on my forehead and that was it.

I felt like I was a rehabilitated animal being released into the wild.

I didn't let myself think too much into why James was helping me. I felt as though I could trust him for now, I believed he genuinely wanted to help me, I was just unsure *why*. Regardless, I'd decided to keep him at arm's length in case he did have some sort of ulterior motive.

A nurse gave me a pair of leggings and a T-shirt that she insisted had been sat in her locker unused for too long for her to miss them. They were way too large for my slim frame but I was grateful nonetheless. I thanked her with a warm smile which she returned.

I collected up my belongings, all two of them, and then a short drive later we stood outside the block of flats listed on my driving license.

It was a neglected looking tall thin building, black bin bags piled high outside with rubbish spilling out onto the street. There was some graffiti sprayed onto the front wall, although it was barely noticeable through the overgrown weeds and grass that had made their way halfway up the wall.

I swallowed hard. This was my *home*?

"You're in flat number 5A," James said from memory. "It doesn't look like there's anyone manning these doors."

I sighed and stepped forward and looked at the three keys in my hand, I guessed one of them had to fit and on the second try was proved to be correct.

There were two flats, A and B, on each floor. We climbed the stairs which didn't smell particularly pleasant, like a mixture of stale sweat and alcohol. I wrinkled my nose and subtly glanced at James who had a neutral expression, but I saw his throat bob, like he was trying not to notice the environment around us. Embarrassment suddenly clenched through my stomach.

"Hit the jackpot here, haven't I?" I joked.

The corner of his mouth twitched into an amused smile but his eyes were laced with concern. I wished more than anything that I had insisted on making this journey alone.

We reached the fifth floor and stood staring at a large brown door with a rusted sign reading 5A. My home. I hadn't recognised a single aspect of our entire trip so far. How could this possibly be my home?

I found the correct key and as I began to turn it in the lock, my stomach twisted uncomfortably as though my gut was screaming at me not to let James in with me. I stopped and frowned but put the feeling down to embarrassment. Based on the sorry state of the outside, I was dreading to see what it looked like inside and I *definitely* didn't want him to see that.

I turned to look at him. "Thank you so much for escorting me here but I think I'm okay now."

I smiled in a way that suggested I was saying goodbye when he smiled back and patted me on the shoulder.

"Nice try but I'm helping you inside. I just want to make sure you get in okay and then I'll leave you to it, I promise. Besides, I'm a detective. I might be able to find something to help you regain your memories, figure out who you are."

His expression was so sincere that I swallowed down the ominous feeling and opened the door, leading him inside.

Both of our eyebrows shot up.

I stepped further into the flat, the door had opened straight into the living room which stretched into an open plan kitchen diner. The first thing I noticed was how *nice* it was. I mean, really nice. If I hadn't just walked through the slums to get up here, I would have thought I was in some sort of penthouse flat in an expensive part of town. I could tell from James' expression that he was thinking the same thing.

The décor was modern and colourful, all tastefully chosen to perfectly complement each other. A suede navy-blue corner sofa pointed to a huge flat-screen television hung on the wall above an equally large electric fireplace. Expensive looking artwork adorned the walls and covered the shelves, all abstract and modern. The kitchen was white with marble countertops and a matching breakfast bar with two high blue suede chairs that matched the sofa. On the opposite side of the breakfast bar to the kitchen was a large glass dining table with four chairs and a chandelier hanging above.

The second thing I noticed was that it was pristine. Not a single item looked to be out of place, there wasn't a single plate or mug or piece of rubbish, there wasn't even a speck of dust. Most importantly, there was absolutely nothing personal. No photographs or personal belongings like clothes or shoes or a laptop, no books or magazines, no mail or letters.

From this room, the only evidence that I lived there was the key fitting in the door.

"Well, if you don't mind me saying," James huffed out a shocked laugh. "This is... unexpected."

I let out a laugh that matched his. "You could say that again. Why on earth would I live in a place like this in an area like this?"

"I will admit it does seem odd," he mused.

It didn't make any sense. "If I could afford to deck out a place with such expensive taste, surely I could afford the rent in a better flat?" I said.

"Well actually I will admit I did have a colleague look up this address and you don't rent it, you own it outright... no mortgage, and this part of Oxford so close to the centre regardless of the area is still expensive."

Interesting. "I wonder what I do for a living?"

He shrugged as he casually looked around. "I'm not sure, there was no current or historical employment records in your file." He pulled open a couple of kitchen cupboards, all of which were completely empty.

"Maybe I've just moved in?" I asked.

"No, you've owned this flat since 2014."

I raised an eyebrow. "How much information on me do you actually have?"

"No more, only what I've just told you. It's easy to get information about an address, Rose."

Something deep inside twisted uncomfortably again when he said my name.

I needed him to leave.

"If you don't mind, I really would like to be alone now," I said honestly. "It's been an indescribable few days and I just need to think and... try to sort my life out."

To my relief this time he nodded. "I understand, I just wanted to make sure you were okay. Sorry I couldn't help any more but your home doesn't exactly give much away."

I gave him a sheepish smile in agreement because no, it didn't give anything away. I was no closer to discovering who I was than when I woke up in the hospital, if anything I was just more confused.

"We'll have a little search around the flat tomorrow, after you've had a proper night's sleep in your own home. You never know, it might surface some memories."

I didn't bother trying to convince him not to come back the next day as I knew my efforts would be futile. I just stared at him with my eyebrows slightly furrowed, wondering why he was going through all this trouble to help me.

He made to leave and then paused by the door. "In the meantime, I'll try to do some more digging and find anything I can and I'll be back here tomorrow afternoon. Okay?"

I nodded. "Thank you."

He looked at me for a couple of seconds, his eyes intense and full of an emotion I couldn't identify. I thought it was a mixture of concern and confusion, it matched how I was feeling.

I forced myself to give him a determined smile. "I'm fine, honestly."

With that he nodded once and left through the door, leaving me completely alone for the first time since I had woken up in the hospital.

-CHAPTER THREE-

I blinked a couple of times as I looked around the flat, it was decorated exceptionally tastefully and yet still felt cold and impersonal. It didn't feel like home. I couldn't imagine myself cosied up on this sofa, watching this television.

I sighed and walked down the small hallway. I had an entirely peculiar sensation at that moment. As I stood at the end of the hallway with three doors surrounding me, I could tell exactly which rooms were behind them. I faced one door, and I knew when I opened it, I would be going into the bedroom, but I didn't know how I knew that, or what it would look like. It was obviously a subconscious memory trying to make its way out, perhaps that was a good sign.

I pushed open the door and as expected I entered the bedroom. It was the same as the living room, decorated in a tasteful but impersonal manner, with none of the mess or clutter that a seemingly normal bedroom might have. It looked like a showroom. There was absolutely no evidence that anyone actually lived here. That *I* actually lived here.

I walked further inside and sat on the end of the large bed, running my fingertips over the incredibly soft satin sheets hoping to remember something, anything. No memories returned, I only wondered why I would have one tiny thin silk sheet; it was soft but didn't look very warm.

I slapped my hands on my thighs and stood up. It was time to do some digging.

A Lotus in the Dark

I crouched down on my knees and looked under the bed to find a completely empty space. I walked to the side table to the left of the bed which held only a single lamp and was unsurprised to find the drawer also empty.

I walked to the chest of drawers, the top two held bras, underwear and socks. It was all black and all looked very comfortable, there was nothing lacy or colourful or even remotely sexy. The next drawer contained only gym leggings, again all black, all the same style. The next drawer contained tops, these were different styles, vest tops, T-shirts, long sleeved. But again, they all looked comfortable and they were all black.

I chewed on my lip. Strange.

I walked over to the large white wardrobe and pulled open the doors. I sucked in a breath and then frowned, even more confused by these contents than I was by the black attire.

In front of me hung a beautiful array of dresses. I stepped forward and flipped through them. They were all different styles and stunning different colours and shades. I looked at some of the labels and when I read them, I knew they were all top-line expensive designer brands. Although why I could remember that and nothing about my actual life god only knows.

I pulled out one dress, it was a tiny tight looking black dress with a plunging neckline and short enough that looked like it would barely cover my dignity. I pulled out another that was the complete opposite, a classy full-length emerald dress with an elegant beaded sweetheart neckline.

I hung the dresses back up and frowned, wondering why I would need such contrasting outfits, some suitable for balls and dinner parties and some barely suitable for a street corner.

As I was flicking through the dresses something at the back of the wardrobe glinted in the light and caught my eye. I parted the dresses to each side to find another row of outfits all hung up.

I leant forward to see what caught my eye; it was a police badge on a police uniform.

So, I'm a policewoman? No... I flicked through the outfits. Cleaner, nurse, doctor... My eyes widened.

Am I a *stripper*?

Although these outfits... They didn't look like stripper outfits or costumes, they looked like realistic replicas of genuine work uniforms.

I closed my eyes and pinched the bridge of my nose, unsure that I could get any more confused, until I opened my eyes to see a neat line of combat boots. None of which were the same size. In fact, I thought some were men's sizes.

I picked up the largest pair to examine them, surprised at how heavy they were. The soles were slightly scuffed so I guessed they had been worn. Did I have a partner?

The boots really did feel heavy, I slipped a hand inside to find it didn't go all the way to the toe.

I frowned and then slipped my foot inside the boot to find it moulded perfectly to my size. It fit and it was *definitely* weighted.

There was only one reason why I would possibly have to wear men's boots, to replicate a man's footprint and weight.

I looked again at the clothes in front of me.

They weren't costumes.

They were disguises.

What the *hell*?

I paused for a moment, unsure what to think or do and then I glanced at the shelf to the left of the dresses to see a pile of fluffy towels.

A bath was exactly what I needed to clear my head.

I stepped closer and grabbed a couple from the pile. I rubbed the corner of one over my cheek and sighed, they were so incredibly soft I wasn't even sure if they'd dry me.

A Lotus in the Dark

I crossed the hallway into the bathroom, again marvelling at how I knew it was the bathroom but not remembering any significant details.

The room was very small, but again the decor was incredibly contemporary and tasteful. The walls were completely tiled with white marble with matching flooring. The huge white bath took up most of the room, with an equally large overhead rain shower. The toilet was squeezed into the corner and the sink was on the wall opposite, with a large mirror above.

I looked around. On a shelf suctioned to the wall above the bath there were bottles of half used shampoo, conditioner and bubble bath. Other than my clothes this was the first sign of anything personal, that I actually did spend my time here. I leaned forward to turn on the hot tap and grabbed the bubble bath as I did so and poured it under the stream of water. I inhaled the sweet scent, vanilla mixed with coconut.

Something inside my stomach twisted again and my throat suddenly felt unbearably dry. I swallowed uncomfortably and took a step back.

I frowned at the familiar ominous feeling settled in my stomach. I recognised that scent, that much was obvious, but why did my body have such a negative reaction?

I shook off the feeling, my body and brain were probably just confused from the conflict of recognising the scent but not remembering exactly how.

I stripped down and shoved my hospital clothing into the corner of the room and then I stood and looked at myself in the mirror properly for the first time.

I had scraped my long dark hair into a messy bun that sat loosely on the top of my head.

I had a neat row of stitches on my forehead and some bruising on my cheek, collar bone and ribs from the accident but other than that I'd come out unscathed.

From the accident at least.

The other scars and lesions that marked my body were older, and I couldn't help but gasp in a breath as my wide, hazel eyes met each one and registered how many there were. I shouldn't have been surprised; I'd heard the doctor list off all my past injuries.

I traced my trembling finger tips over a small scar just above my hip, it was about an inch long. The raised scarred skin felt cold, and although it didn't hurt, for some reason my fingers flinched away from the feeling.

I frowned at myself, I looked an absolute mess from the last few days in the hospital and lack of self-care, but I was definitely attractive, I'd give myself that much credit. I wasn't just slim, my toned body looked fit, like *seriously*. I thought if I did a few sit ups there and then you'd be able to see the outline of a six pack on my stomach.

What the *hell* do I do?

I leaned forward to look closer into the mirror. Aside from the obvious and more than disturbing bruising and scarring, my light freckled skin was shiny and clear. My hazel eyes shone with confusion, covered by a row of long dark eyelashes.

I turned my head side to side as I examined my features and something black caught my eye below my ear. I twisted and pulled my ear forward to get a better look.

It was a small tattoo, just behind my ear of a lotus flower. It was so dainty you wouldn't normally notice it under my hair. Simple but pretty. I liked it.

I blinked and took a step back as I stared at the stranger looking back at me.

I turned around to shut off the taps and slowly slid myself into the full bath, the hot bubbly water rose up to my neck. I tried to shut off my mind and stop attempting to piece together the puzzle that was my life.

A Lotus in the Dark

So, I ignored the fact that when I got out of the bath, I'd have to face my life head on, with no friends or family to support me.

I ignored the twisting in my stomach as the scent of the shampoo and conditioner stirred something deep in my subconscious memories.

I ignored the feeling of my fingertips running over the scars on my scalp and hairline when I washed my hair.

When the water inevitably became cold, I sighed and hauled myself out and wrapped myself in a fluffy towel.

Back in the bedroom I dried myself off, dressed in some of my comfy black clothes, and then I climbed into bed and laid in an almost foetal position as I pulled the cold sheets over my body and fell into a surprisingly deep sleep.

The next morning, I woke up with an empty feeling in the pit of my stomach. It was barely even light outside. I laid in bed until I needed the toilet, having no other reason to get up. I wasn't sure what I was supposed to be doing. I didn't know what life I was supposed to be living.

I had a shower, got dressed into comfy leggings and a hoody with some black trainers I found in the wardrobe and then I just wandered aimlessly around the flat like a dog waiting for its owner to return from work.

I searched through the kitchen cupboards for what felt like the twelfth time that morning, not because I was hungry, I didn't have an appetite at all actually, but just to see if I could find anything remotely interesting. Throughout the entirety of the kitchen, I found some tea bags, some sugar, one box of cereal and some off milk.

I sighed and slumped down onto the sofa which was incredibly hard and not at all comfortable, when there was a knock at the door. I frowned and then realised it had to be James, I didn't know anyone else.

I opened the door to see I was correct. "Isn't it strange you're the only person in the whole world that I actually know."

He blinked. "Hello to you too. I suppose it is yes, but not for long hopefully. We'll get your life back." He smiled and held up a cup holder with two coffees in one hand and a brown bag in the other. "I brought us lunch. I only have an hour before I have to get back to work."

I smiled back in thanks as we walked over to the dining table and he pulled out a sandwich and a pastry each. "I wasn't sure what you'd like so just took a guess."

I shrugged and said dryly, "Me neither, guess we'll find out together."

I took a bite into a chocolatey pastry and put my thumbs up, perhaps I was hungry after all. I took a sip of coffee and grimaced. I poured a couple of the sachets of sugar into it and then took a sip. Much better.

I watched James took a sip of his own coffee.

"Are you married?" I asked.

He put his coffee down then shook his head.

"No, there was a time where I thought it might happen but… it didn't last very long."

"What happened?"

"Just, life happened. We fell apart." He paused and then abruptly changed the conversation. "Did you manage to find anything interesting?"

I sucked a bit of chocolate off my thumb and then shrugged. "Nope. So far, I have figured out that I'm a past foster kid with seemingly no friends or family, I own only black clothes and I like bubble baths and sugar in my coffee. Oh, and I live in a shithole area of town with the nicest possible décor I could have in a flat like this."

I left out the fact that I possibly wore disguises as my day job.

A Lotus in the Dark

He smirked as he swallowed his last bite of sandwich. "Well then I guess we'd better do some proper investigating; I've only got 45 minutes left before I have to get back to work."

He stood up, but I didn't move. I looked at him silently with my eyes slightly narrowed.

He frowned. "What is it?"

"Can you just answer one question, that's all I ask," I said.

He paused for a second and then nodded his head once.

"Why are you so hell bent on helping me when you don't even know me and clearly have more important business to attend to?" I asked bluntly.

He opened his mouth to answer but I interrupted. "And don't give me some bullshit answer like 'curiosity Rose'."

He sighed and sat back down and looked at me seriously, his bright eyes clouded over with a graveness that had me swallowing hard.

"You..." His eyes dropped from mine onto the table. "You remind me of someone, someone who was very important to me."

"Who?" I asked.

"I answered your one question."

I looked at him for a second and decided that I believed he was telling the truth and that his intentions were pure. I'd drop the subject for now, but I'd be bringing it back up later.

"Fine," I said, standing up. "Let's dig."

We worked quickly, starting in the front room and tore apart everything. Literally. Sofa cushions were scattered all around the living room, drawers were all pulled out, chairs tipped over, bins emptied. We examined all vases and pots and artwork and pulled everything off the shelves. We searched the kitchen cupboards again.

When he followed me to the bedroom, I remembered for a split second that I had let a stranger into my house and was now letting him into my bedroom. A stranger who could almost definitely overpower me if he wanted to. But I only doubted James' intentions for one second before I swallowed them down, deciding to trust him instead.

When we entered the room, I turned to face him. "If we find anything incriminating, are you going to report me?"

He pressed his lips together for a second then said, "I mean, if there's a hostage tied up in your wardrobe almost definitely, but I'll have to assess the situation and decide then."

He smiled sarcastically and when I didn't smile back, he sighed. "Rose, I'm here to help you I promise. I know I don't know you that well, but I'm good at my job and I think I'm pretty good at reading and judging people. I don't believe for one second that you will have anything incriminating."

I laughed at that; I couldn't help myself. In answer to his frown, I stepped backwards and pulled open the wardrobe and nodded once with my head for him to look inside.

He stepped forward and looked through the dresses and then like me parted the dresses and looked through the outfits at the back.

"Well..." He cleared his throat and I noticed his cheeks turned a slight shade of pink.

Once again, I couldn't help but laugh.

"I don't think they're stripper outfits if that's where your heads at."

He shrugged and his lips twitched. "No shame in that, it would explain the flat enigma."

I elbowed him lightly in the ribs and then pointed at the boots.

"These boots fit me perfectly on the inside, even the men's sizes. They're also weighted down... and the outfits are too realistic to be costumes."

A Lotus in the Dark

He raised his eyebrows. "You can't be saying you think they're *disguises*." He enunciated the last word as if it were completely ridiculous.

I held up my hands. "I have no idea what they are, I'm just saying they aren't bloody costumes."

James sighed and then took a step back and frowned, his head cocked sideways as he stared at the wardrobe. He walked into the hallway, and then back into the doorway, standing looking half in half out.

"This wall is... unusually thick for an interior wall."

He stood back in front of the wardrobe, we looked at each other once before reaching the same page and we started pulling out the outfits in sync, throwing them on the bed behind us. When the wardrobe was empty James knocked on the back wall before rubbing his hands exploringly all around it.

"There's something behind this wall..." he said quietly, as though just to himself.

My stomach suddenly clenched again and a feeling of dread rose up in my throat until it threatened to bubble out.

I knew then in my gut that he was right, there was something behind that wall and I didn't want him to see it.

And I was too late.

Reaching up he sucked in a breath, his eyes flew to mine, and with a click the wall began to slide sideways.

-CHAPTER FOUR-

The wall slid sideways and then folded in on itself, revealing a hidden section of the wardrobe. It was a small compartment, not big enough to step completely inside, but big enough to open backwards to reveal two thin columns of shelves on either side panel with a much wider set of shelving on the back wall.

My eyes widened as I registered the contents and my heart began to thud painfully in my chest. I stepped forward and then dared to glance at James' expression.

His mouth had fallen open as he stared inside with wide eyes. When he saw me looking, he snapped his mouth shut and ran his hand along his stubbled jawline.

"I'd like to retract my previous statement about you not having anything incriminating." I saw his throat bob as he swallowed hard.

"I..." I stammered; my voice raised an octave. "I'm not lying to you; I swear I don't remember anything. I don't know why I would have this."

And by this I meant an entire armoury of weapons in a secret compartment in my bedroom.

"Rose... Do you know what we're looking at here?"

I looked at him. "I've got amnesia, I'm not blind. We're looking at a bunch of guns and knives and... is that a *grenade*?"

"It's a smoke grenade yes... and that below is a stun grenade." He stepped forward and ran his fingers over one of

A Lotus in the Dark

the larger guns at the top. "This is an M16... There's a sniper rifle in here. These are military grade weapons, Rose. I don't know how you would have access to these."

"What are those?" I pointed to the shelf with little black pieces on it.

"They're attachments, for the guns, silencers and sights and stuff. That's a... reflex sight."

Wrong.

Okay, I was playing it down. Way down. I knew exactly what every single item in this compartment was and that wasn't a reflex sight, it was a holographic sight.

I had no idea why this knowledge still existed in my brain when simple details about my life had vanished. I had no idea how I even had this knowledge in the first place.

What I did know, was not to let James know *how much* I knew.

I glanced around at the "military grade weapons" - the M16 assault rifle, the MP5 submachine gun, the Glock-18 pistol and the sniper rifle. James was right, there was a row of different attachments below, with a row of ammunition beneath that.

On the side panel there was a neat row of knives; daggers, fighting knives and throwing knives. There were different smoke and stun grenades, although no actual explosives thankfully.

On the shelf beneath there was headgear, infrared goggles, a night vision monocular and ballistic safety glasses.

On the opposite panel there was a row of passports, and credit cards and a few piles of cash.

Below them was a neat row of vials of cyanide, arsenic, tetrodoxin -

"That's poison." James interrupted my thoughts. "Why the *hell* would you need poison."

I could only look at him stunned. I had no idea.

"Are you going to arrest me?" I asked.

He blew out a breath and then sank down on the bed and rubbed his hands over his face. Then he looked up at me, his blue eyes clouded with his confliction.

"I should report this," he nodded, although he said it absently as though he was talking to himself.

"But... you're not going to?" I asked, hesitantly.

He shook his head slowly. "Not yet. Not until we know more about the situation."

Frustration grew in my stomach, even though he was helping me, it was just too much.

"Why would you not report it? I don't get it." I threw my hands up. "Why are you helping me to this extent? If anyone found out you knew about this you could lose your job."

"I don't think you're a criminal, Rose. I have a theory."

"Go on then."

"I think you're undercover," he said. "Who for, I have no idea. But it's the only thing that makes sense to me; the lack of close relationships, the outfits, the posh flat in a shitty area, the weapons. I think it's legit and judging on the extent of your arsenal, I think it's for someone high-up way above my pay-grade, and in no way can be compromised. If I'm right, reporting this would be too dangerous."

I pursed my lips. It did make sense.

I had to stop the smirk that threatened to appear. I was kind of a badass. Except for the fact I didn't remember how to do anything.

James stood up and his eyes met mine; they were slightly wrinkled around the edges from age but still shone brightly. They were so sincere, full of concern and a hint of sadness.

"Who do I remind you of?" I asked.

"What?"

"Earlier. You said you were helping me because I reminded you of someone important to you, I want to know who it is."

A Lotus in the Dark

He frowned and turned his back to me. He walked over to the wardrobe and pressed the switch he'd found earlier causing the wall to fold back out, concealing the hidden compartment once again. He closed the exterior wardrobe doors and then turned to face me.

"That's personal," he said, and then paced out of the room.

I followed him into the living room where he gathered up his keys and radio.

I huffed. "I just think that I have a right–"

"Drop it, Rose."

"I just want to know why you're helping me so much." I placed my hands on my hips. "You know just as much about me as I know about myself and I don't know a thing about you! I don't think it's a lot to ask when I'm putting all of my trust into you."

He looked at me and his expression softened but his jaw stayed tense. "You don't really have a choice, do you?"

I didn't have a response to that because he was right. I didn't have choice, I had to have faith in him especially now that he could report me at any second. That and the fact that if I didn't let him in, I'd be completely alone in this.

He walked over to the door, placed his hand on the handle and then turned back to face me with a sigh. "Look... you remind me of someone who was very important to me, okay? I'm not quite ready to talk about it yet, but you can trust me. You have my word. We'll figure all of this out, I'll do some more investigating at work and see what I can find. In the meantime, why don't you take a walk into the city centre, you aren't far from here, just go right out of the building, to the end of the street and follow the signs. Maybe buy a new phone so we can keep in contact, you have enough money." He looked at me pointedly. "I'll be back tomorrow for your hospital appointment, okay?"

"I'll meet you there," I said. "I want to start trying to do things on my own."

He simply nodded and then handed me a little white card with his contact details on before he left me alone once again.

I had managed to navigate my way into the centre of Oxford and had been walking around aimlessly for over an hour. The buildings that surrounded me were a mixture of several different architectural styles, some looked extravagant and gothic like they'd been there for hundreds of years, some were modern and new. It was quite beautiful.

I'd slipped on an all-black outfit as it was my only choice, and the only bag I'd managed to find was a black belt bag that I had clipped around my waist. I'd shoved in a couple of the credit cards that we'd found in my wardrobe and my driving license with my address on it, just in case I forgot the way back home.

I turned onto what I assumed was one of the main streets of the city, it was just one long row of shops, restaurants and cafés. There were no cars allowed down this street, but it was packed full of people. I stopped one of them, a tall woman dressed in business attire, and asked where I could find the nearest phone shop. She kindly pointed me in the right direction, I said my thanks and followed her instructions.

I turned onto an equally busy street and saw the phone shop she had referred to. I smiled at my triumph.

See, I could do this. I could manage by myself.

I headed towards it when something made me turn my head to look across the street. I spotted a man; he was too far away for me to make out his features but he was undoubtedly staring at me intently. He narrowed his eyes when he saw me staring, and I raised my hand in a hesitant wave as my heart began to race.

Was this someone I knew? A friend, maybe a colleague? Was I finally about to get some answers about my life?

I waved more vigorously this time, desperate to find someone connected to my actual life. The man frowned when

A Lotus in the Dark

he saw me waving and looked away. I lowered my hand quickly as he walked away in the opposite direction.

I let out an embarrassed laugh and swallowed thickly. He didn't know me; he must have been looking at someone behind me. I really was alone.

A few hours later I was back in my flat setting up my brand-new phone. It was the latest, most expensive one that I'd bought partly as a test to see how much money I had on my card. I'd panicked when they'd asked me my pin number but when they handed me the machine my thumbs had automatically typed 1312 and it'd worked.

The mind really was a fascinating thing.

I dialled the number on the card James had given me and waited.

"DCI Jones."

I smiled at his professional tone. "Hello, JJ."

I heard him chuckle lightly. "You managed to get into town then?"

"Did you doubt me? I just thought I'd ring you so you had my number."

"So, you still remember how to use technology then?" he asked.

"Yeah, weird isn't it. I remembered my pin number as well, not off the top of my head but my thumbs just knew what to type."

"Maybe it just means your memory is all coming back one little detail at a time," he said hopefully.

"Yeah maybe."

"Well, I didn't manage to find anything on the contents of your wardrobe, I'll have to see if they've got serial numbers on or some-" he paused and I heard someone talking in the background then he said, "Okay be right there. Sorry Rose, duty calls, I'll see you tomorrow."

Then the line went dead and I sighed, wondering what to do with the rest of my evening.

I had another bath, although I kept it short as my stomach twisted uncomfortably once again at the scent of the shampoo and the feeling of my scars. Then I tucked myself into bed hoping James would have something significant to tell me the next day.

I woke up to my phone chiming. I checked the time, it was 10:14. I rubbed my eyes, wondering how I had slept that long, especially as I'd gone to bed so early with nothing left to do.

I noticed there was a message from James.

Hi Rose, so sorry I've been put on a priority case and I won't be able to make it to the hospital with you today. Are you okay to go alone or shall I send a police escort? James.

I rolled my eyes and then typed back.

I'll be okay on my own, thanks though.

Okay, if you're sure. The hospital is close enough for you to walk, just put it into the maps on your phone. If you don't want to walk, ring a taxi.

I sighed, hating that he had to dumb everything down for me. Memories of particular subjects flocked back once prompted, but I never would have thought to use maps until I was reminded.

I got ready quickly and left the flat as my appointment was at 11:30am. It was a very simple route, and I turned the corner to see the hospital in no time and smiled to myself again. Small victories.

I closed the app, looked up from my phone and then stilled, my smile dropping as I recognised the figure standing

A Lotus in the Dark

outside of the hospital. My heart thudded as I thought back to the man from town yesterday who I'd thought I might know. This time he was *definitely* staring at me.

I raised my hand again in a wave and stepped to walk towards him when he frowned and turned on his heel, disappearing into the hospital.

Either that was a strange coincidence, I was seeing things or that guy was following me. I shook my head and marched into the hospital looking around, but he was nowhere to be seen. Sighing in defeat I headed to the waiting room.

I had to wait a while to be seen. I had been hoping to see Dr Saunders again, to ask more questions about getting my memories back, but it was an appointment with the nurse instead. She checked me over, changed the stitches on my forehead to ones she informed me would dissolve in a few days and then I was officially discharged from hospital care.

I signed the paperwork and then exited the hospital and stood facing the road.

Alone in the world.

I took a deep breath. I couldn't possibly be alone, with no friends or family. There was an explanation to all of this, and I'd find it.

Maybe the mysterious wardrobe of death hidden in my bedroom was a good place to start. I decided to have a closer look on my own, sure I'd find something meaningful in there. James had said he may be able to use the serial numbers on the weapons, so I'd note them down for him as well.

I nodded to myself, more determined now that I had some sense of direction and headed towards my flat. I was sure I didn't need maps on the way back as it was such a straightforward route. I left the bustling hospital and headed down a quiet street with small, terraced houses packed together on each side, the odd car driving past me.

I looked down the quiet road, sure it was the same road I had walked down to get here, when suddenly my whole body stiffened. The hairs stood up on the back of my neck as if eyes were watching me. I heard the slight, almost imperceptible shift of gravel behind me as a large foot stepped in my direction and my instincts screamed at me not to stop walking.

I tried to keep calm and walk at the same pace but the feeling that someone was watching me was getting stronger and stronger.

I took a breath, sped up, then took a turn and instantly realised I'd made a mistake. This street was quiet and empty, nobody around but me and the person I was almost certain was following me.

I carried on down the street anyway, and just as I was about to break into a jog, a strong hand slammed over my mouth, and I was roughly pulled into an alley way to my right.

I expected the inevitable panic to build in my chest, but it never arose. Before I could even *think* my body reacted, like natural instinct.

I slammed my elbow backwards into my attacker's rib cage, at the same time I violently swung my head backwards to connect with their nose. They loosened their grip and in that split second, I yanked myself free, span around with preternatural grace and easily kicked upwards into their chest with such force that they stumbled backwards.

I stepped back out of shock. How the *hell* did I know how to do that?

The man in front of me stepped towards me and I realised it was the man from earlier. I *knew* he had been following me, I should have trusted my gut.

Up close I could see him better and he was pretty massive, both tall and muscular, with a strong jawline under a light coating of facial hair and amber eyes that stared directly into mine.

A Lotus in the Dark

Something in my lower stomach clenched and I didn't know if it was recognition or fear.

He took another step towards me and my body naturally reacted again as I kicked upwards aiming for his stomach, but this time he reacted quickly and snatched my ankle out of the air. He twisted my leg, and I flipped over, landing face down on the concrete floor with a painful thud.

I lifted my head up, conscious of the metallic taste of blood in my mouth and rapidly pushed up off the floor and darted back towards the street. I had to get out of this alleyway.

My foot was one step away from the somewhat safety of the street when I heard his strong deep voice behind me, and I stopped dead in my tracks.

"I know who you are, Aria."

As soon as I heard that name it felt like my heart stopped.

I took a deep shaky breath and slowly turned around, willing my voice to come out strong.

"My name is Rose."

He shook his head. "That's an alias obviously, you look nothing like a Rose."

"So, I am undercover?"

He stepped towards me and I instinctively stepped backwards. He raised his hands into a defensive position.

"There's a lot we have to talk about."

My eyes widened in disbelief. "You just attacked me."

"*No*, no if you think about it, I just tried to get your attention. You attacked me... and not very well, you're clearly out of training." He frowned and my stomach twisted again.

"How did I know how to do that?" I asked, rubbing the back of my neck.

He shrugged. "Muscle memory."

He took a couple of steps towards me again but this time I willed myself to stand my ground.

"So, you have lost all your memories?" He asked.

I nodded.

"I thought as much when you waved at me in public like a maniac... *twice*."

I narrowed my eyes at him. "We know each other then?"

He snorted. "You could say that."

At that I wondered exactly how well I knew him.

This was what I had been waiting for, a link to my life and answers to my questions. It was all standing in front of me in the shape of an incredibly intimidating albeit godlike block of muscle that was attempting to give me a friendly smile.

Yet, as his jaw tensed, I realised I already didn't trust him one inch, and it was time I started trusting my gut.

"What's your name?" I asked.

"Ethan," he said.

I stepped towards him. "And just how *well* do we know each other, Ethan?"

I blinked suggestively at him and ignored the flip my stomach gave as I noticed the unusual molten amber of his eyes as he smirked down at me.

He opened his mouth to respond when I suddenly jabbed my knee upwards into his groin and was greeted with the satisfying huff of air as I took his breath away. Taking my chance, I ran into the street.

"Aria!" His deep voice yelled after me, but I kept running.

I ran and ran for miles until I reached my building. I was sure he wasn't chasing me, but I still ran up the stairs and into my flat where I slammed the door shut and slid to the floor. I leant my head back against the door and let out a laugh.

I wasn't even slightly out of breath.

-CHAPTER FIVE-

I remained on the floor with my head leant back against the door for a while, mulling over the events that had just occurred.

I was both terrified and in awe at how my body had reacted. After finding the contents of the hidden compartment in my bedroom I guess I shouldn't have been surprised that I was trained in hands on combat, but everything was still so new. Even though it wasn't new it was just... forgotten.

My body had reacted in combat, but it had also reacted to Ethan. I knew him well, I was sure of it. The feeling that had swept over my body and clenched at my stomach was recognition, I just couldn't remember any more than that.

"Aria," I said out loud. The name tumbled far more naturally out of my lips than Rose, and I knew in my gut that he was telling the truth about that being my name.

I'd known the moment he'd said it.

I didn't know if he knew where I lived but I felt safer in the flat, so I decided to just hide out here until James was off duty. I pondered about whether I should tell him what had happened with Ethan.

On the one hand, I did think I could trust him and I was sure he could help work things out if I told him the whole truth. On the other hand, I had no idea what sort of business I was involved in and wasn't sure I should involve a police officer I barely knew.

I decided that I'd keep it to myself for a while.

I rubbed my hands over my face and was just about to make a move to stand up when I was jolted forward from the door with three loud *thumps*.

"Shit," I muttered as I stood up and looked through the peephole to see Ethan staring back at me.

I frowned as he pulled out a set of keys and made to open the door. I quickly hooked the security latch on just in time, as he opened the door with his own key. It stopped short with a bang as the latch kept it from opening more than a few inches.

"Why do you have a key to my flat?" I asked through the gap.

"Aria, I tried to be nice now open up or I'll break down the goddamn door!" he growled.

I slammed the door shut and looked through the door again. I couldn't help the smile that formed on my lips as the dimensions of the peephole made his head look massive on a tiny little body, which certainly lessened the threatening image he was aiming for.

"I'm giving you until the count of three," he said through gritted teeth and my irritation flared. I was not a child.

I watched as he did his countdown.

"ONE... TWO..." He stepped back and aimed to kick through the door. "THR-"

Just as he attempted to barge his way into my flat, I swung open the door and he tumbled through, saving himself at the last second.

He span to face my smug smile.

"Oh, Ethan hi. Please come in." I smiled sarcastically and anger flashed in his eyes.

He stepped towards me and I instinctively stepped backwards with my hands raised and for the life of me I just could not help the laugh that slipped from my lips.

A Lotus in the Dark

"I'm sorry." I laughed and then took a breath. I plastered on a neutral expression.

"For God's sake this is serious, Aria." His strong jaw tensed as he spoke. "I know you don't remember anything, but I'll explain it all and then you need to come with me."

I pulled the door open wider and gestured at him to leave. "No thanks. I wanted answers but not like this, I'll figure this out on my own."

He moved so quickly I didn't have time to react as he slammed the door shut and pushed me roughly against it, his hands pinned my arms painfully to my sides and his stern eyes drilled into mine.

"That isn't fucking negotiable. But I told you I'll explain everything and then you'll want to come with me anyway."

He stepped back and released me so suddenly I had to steady my legs before I sagged to the ground. I fought the urge to rub my arms where he had gripped them painfully and I plastered on the hardest expression that I could muster, even though my heart felt like it was about to burst out of my chest.

"Fine. Explain."

He huffed out a harsh sigh and his jaw tensed again. I could tell my attitude was irritating him and I was glad. Who did he think he was, putting his hands on me like that?

He sat down on the sofa and his voice softened a fraction even though his hard expression remained.

"Your name is Aria. We don't have surnames where we come from; we're all family in a way, all from the same place called Imperium." He paused and gestured around him. "We own this building, it's one of our safe houses that we use sometimes if we need to come into the city so yes, I know all about the hidden compartments, although I doubt you've found them all," he smirked.

I frowned. "Where we're from? What like, a cult?"

He shook his head. "No not a cult, more like an institution. A very powerful one."

"So, we aren't undercover?" I asked.

He shook his head. "It's hard to explain without showing you. What we do isn't exactly... legal." He looked at his watch and a flash of concern crossed his face before he wiped it neutral again. "We have to go back now because you're too dangerous to be out in public with no memories. That and I've been ordered to terminate you if you don't come in and to be honest, I could really do without that today, I skipped lunch." His eyes flashed.

He was joking. He had to be joking. Why was I dangerous?

A nervous laugh bubbled out of me and I stammered. "I... You... *Terminate* me?"

"No hard feelings, it's just what we do."

My jaw fell open and he rolled his eyes and stared at me pointedly. "Don't look at me like that. Trust me, you've got plenty of blood on your hands."

My eyes widened and a cold sensation passed over my body as I fought the shiver that ran down my spine.

It all just sounded completely ridiculous.

"This is a prank, isn't it? This cannot be real."

He huffed and leant his head back with his eyes closed. "Just let me show you."

"Give me one reason I can trust you and I'll come with you."

He slowly stood up, his gaze sliding to mine, and the look that flashed in his eyes triggered my fight or flight response. I tried to quickly dart past him towards the bedroom, but he grabbed my arm and span me round once again pressing me into the door. I began to struggle when the sudden heat of his body pressing into my back made me stop still.

"You have a tattoo of a lotus flower right here," he said softly, as he lightly moved my hair back to reveal my tattoo behind my ear, his fingers brushed against my neck and I swallowed hard. "It's symbolic," he said, his voice was

A Lotus in the Dark

unbearably close to my ear and I felt this was way too intimate a position to be in with someone I didn't know and yet I couldn't move. "A lotus flower grows in muddy water, rising through the darkness and into the light to bloom, beautiful and strong."

A sensation I'd most *certainly* identify as recognition flushed over my whole body, making my chest tighten and I breathed heavily as he stepped away from me.

I turned to face him and looked into his expression for a couple of seconds and he didn't look away.

I had to know what was going on, one way or another. I had to take this leap of faith.

I swallowed hard and took a deep breath. "Fine."

He nodded and the corner of his mouth twitched triumphantly, then he walked over to the front door. He felt around the rim of the doorway and with a slight click, a tiny panel on the wall opened up, revealing a row of four different keys on hooks.

He raised an eyebrow at me. "You didn't find the cars then."

I frowned, annoyed at myself. I'd looked around this flat so thoroughly I couldn't believe I'd missed that.

We left immediately and locked the door behind us. I had only the clothes on my back and the contents of my bag.

I followed Ethan to an underground garage just around the corner where he put in an 8-digit code and revealed four different luxury cars.

My jaw dropped open as he unlocked a white Lamborghini. "Are we... rich rich?"

"You could say that."

He climbed in and I slid into the passenger seat next to him and took a deep breath, as he reversed out of the garage and sped down the street.

Only about half an hour later Ethan pulled into a similar garage as before and we stepped out of the car.

"Where are we?" I asked.

"A little town between Oxford and London. Are you hungry?" he asked.

I blinked at him over the car, not expecting the question, but my stomach growled in response.

"That would be a yes but I don't really feel like eating, I just want to get on with whatever it is we're doing." I put my hands on my hips and hoped I looked defiant.

"Well, we have to wait a few more hours. We can't enter until it's dark, it's too risky."

Before I could respond he turned and started walking down the quiet road, a row of cute little houses to our left and trees to the right.

I huffed and followed after him.

"Too risky, why? We're out together in broad daylight right now."

He shook his head. "You'll understand later. Come on, I know a place near here."

I pulled on his arm and he stopped and turned to face me with an eyebrow raised.

"Can you at least just explain what the hell is going on? I've come with you without a fuss even though I have no idea who you are, where we're going or what we're doing. I think I've been pretty patient."

He huffed out a sarcastic laugh. "It's cute you think you had a choice in coming here with me."

I put a hand to my chest in a mock gasp. "You think I'm cute?"

His eyes narrowed and then he turned around and started walking again.

I frowned at the back of his head and muttered, "We clearly aren't friends, that much I can figure out for myself."

A Lotus in the Dark

He was silent and I thought he wasn't going to answer but I followed him for a few long seconds, silently admiring the view of his arms from the back, when he said, "You get three questions."

My lips tugged into a smug smile but I wiped it away before Ethan could see. I realised then that I hadn't seen him genuinely smile this whole time; he was so serious I wondered if he ever had fun. I couldn't imagine him laughing. I wondered what our relationship was, if we were friends or just colleagues that barely knew each other and he'd just been sent to collect me. The way I seemed to respond to him told me I knew him better than that.

I thought about what to ask, I didn't even know where to begin.

"Well?" he asked, interrupting my thoughts.

"I'm *thinking*." I snapped and then followed him the rest of the way in silence.

We turned a corner and entered a slightly busier street with a few shops and cafes, he led us into one of them and the smell of coffee and warm pastries made my stomach growl again.

He nodded silently towards a table which I took as an order to sit there, so I purposely sat down in a booth against the wall and gave him an innocent smile. His jaw tensed as he went to the counter to order and I couldn't help but chuckle to myself.

He returned a few moments later and placed a tray in front of us.

"Tea, milk and two sugars and a cinnamon bun." He shook his head disappointedly as though that was what I always ordered and he didn't approve.

I took a bite and couldn't' help the mmm sound that escaped my lips. It was obviously something I loved and he knew that. And he knew how I took my tea.

I asked my first question, "What is our relationship?"

His eyes remained hard and serious. "You have three questions and that's what you want to waste one on?"

Heat coloured my cheeks but I nodded anyway.

He took a sip of his black coffee and stared into the cup. "We are the best at what we do, we have trained together all of our lives and we work together every day."

I narrowed my eyes; it didn't go unnoticed that he dodged the question but I left it alone. I got the feeling he was a bit of an emotionless robot so I changed my line of questioning.

"What do we do?"

"We..." he paused and lifted his eyes to meet mine. "We do whatever Imperium wants us to do."

I sighed. "Can you answer my questions a bit less cryptically please?"

He chewed on a mouthful of his pastry and then swallowed and said, "No, I think this way is much more fun. And that was your third question."

"What? No way that doesn't coun-"

"Stay here I have to make a phone call," he interrupted and then stood up and left without another word.

He was so infuriating.

I angrily finished my tea and bun, annoyed at how accurately he'd selected for me, and began to grow impatient as time went by.

I sighed and got up, walked to the door and looked left and right down the street but couldn't see Ethan anywhere.

"Asshole," I muttered. I considered running away but really, where would I go? What would I even do?

I huffed defeated and sat back in my seat. I pulled out my phone and saw I had a missed call and a couple of messages from James.

How did the hospital appointment go? James.

A Lotus in the Dark

I popped by your flat, but you weren't in, is everything okay? James.

I don't mean to be overbearing but I am rather concerned you aren't home or answering your phone. Just let me know you're okay. Thanks, James.

I couldn't help but smile at how formal he was over text. He did genuinely seem to care about me. I rang him back and he answered on the second ring.

"Rose, hi, how are you?"

I winced at his use of my alias but didn't correct him. I had it for a reason and I had no doubt that meant nobody could know my real name, especially the police.

"I'm okay, I think." I let out a nervous laugh. "It's a long story, an old friend recognised me outside of the hospital. We're just having coffee now and he's explaining a few things."

"Oh," he said surprised. "Has he said anything helpful?"

"Not yet..."

"Just... After what we found in your bedroom, we don't know what or who you're involved with, just be careful Rose."

I smiled. "I know, I am being careful. I will tell you more when–hey!"

My phone was snatched out of my hand and I looked up to see a very angry Ethan towering over me, gripping my phone. He hung up and slipped it into his pocket.

"Who the fuck was that?"

"I made a... friend in the hospital; he was just ringing to check up on me! Give me my phone back." I stood and reached for my phone but noticed a few people in the café turn to stare, so I sat back down.

He sat opposite me; fire blazed in his eyes. My phone suddenly started to ring in his pocket, he pulled it out and went to hang up when he read the name on the screen. I internally cringed as I remembered what I'd saved James as in my phone.

"DCI JJ?" he said through gritted teeth. "Your *friend* is a fucking copper?"

"I... It's a long story."

"We don't need anyone checking up on us Aria, especially not the police! How much does he know?"

"Nothing! I don't even know anything, what could I possibly tell him?"

He pinched the bridge of his nose. "You'd never normally do something so stupid."

"Well, how the *hell* was I supposed to know not to talk to anyone, you weren't exactly there with me helping me in the hospital, were you?" I raised my voice.

"You have no idea what I was doing behind the scenes to fix your fuck up!" He growled, keeping his voice low to not attract any attention. "Do you really think you went from being a suspect in a murder case one day to having the whole case dropped the next? Suicide notes don't usually mysteriously appear overnight, you know."

My blood ran cold as I remembered the police questioning me on the previous owner of my car who'd been found dead. I swallowed hard at his implication.

"So, I was... involved in his death?"

"Shut up," he snapped, looking around us. "Not here, we can't talk about this here."

"You brought it up!" I seethed.

His eyes flashed at me and I sighed and put my head in my hands, my mind racing. When he spoke, his deep voice was surprisingly soft.

"Look, it's pretty much dark now so it's okay for us to go, you'll get all your answers once we're back at Imperium, it's just not safe to talk about it here, okay?"

A Lotus in the Dark

I lifted my head up but refused to meet his gaze, I didn't like his vicious tone, but I certainly didn't like his phony sympathetic tone either.

"Fine. Lead the way," I said.

We left the café and I followed him for only a short walk before we were stood outside of a nightclub with a purple neon sign above the door that read Aces. Two huge bouncers on the door nodded to us with recognition and let us in without a word.

I frowned up at Ethan, confused at why we'd be going into a club but he just nodded and gestured through the door.

We stepped inside and my eyes widened. It was early evening, only just dark and it was heaving already, loud music booming around us. It was dimly lit with a purple hue, booths full of people were placed all around the outside of the room with a large bar against the back wall with a crowd in front of it. In the middle of the room was a large dancefloor with people dancing, talking and laughing with drinks in their hands without a care in the world.

Ethan placed a hand on my lower back, pushing me towards the bar and I let him lead the way, my mind racing with theories about what was happening. He probably could have just explained everything properly before dragging me here but I think he was enjoying tormenting me.

We reached the bar and Ethan held two fingers up at the bartender who immediately stopped serving his current customer and poured Ethan two shots of tequila.

He handed one to me and said, "You're gonna need this," before downing his shot.

I lifted the shot glass to my lips and looked up to meet his gaze. The way his hard eyes glinted made my stomach knot again and I hesitated, pulling the glass back slightly.

"Bottoms up," he said, watching the glass.

It was just tequila, I'd just seen it being poured with my own eyes, and he'd had one himself. I was just being paranoid, albeit justified since I was in a bar with a stranger who I had absolutely no reason to trust.

I huffed, what did I have to lose?

I swallowed the shot down in one. The warm liquid ran over my tastebuds and down my throat and my eyes widened.

Definitely not tequila.

I felt a warm, tingling sensation running down my body, like electricity was flowing through my veins right to the ends of my fingertips. My senses heightened; my brain buzzed with excitement. I felt more alive than I'd ever felt.

I gasped at the feeling and couldn't help but grin up at Ethan. "What is that?"

"It's the Imperium shot, for members only. It's laced with a mood enhancer."

My eyes widened. "So, it's a drug? You just drugged me?"

He shrugged. "I suppose so. But that's sort of what we specialise in, it's a special drug. It boosts your mood without inhibiting cognitive function, so you'll be fine."

"Oh god, we're drug dealers?" I gasped, although couldn't fully get the smile off my face.

He rolled his eyes and tugged on my arm. "Come on."

He led me across the dance floor and through a door at the back of the room with the "Toilets" sign on it.

I tugged my arm back, although a giggle slipped out as the affects of the shot worked it's way around my system.

"I know I don't really know who I am, but I'm sure it takes more than this to get me into the club toilets."

"Really? Because normally all it takes is a cinnamon bun and an Imperium shot."

My eyes snapped up to his, but I saw a glint of amusement.

"You're making fun of me."

His lips twitched but he still didn't fully smile. "Who's the one dragging this out now? Just come on."

"Say please."

A Lotus in the Dark

"What?" he frowned.

"Ask me nicely, something you haven't actually done this whole time. Say please and I will come with you." I put my hands on my hips.

He glanced around the room and then back at me, his jaw tensed and his eyes hardened. In one swift movement he stepped towards me and lifted me up, throwing me over his shoulder. I slammed my fists onto his back as he strode through the door to the toilets, but he continued down the dimly lit corridor for a while, past the toilets and far enough that the sound of the music became a distant hum. When we reached the end, he threw me painfully down onto the floor in front of a large dark purple door.

I sat up, frowning at him.

"I never would have been able to do that to you before, we've got a lot of work to do." He shook his head, his eyes filled with disappointment.

I opened my mouth to speak when he held his left palm to a small silver panel on the front of the door and a green light lit up above our heads. The door clicked open revealing an elevator and I frowned. This was just getting weirder by the second.

I stood up and he pushed me inside and I watched silently as he again put his palm against a small silver panel on the inner wall. The door slid shut and as we began to descend underground, I wondered if my own palm worked on the doors.

As if reading my mind Ethan said, "Yes you're programmed to use the doors as well."

I ignored him, not liking how predictable he found me.

I turned away from him and swallowed hard as we continued our descent, it seemed to be taking forever and the further down we went, the more my palms began to sweat.

Finally, we came to a smooth stop and I released the breath I'd been holding.

"You ready?" he asked, but I didn't have time to answer as the door slid open and he shoved me out of the lift.

I stopped still and stared ahead with wide eyes, not understanding what I was seeing.

Ethan stepped up behind me and I ignored the shiver than ran down my spine as he leaned and put his lips down to my ear.

"Welcome home."

-CHAPTER SIX-

I knew that we were underground, obviously, and yet my brain couldn't quite comprehend the fact that we were inside. Because as soon as I stepped out of the elevator, I was met with a clear starry night sky and a light breeze that blew my hair and tickled my neck.

It was like I had just travelled and stepped out of a train station and into a little town. There were rows of streetlights softly illuminating the paths and although it was night-time and most places were shut, I could still make out a row of shops and cafes to my left. In front of us was what looked like a huge restaurant and I could see people through the windows, sat at tables in the warmly lit diner, enjoying food and conversation. The door swung open and a person about my age and fully dressed in black, casually wandered out of the door with a coffee in their hand and headed away from us. As I watched them walk away, I noticed a street sign saying "School" to the left, "Gym" to the right and "Training Arenas" forward.

There was even a little tram stop with tram tracks inserted into the small road that led into the distance. The only noticeable difference from the real world above our heads was that there were no other vehicles.

My jaw had dropped open and I looked towards Ethan for an explanation but he was looking at me with disappointment again.

"I really thought as soon as you were back you would recognise it."

As I looked around something twisted deep in my gut as an excited, nervous feeling washed over me. I felt like I was home, but like I didn't want to be here. I was conflicted and I knew in my gut that I belonged here but that something had happened to make me leave.

"It's like déjà vu," I said. "Like I've been here before but it feels like it was a dream. How does this all work?" I gestured around us.

He looked up in confusion and then realisation crossed his face, like he was so used to the environment he didn't even question it.

"We're in a sort of dome that uses holographic technology to mimic the outside atmosphere, the time of day, temperature, the weather... only that it doesn't rain and we can't get sunburnt." He shrugged. "We're down here from a very young age and don't leave until we're adults so it's to make it feel real, like a home rather than... an institution."

My stomach clenched uncomfortably again and I stopped looking around in awe to meet his eyes. "How long had I been down here? And you?"

He looked away from me and reached up to rub the back of his neck as he said, "From birth. Both of us."

The world around me seemed to blur and I placed a hand to my chest. "So, our parents are down here too?"

He shook his head. "No. None of us here have biological family, unless we were brought in with siblings which is rare. We are a family in itself at Imperium. We would die for each other if it came to it."

That was rather dramatic and I somehow doubted he would die for me but I moved on.

"So how did we get here in the first place?" I asked.

Ethan huffed, pinched the bridge of his nose and started to walk away.

A Lotus in the Dark

I rolled my eyes. "Oh, I'm sorry that my questions are bothering you, you must be exhausted."

His jaw tensed and he strode towards the cafeteria and swung the door open, I hurried to catch up with him as he called inside. "Isaac!"

Immediately a young man with mousy blonde hair jogged over to us, he had a fresh face and couldn't have been any older than 16. He was dressed in full black attire, the Imperium uniform it seemed, and was quickly trying to finish his mouthful before he had to speak.

He looked apprehensive, like he was intimidated by Ethan but didn't want to show it. Then he looked behind him to me and his brown eyes widened.

"Mentor Aria, you're back." Mentor? "I hope you're well."

I tipped my head sideways and frowned as he bowed his head slightly towards me. Why was he speaking to me like that? I opened my mouth to reply but Ethan interrupted.

"Come with us, I have an important task for you."

Isaac nodded enthusiastically and a few stray curls fell over his eyes. He followed as we stepped back into the quiet street.

"Mentor Aria has unfortunately been involved in an accident above ground and doesn't appear to have any of her memories." I didn't like him speaking about me as though I weren't standing right next to him but I let him continue. "She's been gone a while, so needs to report to the Ambassador. Take her to his office and show her around on the way and answer any questions she has. He's expecting you so make it snappy."

"Yes sir." He nodded.

I frowned again as I wondered who the Ambassador was. My head pounded with the number of questions I had. I still had no idea what was going on or why we were in a little pretend underground town when there was plenty of space up in the real world.

Ethan nodded back and then without so much as a glance in my direction he walked into the cafeteria, letting the door slam behind him.

I frowned after him and then turned to smile at Isaac. "Sorry about this, I know it's a pain. It's just bizarre, there's this whole other world down here that I've supposedly grown up in and I literally don't remember a thing. I don't even know what we do."

He looked at me with wide eyes, like I had just grown another head.

"Is something wrong?" I asked.

"No sorry it's just," he looked around. "There's a set hierarchy here and you don't normally talk to us quite so... frankly."

"You mean nicely?" I asked.

He shrugged, looking down. "I'm an Apprentice and you're a Valda Mentor," he said meaningfully, like I was supposed to understand what any of that meant.

"Isaac, I don't remember a thing. I woke up in the hospital not even knowing my own name, I don't know what you're talking about, so I'm sorry but you're going to have to dumb everything down for me."

He looked incredibly uncomfortable at me talking to him this way but eventually his shoulders relaxed a little. "I understand, where would you like me to begin?"

I had a million questions floating around my head, but the first one that came to mind was about what he'd just said. "Can you explain the Hierarchy?"

He gestured for me to follow, and we began to walk as he explained. "So, it starts with the children, then after school you become an Apprentice."

"And that's what you are?" I asked and he nodded. "How old are you?"

"I'm fourteen, fifteen next month," he answered, and I hid my surprise. I could tell he was young from looking at him,

A Lotus in the Dark

but from the way he acted I had assumed he was older than he looked. "Next month I'll take my assessments to advance to an Operative. There are three levels of Operatives. You've got the Alvara, then the Shamara and then the Valda, they're the best. Above the Operatives are the Mentors. Above them are the four Commanders: one for each Division. Above them is the Ambassador and above him is the President. He runs the whole institution."

I blinked in silence, and I think he could tell that I was thrown by his complete information dump.

"Sorry," he said. "We normally take in information quickly. Perhaps it will be easier to just explain everything as I show you around. We should be quick though; Ambassador Jenkins will not be best pleased if we keep him waiting."

I nodded in agreement and kept up with him as he quickened his pace.

"Imperium is split into four sections; this is the Leisure section," he explained as we walked on. "There are the shops and that's the cafeteria where we eat every day, its open 24 hours and serves breakfast, lunch and dinner."

I followed him down the street taking in my surroundings, the cool breeze blew the hair around my neck again and I shivered. I looked up into the night sky, the bright stars twinkling down at me. It really was amazingly realistic.

"So, this is the school," he said, gesturing to the large colourful building to our left. It just looked like any normal school, with rows of windows to each classroom and a little playground outside. "There's a crèche at the back for the babies and then children go here from three until we're twelve and then we move onto our more advanced education and training. You..." He paused and I felt him glance towards me but when I looked towards him, he looked away.

"I what?" I asked.

"You and Ethan are practically on the wall of fame in there. You're both trained to the highest level and were always the best and top of all of your training right from the beginning, including in the classroom."

I chewed on my lip and looked towards the school, willing any sort of memory to come back, but nothing did.

I forced myself to look away. "What's next?"

We carried on walking down the street, past a little garden area with pretty flower beds and park benches on the outskirts and a large, glorious fountain in the middle. As we walked on, I realised why they had needed to build a tram, this place was *huge*.

"That's the uniform and equipment shop down there." He pointed to a couple of little buildings to the left that looked closed and then gestured to a much larger glass building on the opposite side of the path. "That's the gym and pool. It closes at 11pm and opens at 5am."

We crossed a bridge over an actual little stream with Lily pads bobbing as the water flowed peacefully. I was impressed at the dedication it took to make this place as real-worldly as possible.

I shook my head in awe and breathed, "This place is amazing."

Isaac just looked at me in utter bewilderment before he turned his attention ahead, although I was sure I saw a hint of amusement in his gaze.

We paused in front of a large brick wall and stood at a purple door the same as before with a silver panel on the front. He placed his palm on the front and again a green light lit up above our heads and the door clicked.

He pushed it open and as we stepped through, he said, "This is the second section of Imperium; the Four Divisions."

Once we stepped through and the door slammed shut behind us, the illusion of the outside world disappeared and nothing but a wide corridor with bright white walls greeted us. It was eerily quiet in this section compared to the last and I couldn't see anyone but us. I noticed the tram tracks

A Lotus in the Dark

continued down the corridor into the distance and as I stifled a yawn I wondered if we'd be catching one.

"It's split into four blocks, one for each Division," he said as we walked down the corridor ahead of us with white windowed walls either side.

We eventually reached a cross section where we stood in the centre of the four white blocks, each with a purple door. "There's no time to show you inside each Division now. I can show you tomorrow if you, like but I'm just going to say what everything is and then you can ask questions after does that sound okay?"

I nodded, preparing myself for another information dump and he gestured around each door in a clockwise order.

"Training takes place every weekday from 6:30am, unless you're out on assignment. That section is Intelligence, inside are classrooms for advanced education lessons including maths, science, geography, languages, body language, deception detection and all those kinds of things. Kane is the Intelligence Commander. Next is Cyber-Intelligence, again classrooms full of all hugely advanced technology for lessons in computer skills, hacking and coding. Addison is the Cyber-Intel Commander. Next is The Dojo, where we are trained in Ninjutsu; a mixture of martial arts, hands on combat and stealth training. There's also a room for fitness classes in there. June is The Dojo Commander. And lastly, is Weaponry which is self- explanatory I suppose. We're trained to use the best military grade weapons, inside there is the training arena, a firing range and a secure armoury. Michael is the Weaponry Commander."

He looked at me in hesitation, but my jaw had dropped.

He cleared his throat. "Any questions?"

I looked at him with wide eyes.

"*Why?*" I exclaimed.

He frowned. "What do you mean?"

"Why the hell are we trained like this? It sounds insane, what are we, like an army of Spies... or what... Assassins... Soldiers... *Ninjas*?" I said it all sarcastically, but he shrugged.

"I suppose we're all of that, we're trained to do everything. We do *whatever* we are assigned to do. We have a huge clientele, the elite of the elite and the rich of the rich. We do whatever they hire us to do. I haven't been out in the field yet; we aren't allowed until we advance to Operative level so it's hard to explain... I'm sorry, I've never had to explain it to anyone before, it's just how we grow up, it's what we are born to do. We live and breathe for Imperium, we... we are Imperium."

It was just absurd. Why were we all happy to live down in this underground world, training children like some sort of prison war camp rather than let them live normal happy lives? And why had I been a part of this? It didn't feel right to me. Maybe my accident had altered something in my brain chemistry.

"What if we're not very good?"

He frowned, "What do you mean?"

"Like... I know we obviously have intensive training all of our lives but, surely there are some people who are just not born to be... Operatives."

He rubbed his hands roughly over his face and let out a dramatic sigh. "Mentor Ethan really didn't tell you anything then?"

I shook my head and put my hands on my hips, becoming impatient, so he continued.

"Imperium's speciality is in Nootropics; cognitive enhancing drugs. When we turn twelve, we have an implant inserted into our arms that continuously releases the current drug into our system. Supposedly humans use only 10 percent of our brains in our normal state. With the implants our brains work to about 50 percent of its potential, it gives us a spectacular boost to our brain function, used to magnify memory, intelligence and other cognitive functions. It even enhances physical abilities and the normal pain reserves humans have that restrict our abilities are diminished and so we are far stronger and quicker than average."

I blinked at him, taking in all of the information.

"So, to answer your question," he continued. "We're all good at what we do. We're trained to the best of our enhanced abilities and some of us excel in certain divisions and focus on a specialty. But *yes*, I suppose there are some who still don't quite match up to the rest of us and so they are given other in-house assignments rather than going out into the field. They work in the shops, housekeeping or the kitchen or those whom intelligence massively trumps their physical abilities end up working as biochemists in the lab, working on updated nootropics. They are constantly trying to better the implants."

That explained how I'd nearly managed to defend myself against Ethan in the alleyway.

I frowned, not sure how to feel. Altering children's brain chemistry to be trained into lethal operatives just to be hired by the elite society really didn't sit right with me, but I'd clearly been a huge part of it.

"Something seems to be wrong with my implant then if I can't remember anything," I sighed.

Everything would be so much easier if I could just get my memories back, I knew it was a lot to take in, but something wasn't adding up. I just couldn't get my head around any of it but I could tell Isaac was getting uncomfortable, so I was going to save up all my life altering questions for Ethan whether he liked it or not.

I smiled at him, and his eyes widened, he looked around again like I was doing something wildly inappropriate.

I fought not to roll my eyes and said, "Shall we just continue the tour?"

He nodded with a slight sigh of relief and continued walking. I followed him to another wall and he stood in front of the purple door that matched the others and then looked at me.

"Would you like to try it?" he asked.

I raised my eyebrows.

"Oh sure," I said, and just as I was about to hold up my hand a light caught my attention out of the corner of my eye. I looked towards it and saw another silver door on the far side of the room behind one of the division blocks, just closing as someone went through.

"What's that?" I asked.

"Oh, that's the infirmary. We heal quicker than average but we still get into some pretty dangerous situations so have to have one on site. That's also where the labs are but we... we don't have access to them," he said and quickly turned his attention back to the door and nodded at me to open it.

I narrowed my eyes and took one last look at the door and then turned and held up my left palm to the silver panel the same way I'd seen Isaac and Ethan do. The green light lit up above us, the door clicked open and I smiled triumphantly.

We walked through the door to the third section, this one looked similar to the first and we were once again greeted with a starry sky and light breeze.

"These are the Residence Halls," Isaac said.

There were two huge blocks in front of us painted dark purple with bright white windows. They stretched so far that my eyes widened as I realised how populated this place was.

"The block to the right is for males and the block to the left is for females."

"Is there ever any fraternizing?" I smirked.

Isaac kept his gaze ahead, but his lips twitched as he said, "Sometimes."

I nodded as I followed him down the path between the two blocks for what felt like forever until we reached a little cul-

A Lotus in the Dark

de-sac of actual houses. I counted ten, all with little front gardens with white picket fences. I almost laughed at the absurdity of it all.

"These are the Mentor and Commander houses," he said as he pointed to one in the middle. "That one's yours."

I swallowed hard as something once again twisted deep inside my gut, telling me to run away and get out as fast as I could, but I forced it away.

"There are ten houses?" I asked.

He nodded. "The four commanders I told you about earlier; June, Michael, Addison and Kane. Then there are two Mentors per operative level; Alvara, Shamara and Valda. You and Ethan are Valda Mentors, and I'm sure you'll meet the others tomorrow."

I blew out a breath. Even though it didn't feel like home at all, I couldn't wait to get into bed and be alone with my thoughts. I was mentally drained from the day.

"This is just... It hardly seems worth it. Don't people ever try to leave?"

Isaac looked at me once again like I was insane. "Why would we leave? We have everything we could ever want for here, it's not like we have to pay for anything. Once you have progressed up to Shamara or Valda Operative you can pretty much do what you want anyway, people pay a lot for our services. You can do what you want, even above ground, as long as you still remain loyal to Imperium."

"And what happens if you don't remain loyal to Imperium?" I asked quietly.

He looked around nervously and his voice lowered to match mine. "It doesn't happen."

I swallowed as a shiver ran down my spine. The way Isaac had been nervously looking around, talking as if he was plucked straight out of an Imperium advertisement; I suddenly had the feeling we were being watched.

His eyes met mine and I nodded once showing I understood. He nodded back.

"Through that door is the Ambassador and President HQ," he continued. "When you go through just tell reception that Ambassador Jenkins has requested to see you."

"You're not coming with me?"

He held his hands up and stepped backwards, "Oh no, I'm just an Apprentice."

He looked hesitantly like he wanted to say something but was holding back.

I nodded at him encouragingly. "Go on."

"I know you're a Valda Mentor, but just..." He looked to the ground and lowered his voice so quietly I had to lean in to hear him. "Be careful with your questions, be careful with who you're talking to. Remember the Hierarchy and always trust your instincts about people."

And with that he turned and walked away.

I took a deep breath and held my hand up to the silver panel leading to the final division with the dreaded sense I was being thrown to the wolves.

-CHAPTER SEVEN-

I held my chin up as I walked through the door in an attempt to look more confident than I felt. My head was pounding again, and I couldn't wait to be alone to contemplate my thoughts.

I looked around and my eyes widened in surprise. It looked like we were in a hotel reception, and a posh one at that. There was a glorious crystal chandelier hanging from the ceiling and a huge marble front desk that matched the marble flooring. To the left of the room was a large staircase with golden bannisters and a scarlet red carpet that stretched to a second-floor mezzanine with several doors leading to god-knows-where.

I walked over to the desk where a woman stood with a serious expression, looking towards me over her glasses as though I shouldn't be there.

"Can I help you?" she asked in a tone that made me clench my fists.

I plastered on a fake smile and said, "The Ambassador requested to see me."

She looked at me for a second before she lifted a phone to her ear. "Mentor Aria is here to see you."

I raised an eyebrow, so she knew me? My eyes flicked to her name tag that read "Juliette." I didn't recognise the name, not that I had been expecting to, but we obviously weren't on good terms. Or maybe this was just how she acted with everyone.

She nodded and put the phone down, then turned and pulled open a white cupboard, on the back of the door hung at least 30 keys.

I swallowed, getting the feeling my judgement about it being a hotel had been correct. I wasn't sure why we needed a hotel down here, but I knew we were hired by the "elite of the elite" so despite the fact I may have been jumping to conclusions, an uneasy feeling settled in my stomach.

I suddenly wished that Ethan was with me and then immediately felt annoyed at myself for thinking that, I barely knew him and he was hardly a comforting presence.

She removed the key second left on the top row and handed it to me. I flipped it over in my hand frowning at it, it was a large old fashioned golden key, nothing like the technology of the other doors in this absurd place. Maybe it was purely for aesthetics.

"Go on up," Juliette said impatiently.

"I don't know where I'm going," I said with a shrug. "No memories."

She looked at me like giving me directions was going to extremely impact her day before she huffed and said, "Up the stairs, turn left at the end of the mezzanine, first door from the left."

I flashed her a false smile in thanks and then followed her directions up the stairs, past the row of doors towards the first one on the left. I had so many questions, I needed to find someone in this place who was willing to sit down and answer them properly.

I took a breath and knocked lightly on the door.

A rough voice responded. "Enter."

I used the key the cranky receptionist had given me, pushed open the door and stepped into a what looked like a penthouse apartment. It had huge windows that looked over a

A Lotus in the Dark

beautiful night-time city skyline with lights twinkling against the dark sky. Obviously, it was a complete illusion as we were still far underground, but it looked so real that it almost took my breath away. The rest of the room, however, looked like a typical bachelor pad, all modern tasteless décor in reds, whites, and blacks.

Two men stood in black suits in opposite corners of the room with their hands clasped behind their backs. Their faces were covered with a red mask that stopped just below their eyes. They stood completely still with no expression, only their eyes moved as they followed me into the room.

I'd felt uncomfortable the second I looked around, but something dropped in the pit of my stomach when my eyes fell on the man sat on the red leather sofa.

He leaned forward when our eyes met, and I had to force myself not to turn around and run back out the door. He was wearing a black suit and matching tie, and his watch was so big and ostentatious that I could see it from my position by the door. His dark hair was almost too dark against his pale skin, and I thought Ethan was massive, but he was nothing in comparison to this guy. He smiled at me as I stepped further into the room, although it was closer to a sneer than a smile, and his synthetic white teeth shone so brightly I nearly covered my eyes.

"Please, take a seat," he said, gesturing to the sofa opposite him.

His rough voice made my skin crawl, and I had a terrible feeling my subconscious was trying to tell me something my damn memory wouldn't.

I sat on the sofa opposite him, refusing to break eye contact and show him how uncomfortable he made me feel. He took a sip of his drink from a small whiskey glass, his throat bobbed as he swallowed.

"Ethan informs me you have amnesia?" he said.

I nodded.

"Speak, girl!" he snapped.

I spoke through gritted teeth. "That's right."

"What do you remember?"

"I don't remember anything. All I remember is waking up in the hospital, I remember the names of objects and how things work but not... anything about my life."

His jaw tensed and he suddenly stood up so quickly that I automatically stood as well. He strode over to me and raised his arm and I automatically lifted mine to block him.

He let out a mocking laugh. "Your instincts are still intact it seems. That's good, we can work with that, but don't try to fight me girl. You won't win."

I bit back on my snarky response and lowered my arm as I remembered Isaac's warning.

He smiled at me as if to say, "good girl" and I fought the urge to smack the smile right off his face.

He opened his hand to reveal a small circular device sitting on his palm.

"Do you know what this is?" he asked.

"No." I frowned.

The Ambassador stepped closer, my stomach churning as the bitter smell of alcohol washed over me.

"It's a lie detector," he said. "It was invented here in our own lab by our team of genius engineers. The best of the best."

He grabbed my chin and roughly placed the device on my temple and as he pushed it, it suctioned down so hard that I winced. Suddenly my head filled with pressure as though something had protruded from the device straight into my brain. I couldn't help but squeeze my eyes shut at the sensation, it wasn't exactly painful, just incredibly uncomfortable.

"It uses electrode technology to read signals from your brainwaves and is 100% accurate. I just have a few questions and if I'm satisfied with your answers then you can go."

A Lotus in the Dark

I took a deep breath, mentally forcing my heart rate to slow down and to my surprise, it did.

I looked up to meet his eyes. "Ask away."

"What colour are your clothes?" he asked, testing the waters it seemed.

"Black," I answered.

The device vibrated through my head and then suddenly from the corner of my eye I saw it flash green. *Truth*.

"Are you Mentor Aria, Valda Operative, working solely for Imperium?"

"So I've been told," I answered.

Once again, the device vibrated and flashed green.

"Have you revealed any information about Imperium to anyone outside of the institution?"

I thought about James but still answered, "No."

Green flash. *Phew*.

"How did you lose your memories?"

"A car accident."

Green flash.

His eyes bore into mine and his lips twitched into a sneer as he said, "Last question. Have you truthfully lost all your memories?"

I frowned. "Yes, why would I lie about that?"

The device flashed green and he yanked it from my temple so quickly I gritted my teeth as it suddenly left my head feeling cold and empty.

"Oh, we just had to check you hadn't been compromised is all. No need to worry my dear, you passed." His lips spread into a sickly smile that was about as real as his teeth. "Unfortunately, you really are indispensable to Imperium, so you will need to work incessantly at getting back your memories and keeping up your training. I will be checking and there will be severe consequences if I find you failing to keep up to our standards."

My eyes hurt with the physical strength it was taking for me to not roll them, but I simply nodded and said, "Yes sir."

He nodded back and turned away from me. "You're dismissed."

I turned and walked out the way I'd came without another word to Ambassador Jenkins or Juliette on reception. I had quickly realised that manners weren't really a thing here, so I wasn't going to worry myself with thanks or farewells.

Although, considering I had been raised here all my life, it did seem strange to me that it felt against my nature to not be polite. Surely, I would be used to it like everyone else. I shook my head and added that thought to the box of mysteries in my brain.

I walked back into the Residents section and into the area with the charming houses. I didn't even know what time it was, although it felt late because of the starry sky above my head, and I noticed only three of the ten houses had their lights on.

I walked down the path of the house five in from the left, the one Isaac had pointed to earlier. I wasn't sure when I had advanced to the level I was or how long I had lived in this house, either way I wasn't getting any homely or welcoming feelings from it.

As I stood outside the dark purple door, I suddenly realised I didn't have a key. I raised my palm to the door handle, nothing happened. I ran my palm all around the door frame, all over the walls either side but still nothing happened.

I sighed; I really didn't want to have to have to ask someone in one of the other houses for help. I tried shaking the door handle, thinking maybe I had left it open, but still the door didn't budge.

I groaned and leaned my head back.

In one last attempt, I banged both palms against the door, and finally it opened with a satisfying click.

A Lotus in the Dark

"Yes!" I quietly cheered, happy that I'd managed to open the door without disturbing anyone else, but my triumph was short lived.

"Think you have the wrong house." I heard Ethans deep voice as he pulled open the door and stepped out, forcing me to take a step backwards.

He gestured to his left. "That one's yours."

"Oh," I frowned. I was sure Isaac had pointed to this house.

He stepped out of the dark doorway into the light and heat flushed my cheeks as I realised that he wasn't wearing a top. I allowed myself one quick glance at his incredibly chiselled chest and stomach, but unfortunately it didn't go unnoticed.

"Did you come here to break into my house or purely for the show?"

I looked up and although his words were laced with humour, his eyes were as dark and cold as always. I swallowed, refusing to let him intimidate me. Whether or not I remembered it, in this world we were equals. I had to keep reminding myself of that fact.

I scowled at him. "I just got the wrong house, no memories remember?"

He rolled his eyes and muttered, "How could I forget?"

"What's that supposed to mean?"

"It means that The Ambassador has just re-assigned all of my field assignments for the next month and dedicated my precious time to training you back up to the level you're supposed to be at."

He stepped forward again but this time I refused to step back and I saw his jaw tense.

"It means that any money or freedom I will have earned over the next month has been wasted on you." Another step. "It means you better work your sorry ass off."

He suddenly shoved me backwards and I landed with a hard thud on my backside. He looked down at me in disappointment for the second time that day as he shook his head.

Then he turned and stepped back into the house as he muttered, "Because we've got a hell of a lot of work to do."

-CHAPTER EIGHT-

I woke up in a bed that didn't feel like mine, but that I had to admit was so incredibly comfortable I didn't want to move. I'd finally made it into my own house last night, the door had opened at the first touch of my palm, and I'd stumbled through the dark rooms and dropped into bed in the clothes I was wearing. I'd had what felt like the longest day in history and had been so mentally exhausted that I'd fallen asleep as soon as my head had hit the pillow.

I looked at the clock on the bedside table next to me and saw it was 6:17am. I rubbed my hands over my face and groaned. I knew my day was going to consist of Ethan brutalising me and I wasn't sure I was ready for it. I still had so many questions and I felt I wouldn't be able to do anything until I understood why we were even doing it in the first place.

I suddenly sat up as I thought of James. It felt like a lifetime ago that he had been trying to help me figure out my life, had it only been a day? Ethan still had my phone from when he'd confiscated it in the café. I'd have to ask to ring him and get him off our case else there's no way he'd let it rest and I didn't want to put him in any danger.

I sat up and looked around, the room was a lot lighter this morning so I could take in my surroundings. It was surprisingly warm and cosy, all decorated in neutrals and browns, it felt homier than the apartment in Oxford. I forced myself to climb out from under the large cream duvet, even though it was so soft all I really wanted to do was wrap myself in it like a human burrito.

I found the ensuite to my bedroom and stripped down before stepping under the huge shower hanging from the ceiling. I looked around for any controls but all there was on the wall was a silver panel. I held my hand up to it and the shower immediately rained down at the perfect temperature.

I washed my hair with the shampoo and conditioner I found on a little shelf on the wall of the shower, the scent of vanilla and coconut once again stirring something deep inside my stomach. A feeling I had started to get wearily accustomed to. With a sigh, I held up my palm to stop the shower. Instead, the shower flipped and turned into what can only be described as a massive human hairdryer. It bellowed down over me, almost too hot, and seconds later it stopped and I was completely dry.

I let out a light chuckle and shook my head. This place was wild, it had some seriously advanced technology that they didn't seem interested in sharing with the rest of the world and I wondered why. Another question to add to my never-ending list.

I stepped out of the shower and wrapped myself in a huge towel purely for comfort purposes and then walked into my bedroom and over to the large wardrobe on the far side of the wall. Before I even opened my wardrobe, I knew it would all be comfortable, practical, black clothing. I dropped my towel and rummaged around, wondering if I should go for a black vest top or hoody.

"Go for the vest top."

I squealed as I spun round, inadvertently giving Ethan a full show, and then grabbed the towel at my feet and yanked it up to cover my dignity.

"What the *hell* is the matter with you?" I gaped.

A Lotus in the Dark

He shrugged casually as he walked into the room towards me. "It's nothing I haven't seen before. Go with the vest top, you'll need to be comfortable."

I was still looking at him with wide eyes. "How did you get in here?"

He just rolled his eyes and said, "Be outside in two minutes."

Then he walked out without another word.

"Pervert!" I called after him and would have sworn I'd heard a light chuckle if it hadn't been for the fact that I hadn't even once seen him crack a smile.

We had taken the tram straight to the Four Divisions and sat in silence for the duration of the 4-minute journey. I had tried to make a start on my never-ending list of questions, but Ethan had just responded with a shake of the head and a raised finger each time I had tried to speak.

I'd fought the urge to break his finger and instead stared out the window, deciding perhaps that wasn't the best way to start off the day.

It was a completely different atmosphere outside now that it was lit up and resembled daytime. As I looked out of the window, we passed by hordes of people leaving their residences all dressed in black, chatting away to each other. When we entered the Four Divisions, they all went their separate ways towards the different divisions, like students all heading to their assigned classrooms.

We got off the tram and I apprehensively followed Ethan towards the block I remembered Isaac had told me was The Dojo.

"We're doing hands on combat today?" I asked.

He nodded and I followed him through the door. We passed through the first main hall where students were training in various physical activities. I looked around in awe as they practiced either on punching bags or each other. They really were impressive, there were no sloppy unpractised movements, they were swift and graceful, moving without hesitation, so fast my eyes could barely keep up.

My stomach twisted, but not with nerves like I had anticipated, rather with excitement. There was something thrilling about knowing not only I could do that, but I was supposedly better than all these students. I *mentored* these students.

A slight smile tugged at my lips and Ethan caught my eye but looked away quickly. I wondered what his deal was. His mood seemed to fluctuate constantly. There was more to this story than I was being told and I knew I'd get to the bottom of it sooner or later. But for now, I would play along and do as I was told.

I followed him into a smaller empty room off the side of the main hall.

"I thought it would be better to work in private to start with," he said.

He turned to face me, and something suddenly flashed deep in my subconscious, like a reel of blurred memories playing back to me.

I blinked a few times and took a step back.

"What now?" he asked, his jaw tense.

"I just... You standing there... It's like DeJa'Vu. Like I have a memory but can't get to it."

"We train in this room together all the time Aria, you'll have loads of memories in here," he said as he turned back around.

His voice was flat and void of all emotion which only confused me more as my brain was assaulted with images of Ethan standing in this room, he was goading me on but he was... laughing. Not full belly laughing just lightly chuckling, but his whole face lit up and his eyes were full of humour and mischief rather than the cold, empty eyes I had become accustomed to the last couple of days.

A Lotus in the Dark

The broken memory filled my chest with joy, it made me want to laugh back at him and I knew in that moment that there used to be happiness here.

Something had happened. Something had gone very wrong since that memory.

I swallowed hard; unsure whether I should ask what had happened, but I decided against it.

Ethan turned back to face me, he planted his feet slightly apart, his expression turned dark, and he raised his hands.

"You ready?"

My eyes widened. "Ready for what?"

"This is what we do, this is how you and I train the best, we fight until submission. I want to see how much you remember."

I put my hands on my hips as I looked at the size of him compared to me. He was literally twice my size; I wasn't even sure both of my hands would go around one of his biceps.

"I don't remember anything," I said through gritted teeth. "Why can't you idiots understand that."

"You did fine back above ground the other day. Your body reacted without even trying. I want to see what you can do when you *do* try. Oh, and remember to tap out when I win." His lips twisted into a slight smirk that made my stomach jolt.

I huffed. "This is ridiculous I don't even – Ow!"

He had smacked me across the face so suddenly I hadn't seen it coming, I lifted my hand to the spot where my lip was tingling and pulled back to see he had drawn blood.

Asshole.

He smirked and gave me a "bring it on" gesture. I shook my head at him in disbelief, this is where he seemed most comfortable, most at ease.

So, I'd play along.

I lunged forward quickly, hoping to take him off guard and punch him in the throat but he moved quickly to the side, gripping my upper arm as I missed him and then threw me down to the floor. I landed with an undignified huff down on my stomach but pushed myself quickly up off the floor. I turned back towards him and attempted to kicked upwards into his stomach, but again he anticipated my move and grabbed my ankle.

"Way too predictable," he shook his head as he twisted my leg and I inelegantly flopped down on the floor again.

Once again, I pushed back up off the floor, this time I took a step backwards rather than going to him. He lunged towards me with a giant fist and I instinctively dodged it with grace, although it was close. I swallowed as I realised he wasn't holding back, if he'd connected with my nose then I was sure it would have broken.

He jabbed with his other fist and once again my body reacted and I dodged to the right, I kicked my foot straight into the top of his thigh and his leg nearly gave way, but he quickly recovered, grabbing the tops of my arms and throwing me down on the floor so hard my vision blurred.

I took a couple seconds to allow the room to stop spinning and then once again pushed myself up off the floor. I looked at him, determination plastered on my face, blew out a breath and lunged for him again. There was no way I'd give him the satisfaction of tapping out.

The next hour consisted of the same routine, I'd try my best for a few minutes and then end up on my face on the floor. I'd been punched, kicked and slapped, my lip was split, my eye was so swollen I could barely see out of it, and I was sure he'd broken one of my ribs.

He had gotten me down to the floor for the hundredth time, his forearm pressed painfully down onto my neck. I scratched and pulled at his arm, but he was too strong and I was starting to panic as I couldn't take a breath. My vision started to blur and I thrashed underneath him, trying to throw him off but he barely budged. In fact, after this whole time he was barely even out of breath.

A Lotus in the Dark

"Tap out Aria," he growled as he pressed harder into my throat.

I punched his sides, but my arms were growing weaker as my oxygen supply began to run out. My vision completely blurred and began to darken around the edges.

I was going to pass out.

"Aria. Tap. *Out*." Ethan said through gritted teeth.

Any second now.

"Ah, *fuck*," Ethan growled, he shoved away from me, and I immediately and quite dramatically gasped for air.

I pushed up to on all fours and coughed and spluttered, gasping until I managed to level my breaths.

"You're supposed to tap out unless you actually want me to kill you," Ethan's sharp voice came from behind me.

I managed to finally compose myself and looked up at him with a big smile on my face.

"Does that mean I won?"

He frowned down at me, his cold eyes suddenly shifted as a glimpse of amusement entered them and he seemed to fight a smile. He reached out a hand which I accepted, and he pulled me upwards into him.

"Far from it," he smirked.

Then just as quickly as the light had entered his eyes it disappeared, and he stepped away from me. I ignored the sinking feeling in my stomach and folded my arms.

"Your technique is sloppy; you're not focused enough. At no point were you close to getting the upper hand," he said seriously.

I gestured to his body. "Have you seen the size of you, what do you expect?"

He shook his head. "You repeat this to anyone and you're as good as dead, but in this room, we're equals Aria. You've got me to the submission point just as many times as I have you. I use my strength and yes, strength is important and you're by no means weak, but technique is just as important."

He looked up to meet my eyes. "You're a smaller fighter, you are focused, graceful and tactical. You fight with more determination and ferocity than anyone I know to bridge the gap between us and that makes you just as strong as I."

I swallowed hard at his words as my heart started to thump in my chest.

I looked down at my feet. "I still don't understand why we have to do any of this. What we're trained this way for."

He sighed and pulled a phone out of his back pocket. I was going to ignore the fact he'd not even felt the need to put his phone away during our training.

It also reminded me again I needed to ring James.

He tapped a few times on his screen and then passed the phone to me.

On the screen was a photo of a little girl, with blonde pigtails and cute freckles over her cheeks. She couldn't have been any older than five. She smiled up at the camera, her face full of happy innocence. I frowned down at the photo and then looked up to meet Ethan's eyes.

"That's Janie.... Our last mission, the night you crashed your car, we were hired by Mrs Rogers. Frank Rogers' wife."

My mind whirled back to the night my memories began, with the police questioning me about the murder of Frank Rogers.

"The police said he committed suicide."

He let out a humourless chuckle. "That's because we're good at our jobs. Like I said before, suicide notes don't usually mysteriously appear overnight. He was a powerful politician; his wife had been trying to escape his abuse for years, but he always found a way to get her back. One night she found him sneaking into their daughter Janie's bed. She stopped him, but you best believe he put her in the hospital for it."

I swallowed the bile threatening to rise from my stomach.

A Lotus in the Dark

"One night sometime after she had returned home, she went to comfort her daughter after she had wet the bed. Janie told her mother all about her nightmares entailing the monster that sneaks into her bed. It would appear her father had managed to steal her innocence while her mother was fighting for her life in the hospital... She's only *five*."

I dragged my eyes away from the photo, nausea sweeping through my stomach.

"Mrs Rogers packed her bags in the night and ran away with Janie, but he's a powerful man with powerful contacts. His men found her, and you can imagine how he retaliated when they got home." He took a deep breath. "Finally, she decided enough was enough and through our contacts she found us. We did what we were hired to do and... now he will never hurt that little girl or anyone else, ever again."

He nodded down at the phone, and I looked at the beautiful face looking up at me, her wide innocent eyes now telling a completely different story.

"That's the reason we do what we do."

-CHAPTER NINE-

We cleared up the training room in silence, my mind reeling from our previous conversation. My feelings were suddenly completely conflicted, I was unsure how to feel about any of it. I wasn't sure what was right and what was wrong. I was even more unsure of who I was. I followed Ethan out of the room as I chewed on my lip, deep in thought.

He glanced over to me and sighed. "You have until we reach the lunch hall to ask as many questions as you want."

I was silent for only a moment as we walked back through the now almost-empty main hall of Dojo. I had so many questions I wasn't even sure where to begin, but I opened with the question that had been eating away at me the most.

"How are we all so okay with implanting children and forcing them to become these deadly soldier-like killers?"

He looked over to me with a slight frown, as though he hadn't been expecting that question and he certainly didn't know how to answer it.

"We're giving their lives a meaning; we give them a purpose. Most, if not all the babies brought in are orphans or from abusive homes or going through withdrawal from whatever shit their drug addict mothers pumped into their bodies while carrying them. We take them in, care for them, give them everything they could wish for. We give them a family and we give their lives a purpose."

A Lotus in the Dark

I followed Ethan onto the tram that was already waiting at the stop outside the Dojo.

I sat in the seat next to him as I quietly said, "They should have a choice."

"We didn't," he responded, and I looked up at him. He was right. We were brought in as babies, raised through childhood here. Yet I didn't remember any of it.

"Next question," he said.

"The implants, do they change who we are?"

He shrugged. "They just make us better. Isaac told me he explained the implants to you."

I nodded, he had. "It just seems weird to me that there's something coursing through our veins that can have that effect."

"Well, yours seems to be broken," he said, sarcastically.

I rolled my eyes but lingered on that thought for a second before I mentally shook it away.

"They aren't a bad thing. They make us better and enhanced in every aspect – we're stronger, we're faster and we have immense brain power. We move quicker, we react quicker, we can even heal quicker. How did you think you came out of that car crash practically unscathed? Medical miracle my arse." He scoffed. "Without that implant in your arm, you'd be dead."

I swallowed as I remembered the unbearable, excruciating pain I'd felt compared to the lack of injuries the doctors had found.

"It's why we have our own hospital down here, it's too risky for the doctors above to treat us, they'd start to notice. But you happened to crash just as a bloody paramedic was passing by and she called it in before we could get to you. We had to leave you a couple of days to avoid suspicion, it was only when I came to pick you up that I realised you didn't have any of your memories."

I just nodded, taking it all in as I looked out the window. We were just passing through the divisions, almost at the lunch hall, so I moved on to my next question.

"Why children, why start us so young?"

"Children's minds adapt easier, they learn quicker. But mainly, nobody suspects children."

I looked at him as my skin suddenly felt cold. Until that moment I'd assumed we had just trained our whole lives and then when we reached maturity, we were sent out into the field to carry out whatever it was we'd been hired to do.

"So, we send children out... to...?"

He nodded. "We were fourteen on our first field assignment. I can't believe you don't remember... it was such a thrill for us." He shook his head. "We'd been training our whole lives for that moment."

Fourteen. Still a child.

"What was our assignment?" I asked quietly.

"We'd received intel about a child trafficking ring. We went undercover, me you and a couple others, pretending we were younger than we were. They thought they were grooming us, but we purposely let ourselves get caught and they took us to these units where they were auctioning hundreds of terrified kids, boys and girls, all aged about 6 to 12. We got every single one of those kids out of there."

"And the people running the ring?"

"What do you think?"

"So," I had to just say the words. "My first... murder, was at fourteen years old?"

"I prefer assassination, but yes."

My heart thumped hard against my chest.

"Death isn't always the worst thing that can happen to a person."

I frowned at him, and he continued.

"We saved a lot of lives that night, Aria. You didn't even hesitate. Yes, we assassinated the scumbags running the ring, but in doing so we prevented hundreds of children from being subjected to a fate far worse than death."

I thought about it for a second.

Death isn't always the worst thing that can happen to a person.

We all lost our childhoods down here; it hadn't seemed fair, but now I wasn't sure. Perhaps he was right. We were all part of something huge, this was our purpose in life. In sacrificing our childhoods to this cause, we were saving thousands more.

"So, we're vigilantes?"

He shook his head and looked at me with his dark eyes, although they were laced with that humorous glint that seemed to always be trying to fight its way out.

"Call us what you want, Aria, whatever helps you sleep at night."

I opened my mouth to respond with something sarcastic, but he interrupted me.

"Question time is over."

I looked up as the tram pulled to a stop outside the lunch hall. Everyone on the tram got up and made their way out. Some stared at us, some uttered their greetings, some even bowed their heads slightly.

Ethan ignored them while I smiled politely back, which only turned their expressions to a look of horror. I looked up at Ethan and he rolled his eyes at me and stepped off the tram without a word.

I looked around as I followed him. The Leisure Section looked completely different now it was the middle of the day. The sky above was bright blue with a few clouds dotted around and there was a slight warm breeze tickling my skin. The shops and cafés that had been closed the night before were bustling with students, all dressed in black.

I frowned as I looked around again. Something was off. Something more than the fact we were living in a completely simulated underground world of assassins.

I just couldn't put my finger on it.

I followed Ethan into the lunch hall where he headed towards a table with two young men already seated, they looked in their young twenties, about the same age as us.

That's when it hit me.

I looked around again, we were a few of the oldest here. Everyone else, they were all children, but this place had been going for years.

"Where are all the others?" I whispered to Ethan quickly before we reached the table.

"What others?"

"It's just us and kids here, there's a few people our age, I'm assuming we're all Mentors. Where are all the kids who have grown into adults here? That have been here all their lives like us and the ones before us?"

"We are let go when we reach 18, unless our services are particularly requested or we are needed as a mentor or higher, like us."

"What do you mean, let go?" I asked, confused.

He shrugged. "Like I said, nobody suspects children."

"But-"

He spun to face me, his jaw tensed, and his eyes flashed. He didn't say a word, but it was enough for me to know he was telling me to shut up. I gritted my teeth to stop from snapping back at him and instead silently gestured for him to continue to lead the way.

We reached the table and sat down opposite the two men who nodded to me in greeting. They were both ridiculously muscular, not quite as large at Ethan, but still pretty huge.

"Is it true then?" The one on the left said, his brown hair was tussled and his lip was slightly split, as though he had just been fighting.

A Lotus in the Dark

I realised then that I could now see out of my eye that was swollen shut only a few moments ago, and my lip was no longer bleeding, thanks to the implant.

"Is what true?" I asked.

"There are rumours going around that you got yourself into a car accident and turned your brain to mush," he said, his lip slightly curled as though he was disgusted at the thought. I looked at the other one who just looked at me, with cold vacant eyes.

I felt Ethan slightly shift in his seat beside me, but I refused to let them intimidate me.

"I've lost my memories, that's it. The rest of me is just fine."

"That's not what we've heard, looks like there won't be any use for you here soon. You'll be let go just like all the other Mundanes."

My eyes flicked to Ethan, he knew I didn't recognise the word, but he wouldn't jump in to help me, not here.

"Don't you think I would have been let go already if that were the case? The Ambassador told me himself I was indispensable, unlike the rest of you."

Something flashed in their eyes and I could tell I'd hit the nail on the head. They were resentful, I had been better than them. I *was* better than them.

They both stood and walked away with a final cold sneer in my direction. Everyone here was so robot-like, like they lacked any sort of humanity. I suppose growing up in a place like this would make anyone institutionalised, but then why did I feel so different?

I blew out a breath as they walked away and muttered under my breath, "Dicks."

Ethan stood up quickly and looked down at me. "I'll get us some food; it will be quicker than you trying to remember what you actually like."

I nodded and mumbled my thanks, although I knew he was acting out of efficiency rather than generosity. I rubbed my hands through my hair as he walked away.

There was so much to take in.

I had completely healed from our session earlier; my previously painful shoulders were now moving with ease, as though I'd not just had the shit kicked out of me.

I couldn't imagine a time when I had ever been able to beat Ethan in that room. He was just so quick and graceful, always ten steps ahead of me like he knew what move I was going to make before I even knew it myself.

Something competitive flared up inside of me, and I had to admit to myself that I'd gotten a weird sort of thrill from our fight and knowing what I was capable of. I already wanted to get back to training to learn what I'd forgotten.

I was still conflicted, something seemed off about this place, something I still couldn't put my finger on. But everyone seemed content with their place here and their role in this world.

My mind flashed to the photograph of the little girl Ethan had showed me, as well as the thoughts of the poor innocent children we'd saved from being trafficked, even though we'd only been children ourselves. Being down here and training all our lives meant that we saved countless others, but in doing so, we all lost our own childhoods.

Lost deep in my conflicted thoughts, I nearly jumped out of my skin when someone roughly grabbed my arm. I looked up at the culprit as they slid into the seat next to me.

It was a woman I guessed to be in her mid-thirties, the oldest person here that I had seen aside from the Ambassador. She had her blonde hair pulled into a ponytail and was wearing the same tight black attire as us, which accentuated her feminine but muscular physique.

Most notably though, her bright blue eyes were drilling into mine with a sense of panic I felt instantly.

A Lotus in the Dark

"Where the hell have you been?" she hissed quietly as she leaned in closer, looking around to make sure nobody was listening. "When we heard about your accident, we were worried sick, we even had to delay the last drop!"

I frowned at her. What the hell was she talking about?

She frowned back, her eyes filled with emotion, and placed a gentle hand on my arm. "I mean, don't get me wrong I'm beyond relieved you're okay, but you know you can't just drop off the grid like that! What on earth happened after your crash?"

I opened my mouth to tell her I had no idea what she was talking about, when she suddenly pulled back her hand as she straightened up and looked behind me.

I turned in my seat to see Ethan arriving at the table with a tray of food in each hand. He put them down and dropped into the seat opposite us.

I looked to the woman, who had plastered a completely neutral, almost bored expression on her face. Her eyes were now empty, matching the hollow expression that filled all the other eyes in the room.

Ethan nodded towards her in greeting. "Good afternoon, Commander June."

I thought back to yesterday when Isaac had given me the tour of the divisions.

June was the commander of The Dojo, so basically, a total badass.

She nodded back with a neutral expression.

"Good afternoon. I was just here to check why Mentor Aria had not shown up to teach her class this morning."

She was outright lying and something deep in my soul told me I couldn't give her away.

"I-" I began but Ethan interrupted me as usual.

"I thought you were informed of her accident?"

"Can you not talk about me like I'm not sat right next to you," I snapped.

June raised her eyebrows and then quickly lowered them again, as though it was a completely involuntary action.

Ethan ignored me entirely as he spoke again. "She has no memories, she lost them all in the accident. The Ambassador has assigned me the task of training her back up to standard and hopefully regaining her memories."

June looked towards me with concern. She was sending me a message with her eyes, but I couldn't understand what she was trying to say. The expression was only there for a second before she wiped it blank, but it had definitely been there.

"No memories at all?" she asked.

This time I answered before Ethan could. "None, I'm starting to get flashes though, maybe that's a good sign."

She nodded at me once. "I see. I will arrange to get your classes covered for the foreseeable."

Then June stood and, with one final meaningful glance towards me, walked away without another word.

-CHAPTER TEN-

Ethan and I ate our food in silence which for once I was happy with. He had chosen a chicken salad for the both of us which was actually quite nice, but where there was an apple on his tray, on my tray was an additional chocolate cookie. I was obviously serious about getting my sugar fix and he knew it too. I ate it all hungrily and then sat back and sipped my water as I looked around the room and waited for Ethan to finish.

I was still pondering the previous conversation with Commander June. She was obviously talking to me about something she didn't want Ethan knowing, I knew I had to get her alone to find out exactly what she had meant.

'We even had to delay the last drop'

I had so many questions. What drop? Who's we? Why did they have to delay it because of me?

The question eating away at me the most though, was why she seemed so... *alive*. It was the best word I could think of. Her eyes had more emotion and humanity in them than all the other eyes in the room combined. Like she was alert and the others distant, with their eyes cold and empty.

Like Ethan's.

I felt alive though, like her, and the fact that she had tried to hide it made me wonder if should be trying to do the same. I was just so confused.

I sighed and looked back towards Ethan to find he was already looking at me. His empty eyes laced with a little curiosity.

"What?" I snapped.

"This is the longest you've been quiet since we got back here."

"Yeah, well don't get used to it," I smiled sarcastically. "I'm just formulating all my questions so I can ask them all at once."

"Lucky me," he said like he didn't quite believe me.

He finished the last of his water, his throat bobbing as he swallowed. Even his neck was pure muscle. I looked away, silently cursing myself for admiring him once again.

My eyes caught the two operatives who were sat with us earlier as they spoke to a couple others.

"Who were the guys sat here earlier?" I asked Ethan who followed my gaze towards them.

"Shane and Karl, they're brothers. One of the only actual biological sibling pairs in this whole place, they were brought in together. They're Shamara Mentors."

My brain whirled back to the hierarchy. The three levels of operatives were Alvara, Shamara then Valda. "So, they're the ones below us?"

He nodded. "Yep. Gunning for our positions though and have been for ages. Don't take too much notice of them."

I looked towards him. "What's a Mundane?"

"Like I said, when we turn 18, we're expendable. More noticeable, suspicious. Less stealthy and certainly less requested. You and I were always the best, always top. We bring in more clients and money than anyone else, and we're still requested more than anyone else, so we could stay on as Mentors. The others are let go, stripped of their chips and their ID passes," he indicated to the chip in his palm.

"So, after everything they've done, sacrificing their entire lives to Imperium and risking their lives on whatever jobs

A Lotus in the Dark

they've been assigned, they're then just dumped and never allowed to return to their homes and only family they've ever known?" I shook my head.

"Exactly, they've done enough. They're let go with more money they can ever wish for and more freedom than people would pay all that money for before they're even out of their teen years. It's hardly unfair."

"And they're just let go with all the knowledge and power they hold?"

"I mean, they're closely monitored. There may be a little chemical tweaking on how much they exactly remember once they're released, I'm not sure on the exact science of it though, that's not our area."

My heart began to race a little bit. "You're saying they erase their memories?"

"Something like that," he frowned as he took a sip of his water. He genuinely wasn't sure how it worked.

"That doesn't seem right." I shook my head again. "How do we know my memories haven't been erased?"

He rolled his eyes. "Because your amnesia is because of your car accident, we know that. Don't be paranoid, they have no reason to erase your memories."

I chewed my lip; I could only trust he was correct. I didn't get the sense he was lying anyway.

"It just doesn't make much sense, to lose our entire lives being trained this way to be used for a few years at most."

He just shrugged and looked around almost nervously.

I frowned and suddenly felt the need to be reminded why we did this.

"Tell me about some more assignments we've been on."

He stood up. "That would be a waste of time, come on. We've got more training to do."

I didn't move. "Just tell me one, a good one, with a happy ending."

"I'm not sure 'happy ending' would the correct way to describe any of our assignments."

"You know what I mean."

His jaw tensed and he didn't sit down, but then he rolled his eyes and thought for a moment.

"When you were 14 you started talking to a predator who was well known in circles on the dark web. He used to groom children online, even younger than you at the time, pretending to be a child himself. He used photos of his nephew to keep up the pretence. He'd eventually convince the girls to meet him at his home, where he would then create pornographic material, against their will, and sell it on the dark web."

Nausea washed through me again, the world was filled with some seriously sick people.

"You arrived at his house as an innocent, beautiful young girl, he thought he'd hit the jackpot. You secretly filmed every moment you were there, so you had evidence of the disgusting things he was trying to get you to do."

Ethan rubbed a hand over his mouth, and when he pulled it back, he was smiling. A genuine smile that reached his eyes like he was trying not to laugh. I couldn't help but smile back as I wondered why he could possibly be laughing at such a dreadful story, but I daren't say anything that might snap him out of it, so instead silently took a sip of my water.

He shook his head at the memory. "Ten minutes later when you sent us the signal, we barged into the bedroom to find him pinned to the bed, completely naked, tied up like spit roast pig with an apple in his mouth."

I nearly spat out my water but just about managed to swallow it and let my jaw drop open. He smiled back and I couldn't help the laugh that burst out of me.

A few people turned to look which instantly sobered Ethan, his smile dropped, and he straightened. He frowned at himself, as though he was confused that he'd allowed himself to relax for a second. I sighed, the moment was over.

A Lotus in the Dark

"We sent the photos of him in that position to everyone he knew, and then sent all the evidence to the police. He'll be in prison for a very long time."

"I guess that is a happy ending," I said quietly.

He nodded sombrely. "If you ignore the 27 girls he violated prior to his arrest."

I swallowed. He'd gotten everything he deserved then.

"Okay story time is over," he said, starting to walk away. "We've got a lot of work to do else I'm never getting my freedom back."

I nodded as I followed him. "What's next?"

"Back to The Dojo, we're not stopping until you win a fight."

I huffed. "That could take forever. "

He nodded in agreement.

I frowned at his back, but still followed him to the tram stop towards The Dojo when another question popped into my head.

"That assignment you just told me about, who hired us? And the traffic ring and big jobs like that, who hires us then?"

"We have a few contacts in official law enforcement who hire us off the record. They can't exactly publicise using children to take down criminals."

My stomach tensed; we were bigger than I thought. We had contacts everywhere, even official law enforcement. I wasn't sure if that made me feel better or worse, it almost felt corrupt.

I had another sudden thought.

"Where's my phone?"

He ignored me as we stepped onto the tram and took two empty seats at the front.

"I need to call James."

He tensed. "No, you don't. You barely know him, it's too risky."

"I think it would be riskier to not call him and throw him off our scent. Trust me, he's incredibly persistent."

He looked at me intensely for a few seconds. My palms began to sweat, but before I made myself look away, to my surprise he nodded.

"Fine, we'll have to go above ground though as normal phone service doesn't work down here at the risk of being tracked. We'll go later after training."

I nodded in thanks. It was true, I believed James would think something had happened to me if I never spoke to him again and I hadn't told Ethan he'd seen the contents of our personal weapon collection. It was too risky not to let him know I was okay. That and the fact that he had just been incredibly kind, I felt like I owed him that much at least.

We had spent the entire afternoon training in The Dojo. The first few hours were a repeat of the morning, Ethan kicking my ass and then pinning me to the floor time and time again.

My defence instincts seemed to kick in the most without my memories. After just a day's training I was able to swiftly dodge some of his strikes. Some. Not enough.

I certainly didn't manage to land any attacking blows; I barely laid a finger on him.

I was pinned to the floor for the 87th time, Ethan pushed himself off and shook his head.

"I think we're done here for the day."

Disappointment laced his tone which irked me to no end.

"You're not the best teacher, let's face it." I huffed as I pushed myself off the floor and stood to face him with my hands on my hips. "You're just expecting me to fight over and over and pick it up or remember something, but it's not working. You're not teaching me; you're not telling me where I'm going wrong."

He frowned back, annoyance flashing in his eyes.

A Lotus in the Dark

"It's not something I can teach at this stage. You either get it, or you're out. This is who we are, these skills are embedded inside us, they've been drilled into us our entire lives. I can't teach you now, it's too late, you just have to remember. You must let your instincts take over and remember this is who you are, this is what you were made to do."

I gritted my teeth in frustration. "But that's not *working*."

He shrugged. "Then I'll have to find myself a new partner when you get let go."

I folded my arms. "Maybe I want to be let go. I don't remember anything; I have no loyalty or passion about this place. What's the point?"

He was on me in a heartbeat, his front pressed against mine and his hand clamped over my mouth.

"Don't say shit like that," he snapped, eyes boring into mine.

I paused for a second, almost losing myself in the blazing pools of amber before I swallowed hard and shoved against his solid chest with all my strength. To my surprise he involuntarily stepped backwards.

"What's your deal?" I snapped.

"What do you mean?" he snapped back.

"Sometimes you almost act human, like there's an actual living person underneath all that muscle. Other times it's like you've vanished. Same as everyone else in this place with their cold eyes like lifeless robots. It doesn't seem right to me; I don't feel like I belong here."

He stepped forward and raised a hand to cover my mouth once again but I slapped his hand away.

"Will you stop that!" I yelled.

He silently gestured at me to calm down, held his hands up in the defence position and then placed a finger over his lips in a shushing signal.

I breathed heavily as my frustration worked its way out, and my skin started to turn cold as I thought back to when Isaac had acted the same way.

"I think it's time we called it a day," he said again. "We'll go shower up, have some dinner and then you can make your phone call."

He shot me a meaningful look. I nodded back to him showing I understood. Someone was listening.

All the time. Constantly. They were listening to us.

-CHAPTER ELEVEN-

We were part of a large group who boarded the tram outside the cafeteria, back towards our houses. Ethan sat in the middle, where I slipped in next to him. The rest of the group made their way to the back of the tram, but I noticed Isaac and another young operative who sat on the seats across the aisle from us.

"Mentor Aria, Mentor Ethan." Isaac nodded in greeting to each of us.

"Hey!" I smiled and waved at the sight of a familiar face. Isaac *actually* smiled back with a slight shake of his head, as though he found my behaviour to be amusing. He quickly let it drop as he noticed the look of confusion on the face of the boy next to him.

"This is Jacob, he's an apprentice like me." He turned to Jacob. "Mentor Aria lost her memories in a car accident, they're currently re-training in hope she regains them."

Jacob nodded like that explained my behaviour.

He opened his mouth to say something when our attention was brought to a commotion at the doors of the tram.

I noticed Ethan next to me raise his wrist as he checked the time on his watch.

"For fuck's sake," he mumbled.

I frowned, wondering what had annoyed him when the commotion at the doors tumbled onto the tram in the form of about twenty chattering children, aged from two to ten I'd have guessed.

They were ushered on by two young women who I assumed worked as the childminders of Imperium from the way their clothes were ruffled and covered in an assortment of paint and food.

The children piled on, sitting in pairs in the rows of seats in front of us. The youngest child, a little boy about two, plopped himself down on the seat right in front of me and Ethan. He turned to kneel in his seat, staring at us with the biggest brightest blue eyes. He had freckles dotted all over his cheeks and little button nose, and huge curly blonde hair that someone had attempted unsuccessfully to tame with a hairband.

"Well, hi there," I cooed, which earned a huge cheeky grin in response.

"Gosh I'm so sorry," said one of the women as she hurried over with a stern expression.

His grin dropped and his bright eyes widened. I frowned.

"Zachary, sit down. Don't bother the Mentors."

"Leave him," I ordered louder than I had intended to. She awkwardly bowed her head and immediately sat down on the empty chair in front of him with her back to us.

I wasn't sure what had made me snap at her, it just didn't seem fair that these children were in a place like this.

I watched as the younger children of the group chatted or pointed with smiles on their faces, just innocent children with their natural curiosity, no idea of the dramatic course their lives were going to take.

I then looked over to the older end of the group, still children not even in their early teens, and yet they sat still, eyes forward, unmoving, unspeaking. No childlike qualities.

It was so disturbing it made my stomach turn.

It made me wonder who raised us, I saw the school so yes, we had teachers. But who *raised* us?

A Lotus in the Dark

All children really need in their lives is love, attention and a bit of fun, who was providing that?

Zachary, reached forwards and grabbed the bottom of my low ponytail with a sticky hand and tugged on it gently.

I made a big gesture of pretending he had yanked me forward, and he tipped his head back and giggled loudly.

I smiled and then couldn't help myself; something came over me and I lifted a hand to cup his little face and brushed my thumb gently against his soft cheek.

He stilled, like he had never felt such a gesture. But then he looked up at me curiously, with those big blue eyes, and after only a moment he closed them and leant into my hand with a sigh.

It broke my heart into damn pieces.

I felt Ethan shift in his seat next to me and look away from us, out of the window.

I realised in that moment which side I was on.

These children didn't deserve this, they needed love and care.

They needed to live.

Instead, they were being raised like cattle, for a purpose, a monetary gain. Instead of love they were getting discipline, instead of toys they were given weapons, instead of games they were being taught to fight, instead of compassionate, curious, happy children... they were stone cold killers.

Yes, we saved lives, we carried out good deeds. But there were better ways to do it, all the assignments we were hired to do, surely, they could be done in an official, legitimate way.

This wasn't right, and yet I was a huge part of this. I *trained* these kids.

Had my accident changed my brain chemistry? Had I always felt like this? Why did it feel so wrong now?

We reached the stop outside the Residence Halls where all the children clambered off. I looked out the window as

Zachary raised a tiny hand to wave back at me, until he was roughly pulled to stand in line with the others.

I looked away.

The group at the back, as well as the two apprentices, also stood up to leave. On their way past my seat, Isaac lightly brushed the back of his hand against the top of my arm.

It was subtle, so nobody else noticed, but it was certainly intentional.

He was telling me he knew what I was thinking, and he agreed. I wasn't the only one to disagree with what was going on here.

I wasn't quite sure what to do with that.

We had arrived back at our houses, showered and freshened up and then made our way back to the cafeteria for some dinner. My appetite had completely vanished, so I had just sat silently picking at my lasagne while Ethan spoke to a group of Valda Operatives about their classes, his gaze intermittently flicking over to my direction.

I probably should have been paying attention, I needed all the help I could get. I just suddenly didn't have any interest or motivation to excel in something I didn't particularly agree with.

Afterwards, I followed Ethan to the lift we had descended in not too long ago. As we passed the school my stomach clenched, and heat rose to my cheeks. The more I thought about the situation we were in, the angrier it made me. These children should have a choice, to grow up and to live their lives how they wish.

We should have had a choice.

I looked to Ethan as he walked next to me, his jaw was tense and his eyes hard.

I began to casually ask him how he could live with himself when he spoke first.

"I know what you're thinking, but not here," he growled.

A Lotus in the Dark

Of course, I internally sighed. The ever-listening ears.

I gritted my teeth in frustration. This was hardly freedom.

Once we were in the lift and making our ascent back to the real world, I leant my head back against the panel with my eyes closed and sighed.

I needed a plan, I needed to do *something*. Could I really just stay here playing assassin until I figured out what was going on? Until I figured out why I had been so involved in training children to become killing machines when it didn't sit right with me now.

My thoughts flew back to Zachary on the tram, he was still innocent, he hadn't been converted into a mindless assassin yet, he still craved human affection.

Could I get him out of here, was there a way to help them? I didn't know the place well enough, I desperately needed to get my memories back.

"You're plotting."

I looked up to see Ethan's cold eyes on me.

"I'm just enjoying the peace and quiet before we have to go back to you breaking my ribs." I smiled innocently.

He narrowed his eyes and stepped towards me. "I know that look."

I swallowed and silently cursed the rush of heat that flooded through me at his proximity.

"It's quite sadistic actually how much you enjoy torturing me." I put my hands on my hips. "And again, it's clearly not working. I think we should try a different approach tomorrow."

He rolled his eyes and thankfully stepped back. When he spoke, his voice was as cold as his eyes.

"You're deflecting. I know when you're getting your mind set on something and I'm telling you now, whatever it is, forget it."

"I don't know what you're talking about."

He scoffed. "I know you, Aria."

"Well, I don't know *you*," I snapped.

I watched to see if any sign of emotion flickered over his face, but he just blinked and looked away.

"Stone-cold robot," I muttered under my breath, his eyes flicked once in my direction, but he ignored my remark.

We had reached above ground and exited back through Aces nightclub. It was only early evening, but the club was jam-packed, I guessed they kept it busy all the time to hide what was going on downstairs. On the way out I looked longingly towards the bar, a shot or two of tequila would go down well right about now.

We headed towards the café we had gone to when we arrived here. When we reached the entrance Ethan turned towards me and handed my phone to me.

"I'll go and get us a coffee. You have five minutes."

I smiled in thanks, and he hovered for a second, like he wanted to say something else, but then turned around without another word.

I sighed and turned on my phone.

7 missed calls and 5 text messages, all from James asking where I was and if I was okay.

I pressed the little video camera button on the top of our message thread and waited a few rings before his face popped up on the screen. I couldn't help but smile.

"DCI JJ," I said in greeting.

He smirked and rubbed a hand over his face. "Rose, good to see you're alive."

I bit down on my smile at the use of my pseudonym, Rose had never felt right to me.

"I know I'm sorry, I should have called sooner; it's just been hectic." Understatement of the century.

"What's been going on?" he asked. "Have you regained your memories?"

A Lotus in the Dark

"It's a long story, but no I haven't. I'm trying to get them back though, my... colleague is helping me."

"So, are you some kind of undercover agent or am I going to have to arrest you for weapon trafficking?" he joked, his voice light.

I smiled back at him and made the gesture of zipping my lips and throwing away the key.

He smiled for a second before it slipped from his face and he stared at me through the phone for a few moments.

"You can't tell me what's going on, can you?"

I sighed and shook my head. "I just wanted to let you know that you were right, I'm involved in some confidential stuff but I'm fine, I'm safe and I appreciate your help more than you can know. It's probably for the best if we don't have any contact for now. For both of our safeties, I... I can't say any more."

He nodded and raised an eyebrow. "You understand I'm in a position where I should report this, especially after seeing the contents of your wardrobe."

I swallowed. "I know, that's up to you. There won't be a lot to report though."

My stomach knotted. I'd have to tell Ethan the apartment had been compromised and I had no doubt it would be cleared out in a blink of an eye, all records wiped, but he wouldn't he happy about it.

James smirked at me. "I'm just glad you're safe." He paused for a moment and looked around wherever he was. I saw him sit down at a desk and then he lowered his voice. "Are you alone?"

I looked through the glass door of the café, Ethan was still in line, and I didn't think he could hear me. I nodded.

"Look I know you think I'm just an overbearing stranger, but... If you ever need any help, anything at all, you know where I am, okay?"

I nodded seriously. "Thanks James, I don't know what I did to earn your loyalty but I'm glad to have you as a friend."

"Like I said, you remind me of someone." He smiled genuinely, his sapphire eyes shining. "Maybe it's in my nature to help people, but listen I need to say this and it's going to sound a bit absurd..." I frowned as he leant forward and lowered his voice. I glanced again towards the café; Ethan was at the front of the line. "My father owned a ridiculous security tech company, by ridiculous I mean worth millions. Before he passed away, he went a bit... senile." He smiled like that was the polite way of saying it. "He bought this mansion in the middle of nowhere on the outskirts of London, convinced he had God-knows who out to get him, and kitted it out with some of the highest security you've ever seen."

I nodded. "Woah, that's... cool?" I was unsure where he was going with this.

"When he died, I inherited everything. So, what I'm trying to say is if you ever need somewhere to go like that. Just say the word. I've got you."

My chest swelled at his words, and I cleared the lump in my throat. "Well JJ if I'd have known you were a multi-millionaire I might have stuck around."

He smiled and shook his head in a way that said he knew I was deflecting from my emotions with humour.

I looked up to see Ethan walking out with a coffee in each hand. "Thank you, James. Seriously. I'm sorry but I have to go."

He nodded. "Stay safe."

"I'll try."

-CHAPTER TWELVE-

"Is the policeman off our case?" Ethan asked as we walked back to Aces with a coffee each. He'd ordered mine with a vanilla shot, for extra sweetness, just how he knew I liked it.

"I think so, he seemed satisfied that I was okay," I answered. I left out the part about the fancy high tech mansion just in case I ever had to take James up on his offer one day.

He nodded and sipped his coffee.

"I have a question," I said.

"When do you not?" I could almost hear his eyes rolling.

I ignored his jab and asked anyway but kept my voice low. "Down in Imperium, are there people listening to us?"

He kept walking but his whole body tensed as he subtly looked around. He rubbed a hand over the back of his neck as though he was contemplating how much to reveal but then he nodded slightly and matched my hushed tones.

"All the time, you can't even be too careful up here. They're always listening, but they get an alert if a certain buzzword is spoken aloud."

I frowned. "Buzzwords, like what?"

He rolled his eyes at me. "I'm not going to say them out loud am I, dumbass."

At his insult I attempted to slap the top of his arm with the back of my hand, but he instinctively caught my wrist as easily as if I had been moving in slow motion. He gave it a painful squeeze before pushing me away and shaking his head.

"Who is listening?" I asked.

He shrugged. "The President's team, I guess. Or maybe the labs, or the technicians. I'm not sure, we just know someone is."

"What do you mean his team?"

"The Presidents guards, they all reside in the headquarters with him and the Ambassador half the time. They're loyal to a fault, and ruthless too. You don't want to get on their bad side. We think the President recruits them personally or selects from the best of our Operatives instead of letting them go."

I suppressed a shudder at the fact it was Ethan saying those words. I thought he was the ruthless one.

"You think?" I asked.

He shrugged. "They all wear masks; we've never actually seen their faces."

I frowned at this and then asked. "What about the other half of the time, where do they go?"

He shrugged again. "Who knows? Official business, *holidays*," he scoffed. "They've got unlimited funds; I'm sure they do whatever the hell they want to."

I shook my head in disgust. The President was the one running this whole operation yet him and his "Guards" didn't give a shit about the children in this place. As long as they brought in the money, that was all that was important, all they cared about. I bet they never got their hands dirty doing half the shit we were all subjected to.

As we reached Aces, I stopped and looked down the empty road. I wasn't sure how long I could continue down there, and I was sure I didn't even know the half of it.

A Lotus in the Dark

"Why don't people just leave? If we can come up here whenever we want?"

"Only Valda Operatives have access to the lift's functions. But even so, I don't think people could leave."

He looked at me.

Not "would" leave, *"could"* leave.

I didn't even bother asking what that meant as I knew I wouldn't get a straight answer. Or I'd get the shut-up-they're-listening look.

I sighed out loud.

I still had to find Commander June to discover what the hell she'd been talking about in the cafeteria. Maybe she would have an insight into what was going on, why I seemed to feel so differently to everyone in this entire place.

I made that the first step of my plan.

We'd made the descent back to Imperium, my chest growing tighter the further down we reached. We began to head back to our houses but as we walked, we both started to slow our pace.

Something felt... *off*.

The air felt thick with tension.

We looked around, people gathered in groups, talking in hushed whispers, throwing glances around. It was the most animated I'd seen anyone in this place yet.

"What's going on?" I asked Ethan.

He frowned just as Isaac spotted us and he beckoned him over.

"Have you heard?" Isaac asked.

We both spoke at the same time.

"Heard what?"

"What's going on?"

He answered, "Another group have gone missing, just vanished."

My eyes widened. "I thought you said people didn't leave?"

Ethan glowered. "People don't leave, this is a new development. What do you mean *another* group?"

Isaac frowned at Ethan and looked him up and down. "This... This happened last month, and the couple of months before that. Don't you remember?"

Ethan swallowed and his expression hardened, his amber eyes flamed. Isaac shrank under the weight of his stare, and rightly so.

"Of course I remember," he snapped. "I thought you meant another one this month."

I frowned, sensing that he was lying, but why would he lie about that? I ignored it in case my instinct was wrong.

"Who has gone missing? This happens every month?" I asked.

Ethan looked to Isaac to answer, who quickly obliged.

"It's only just started happening but it's the first time in the history of Imperium. The last few months a random group of ten have just disappeared overnight, no sign of where they went. It happened again last night but news has only just got out."

I rubbed my temples. I didn't think this place could get any more confusing.

He leaned forward. "Apparently, the President is furious. He has assembled a full team dedicated to finding the missing operatives."

We all frowned, lost in our own thoughts for a second.

"You don't think they're just escaping themselves?" I asked.

A Lotus in the Dark

Both Ethan and Isaac whipped their heads towards me with wide eyes.

Ah, buzzword.

I winced and made a silent gesture as if to say, "Oops sorry."

Ethan's eyes blazed as Isaac sighed and slowly walked away.

"Nobody would escape," Ethan said pointedly, through gritted teeth. I knew it wasn't for my benefit. "We aren't in prison, and nobody would choose to leave."

"Gotcha."

For some unknown reason as I said this, I gave him a thumbs up. I cringed but stuck with it.

He looked utterly disgusted at my thumb, as if I'd just offered to shove it somewhere and not simply offered a friendly gesture. He turned swiftly toward the tram stop and I hurried after him.

"We'd better turn in," he said. "We have a meeting with Kane in the morning, the Intelligence Commander. He's going to see if he can use some techniques to help get your memories back."

I blanched. "Do you really think he could help?"

He shrugged. "It's worth a shot."

I chewed on my lip.

Would everything change if I regained my memories? Would I go back to being a complicit part of this institution, ignoring the brutality of it all?

I rubbed my temples again; I felt a headache brewing.

After an unbearably silent journey back to our houses, Ethan and I parted ways without so much as a goodbye and I made it through my front door.

I kicked off my shoes and had every intention of immediately passing out on the bed.

That was, if it hadn't been for the woman sitting on the end of it, looking towards me with a huge grin on her face.

I opened my mouth to speak when she stood up and put a finger to her lips. I clamped my mouth shut and she pulled a device out of a little belt bag she had round her waist. It looked like a mini remote control with only a few buttons, one of which she pressed down on with a manicured finger.

There was a slight high-pitched ringing, and then suddenly from the device shot a bright red laser beam that shone directly to the corner of the mirror hanging on the wall.

She waltzed over to where the light aimed and pointed to something that looked like a small black button hidden in the corner of the mirror. She pressed another button on the device and held it to the mirror, and it suddenly snapped with an electric *buzz*.

She let out a satisfied huff and turned towards me and smiled again. She was about my age and beautiful, tall, and slender, her full pink lips were smiling at me. Her long blonde hair was in a high ponytail that swayed sassily down to her hips.

I knew her, I knew in my gut that I knew her, I just didn't know how.

"Those bastards bugged your room again." She put her hands on her hips and stepped towards me. Her smile faltered slightly. "The others told me you have no memories, please don't tell me it's true?"

I swallowed my shock and spoke for the first time. "It is true unfortunately, so if you could start with telling me who the hell you are that would be great."

She tipped her head back and let out a laugh that somehow still sounded musical even though it was humourless.

"Oh god," she groaned, still smirking at me. "You're gonna need this."

A Lotus in the Dark

She pulled out a flask from her belt bag and handed it to me. When I didn't reach out to take it, she huffed dramatically. "It's just tequila."

Yeah, I've heard that before.

I scowled at her. "I'm not taking a drink from a stranger."

Her eyes flashed with hurt for a second before she covered it up with a smile.

"Oh Aria, I'm not a stranger," she said with a wink, and took a huge swig from the flask. "I'm your best friend in this whole crappy world."

My stomach twisted. I had a best friend?

I put my hands on my hips.

"Why would I believe you?" I asked with narrowed eyes.

I was getting sick of not knowing who I could trust in this damn place.

She smirked and walked over to stand directly in front of me, then pulled back her sleeve to reveal a small tattoo on her wrist.

I looked down at it and read aloud, "Live by the sun."

I frowned back up at her. "Is that supposed to mean something to me?"

"It's... never mind. What about this one?"

She turned her head to the side and flipped her long blonde ponytail over to the other shoulder. Behind her ear, in the exact same place as mine, was a small lotus flower tattoo. I lifted my hand and rubbed the spot behind my ear and looked into her eyes that were glinting with wild excitement.

"We're really friends?" I asked.

She nodded. "Yes, and there's so much to tell you and not much time." She glanced at the black watch on her wrist and then tucked the flask back into her bag. "I only have a 15-minute window before I have to get out of here, so we have to make this quick."

I blew out a breath. I was still sceptical but if she had answers for me, I wasn't going to turn her away. I'd learned to trust my gut since being in this place and so far, it wasn't screaming at me to run for the hills.

I sighed. "Okay, I have so many questions I don't even know where to begin–"

She held up a hand to interrupt me. "Sorry no time, I've just got to relay all the most important information at the moment but trust me, you'll understand everything soon, okay?"

I nodded and she leant back so she was perching on the set of wooden drawers at the side of the room.

"Okay, God it's such a long story I don't even know where to start." She sighed and then looked at me. "Our tattoos, they have a meaning. Lotus flowers grow in muddy, murky waters and still bloom beautiful and strong. That symbol, the lotus flower, it represents rising out of the darkness and into the light... It represents the Rebellion."

My chest tightened at the word. *Rebellion.*

"And," I said slowly. "I'm a part of this Rebellion?"

She chucked lightly. "A part of it? Aria, you started the whole damn thing."

-CHAPTER THIRTEEN-

I pinched the bridge of my nose. "I started a Rebellion?"

"Yes, I'll explain as well as I can in the short time we have," she said.

I realised I still didn't even know her name but I wasn't going to interrupt. I was finally getting some answers.

"Imperium started here, years and years ago, way before you and I were brought in. At first it was small and experimental, although I think it has always been about the money. They've hired out operatives since the start even before they introduced the implants. Then the President took over and expanded the whole operation.

Imperium is still the Headquarters but we think there are institutions everywhere now, world-wide. Once he'd expanded and started to bring in the funding, he got rid of all the old biochemists and introduced a new team who were far more radical and began to experiment with more unorthodox practices. The implants we have put into our arms at twelve, you know about them?"

I nodded so she continued. "They're incredible inventions, truly the highest nootropic technology in the world. They're inserted into us when we're children because our brains are still so malleable at that point, they increase our cognitive functions and physical abilities tenfold."

She paused and smirked at me. "I'm sorry I know this is a lot of information at once just bear with me."

"It's fine, I'm following," I replied.

My heart was beating so fast it was about to burst through my chest, but I was keeping up.

"I was told the implants allow us to use a higher percentage of our brains?"

She nodded. "There's an old myth that there are untapped cognitive reserves in our brains and that we could accomplish incredible things if we could access them. Supposedly humans use only 10 percent of our brains in our normal state. With the implants our brains work to about 50 percent of its potential. The President he... to put it bluntly he's a complete and utter psychopath. He wants to up that percentage even higher, working towards superhuman levels, but he doesn't give a shit about the welfare of the people in this place."

That much I'd figured out myself.

She stood and began to pace, her eyes flaming with anger. She was passionate about this, that much was obvious.

"But as you've probably figured out by now, not everything is perfect with the drug. As it gets stronger and intelligence increases, the empathetic side of the brain decreases. It starts to shut down the hypothalamus and inhibits the release of hormones such as dopamine or oxytocin, all the hormones associated with happiness, empathy, love... you get the gist... and it replaces them with serotonin, adrenaline and cortisol, essentially creating mindless killing machines."

"Stone-cold robots," I said quietly.

She nodded sombrely. "Exactly. Except for some reason, it didn't have that effect on you. Your emotions have always been stronger, your empathy always remained intact. Not just you, a few others as well, but the President has no idea, he's happy to turn these children into soldiers. They're completely brainwashed to do anything Imperium tells them; they don't have the emotional capacity to think any other way."

"What about you, you seem more alert than everyone else? In fact, I've not seen you around Imperium since I got back from my accident," I said.

"I was affected by it, but not as deeply as the rest. Most of us who join the Rebellion are that way, it's like we always knew something was off but couldn't figure out what. It's a strange phenomenon, but once our minds click and become aware of the implant it's almost like we can break out of its spell or something. It's impossible to explain. You're the only one we know of that it didn't seem to affect at all, well... you and–" Her watch suddenly let out a high-pitched beep which she silenced immediately and stood up straight. "Five minutes left... Listen, the kids, the ones going missing, I'm sure you've heard about it by now, they aren't missing... It's us. A while back we set up a huge safe haven, we've been gradually rescuing small groups at a time and taking them back to Haven, that's what we call it. It's where I'm living, that's why you've not seen me around. We decided I'd run the ship from there. We've got a full operation going, dorms and our own labs and everything."

"Christ, how did we manage-"

"No time!" I supressed an annoyed huff and let her continue. "You obviously don't remember but that's what I've always specialised in, the biochemistry aspect of things. At Haven we've been experimenting with implants that have the same cognitive enhancements but don't impair the emotional side of the brain."

It all sounded ludicrous.

"Why don't we just, *stop*? I don't understand. Why don't we just go up into the real world and tell everyone what's going on?"

"You don't understand, I meant it when I said Imperium is everywhere. You so much as breathe a word; you'll be dead before you even finish your sentence."

We both paused for a second, and I swallowed hard as I met her stare. "So, I really wasn't a part of this? I hadn't been a part of stealing away all these children's lives... their innocence?"

"Quite the opposite," she raised an eyebrow.

I shut my eyes and blinked away the tears that were threatening to form. "That... is the first thing anyone has said that's actually made sense to me."

Her eyes softened and she made to reach out to me when her watch beeped again. "Ah, I've got to go but you need to know these last things before I do..."

She took a breath and looked towards the window and then looked back to me, she started speaking in such a rush I could barely keep up. "Ethan, he... he was a huge part of the Rebellion with us until your accident, he acted like he had no memories of the whole thing, and it was like he was suddenly one of them, he was cold and distant when he hadn't been before." She paused and smirked at me as though we were sharing and inside joke. "I mean he's always been a bit of an arrogant egomaniac but at least he was on our side. We couldn't risk approaching him while you were gone in case he blew the whole operation."

I thought back to the flashes of memories I'd had of us laughing in the training room, compared to the way he acted with me now.

I ignored the sudden somersaults in my stomach at the mention of his name and asked, "What happened?"

A Lotus in the Dark

"We think they were getting suspicious and took control of the situation."

She walked over to open the window in my bedroom and casually and effortlessly swung a long leg over, so she was straddling the ledge.

"Look... we don't think it's a coincidence similar happened to you. We think you both might have had your memories erased and we're working on something in the labs that might help. We have intel that the President and his team are away on business at the end of the month, we have a small window to come and get you but only for a short while."

She looked behind her shoulder and then looked back to me and held a handout. Instinctively without thinking I took it. She smiled at me, and I couldn't help but give a small smile back, but pulled my hand back nonetheless.

She frowned slightly. "In the meantime, just keep your head down, okay? Stay out of trouble, play the part they want you to play and keep your ears open. I'll see you soon."

She began to swing her other leg over to drop out of the window when I grabbed her arm. She looked back at me.

I wanted to thank her, to ask her to take me with her and answer all my many questions but instead I just said, "I don't even know your name."

She let out a light laugh and said, "It's Ivy," before she dropped out the window and disappeared into the darkness.

It was safe to say I didn't get much sleep that night, regardless of how comfy the bed was. My alarm blared at 6am and I groaned, I'd barely even shut my eyes. I shuffled to the shower and stood under the hot stream of water as my mind reeled with all the same thoughts that had kept me up all night.

On the one hand, I was overwhelmed with all the bombs Ivy had dropped. On the other hand, I was relieved to finally have some actual answers, and everything she'd said had made sense to me. It was like she'd arrived with the final piece of the puzzle I'd been struggling to finish.

It explained why I'd felt such a sense of dread in the pit of my stomach when I'd had to go to the HQ section to meet the Ambassador. I knew in my gut there was more to the story, I knew I didn't agree with what was going on here. I had already felt uneasy at the thought of implanting children to train them into assassins, let alone shutting off the part of the brain that actually makes them human. The President and his team knew of the effects of the implants and still injected us with them anyway.

They didn't care at all that they were essentially creating an army of brainwashed, obedient child soldiers. Not only did they not care, that was actually the goal they'd aimed to achieve.

Of course, it was easier to kill someone if you couldn't feel guilty about it. Easier to blindly follow orders if your moral compass didn't object.

It was so corrupt, so amoral, that I had absolutely no doubt in my mind there was more to Imperium than working as vigilantes.

I had to find out.

I thought about Zachary again, I wasn't sure what it was about him that had stuck in my mind. Maybe his innocent, untainted eyes or the way he'd leaned into my touch, starved of all affection.

If what Ivy said about the Rebellion was true, and for some reason I didn't doubt it was, then that was something I was happy to be a part of.

Play the part they want you to play, she'd said.

If I was going to help get Zachary and all those other innocent children out of here, I was going to have to start

A Lotus in the Dark

working harder at training. There was no guarantee I'd get my memories back, even though Ivy had said they were working on something, I couldn't rely on that.

I'd been the best of the best, Isaac had said.

And the best of the best wouldn't let herself be affected by a teeny bit of amnesia. I'd spent my life learning these skills, they were imbedded, rooted deep inside me. I'd been the only one to not have their humanity affected by the Implant.

I was stronger than that.

I could do this.

I got out of the shower, quickly dressed and then scoffed down a protein bar and banana from the food stash I'd found in the kitchen. I stepped outside of my house and headed towards Ethan's more determined than I had been since I'd lost my memories.

The conversation with Ivy had left an impact, I felt like I finally had a plan, a purpose.

I was a badass, Valda Mentor. I was going to re-learn all my skills quicker than anyone would have thought possible, and I was going to get all these people their lives back.

My sudden determination was short lived, however, because as soon as I arrived at Ethan's his sullen face greeted me at the door to explain Kane had cancelled on us.

"His exact words were 'something has come up that is far more important than helping someone stupid enough to lose her memories'." He looked at me pointedly.

I stared at him. "Oh yes how silly of me, how could I have been so stupid to lose my memories. By the way, how many times is it that have people gone missing from Imperium?"

I said it sarcastically, to let him know I was on to him. His eyebrows twitched into a slight frown, he obviously knew he didn't remember, but didn't know why. If Ivy was right and our memories had been erased because they were onto us, I'd have to tread carefully as to not raise any more suspicion.

He glared down at me and I looked into his amber eyes, sparkling as though he was in there, deep down. I softened my expression as my heart squeezed slightly at the knowledge that he had been against this just as much as I was, he'd been helping to get these kids out of here too.

How could I find out how much he knew? How could I find out how he lost his memories of Haven and the Rebellion? How could I find out why his humanity had been impaired when it seemed to be unaffected before?

And most importantly, how could I get it back?

Maybe they'd messed with his implant when they had his memories removed. Maybe they'd messed with mine too.

My sympathy was also short lived as he suddenly interrupted my thought train with a painful flick to my forehead.

I batted his hand away and rubbed the spot where he'd flicked. "You can be a real asshole sometimes do you know that?"

"You've told me enough times yes."

The weight behind his words told me he meant throughout the course of our lives together not just over the last few days.

I snorted. "Somebody's got to."

-CHAPTER FOURTEEN-

We were just about to enter the Dojo when I noticed Commander June heading in our direction.

I bent down to pretend I was tying my shoelace and said to Ethan, "I'll meet you in the training room."

He huffed in silent agreement and pushed through the door, when it closed behind him, I stood up and turned to face June.

She walked confidently, with her head high, exuding authority as her long ponytail swayed behind her. The few students around us lowered their heads when they walked past her.

She looked around with a serious expression, her lips set in a hard line. When the last of the students entered the Dojo, she stopped in front of me, and I saw her relax slightly.

"How are you doing?" she asked. Her voice was gentle, so opposite to her hardened exterior that I couldn't help but breathe a sigh of relief. I was desperate to ask what the nature of our relationship was.

"I'm okay." I gave her a small smile. "But, still confused, and still have no memories. I have no idea what you were talking about the other day. What did you mean about delaying the dro-"

"We can't talk about that here," she interrupted me with a hard look. "How is your training coming along?"

I sighed. "Not so good, it's not coming back to me like they hoped, and the Ambassador made it clear what would happen if I failed."

June's dark eyes flashed at the mention of the Ambassador. "There is one thing you and I both know makes you stand out in this place."

She looked around again and delicately tucked a loose strand of hair behind my ear, and then gently touched the spot with my tattoo. It was such an unexpected, affectionate, almost motherly gesture that my eyes widened. I was sure it was also her way of telling me she was a part of the Rebellion.

"The lotus flower plunges to life from beneath the mud, it does not let the dirt dampen its strength or beauty. Be like the lotus flower, trust in the light inside you to grow through the dark. Remember who you are and find the fire that fuelled you before they tried to tame you."

I swallowed hard as I looked into her eyes, and I understood what she was saying.

I nodded once and she cupped my cheek for one second, before she once again stood tall, held her head high and winked at me. She plastered a dangerous expression on her face and paced towards the door.

It was as though she had been replaced by a completely different woman.

"I'll find a better time for us to discuss this matter properly," she said and then strode towards the group of students waiting for their class, who all stood up straight and silent in her presence.

I headed straight past them, towards the private training room, where Ethan had already set up.

A Lotus in the Dark

"We'll try this again for the last time today, then tomorrow we'll move on to a different technique," he said, his voice flat.

I manifested my earlier determination to regain my abilities that were lost somewhere along with my memories.

Remember who you are and find the fire that fuelled you before they tried to tame you.

I smiled brightly at him; I wasn't going to hide my emotions in this room. He blinked and turned away from me to lay the training mats down on the floor.

"Finally, he takes my advice," I said.

"Mainly because kicking your ass every five minutes has become quite tedious," he said without turning round.

I rolled my eyes at his back and then quickly tied my hair into a high ponytail, ready for action.

He turned and looked at me then up to my hair, he seemed to pause for a second, then looked away.

"What?" I asked.

"Nothing."

I punched him in the ribs. "What?"

He huffed, taken off guard, and looked at me again. "Your hair… you always used to wear it like that. You haven't since you got back from your accident is all."

His eyebrows furrowed as he looked down at me, he looked almost confused. His eyes searched my face for a moment too long before he turned and stepped away again.

I swallowed and fought the frustrating urge to smile.

I decided in that moment to seize my opportunity while he had his back to me.

I ran and jumped onto his back, wrapping my legs round his waist from behind and linking them together with my ankles around his front. I did the same with my arms around his neck, and squeezed as hard as I could.

He rapidly leant forward so I was practically upside down and reached up to put his hands over the back of my neck and threw me forwards.

To my surprise, instead of landing on my back in an undignified heap as usual, I flipped and landed gracefully on my feet, spinning to face him with my fists raised.

His eyes brightened in excitement which only encouraged me further, and I advanced forwards again.

I had to not overthink this. My body and my brain knew what they were doing, my abilities were rooted deep inside, I just had to let them emerge naturally like I had done in the alleyway before.

I let out a breath to calm myself, and I let my instincts take over.

I swung with my right hand, he blocked me with his and swung with his left and I blocked him with mine.

From there we engaged in a series of swift, graceful movements, both of us powerfully punching, slapping, kicking, but easily blocking each other.

We both managed to land equal blows on one another, his eyebrow was bleeding, as was my lip. I wasn't even sure how; we were moving so quickly.

It was as though we knew exactly where the other was about to strike so knew where to defend. It was like a dance.

It was beautiful.

He jabbed a strong fist towards my jaw, to which I swiftly dodged by squatting down, and as I did, I swung my leg round in a circular motion, kicking both of his legs from beneath him, sending him crashing to the ground.

He landed on his back, and I launched myself up to straddle him and bashed my elbow down onto his nose which sent blood splattering down his face and chest. He roughly

A Lotus in the Dark

grabbed my arms and pushed and rolled so my back was now to the ground, and he had the advantage over me.

He lifted me up with my arms again and slammed me back down, my head banged painfully into the ground, and I flinched as some of his blood dripped across my face. He swiftly flipped me over and wrapped a strong arm around my neck while he pinned me to the ground with his solid knee pressed into my back.

I had no choice as the world started to fade around me.

I tapped out.

He let go immediately and stood up, lifting me up with him and spun me to face him.

We were both breathing heavily, covered in a mixture of each other's blood, and sweat.

And he was *smiling*.

It was a sight to behold, it made his whole face light up. He was beautiful enough when he was his usual sullen self. But smiling, his eyes full of excitement, he was incredible.

It took my breath away.

The lights in the room suddenly began to flicker, drawing our attention upwards for a second before they returned to normal.

"You fucking did it!" he beamed, looking back towards me. "I mean I still won obviously but that was incredible... *you* were incredible."

I smiled back; I couldn't help myself. "I thought about what you said, about the training being drilled into us, about it being a part of who we are. I had to stop overthinking and just let it happen."

He nodded encouragingly and walked to the side of the room to throw me a towel and a bottle of water. I wiped my face and arms and then guzzled down the bottle, as he did the same.

"Let's go again," he said.

So, we did.

For the rest of that day and the three days following.

We'd wake, train, sleep, barely having a minute between sessions, barely even seeing anyone else.

I was improving by the day and sleeping like a corpse each night.

Repeatedly we fought, each time our wounds from the previous fight had healed before we began again.

Each fight was the same, an elegant sequence of swift, unfaltering movements that matched each other until the last moment. Each time Ethan had managed to overthrow me, a hundred different ways, but it hadn't mattered. Even if I had tapped out hundreds of times.

We were almost equals.

He'd kept it professional; he'd not smiled at me like that first fight, not made any jokes or snarky comments. I hated to admit to myself, but I'd been disappointed. I'd thought maybe he was breaking out of whatever hold had been put on him to shut off his human side, like everyone else in this place.

Regardless, even though he wasn't smiling and joking, he still seemed more alive than before. His eyes flashing warm with encouragement and excitement, before he'd frown and turn cold again, like he was in a constant mental battle with himself.

On the end of the third day, we both laid on our backs on the mat, breathing heavily after a particularly long fight. I was holding him off for longer each time, and he was covered in more cuts and bruises than ever.

He sat up and opened his mouth to say something when the door slammed open. I looked up to see Shane and Karl storming through the door.

"We need the room," Shane said.

A Lotus in the Dark

"We were just leaving," Ethan replied as he stood up and I did the same.

I made towards the door when Karl stepped in front of me. He was the wider of the two.

"You can stay if you like, I can show you everything you need to know," his words were full of suggestion, but his voice and eyes were still void of life. I suppressed a shiver.

Ethan placed a hand on Karl's shoulder in warning, but he shrugged him off.

"Or is that what you've actually been using the room for all week?" he sneered and my eyes widened at his implication.

I suddenly had a thought that hadn't crossed my mind yet. Were relationships allowed in Imperium, did they ever happen? Ivy had said the emotional side of the brain that allowed us to feel love was impaired because of our implants, but what about... sexual desire?

It was a natural part of growing up, surely it happened, unless the implants shut off that side of us as well.

My cheeks flushed as my eyes involuntarily flicked to Ethan and I wondered if I had ever been with anyone in that way. I was both annoyed and embarrassed that I had nobody to ask and even more annoyed I couldn't remember in the first place.

Ethan just rolled his eyes, not bothering to entertain Karl's comment with a response.

I made to step round him when he stepped in front of me again.

"She's going to make you weak," he said flatly to Ethan, although his eyes remained on mine. "Did you know we've been covering both of your classes and assignments since your accident? Word is, you still don't remember a thing, including any of your training. Won't be long until they realise that you're not worth the hassle and you end up with the rest of the Mundanes."

I scoffed. "You'd love that wouldn't you? Pretty pathetic though, making your way to the top purely because I've lost my memories, not because you're *actually* better than me."

"I'm a thousand times better than you," he snarled. "You're just requested more because of those things." He gestured to my chest.

"You think I'm requested more because I'm a woman?" I laughed sarcastically but hid my confusion, unsure what he meant by that. "You might be better than me for now, but I'm going to get it all back, so enjoy it while you can."

I patted him patronisingly on the cheek and he grabbed my wrist and pulled me into him so I was pressed against his chest.

"Oh, I'll enjoy it alright," he breathed, his hollow eyes replaced with feral hunger.

Ethan and Shane stepped towards us just as I slammed my knee up into Karl's crotch. He huffed as the air rushed out of his lungs, and as he involuntarily bent forward, I threw my forehead into his nose and smiled as I was greeted with a satisfying crack as it broke.

"*Huh*, turns out I'm better than you even without my memories," I taunted.

He aimed a strong fist towards my face which I blocked easily before Ethan pulled me back at the same time as Shane yanked Karl back by his arm.

"You fucking bitch," Karl snarled as he struggled against his brother's grip.

Ethan pulled me towards him and then shoved me out of the door before turning round with a dangerous look in his eyes.

A Lotus in the Dark

"Touch her again and you're as good as dead," he growled with a sinister coldness to his tone, then he turned and pulled me with him to walk away.

I looked at Ethan, trying not to think too much into it, when Karl's voice followed us just before the door shut.

"Like I said, she's going to make you weak!"

Ethan was still pulling me through the main hall of The Dojo, others turned to stare as I yanked my arm out of his grip.

"You don't have to do that you know; I can defend myself," I said.

He rubbed a hand over his face and looked back at me, I was surprised to see a glint of humour in his eyes.

"Yeah, that much is clear." He looked pointedly to Karl's blood down my front. "I'm obviously a better teacher than I realised."

I smirked at him. "He deserved it anyway."

"I can't argue with that," he said, and his lips twitched slightly before he plastered a neutral expression back on his face, but his eyes lingered on mine for a moment.

I couldn't bring myself to look away, so we just stared at each other for a second before his eyes dropped down to my lips. He turned away quickly, his throat bobbing as he swallowed hard, and my pulse quickened.

"Come on," he said thickly. "Let's get cleaned up, have some lunch and then we'll spend the afternoon in the Weaponry division."

"We're done with combat training?" I asked then cringed as my voice came out all breathless and weird.

I had to admit, even if my mind wasn't, my body undeniably seemed to be reacting to Ethan.

"Not *done*, you still haven't beaten me, we're just taking a break from it. You're nearly there in that department and the

Ambassador was clear that you needed to be excelling in *all* areas of your training."

-CHAPTER FIFTEEN-

The tram ride from The Dojo to our houses took only a few minutes, we exchanged brief words about meeting for lunch and then discussed the training plan for the afternoon.

Ethan was going to be explaining the firearms basics before we were going to do some simple target practice. I'd be lying if I said I wasn't looking forward to it, although I was against the whole operation, I still couldn't hide the thrill of adrenaline from training. It was addictive.

We hopped off the tram and just before we entered our houses I had a thought, so I called to Ethan. "Don't wait for me, I'll meet you at training."

He waved in response, entered his house and shut the door behind him, all without turning to look at me once.

I rolled my eyes. The sooner we sorted out this mess the better, I was getting tired of Ethan's hot and cold routine. Although I had to keep reminding myself it wasn't his fault, there was something more going on. I desperately wished we both had our memories; he didn't even know he was missing any of his, but I could tell from his reaction that he didn't remember the recent groups of kids going missing and I was sure he couldn't remember Haven. Surely, he would have mentioned it to me.

I quickly showered, cringing a little as mine, Ethan and Karl's blood washed off and pooled around my ankles. Once satisfied that I was completely clean, I dressed in our usual black attire and headed out of the house. I jumped on the tram that was luckily just pulling into the stop by our houses and sat in silence looking out the window until we pulled up to the last stop in the Leisure section.

Instead of turning left to the cafeteria however, I turned right and headed straight to the school.

I had to remember my position in Imperium, even though it hadn't felt right to me, the childminders on the tram the other day had acted as though I had authority. So, I would act the same.

Since seeing the small group of children on the tram the other day I just hadn't been able to get their faces out of my head. Little Zachary leaning into my touch, and the older children staring blankly ahead. I needed to see the school for myself, to remind myself why the Rebellion was so important. To remind myself there was a purpose to all of this, a reason to excel at my training and not just disappear back into the real word and leave all of this behind.

The school looked so real. I mean, I knew it was real, but it looked so similar to above ground. I pushed open the large green gate, which opened with no resistance. There was no security to get into the school. I closed the gate behind me and walked through a big garden towards the school. The grass was vibrant green, with bright beautiful flowers and water features lining a pathway towards the entrance. Although I could smell the freshly mowed grass, and could feel the light breeze tickling my skin, I knew it was all artificial.

None of this was real. None of these children were free.

I pushed open the door and walked into the main corridor. It was lined with doorways into classrooms, and with nobody to show me where to go, I held my head high and pushed into the first door on my right.

A Lotus in the Dark

Immediately, everyone in the room stood up. I looked around at the dull classroom, with barely any decoration or colour. Children aged about ten were stood behind three rows of five desks and I swallowed hard as they stared at me. None of the children smiled or waved, or even looked at each other to giggle as children should when their class has been unexpectedly interrupted.

The woman at the front of the classroom spoke sharply.

"Can I help you Mentor Aria? We were in the middle of a test."

I dragged my gaze away from the multiple sets of hollow eyes staring back at me and looked to the woman.

"Where's the nursery?"

"Down the end of the hall to the right."

I stood for a second, and then curiosity got the better of me. I walked over the desk closest to me, picked up the test and read the first question.

"From which chamber of the heart does blood travel to the lungs?"

I sighed and glanced at the rest of the questions; this was a biology test. Advanced for this age group, but it was just biology.

I wasn't sure what I had been expecting: "After killing someone, what is the easiest way to clean up all the victim's blood?"

I mentally rolled my eyes at myself and then without another word I turned around and let the door slam behind me, not wanting to see their faces again.

That's when it hit me.

These children weren't even twelve yet, they hadn't had their implants yet. They still had their full emotional capability, and yet were so without love and affection they were lifeless anyway. It made my stomach turn so much I couldn't even bring myself to go the nursery.

I had wanted to see Zachary again, but I couldn't get too emotionally involved at this point. I needed to just focus on the task at hand, so I turned on my heel and headed in the opposite direction.

I sheepishly entered the Weaponry section, not remembering my way around at all. I began to walk down the corridor in front of me, huge glass windows lined either side. On the left side, the room was empty of people, although the walls were full of all kinds of different, intimidating weapons.

I turned away and looked to the right to see a firing range. Several students were positioned in their own sections, some holding pistols, some holding rifles, but all of them hitting their targets in front of them. This group were all on the older end of the students I'd seen around Imperium, and from the way they stood dead still, barely even flinching as they sent rounds flying through the centre of their targets, they were obviously experts by now.

I began to head for the door when I noticed Ethan stood on the far left of the group. I watched as he picked up a pistol, swiftly reloaded it and aimed upwards towards the target and fired. The first round went through the dead centre, and every single one after went perfectly through the one before.

I shamelessly watched as his strong forearms tensed every time he pressed the trigger, his biceps bulging as he held it up with steady, unwavering arms.

"Enjoying the show?"

I violently flinched at the voice next to me and placed a hand on my chest where my heart thumped.

I turned to see Isaac looking between me and Ethan, with a slight smirk on his face.

A Lotus in the Dark

I narrowed my eyes at him. I was sure he was like Ivy and I. His eyes, although mostly serious, were not cold or empty and right now they shone with humour. I couldn't help but smile at him and he gave a small smile back before he gave me a pointed look and plastered a serious expression on his face. I did the same.

I wasn't sure he was part of the Rebellion, and I couldn't exactly ask outright with the ever-listening ears on us. But I knew in my gut he'd want to be, and I made it part of my plan to get him on board with us.

"I was just watching for... training purposes."

He nodded, and I noticed the way his eyes also slipped over Ethan with appreciation, and he lifted his hand to rub the back of neck before looking away.

I couldn't help my smile and I pointed to his lip as I said, "You've got a little drool, right there."

His head snapped towards me, and I saw him visibly relax when he saw I was smiling at him.

"I get it," I shrugged, looking back towards Ethan. "I think it's very beneficial to our education when the trainers look like... *that*."

I saw Isaac's chest move as he chuckled silently, before his eyes went wide as though he'd not been able to help himself. He looked around to check nobody had seen him laughing.

I rolled my eyes and patted him on the back. "You're good."

He turned and looked at me for a second, studying my face before he lowered his voice.

"I'm falling behind in this section. I'm excelling in all the intelligence classes, but I just... I can't do *that*." He nodded towards the row of students. "I should be able to by now."

I looked up at him and realised he was scared, and he was opening up to me. I swallowed as I realised that meant I was right, the emotional side of his brain was definitely still working, and he knew mine was too.

I forgot how young he was, he was so mature and serious, put together, like everyone else in this place. I kept forgetting that really, he was still a child.

"We can't all be good at everything, even with these implants in our arms. Isn't that why we work in teams? So that each role can be filled with the person best suited, and every strength is covered?" I said softly. "If we were all good at everything, we would have no need for each other."

He gave me a slight appreciative smile which I returned. I gave his arm a light squeeze before I walked past him and headed through the door towards Ethan. I'd delayed this long enough.

He turned to look at me as soon as I walked through the door and his jaw tensed. I walked over to his position and his eyes flashed in anger.

"Where have you been?"

"I had to wash off all that blood, it took ages to get out of my hair," I said.

"You don't have time to worry about your hair," he sneered. "The Ambassador is hounding me to get you trained back up to an acceptable level. God knows what will happen if you fuck this up for us, but we're not going to find out."

I just shrugged. "If I'm gonna keep getting my ass kicked, I'm at least going to do it with clean hair."

"This isn't funny, Aria."

"I'm not laughing."

He let out a frustrated noise and then painfully flicked me in the forehead again, right between my eyes.

"Ow." I batted his hand away. "Will you stop that! You're a Valda Mentor with all these awesome skills and you keep flicking me like a child."

A Lotus in the Dark

"Because you keep acting like a child!"

"Is there a problem here?"

We both turned to see an absolute beast of a man towering over us. Seriously, he was so huge I couldn't help but glance over to the doorway to see how he'd fit through it. He must have at least had to bend down and turn sideways.

"I asked you a question," he boomed, and my eyes snapped back towards him.

"Sorry... I–" I stammered.

"Aria," Ethan interrupted. "This is Commander Michael, head of the Weaponry Division."

"Oh, that's right," Michael sneered. His emerald eyes drilled into mine with such disdain that I had to force myself not to look away. "You've lost all your memories, and they're wasting more resources to try to get them back. I'm not sure why they're bothering myself, but you must have something special we don't know about."

He crossed his arms over his ginormous chest and nodded towards the target Ethan had been firing at.

"Come on then," he said. "Let's see what's so special about Mentor Aria that she couldn't just join the rest of the Mundanes."

I saw Ethan's fist clench by his side, but he spoke calmly, "Sorry sir, but she really doesn't remember anything. I'm not sure she'll even remember how to-"

"Shut it."

He did, but his nostrils flared, and he turned to me with a look that said, don't fucking embarrass us here.

Which of course I was about to do. Epically.

I awkwardly picked up the pistol resting on the table and moved to stand in the spot Ethan had. I raised the gun, relieved to find my hands were steady and not trembling like I was on the inside. I aimed as best as I could and took a breath before I pulled the trigger.

I frowned as the gun let out a low, unsatisfying click.

I went to fire again, then startled as Michael stood behind me and dropped his voice to my ear.

"Usually, for target practice, I would recommend using a loaded weapon."

I wanted to crawl into a hole and die.

I turned to see Ethan pinching the bridge of his nose, facing the opposite direction, as though he couldn't bear to watch the scene unfolding in front of him.

"Right, sorry," I murmured.

I awkwardly held the pistol in my right hand as I picked up a full magazine from the table with my left.

What the hell do I do here?

I breathed and turned over the gun, then noticed a little button on the left-hand side just below the trigger. I pressed it and then physically cringed as the empty magazine fell out of the bottom of the gun with a loud, embarrassing crash onto the floor.

This was probably the only time in my life I was willing for a sudden heart attack to take me away from the situation. Or stroke, or brain haemorrhage. I wasn't fussy.

Michael snatched the gun and magazine from my hands, and gracefully reloaded it in less than a second, then held it back out to me.

I swallowed and took the gun, not daring to look up at him. I turned, aimed again, took a deep breath in and blew it out. I could do this, I just had to relax and let it happen naturally like I had before.

I took one more breath, looking at the target and was about to fire when suddenly the room around me blurred except for the target and my vision quite literally zoomed in. It was as

A Lotus in the Dark

though the target was right in front of me, I felt like I could press the tip of the gun against the centre.

So, I breathed, aimed and pulled the trigger and watched the bullet fire straight through the hole directly in the centre that Ethan had made before. Then I fired a second and third round through it again, just for good measure.

I barely registered Michael as he reached forward and clicked a button on the wall next to me. The target began to move side to side rapidly, in no particular pattern.

I breathed, aimed and fired over and over again, each bullet passing beautifully through the centre until the gun was emptied once more.

I stood back breathing heavily and blinked, the room and my vision returned to normal. I wanted to punch the air in triumph but forced myself to remain cool.

So, I turned calmly and looked to Michael and Ethan and was surprised to find them both smirking at me.

Michael nodded at me once, in approval, and then turned and headed back out the door.

I looked to Ethan who held up his finger and thumb together.

"This close," he said. "I was this close to faking a stroke before you humiliated us even more."

There was no humour in his eyes as he said it, but his thoughts were so similar to mine that I couldn't help but let out a surprised laugh. His mouth twitched slightly as he gave me the smallest smile back, and even at that I had to shove down the pure delight in my chest.

I looked away from him.

I was in trouble.

-CHAPTER SIXTEEN-

We stayed a while longer, I excelled at target practice each time. For some reason, my brain remembered that part of my training as though it was second nature, as easy as brushing my teeth.

"How does that work?" I asked.

"What?"

"When I was aiming, it was like the target came closer to me, like there was nothing else in the room."

He nodded knowingly. "That was the implant. With some things they don't work on their own, you have to work with them. But when you do, when you work your brain with the enhancements of the implant, the results can be pretty epic."

I nodded; it was pretty cool.

Ethan then went through the basics of the different weapons and how to reload each one. When we got to the assault rifle training, I stopped him.

"Why do we have to learn about rifles?"

He looked at me confused. "It's just a part of our training?"

I tilted my head. "I understand why we'd need a pistol, its stealthier for the type of work we're hired to do. When would we ever need to use a rifle?" My mind flicked back to the stash of weapons on the other side of the building. "And I saw

A Lotus in the Dark

grenades out there too, when would we ever have to use those?"

He shrugged. "I mean, we haven't yet, but it's just a part of our training regime."

I frowned and bit my lip; it didn't make sense to me.

When I looked back to Ethan his eyes were on my lips, but quickly snapped up to meet mine.

He swallowed and turned away. "We're done here for the day. We'll do knife training tomorrow."

"Knife training? Throat slashing 101," I joked.

He shook his head. "Slashing a throat would make way too much mess, not to mention just drags out the kill. Instead, one quick stab to the base of the skull or behind the ear, done."

I wrinkled my nose at him. "You're a little scary you know that, don't you?"

He blinked at me, then turned and silently walked away.

I rolled my eyes at his back for the hundredth time and followed him out of the Four Divisions to the tram stop to spend yet another silent journey back home.

I was just thankful it was so quick.

We climbed off and I headed down the little path in the front of my house when I noticed from the corner of my eye that he'd paused at the top of his.

I turned to look at him to see he was already looking at me.

"You okay?" I asked.

"Yeah," he said slowly, his eyebrows knitted. "I just... Never mind, I'll see you tomorrow."

I sighed softly. I did feel for him, it must be confusing; his memories and emotions being suppressed by the implant without his knowledge.

But I had to play the part, so I simply nodded and walked into my house and shut the door behind me.

I kicked off my shoes by the door and then padded to the bathroom. I leaned into the shower and turned it on.

Before I had the chance to even begin to pull off my clothes, I was suddenly shoved forwards into the shower.

I spluttered, taken off guard, as the powerful overhead shower rained down over me and into my mouth.

I span around, about to raise my fists when I was shoved roughly into the wall. Hard hands gripped my arms tightly as they pinned my back against the wet tiles, and I blinked through the shower droplets.

I stopped still.

"*Ethan*?" I choked through the water that was pouring down over the both of us. "What the hell are you *doing*?!"

Ethan's blazing amber eyes stared down at me, even through the droplets I could see they were alert and clear. The water crashed down loudly around us, soaking us completely, our hair and clothes clung to our bodies.

He was still holding my arms, pinning me to the wall, but his grip was loose and his hands were shaking.

"Ethan?" I said again, struggling to talk through the water. "What's going on?"

He stepped back, but only an inch. His usual dangerous expression was replaced with something far more vulnerable and I had to stop myself reaching out to him.

"This is the only place where I don't think they can hear us. I just... I need to say this before..."

"Before what?" I asked, my heart pounding in my chest.

"I don't know. It sounds crazy but before my mind goes *blank* again. My head's fucked Aria. It's like I'm in a constant battle with myself. I feel numb half of the time, like I'm just walking around drifting through life." He rubbed his hands through his soaking hair and then down over his face.

A Lotus in the Dark

"Then sometimes I have these moments of clarity, like there's something more, deep inside, trying to fight its way out."

"Ethan..."

"I know, it sounds crazy."

"Ethan."

"I don't even know why I'm telling you this," he said, gruffly.

"Ethan will you just *listen*," I snapped. I tried to blow the water away from my mouth. "It's not crazy, it's the implants."

"What do you mean?"

"The implants, while boosting our abilities, they're messing with the part of our brain that produces positive emotions, the part of our brain that makes us human."

"What are you talking about?" he said roughly.

"Think about it! Think about everyone in this place, they're all cold, lifeless robots, including you most of the time." I wiped the soaking hair back from my face. "It's exactly what they want... It's easier to kill, easier to be obedient, senseless murderers if we can't feel it. No remorse, no regret, no emotional attachment. But we're stronger than that, they don't know it, but we are stronger, we can fight it."

"How do you know this?"

I didn't know how much to reveal. "I... I just do."

He shook his head. "You've got it wrong; they wouldn't mess with our brains like that... with *children's* brains."

"Those moments of clarity, it's your humanity fighting its way out. The implant tries to supress your emotions but they're still there."

I placed my hand over his chest, and he wrapped a hand around my wrist. The water rained down over us as we stared at each other, his eyes more alive than I'd ever seen them.

"It only happens when I'm around you," he said, his deep voice so low I barely heard him.

But I did, and it sent a thrill up my spine.

He stepped towards me again. "I don't know why, but it's only when we're together, like you wake something inside of me. The part of me fighting its way out that feels... alive. You bring it to the surface."

Whether it was at his words or his proximity, my heart literally skipped a beat. I looked up at him, completely speechless. My words were trapped in my throat, mesmerised by his face that I thought was leaning down to close the space between us.

I involuntarily tipped my face up towards his, but in the next second he shoved himself away from me. The small space between us suddenly felt miles apart.

He shook his head and frowned as he looked down at me breathing heavily.

The fire in his eyes turned to ice.

He turned to walk away and I reached out to grab his arm. "Ethan–"

His jaw tensed as he yanked his arm back, pulling away from me. He gave me one last stare, cold enough to freeze the blood in my veins, before he stormed out of my bathroom without another word.

I swallowed hard, surprised to find my eyes stinging. I allowed myself a couple of moments to compose myself before I stripped off and finished showering.

I wasn't sure whether he had immediately regretted what he'd said, or his implant took over. Either way, I decided to momentarily shove all thoughts of Ethan into a dark, inaccessible corner of my brain.

I wrapped a towel around me and headed into the bedroom, where I sat on the end of the bed.

A Lotus in the Dark

A low whistle sounded from the corner of the room, and I whirled around, snapping my neck in the direction of the sound and gripping my towel tighter to my body.

"That was intense," Ivy said as she sat cross legged on top of my set of drawers, examining her fingernails. "Like really intense."

"What are you doing here?" I shook my head, ignoring her comment.

She looked up from her nails to grin at me.

"Fine, we'll talk about it later." She hopped off the dresser landing gracefully on her feet. "Get dressed quickly, something's come up and the Ambassador and President had to leave, they'll be back tomorrow. We weren't expecting them to go so soon but we may as well make the most of the opportunity. We need to get you to Haven, and it's now or never."

I blew out a breath as I grabbed some clothes from the wardrobe and began to dress.

"I can't," I said. "I have training with Ethan in the morning, he'll know something's up."

"Oh, he'll just think you haven't shown up after that mortifying shower episode." She winked at me.

I suppressed the embarrassed groan that threatened to bubble out of me and instead rolled my eyes. "You heard all of that?"

"Some, I thought it was just you so thought it would be funny to scare you but then saw you both in there and thought I'd leave you to it." She wiggled her eyebrows and then turned to open my bedroom window.

I slipped on my comfortable black trainers and joined her at the window. "How do we even get to Haven from here without being seen?"

She smirked at me. "Secret tunnel."

I snorted. "How cliché."

"I know right? It's an old hidden passage they used to get stuff down here I think, before the lifts were installed. It's monitored by one low security camera but we have Jackson hacking into it from back at Haven, each second that we're on it he'll be deleting before we've even shown up, I just have to give him the signal."

I chewed my lip. "Seems too easy."

"I know, the President is such an arrogant bastard he'd never even suspect that his experiments might actually fail enough to end up escaping through his very own secret tunnels."

My lips twitched upwards. Speaking to Ivy was like a breath of fresh air compared to the rest of the people in this place.

She put her hands on her hips, looked me up and down and then frowned and pushed past me to my drawers. She pulled one open and rummaged around for a few seconds before she huffed and moved to the next one.

"What are you looking for?" I asked, but she ignored me as she continued searching through my drawers and pulling open my cupboards.

She moved to the bed and pulled up both sets of pillows, and then slipped her hand down between the top of the mattress and the headboard. She let out a small gasp and pulled out something black.

"Yes!" she cheered quietly and then handed it to me.

It was a knife, in a beautiful black leather sheath.

"What's this?" I asked.

"What does it look like?" she tutted and took it off me again and bent to clip it to my belt on my right-hand side.

A Lotus in the Dark

My hand automatically reached down to pull out the blade; silver, double edged and deadly. A beautiful lotus flower was engraved into the hilt.

"You don't go anywhere without your dagger," she grinned. "You didn't look right without it."

My hand lingered as I slipped it back into its sheath. It's weight on my hip felt like a comfort blanket rather than a foreign object and I knew she was right.

She pulled out her phone and pressed the screen a few times before she slipped it back into her belt bag.

"We don't have long; Jackson can only hack the system for a few minutes before being noticed."

I nodded and followed her lead as she slipped out of the bedroom window. We both landed gracefully and silently, and began to move behind the row of houses with stealth.

I swallowed as I remembered who these houses belonged to and my heart rate began to speed up. Just as I'd had the thought, I almost crashed into Ivy's back as she stopped still and raised a hand.

I followed her gaze and we both crouched down at the sight of Commander Michael walking from the tram stop to his house. We were in the dark and hidden behind the wall, I was sure he wouldn't find us, and yet my heart felt like it was trying to jump out of my throat.

A few long seconds later we heard his door slam shut, and each released a small sigh of relief. I stuck close to Ivy as she continued on.

Before we reached a clearing, Ivy hopped the small fence behind the last of the houses. I frowned but followed her lead anyway as she crouched down, pushed back some of the artificial grass and grabbed a small metal handle, pulling open an actual trap door.

"So cliché," I mouthed.

"I know!" she mouthed back with a smile and then leant in and whispered. "Wave to Jackson."

She looked up to the small camera placed on the corner of the house that I wouldn't have noticed myself. I smirked and gave it a little wave at the same time as Ivy stuck her middle finger up to it.

She gestured at me to go first, and I hesitated for only a second before climbing down a short ladder. I was on safe ground in a matter of seconds. Ivy followed my lead, shutting the door above and plunging us into complete darkness before I heard the click of her torch.

I followed her down a long, dark tunnel for a few minutes before we reached the end, and she shone the torch at the wall. There was a hole with a little platform in it, only small enough to fit one of us in at a time.

I looked to Ivy, and she shrugged.

"Like I said, it was used to bring down supplies not people. Hop in."

I stared incredulously. "I still have no idea who you are, and you know that, this could all be a trap."

She shook her head, humour glinting in her eyes and gestured to the platform again. "Well, there's only one way to find out."

I sighed and rolled my eyes before climbing onto it, sitting on my bottom with my knees tucked in.

"See you on the other side," she saluted to me.

She yanked a lever to her right and I began my ascent back up to the real world. It seemed to take forever, the conveyer platform being considerably slower than the lift at the main entrance.

I wondered if my return to Haven would help bring back my memories. If I had started the whole Rebellion, it was obviously something I was passionate about. I cared enough

A Lotus in the Dark

about getting everyone out of this place without my memories. So surely, I would remember the hub of the operation when I saw it.

Although, I pondered to myself, I didn't even recognise Imperium and I had lived there my entire life. I sighed, at least Ivy had said they were working on something to help bring them back.

The platform clunked to a slow stop, interrupting my thoughts and my body naturally readied itself for action, my hand hovering over my knife, preparing for whatever or whoever was waiting for me at the end.

The wall in front of me slid away and I squinted as a bright torchlight shone into my eyes. A strong but delicate hand reached out to me, so I took it and hopped off the platform and looked into the smiling face of Commander June.

"I knew you were a part of this." I smiled back to her.

"Of course I am, how else would you have afforded a place large enough to harbour all the *fugitives*."

She laced the last word with sarcasm, because of course we were only rescuing innocent children.

I looked around; we had ascended into a random back ally in the middle of nowhere. Completely alone, although I could hear cars and noise in the distance, so I assumed we weren't far from the city centre and the main entrance at Aces.

I shook my head. I had so many questions. "The implant doesn't affect you either?"

"You and I are the only two people we know of so far whom the implant seemed to have no noticeable effect *at all* on our emotional capabilities. The others who join the Rebellion needed more persuading; they were affected but not as deeply as the rest."

She placed a hand on my shoulder. "I was on my own for a long time before I realised you were the same as I. I had always thought it was just the mother's instinct taking over, more powerful than any synthetic control."

I frowned at her. "Mother's instinct?"

She shook her head and let out a light laugh. "Of course she didn't tell you; my daughter is a fan of the theatrics. Speaking of…" She turned and pulled the lever on the wall to lower the platform back down and then turned to smile at me. "We should probably get her up here."

-CHAPTER SEVENTEEN-

I blinked at June.

"Ivy is your daughter? How is that possible?"

She nodded and looked to the ground.

"It is a long story that I do not wish to divulge at this moment. Hopefully Dr Boman has been successful in his work back at Haven and you will gain all your memories back so that I don't have to."

I frowned. "Ivy trained at Imperium with us though, right? Surely, she was one of those they've assumed *missing* recently? Would they not suspect your involvement straight away?"

"They did, but apparently my mind is stronger than their lie detector so, we got away with it." She shrugged.

June looked to her watch and then up at the security camera above us.

"Are we okay?" I asked.

She nodded. "For now, Jackson has this one covered for a few more minutes, we do need to get a move on though."

The platform clunked to a stop at the top once more and Ivy hopped out.

"Oh no don't worry about me, you guys take your time, have a catch up, I think there's a nice café down the road, why don't you get a bite to eat whilst you're at it."

Her mother shoved her arm and they both laughed lightly, I couldn't help but smile.

Ivy pulled out her phone and sent what I assumed was another signal to Jackson. I followed as they headed down the alleyway and at the exact moment we reached the end, a black van pulled up. Ivy yanked open the sliding door and climbed in. I followed her in, sitting on the black leather seat next to her, June climbed in last and shut the door after us as I looked around.

It was obviously a surveillance van, kitted out with a number of screens, wires and computers. A young man sat facing one of the monitors with a headset on, tapping away on a keyboard so fast I could barely see his fingers moving.

"Aria, if you don't remember, this is Jackson," Ivy said.

He looked up with a kind smile that reached his brown eyes, his dark curly hair slightly ruffled from the headphones he had on. I smiled back and without a word, he went straight back to tapping away on the keyboard.

Ivy smirked. "He has to erase every second of us on every single camera on the way to Haven so that we get there undetected, its precise work."

The van jolted as we pulled away and I turned to see another man in the driver's seat, strong hands gripping the wheel as we sped away. I raised my eyebrows at the sheer size of his arms, covered in tattoos that were barely noticeable against his dark skin.

"And again, if you don't remember, this is Ben," Ivy said.

He turned and nodded to me quickly with a small smile before looking back to the road. "Glad you're okay, Aria."

His face fell into a slight frown. "You took longer than we expected," he said it lightly, but his voice was laced with concern.

A Lotus in the Dark

"Aria had a particularly awkward moment in the shower that could not have been interrupted. I knew we'd still get out in good time, which we did, I had it all under control."

I physically cringed at the mention of that awkward moment and quickly changed the subject to avoid thinking of Ethan. "How far away is Haven?"

"About an hour," she yawned. "May as well close our eyes until we get there, it's gonna be a long night."

I covered my mouth as I caught her yawn; she had intercepted me just as I was about to go to bed, and I had no doubt we were going to be up all night making the most of the time we had before I had to go back to Imperium. So, I followed suit and closed my eyes, surprised at how quickly consciousness began to fade.

I woke with a jolt as the van pulled to a stop and I leaned forwards, rubbing my eyes. There were no windows in the back of the van, so I turned and tried to look out the windscreen. It was completely dark now as it was the middle of the night, but under the soft street lighting I could see that we had stopped in front of a pair of large black iron gates.

Ben opened his window and pressed a button on the intercom next to him. A second later the gates buzzed and began to swing open so Ben could drive us through and down a long gravel driveway. When we pulled to a stop at the end, he turned to look at us over his shoulder.

"You guys hop out here and I'll go park the van."

We did as he asked, Jackson staying behind in the van, and as they drove away my mouth dropped open. I looked up at the enormous, old country style mansion in front of us.

It looked like something straight out of a fairy tale, with beautiful arched windows with French shutters and ivy growing up the red brick walls. It was breath-taking.

"Welcome to Haven," Ivy said as she walked past me and straight to the front door, June close behind her.

Even though the house was clearly very old and kept in its traditional architecture and décor, up close you could see it had been kitted out with modern, high-tech security systems.

Ivy stepped up to the large wooden door and tapped a number into a keypad with her right hand at the same time as holding her left palm up to a metal panel on the wall, similar to Imperium.

She turned to look at me as the front door clicked open. "We don't agree with the practices at Imperium, but their technology really is amazing."

I followed them through the door and into the hallway, it was about as grand as I had expected it to be, but also warm and inviting.

"And Imperium doesn't suspect anything about this place?" I asked.

June tilted her head. "They are aware children are going missing, the first group they assumed were a one-off, lucky escape. When we rescued the second and third groups, they realised something bigger was going on, they presume a rescue mission rather than full Rebellion, probably from someone working on the inside which is why we must remain extra vigilant from now on. But no, they don't suspect anything about Haven. We are hidden under a few miles of forest; Jackson has deleted every sighting of us possible and our names can in no way be traced back to the property. Not only is the place equipped with the highest surveillance and biometric systems, cameras and motion detectors on every angle, we also have the strongest signal jammers in place to ensure we cannot be tracked or hacked."

I blew out a breath. "We're pretty safe then."

A Lotus in the Dark

"You could say that," Ivy chuckled. "We're hoping to have security guards eventually when we have more manpower, but first we need to figure out who would be willing to join us."

I nodded. "So who–"

"We don't have all night you know," Ivy interrupted me. "You'll remember all of this when you get your memories back anyway."

"*If* I get them back," I responded.

"Oh no, not if... when."

She shared a look with her mother and then they both looked at me with shining eyes, their similarities so obvious now I felt like an idiot for not seeing it before.

"What are you not telling me?" I narrowed my eyes.

"Come on." Ivy skipped over to me and linked her arm through mine. The gesture was so comfortably familiar I couldn't bring myself to pull away. "Let's go get your memories back."

I followed as she pulled my arm, giving me a slight guided tour as we made our way through the house.

"Kitchen and dining area." She pointed through two wooden double doors. "We hired a couple of live-in caterers who had nowhere else to go; well vetted, paid extensively. We converted the top two floors into bedrooms, most are shared dorm rooms with bunk beds, a few single or double rooms for the older kids, we have capacity for about 400."

"At a push," muttered June.

I raised my eyebrows, but I wasn't surprised at that, this place was *huge*.

"How long had we been planning this before the first rescue mission?" I asked.

"About three years," June answered. "As you can imagine, it took a while not only to discover who was going to be on board with the Rebellion, but to get this place ready. It needed to be the safest, most undetectable place imaginable. If the President found out any of us had betrayed Imperium, we'd be executed without a second thought, he shows no mercy."

Ivy and I shared a look. I didn't know how June did it. How she could be such a huge part of this and then act Commander at Imperium with people that would likely kill her if they ever found out.

We went through a huge lounge area with a few fancy old-fashioned sofas, although it looked mostly unused, and then through a door on the other side. Through that door I followed them to the end of a long corridor, and we stopped outside a huge industrial metal door.

"These are our own labs," Ivy said, she punched in a code and held her palm up to the panel again. This time an extra device appeared from a panel in the door and Ivy leant her face forwards into it. It scanned her face and then a small, automated voice came through the speaker.

"Access Granted, Ivy-004."

"004?" I asked.

She shrugged as she pulled open the unlocked door. "We had to put in Access codes when we set up the system. You're 001 and mother is 002."

"Who is 003?" I asked.

Ivy walked ahead, her ponytail swinging behind her as she said quietly, "Ethan."

I swallowed. So, he really was a huge part of this. We needed to get him back. I would get him back.

We walked down a short staircase and Ivy made us sanitise our hands before we went through a large glass door at the bottom. The lab was huge and looked exactly how you'd expect a biochemistry lab to look, white and clinical with rows of desks full of large scientific equipment.

A Lotus in the Dark

"This is where I spend most of my time," Ivy said as she looked around with pride.

There was a section separated through a glass wall with a sign that read "Animal Facilities" on the front. Ivy caught my eye.

"That is where we do our animal testing, I know its controversial but unfortunately there is no other way... We only use mice."

"What are we testing?"

"The revised Implants. Remember I told you we've been experimenting with implants that have the same cognitive enhancements, but don't impair the emotional side of the brain. That's what I've mostly been working on down here, we think we're there we just... haven't implanted a human yet."

I frowned at her. "Why don't we just remove their implants?"

Ivy shook her head. "We don't know the risks; the implants have been altering our brain chemistry for years. We don't know what effect removing the implant may have." She shrugged. "Anyway, like I said before it's a strange phenomenon, that of course we are researching as well, but it seems that once we become aware that the implant is affecting us it seems to... reverse the effects?"

"How could that possibly work?" I frowned.

She shrugged and bit her lip. "I wish I could answer that. I'm just more... awake than I was before. It's the only way to describe it. It was like I was under a fog, like the real me was inside fighting her way out but with no choice other than to follow orders, no way to express the way I felt inside." She shook her head. "It's impossible to describe, but soon after you guys told me about its affect, I was completely different."

June nodded as she squeezed her arm. "We always had an amazing bond through Ivy's childhood and when they implanted her at twelve it was like she completely disappeared. That was the first time I really took notice in what was going on, I knew something wasn't right. I was against the whole operation from that moment."

June looked to me. "That was also when I noticed you hadn't been affected. You and Ivy were friends as children, all through school, and although you were implanted at the same time, nothing drastically changed. Ivy and the others were becoming empty shells almost instantly, with only moments of clarity like they were trying to break through. We both noticed it and it's taken a long time to get where we are now." She sighed and looked back to Ivy. "Even with the implant we were closer than normal though, regardless of any supressed emotions. But when the effects of the implant were gone it was like I finally had my daughter back."

She smiled and looked away as her eyes shone with emotion. Ivy rolled her eyes at her, but I couldn't help smiling when I saw she also looked away, blinking rapidly.

I blew out a breath as I looked around. This was heavy.

"So, we're creating implants to keep all of our enhancements anyway?"

June cleared her throat and nodded. "Yes, the children we rescue first will never be forced to have an implant of course, we're working on a future solution to their freedom. But everyone from apprentice level and above will be given their choice whether they want to have the replacement in and fight with us to end Imperium or not. They don't have to though, that's the point. They have the freedom and choice."

I nodded; it sounded like a reasonable plan.

"So, we get as many people out as we can before we try to take down Imperium," I confirmed.

A Lotus in the Dark

They both nodded but then I frowned.

"There will be a lot of collateral damage, there are still hundreds of operatives there who have the implant too, is it fair to let them get caught up in the crossfire. Even if they fight against us, is it really their choice?"

They looked to each other.

"That is the flaw in the plan," Ivy said.

June nodded. "Yes, we haven't quite come up with a solution to that predicament yet, but we will get there. We have a thousand other tasks to focus on first, getting all the children out is our priority. We're starting with the older children at the moment, who don't need such hands-on attention."

"We need to kidnap a few of the childminders before we can get the younger ones," Ivy said.

"We are not kidnapping anyone," June said pointedly. "We will be rescuing them."

"And then putting them back to work to look after the kids." Ivy smirked.

"They will have a choice," June chewed her lip. "Although I am hoping they choose to help, until we figure out a more permanent solution."

"They will," I said. "They don't know any different, they don't have any other way of life. They will want to help, I'm sure of it."

I knew that even without my memories.

"Anyway, you'd know all of this if we could just make it two meters without having a full conference." Ivy huffed and she walked on ahead again.

"You seem so sure I'm going to get my memories back."

"Well Dr Boman said his work is ready and he is one of the best Biochemists and Engineers in the world. He worked at Imperium, and they made the mistake of not Implanting him, just paid him a ridiculous amount of money thinking that would be incentive enough for him to turn a blind eye. Luckily for us his morality overtook, and he happily came with us when we approached him. It was a huge win for the Rebellion cause," she grinned.

We reached the far end of the lab where Ivy tapped in another code in yet another metal door. She pulled it open, and we all entered the small room that was cramped with huge equipment. A gentleman was sat at a desk, his nose in a book. but he stood when he saw us enter.

"Dr Boman," Ivy beamed as a way of greeting.

"Ah, finally you have arrived," he said in a strong accent that my brain managed to identify as Polish.

He looked to me. "I am glad to see you are well."

His genuine smile met his bright but serious blue eyes. He had a long grey beard and wore a blue shirt with a white lab coat.

"Thank you," I said. "Ivy has told me that you think you'll be able to get my memories back?"

He nodded. "I do hope so. Please, take a seat."

-CHAPTER EIGHTEEN-

Dr Boman gestured to the chairs dotted around the organised chaos of the room. We grabbed a chair each and took a seat around his desk where he also sat back down.

The three of them looked to each other, as though sharing a secret I was not a part of.

I shifted in my seat. "What is it?"

They were all silent for a moment before June spoke. "We know the President and his team were getting suspicious after our first few rescue missions. They were being even more hypervigilant than normal."

Ivy turned to me. "We don't believe you lost your memories in the accident. We're not even sure you were in an accident at all."

I nodded. "You've said this already, you think they erased my memories, and Ethan's too."

They nodded and she continued. "We just want to make you aware of what this means. If this works, you must act like you have no memories at all. Staying in Imperium whilst they are so suspicious is dangerous enough as it is, especially if they believe you have your memories back."

"There is also the question," Ivy said. "Of why they felt the need to erase your memories, and not just eradicate you completely."

June sat up straighter in her seat, I glanced in her direction, but she averted her gaze. I frowned slightly but then looked back to Ivy who hadn't seemed to notice.

It was true. What had they felt the need to erase? And why hadn't they just killed me? Surely it was more hassle than it was worth to keep me around.

"Maybe they thought I might lead them to the rebels as I gradually started to remember? Or they're watching to see if anyone approaches," I shrugged.

"Possibly," June answered. "They will definitely be keeping a close eye on you, that is for sure."

"Perhaps we will find out more if we get started?" Dr Boman asked, not impatiently.

The three of us nodded and he cleared his throat.

"Years ago, in the labs at Imperium, as well as the nootropic technology, one of their main focuses was memory alteration technology. I was not a part of this particular study myself, but I heard a few things in my time there about a substance called Nepenthe, literally named anti-sorrow. Consumption of the substance causes sorrowful memories to be forgotten. Even back then I believe they were working on a somewhat equivalent, I think they may have almost achieved it."

He sighed gruffly and ran a hand over his beard. "However, I think they were still experimenting and used the technology on yourself out of desperation. I don't believe that they intended to erase all your memories, just some very specific ones and they failed. And I think it is imperative that we find out what it is they wanted you to forget."

I swallowed and pressed my palms into my thighs to stop them from shaking. He stood up and walked over to the huge machine to the side of the room, that essentially looked like an MRI scanner you'd find in the hospital.

A Lotus in the Dark

"I already had all the scans I could possibly have at the hospital, they found nothing except years' worth of training wounds," I explained.

He nodded. "Another study of theirs was on a synthetic material that could not be detected on standard hospital technology. Commander June has been sneaking prototypes back to our labs here, so I believe I know exactly what it is they have created."

Ivy looked to her mother pointedly. "Risky."

"Necessary," she replied.

They nodded to each other once in agreement and then looked back to Dr Boman who continued.

"I have been working extensively on the configuration of this particular scanner, and I believe if I am correct, after just one scan we should find exactly what it is we're looking for." His eyes shone with the same excitement as Ivy's, they were both proud of their work.

I nodded and jumped up. "Let's waste no time then."

I walked over to the machine with Dr Boman who handed me a hospital gown.

"You'll have to remove everything and only wear this for the duration I'm afraid, at risk of any interference."

I nodded and began to undress shamelessly and change into the gown. The quicker I regained my memories, the better it would be for everyone involved.

I followed Dr Boman's instructions and laid down flat on the bed and kept as still as possible. The bed slid slowly backwards into the donut shaped machine, and I closed my eyes at the whirring and humming of the process. I fought not to fidget for the entire five minutes I was inside, before the machine clunked to a stop and the bed slid back out.

I sat up and looked to Dr Boman who was looking intently at his computer monitors, waiting for the images to appear.

Ivy had moved to stand behind him, looking over his shoulder at the screen.

I could tell from their expressions the moment the images appeared in front of them. Dr Boman examined them only for a few seconds before pointing to something on the screen. Ivy gasped.

"What?" I asked. "What is it?"

June and I both moved over to take a look, he continued to point at one particular white spot.

"That, is in your neck, and by the looks of the scar tissue around it, even with your quick healing, I would estimate it has only been there for a couple of weeks at most."

My hand instinctively went up to my neck. "What is it?"

"That is where we move onto the second part of my work. I won't bore you with all the science, but essentially, I have created a device that can target any foreign substance and identify it immediately."

He almost bounced out of his chair with excitement and moved to a large cabinet where he pulled out what looked like a tiny laptop with a probe coming out of it.

"Please take a seat." He gestured to the chair. "This will hurt a touch."

"It's fine, let's just get this over with."

He didn't need to be told twice. He stepped towards me and shoved the probe straight into my neck. I squeezed my eyes shut at the sensation, but I didn't flinch.

He monitored the laptop closely as he moved the probe around, until his hand stopped still, his eyes moving left to right.

My knees bounced up and down and I fought the urge to ask him to hurry the hell up.

"What is it?" I asked, impatiently.

A Lotus in the Dark

He grimaced. "It seems to be some sort of chip, similar to the implant, but instead of releasing the nootropic enhancements it's releasing a mixture of benzodiazepines with something new, something my device does not recognise. They must have created it at Imperium. Together they seem to be slowing your brain functions and blocking the neurotransmitters associated with memory. It's basically the same experience as a black-out from drinking too much alcohol, except it's happening continuously."

"Those bastards," I seethed, my hands visibly shaking. "This whole time I've been trying to cope, trying to find my way in the world with no memories and they did this to me."

Ivy was as angry as I. "Oh they'll pay for this, Aria, we will make sure of it."

Her eyes flashed as they met mine, I knew by we she meant the two of us. Together.

"Get it out," I demanded.

"I am not sure of the effect it would have to remove it immediately; they are strong drugs," Dr Boman said gently.

"I need it out," I pleaded.

June softly put her hand on my arm. "We will remove it, but we need to do it safely. It would be best to wait–"

"I am not waiting another damn minute!" I stood. "I woke up in that hospital and I was completely alone. I was terrified and I thought I had no one." I looked to the three of them. "Even with no memories I still found my way back to you, back to where I belong and I'm still utterly useless... I'm still not me!"

I took a breath to level my voice. "There is more to this. There is something bigger going on here, I can feel it in my gut, and I need my memories to find out."

With a trembling hand I reached over to my pile of belongings, grabbed my knife and yanked it from its sheath.

"If someone doesn't get this thing out of me right now, I will do it *myself*."

Dr Boman raised his hands in a defence position. "Will you at least let me prep some anaesthetic?"

I raised the knife to my neck and gave him the *'what the hell does it look'* like stare. To which he sighed and grabbed a scalpel and some surgical tweezers. He pushed on my shoulders so I would sit back down, and he began to slice into my neck.

I grimaced at the pain, but it was no worse than anything I had felt before. The warm sensation of blood trickled down my neck, over my shoulder and down my arm as he dug deeper and deeper until finally, he squeezed the tweezers and pulled out the device.

I blew out a long breath as the pain subsided.

"We don't know how long it could take for the effects to wear off," he said softly as he bandaged the wound on my neck.

I nodded but couldn't help squint at the pain that was suddenly filling my head.

"Aria?" June said, her voice filled with concern.

I gasped as the pain worsened, I leant forwards and put my head in my lap, gritting my teeth. I fought the increasing need to sway forwards and collapse on the floor in front of me.

"See," Ivy snapped as she rushed over to me and placed her hand on my back. "This is what happens when you have a bitch fit and don't listen to the professionals!"

I yelled out in pain as my brain filled with excruciating pressure to the point where it felt like it was about to explode.

Just as the pain became unbearable and reached its climax, it stopped. It rushed out completely, and I panted in relief, composing myself for a few seconds before I stood up.

A Lotus in the Dark

My heart pumped furiously beneath my chest as I looked between Ivy and June. My hands shook wildly and tears beyond my control flooded my eyes.

Ivy looked to me apprehensively, her eyes searching mine, and then she once again revealed the tattoo on her wrist and said softly, "Live by the sun."

Without moving my eyes from hers, I lifted the knife still in my hand and I traced my thumb along the words I had forgotten were engraved across the blade, but now I didn't need to look down to know what they said.

"Love by the moon," I whispered in return.

She gasped and beamed at her mother and then at me, tears filling her eyes.

My best friend. My soul sister.

Whose face fell when she saw my expression didn't match her own.

Because yes, I had my memories. They had hit me like a sequence of flashbacks assaulting my brain, over and over they rushed back in until finally it was like they were never even gone.

I remembered everything.

And the truth was far more disturbing than we could have ever possibly imagined.

Part Two

All We Have Is Now

-CHAPTER NINETEEN-

Four Weeks Earlier

"Target acquired; third floor, East, three windows from the left," I heard Ethan's voice in my earpiece.

"Watch out for the–"

"Cameras on the entrance of the third staircase, I know you've told me already," I whispered back in return, my voice slightly muffled from the black mask that covered half my face, stopping just below my eyes.

"Okay smartass, I won't do my job." I could hear the humour in his voice. "You go at it all alone if that's what you want… I will not tell you to watch out for the two, armed security guards reaching your position in… 3…2…"

"Shit," I hissed and pulled my knife from its sheath just in time as they rounded the corner about a meter in front of me and I saw two pistols raise in my direction.

"Stop right there!" One of the guards shouted.

I wouldn't kill them, that's not what we were here for.

I leapt forwards without giving them a chance to react, I spun and kicked the guard on the left in the chest with such force he flew backwards, landing with a thud on his back. He gasped as the wind rushed out of his lungs.

Simultaneously, I slashed out with my knife, wounding the other guards weapon baring arm so deeply he dropped it to the ground and shrieked out in pain.

"Is the second guard a woman?" Ethan asked in my ear, and I fought a smile as I kicked both of their pistols behind me, far out of reach.

I spun and slammed my knee into the squealer's groin, then grabbed his head and slammed it against the wall beside us with a loud crack. He passed out, landing in a heap of blood on the floor, but he'd recover.

"Not very stealthy," Ethan said.

"This wasn't a stealth mission," I hissed back. "They have so many enemies in this place it was bound to happen at some point."

The first guard had only just managed to get his breath back and was striding towards me, fists raised. He swung towards me with a strong fist, but far, far too slow. They were untrained.

I rolled my eyes as I easily blocked his fist with my left hand and with my right punched him square in the throat. He gasped for air again as I slammed the handle end of my knife into the weak spot in his temple and he dropped down on top of his partner.

I slid my knife back into its sheath, wiped my hands on the backs of my thighs and then casually stepped over the two unconscious bodies in front of me.

"Door to the stairwell on your right, you can go all the way to the third floor undetected from there," Ethan said.

I followed his directions from there all the way to an office on the third floor. I pulled out my pistol and shoved open the door, stepping inside with my weapon raised at the grey-haired gentleman sat at his desk.

A Lotus in the Dark

He looked up at me and raised his hands, fear crossed his expression for only a second before I put a bullet straight through his head.

"Target down."

We hadn't bothered cleaning up after this contract-killing. He was a rogue judge with a history of sexual assault, who also put a lot of innocent people behind bars for money or just for the hell of it. He had a lot of known enemies, one of which had hired us on his release out of prison, where he served ten years for a crime he did not commit.

Ethan and I had met back up at our pre-arranged rendezvous point and were already in the lift back down to Imperium.

"I could have come with you on that one," Ethan muttered.

I raised my eyebrow at him. "Come on, that was a simple contract killing and you know it, it didn't need two of us and besides, the Ambassador benched you for a month."

He huffed. "I know he did but my knee is fine, a month is ridiculous."

He jumped up and down to prove his point, his huge body shaking the lift.

I shook my head. "We heal quickly Ethan, but your leg was nearly severed at the knee just a week ago. Just give it the time to heal and you'll be back out there with me, else you'll just do more damage than good."

"But it's literally fine, I can–"

My foot shot out and kicked his knee in his weak spot, just above the scar. I didn't even kick hard, just on target.

His leg completely gave out and he gritted his teeth as he crashed forwards against the wall of the lift.

"Bitch." He quickly pushed himself up and flicked me in the forehead but didn't argue any further. I had made my point.

His face fell and I suddenly felt bad.

"Remember, the lotus is blooming tomorrow night, I'll still let you help with that," I said with a patronising smile.

"Oh, thanks I'm glad I have your permission." He smirked but his eyes did brighten at the coded mention of our third rescue mission.

The first a few months ago had gone perfectly; we'd rescued ten people we thought we'd utilise the most. We'd made the decision Ivy would stay at Haven, running the operation from there. Her, Jackson and Ben were the only three field operatives taken, the rest were lab technicians.

The second, a couple more operatives were rescued who we had noticed were less impaired by their implants. The rest were recently implanted children, about to move into their first week of Apprentice training.

All of them had everything explained to them when they had arrived at Haven. It had been truly magical watching them gradually escape from their mental prisons. Once fully recovered they were all grateful, and fully dedicated to the Rebellion.

Our third mission in a days' time, we were due to rescue ten others, five technicians and five skilled field operatives.

It felt right after all the killing we did, even if most of it was somewhat justified, it felt gratifying to finally be doing something *good*.

As the lift slowed to a stop and the doors opened to Imperium, I shoved down the heaviness in my chest that seemed to weigh more every time we came back to this place. I took a step forward when Ethan stopped me.

A Lotus in the Dark

I looked up to him and he reached up and rubbed his thumb across my cheek near my hairline.

His mouth lifted at the corner and he shrugged as he removed his hand. "You still had a bit of blood."

He strode out of the lift as though nothing had happened, which I suppose it hadn't. We'd grown up together, we were practically family and we'd touched thousands of times.

So why was the spot on my cheek still warm and my heart still pounding in my chest?

I frowned at his back as I watched him walk away. He turned back towards me and observed my expression.

"What?" he asked.

"Nothing... You go ahead, I've got something to do quickly."

He shrugged and headed back on his way towards our houses when I called after him. "Ethan."

He turned back around.

"Remember I've got that solo assignment tomorrow, Frank Rogers." We both grimaced at his name. Scumbag. "I'm heading out first thing, but I'll catch up with you after."

He nodded. "Okay... Be careful."

I made a point of rolling my eyes then turned and headed towards the cafeteria and grabbed a quick decaf coffee to go. Caffeine at this time would keep me up all night and I really just needed the excuse to put some distance between us.

I wandered slowly to the tram stop, it was quiet as it was about one in the morning, so I was both lost in my thoughts and trying to shove down the feelings for Ethan I was pretending didn't exist.

I climbed on the night tram already at the stop and took a sip of my coffee as I sat down. I leaned my head against the window as the tram began to move, but as we entered the Four Divisions something caught my eye, and I looked up.

It was the light from the door leading to the labs that had captured my attention. It wasn't unusual for the technicians or scientists based in the labs to be working at all hours of the night. I squinted as the door opened and the light from other side showed three men in suits. I instinctively ducked down as they looked around to see if anyone had seen them. I frowned to myself as I wondered who they were and why they were acting so suspicious.

The tram pulled to a stop just before entering the third section. I chewed my lip for only a second before curiosity got the better of me and I decided quickly to climb off and see for myself what they were up to. I ducked down behind a fence. Once I was sure I couldn't be spotted, I moved stealthily towards the doorway which the men were now disappearing through. It shut behind them, plunging me further into darkness as the light was trapped behind the door.

I stood up, wondering if the regular chip in my palm would grant access to the labs, when I noticed movement to my left. I crouched again, still hidden, as a regular technician hurried to the door carrying a bunch of equipment. He didn't look suspicious like the other men as he raised a palm to unlock the door and pulled it open.

I waited for a few beats as he hurried through the door, not bothering to look behind him, and I sprung forward, catching the door just before it locked shut again. I held the door as it was for a few minutes, my heightened senses listening for any movements. When I was sure there was nobody on the other side of the door, I pulled it open and stepped into the long white corridor inside.

I crept forward, my senses still on high alert. My entire life I had lived in Imperium, and I had never been into the labs. My heart raced at the thought although I wasn't sure why.

A Lotus in the Dark

I peered through the windows of the first few doors I passed, seeing only standard labs full of science equipment. I wasn't even sure what I was looking for.

I had just reached the last door before the corner at the end of the corridor, when I heard several deep voices coming in my direction. I held my breath and silently opened the door next to me and hurried inside.

I closed the door and turned, and my heart nearly leapt out of my throat as I quickly surveyed the research lab in front of me.

There were six hospital beds, each with a person tied down with black belts strapped across their upper arms, waist, and ankles. There were three boys and three girls, all aged around 18 if I had to guess. All six had on hospital gowns and their heads were completely shaved.

Stuck to their scalps were an array of sensors and wires, each one linked to an individual screen next to their heads. My eyes widened and I stepped into the room, trying to make sense of what I was seeing.

I stood over the boy closest to me and gasped as I recognised him from the classes I taught. He was a Shamara operative; he was tough and ruthless and yet lying here he looked so vulnerable. I placed a hand on his chest, relieved by the gentle rise to see that they were only unconscious.

My heart pounded in my ears and when the door handle clicked behind me, my eyes darted around the room. I had no choice other than to climb into a large silver cabinet placed against the far wall. I closed myself in and held my breath, peering through a slight crack to look into the room.

I watched as the three men I had seen earlier all strolled into the room, wearing fancy black suits. The last into the room shut the door and turned to face the other two men. My eyes widened.

Shit.

The Ambassador smiled at the two men with his stupid fake teeth, and I was surprised they didn't shield their eyes.

"Well gentlemen, this is where the magic happens."

He gestured to the beds in the room, where the other men looked around and nodded approvingly. As soon as they had their backs to the Ambassador, his smile dropped and his eyes flicked around the room. I frowned and instinctively pressed back further into the cabinet.

"And the President won't be joining us today?" one asked.

"Not today, he was pulled into a rather important meeting overseas," the Ambassador replied, his fake smile plastered back on his face. "But he is happy for all communications to go through myself. Commander Kane should be joining us shortly as he is the intelligence behind the operation." His jaw tensed as he spoke.

I squeezed my eyes shut at the thought. The Ambassador was powerful and corrupt, but the pure evil that emanated from Kane made my blood run cold.

I had flown through all my intelligence exams years early, most thought I was ahead, a know-it-all, but the truth was that I had wanted to get away from Kane as soon as I possibly could.

At his words the door swung open, and Kane strolled through.

The Ambassador turned. "Ah, speak of the devil."

Literally.

Kane paced forwards into the room, his black hair and dark eyes a complete contrast to his pale white skin that covered his large muscular body.

Kane greeted the men, his jaw set, and his eyes serious and then gestured to the beds. "The nanobot technology is in the final stages of development, but rest assured, the president and I are working to finalise imminently."

One of the men turned to look over the bodies. "And these betas are currently connected to an alpha mainframe?" he asked. I scowled again.

Kane nodded and reached for a tablet next to him. He tapped the screen, and I fought a gasp as all six of the individuals on the beds opened their eyes. He tapped again and in perfect sync they all turned their heads to face the men in suits.

My jaw hung open.

Kane glanced at the indifferent faces of the two suited men and his jaw tensed.

He took one long stride and unclipped the restraints on the boy I had recognised, pulled a knife from his side, and slipped it into his hand.

Kane tapped a sequence into the tablet, and I watched in absolute horror as the boy jumped off his bed with preternatural speed and launched himself onto the girl next to him.

She didn't even flinch.

He looked down at the girl with cold, lifeless eyes for only a second before he plunged the knife straight down into her throat. Blood pooled over his hands and over her body

I couldn't help the small gasp that escaped my lips and Kane's eyes flicked over to my direction briefly. I clamped a sweaty hand over my mouth, and he turned his attention back to the task.

I looked around in panic to see if someone was going to step in. The men watched eagerly, and I scrunched my nose in disgust.

The Ambassador had looked away.

The boy held the knife there for a couple of long seconds before he twisted, blood spilled from the girl's mouth and my stomach turned as she made a horrid gurgling sound that grew louder and louder until it just, stopped.

The silence was deafening.

-CHAPTER TWENTY-

I held a trembling hand over my mouth as my shock turned to pure anger at what I had just witnessed.

How could they let this happen? At that moment I was happier than ever that we had started the Rebellion. We had to get everyone out of here.

The two suited gentlemen began to clap.

Clap!

Kane strapped the blood covered boy back to the bed next to the girl he had just murdered. With a single tap on the tablet, they all closed their eyes, falling back into their unconscious states.

What the hell was I seeing here? My whole body trembled as it all sunk in.

Nanobot technology.

This could not be happening.

Is this what we were being trained for our entire lives, under the pretence we were working as highly trained vigilantes?

The two men looked to each other and then back to Kane. The larger of the two spoke first. "It's impressive. The Nightstone Captain will be intrigued by this, that's for certain. We would be happy to start negotiations."

Nightstone? Negotiations? As if I could feel any more nauseous. Were they... *selling* these kids?

"That's not all," Kane said, flashing a smile that made my skin crawl. The Ambassador had moved somewhere in the room out of my view from the small crack in the cabinet.

"Go on."

"These prototypes have each undergone an extensive neurosurgery to infuse synthetic nanobots to the top layer of their brains, not only enhancing all parts of their brain to use its full potential, but as you can see making the subjects completely susceptible to compulsion."

He picked up the tablet again and my heart stuttered. Blood still oozed from the girl on the table into a scarlet pool on the floor from his last demonstration.

"We had connected their brains to our main electronic systems. However, in the process we discovered that the nanobots are also capable of wireless communications with other nanobots in another brain, opening the door to telepathic communications and the fusion of single minds into group minds."

"Okay, so what does that mean for us?" one of the men said in his gruff voice, and I was glad he'd asked.

"Once an Alpha is established, it appears if the subjects are linked to the Alpha brain, they follow commands at just a simple thought, no need for this," he dropped the tablet down on the desk. "The Alpha thinks jump, the Betas jump."

I gulped.

Kane looked away from the men and busied himself collecting up his items. "It would appear though; the Betas only respond to certain Alphas, so we still need to do some tweaking in this area. But the rest of them are good to go."

He turned to face the men. They looked at each other for a second before one said, "You have a deal, we will await your confirmation that the research is finalised. In the meantime, I hope our regular wave of operatives are ready for us?"

A Lotus in the Dark

"Of course, the next group of Valda operatives are of age, they are being prepared for transportation to Nightstone immediately."

I squeezed my eyes shut. There was so, *so* much to process here. I needed to speak to Ethan straight away while it was still fresh in my mind. I silently cursed the sudden need to have him close by.

We needed to get to the others at Haven to explain the increased urgency to complete our next few rescue missions.

They weren't training us as vigilantes and then giving us the freedom to live our lives as we wanted at eighteen, of course they weren't.

They were training children all their lives to become ruthless killers, implanting them and stripping them of any humanity and control they had left, then selling them on to this Nightstone place.

They were creating an indispensable army of human weapons.

But why? It couldn't all be for the money, there were easier ways to make money, surely.

I shook my head of all the thoughts flying round my brain and brought myself back to the room.

The Ambassador was gesturing the two men out of the room.

"Gentlemen, it was a pleasure doing business with you, if you wouldn't mind making your way back to the entrance down this corridor and Commander Kane will be along in a moment to see you out."

They all shook hands and then the two men left, letting the door shut behind them.

Kane smirked at the Ambassador, there was nothing friendly in his expression.

"Impressive don't you think? The President will be happy with the deal."

"Cut the shit, Kane."

The veins in Kane's neck looked like they were about to burst. "What are you talking ab-"

"I *said* cut the *shit*," the Ambassador spat. "People are going missing. Something is going on and I think you know about it."

"I don't know what you're talking about. That's under your charge, don't try passing the blame to save your neck," Kane snapped back.

The Ambassador stepped up to him so that their chests were almost touching.

"You know something, and when the President finds out, do you know what he'll do to you?" He lowered his voice. "His chambers have been unoccupied for a while; I'm sure he's itching to fill the spot."

If any colour existed in Kane's face, it had just drained.

He swallowed. "Fine, full disclosure. We have discovered a whole section of the brain imbedded in the hypothalamus, you already know the effects of the implant, it shuts down the brain's ability to feel happiness, empathy, love... all that shit."

I rolled my eyes.

"But this new part of the brain we discovered, it's…getting in the way."

The Ambassador gritted his teeth. "We don't have all night Kane, start talking."

"Essentially, every brain is wired right from childhood by this tiny part we've named the Morallus, termed as it seems to be controlling a person's morality. But… it appears no amount of chemical engineering can alter it. We've started vigorous research targeting this area of the brain, but it seems that once a person becomes self-aware of their own morality,

A Lotus in the Dark

if they genuinely have pure, good intentions...then we can't change that."

The Ambassador rubbed his hand over his jaw.

"They can overcome the implants?" he breathed.

My heart was beating so loud I was sure they'd hear it.

This is why it didn't affect some people the way it did others. This is why our group at Haven had overcome the Implants... because we wanted to. Because we were good, and pure.

The likes of Kane, Shane and Karl could be controlled easier because they were evil inside, they didn't want to feel any emotions, they *wanted* to kill.

"I believe that is what is happening," Kane answered. "But not for long, we're tweaking the chemicals in the Implant and we're not far off, we'll roll out new Implants as soon as we can. Just give me a few weeks."

"I should go straight to the President with this. Do you know what you're saying? The whole operation could be compromised if anyone on the outside finds out."

"We have our best of the best out searching for the missing operatives, we've even recruited Nightstone ops. We will find them. Just keep your mouth shut for a few weeks."

His words were filled with venom, but his eyes were pleading.

The Ambassador shook his head and tensed his jaw.

"Find them," he hissed.

They nodded once to each other, before marching out the door, and finally leaving me alone.

I held my breath for as long as I could, until I was sure they'd gone, then let it out in one long huff. I didn't have time to let myself get wrapped up in my thoughts right now.

I pushed out of the trusty cabinet and stepped around the blood now pooling towards me. I moved over to the innocent girl who was senselessly murdered only moments ago and forced myself to look down at her face, to remember why the Rebellion was so important. I swallowed the lump in my throat, more determined than ever to get every last innocent person out of this hell.

I crept back towards the door and cracked open the smallest gap. I listened around my heart thumping in my ears, and opened it fully, satisfied nobody was outside.

I quietly hurried down the corridor towards the door leading back to the Four Divisions when time seemed to slow down in front of me.

The door to my left swung open and out stepped the Ambassador. I frantically looked for somewhere to hide but it was too late, his wide eyes were on me.

"Mentor Aria, what are you doing here?" He looked around and then back to me.

I forced my voice to come out strong, I was trained for this. "I thought I saw you come this way, I was just coming to inform you our latest mission was a great success, it was one with a huge pay-out. I thought the President would be pleased."

His eyes searched my face and my heart drummed in my ears as his jaw tensed, but then he looked around again.

"Fine, you should get to bed, it's late."

My jaw nearly hung open. Was that it? I'd seen people punished for far less. Perhaps he just wanted to get me out of there quickly in case I saw what they were up to.

I nodded. "Of course, goodnight."

He moved so I could step past him, but I paused when I heard his sharp intake of breath.

I turned to where his eyes looked behind me. *Shit*.

Commander Kane was strolling in our direction, a face like thunder.

A Lotus in the Dark

"Mentor Aria, what business do you have in this department so late?" he asked, coldly.

I opened my mouth to speak when the Ambassador spoke first. "Our business is handled; Aria was just leaving."

Kane's thin lips slowly spread into a sickly, threatening smile that would haunt my nightmares.

Then it dropped and he shrugged and headed through the door.

The Ambassador looked down at me, his eyes met mine with an expression I couldn't read before he snapped, "Go *home*."

I wasted no time doing exactly that.

I slammed a hand down on the alarm beeping on my bedside table, but I'd not long stepped through the door. I'd learned so much last night, but it had been far too risky to try and make contact with anyone from Haven after both Kane and the Ambassador had seen me.

It was only 2:30am, but I had my solo assignment this morning. It needed to be completed in the dead of the night and I'd gotten everything prepared already.

I quickly showered and dressed in my full black, stealthy attire with my dagger in its usual place on my hip. I picked up my bag with everything I needed and began to head out, pausing as my eyes flicked to Ethan's front door.

I swallowed and looked around; all was quiet. I glanced at the time on my watch, I had a few minutes to spare. I hurried over and knocked lightly on his front door and then again on the window I knew led to his bedroom. I heard shuffling inside and then the front door unlocked with a click.

I pushed my way inside before he could even open the door fully. I pushed the door quietly shut behind us and turned, he looked down at me, eyes full of sleep yet still on alert as we were trained to be.

"Aria, what's going on?"

I breathed heavily as I looked at him, his concerned eyes searching my face.

"What's going on?" he repeated.

"I… I don't even know where to begin." I breathed and ran my hands over my face. "I've had such an insane night, you wouldn't even believe half of the shit I've seen."

He frowned. "You just went to get coffee?"

"I know that," I snapped. "And then ended up hiding in a cabinet in one of the labs while Kane and the Ambassador had a *very* interesting meeting."

His eyes widened in both surprise and curiosity and he gestured at me to continue.

"I don't have time to tell you everything now, but god it's so fucked up Ethan. What they're doing to these kids is even worse than we could have imagined." I took a deep breath. "They're experimenting with some crazy neurotechnology to have them completely under their control and then they're selling them to some place god knows where."

"Woah, woah." Ethan held his hands up. "Back up, what are you talking about? They're being sold? What neurotechnology?"

The watch on my wrist beeped twice, I had to go.

"There is so much to tell you, I'll meet you back here after this mission, okay? I should only be a couple of hours."

He stepped forwards and placed his hands on the top of my arms and rubbed them encouragingly.

"You've got this. We'll get them out, every last one."

I swallowed the lump in my throat and along with it any words I may have wanted to say, and instead gave him a curt nod and turned to leave.

A Lotus in the Dark

I had a job to do.

A couple of hours later I was sat in Frank Rogers' car having just ended his life, but for all the right reasons. I didn't have time to feel bad about it.

I started the engine and pulled out of his driveway, finding comfort in the peaceful sleep the family in that house were now bound to have.

It hadn't gone as smoothly as I'd hoped with my mind completely elsewhere, but the job was done. I just had to get rid of the car and make it look like a car theft gone wrong, easy.

I was aware that I was rushing everything, I needed to get back to Haven as soon as possible to inform them of everything I'd witnessed. Maybe there was a way of reversing the control over them, we'd have to look into recruiting more lab techs...

My internal monologue was suddenly interrupted as one of the tyres burst and the car veered off to the side.

"*Shit!*"

I frantically tried to steady the car, still going at high speed when I felt another tyre go. The front end of the car swung round, completely out of control. I gripped the wheel and slammed on the brakes, but it was too late.

All the air rushed out of me as the car slammed straight into a tree and I gasped as I felt my ribs crack.

I lay my head back and coughed a little. This was not good. I gave myself a moment to compose myself before I pulled out my phone.

I pursed my lips at the thought of Ethan's smug tone when I had to ask him for help, but I had no choice.

I was just about to dial his number when the phone was ripped out of my hands.

I looked up and my blood ran cold as I saw Kane's lifeless eyes staring down at me with a sinister smirk on his lips.

"Do you really think we're that stupid?" he sneered. "We know what you heard."

I shivered at his words, sure I was going to die.

"Unfortunately, the President is insistent you're indispensable." He spat the last word and then sighed. "But I suppose I understand his reasoning. Anyway, it'd be too risky to leave you with your memories."

He pulled out a device that looked like a tranquiliser gun. I fought to move but I was well and truly trapped under the weight of the crushed metal.

"I don't know what you're talking about," I pleaded.

"That might be true, but it's just not worth the risk."

He clicked something on the side of the gun and muttered more to himself than me. "A couple of days should be enough; this shouldn't hurt much." He pressed the end of the gun painfully into my neck, I tried to pull away but had nowhere to go. I took a deep breath as I prepared myself when he said. "Oh, and I saw you leaving Mentor Ethan's house no doubt having discussed your recent discovery, so don't worry, we'll sort him out too."

He let out a manic laugh as he pressed the trigger and I felt pain shoot down my neck. I wondered when it would kick in as he roughly grabbed my hair and slammed my head against the steering wheel.

Blood coated my cheeks as he slammed my head over and over into the steering wheel, until I had no choice but to succumb to the empty abyss waiting for me.

-CHAPTER TWENTY-ONE-

Now

I looked at the three faces opposite me as I finished relaying the events of the last few weeks, all the memories that had been torn away from me in the hope they'd get away with everything.

Their first mistake was underestimating us.

June and Ivy stared at me with matching expressions of horror while Dr Bowman let out a long breath, shaking his head.

"Mind control," he breathed.

June raised a hand up to her lips. "They're creating an army."

"And they had no control at all?" Ivy asked softly.

I shook my head and swallowed.

"You should have seen it," I breathed.

I was assaulted again with the image of the boy's cold unconscious eyes as he stared down at the lifeless body, blood pooling around them.

They paled as I described exactly what I'd witnessed in that lab and the room went silent. There were no words to describe the horror fated to every one of the children we left at Imperium.

My heart drummed in my chest. "We have to get those kids out of there, but not just that… the hundreds of operatives raised and trained in the past, none of them are being let go when they turn eighteen. They must all be at this Nightstone place. We have to rescue them all."

They all nodded along with me.

"I agree," said June. "But we have to play this carefully, we have to be smart about this. We can't just rush it now; I know how tempting it is but we are wildly outnumbered and unequipped."

I nodded. I'd love more than anything to destroy Imperium tomorrow and get as many people out as I could in the process, but I knew she was right.

"I know. We have to be prepared." I nodded.

"We need a solid plan. We need more resources and we need more people." Ivy agreed.

I sighed; my chest heavy as I knew what I had to do first.

I raised my eyes to meet Ivy's, knowing my best friend knew me better than anyone in the world, and my lips twitched a little. Understanding crossed her face and she smirked back at me.

"You're going to get Ethan back," she said, it wasn't phrased as a question.

I nodded and shrugged casually. "Somebody's got to."

"You'll have to remove the chip in his neck, if they've put in the same one as yours." Dr Bowman said, as he picked it up from the tray and turned it over. "They must have got the dosage wrong or something, it sounds like they were only trying to erase a few days and it affected you both so differently."

I nodded. "Ethan seems to have all memories of Imperium, but none of the Rebellion. I could tell in his face he had no recollection of our rescue missions. How can that happen?"

A Lotus in the Dark

Dr Bowman blew out a breath. "I think it's all experimental, someone over there has no idea what they're doing. Maybe they're experimenting with erasing certain memories or certain time frames, either way, they messed up."

I reminded them of the conversation I'd overheard between Kane and The Ambassador.

Dr Bowman frowned. "The Morallus... I'll have to do some research into this, but it sounds hopeful. If it appears that we can break out of the control of the implants simply from becoming self-aware of our own morality, then we have hope."

Ivy agreed, looking off to the distance as if lost in thought.

"We can get through to anyone like us," she said quietly. She looked to us all now and stood up. "Anyone who wants us to, anyone with good, brave hearts. It makes us stronger than the others, while we're fuelled by fire, they are frozen by malice. It makes them weak."

I nodded and gave her a soft smile as I placed my hand over hers. "That's why we're going to win this."

After a beat I said, "Although... that just applies for the implants, I think the ones forced into neurosurgery are under complete control of the nanobot technology, they'll be harder to get back."

"We have to stop them before they do it to anyone else," June spoke for the first time in a while.

"It seems like they are having issues with this though," Dr Bowman said. "Struggling to establish an "Alpha" their Betas will respond to fully. This could work in our favour."

We sat pondering for a moment before I stood up.

"I've got to get back to Imperium."

"You should stay, just for tonight," June said, softly.

I looked to Ivy; her eyes shone in agreement with her mother, but she knew better than to argue.

"No, I... I need to go now. I think it's best for everyone if nobody discovers I have my memories back for now. They won't suspect me at the moment and I can get Ethan back on board."

"You'll still have to remove the chip from his neck, its blocking all his important memories," Dr Bowman said.

I sighed; we needed a plan.

About an hour later, after countless discussions and debates, I was on my journey back down to the depths of Imperium.

We'd sat as a group; myself, Ivy, June, Dr Bowman, Ben and Jackson, and had formulated a solid plan.

It was going to work. It had to.

I reached the bottom with a quiet thud and took a deep breath. The last couple of weeks had felt like a blur, like I was an empty fraction of myself. But I was back and I knew what I had to do. For us, for all the innocent children in this place.

I crept silently down the tunnel, in tune with my abilities that had crept back in since having the memory suppressant removed from my neck. I could feel the implant working its magic, but it wouldn't affect my humanity. I wouldn't let it; I was stronger than that.

I reached the end and began to climb the ladder I had so many times before, listening with my heightened senses I slowly and carefully made my way through the tunnels and past the mentor houses, until I was safe in the warmth of my bed. I closed my eyes even though the light of a new day was beginning to brighten the room.

It seemed impossible that it had been only a few hours ago that Ethan had ambushed me in the shower. I felt like a whole new person since then, as though I'd been freed from the mental prison the chip was keeping me in.

I couldn't help but remember his words, the way his eyes had blazed as they'd looked down into mine.

"It's only when we're together, like you wake something inside of me. The part of me fighting its way out that feels... alive. You bring it to the surface."

I ignored the twisting in my stomach and put it down to guilt. Ethan was still stuck in that mental prison and I needed my partner back.

I tossed and turned until my alarm rang, I'd barely had an hours sleep and yet didn't feel the effects of exhaustion, either down to the implant or the adrenaline of the tasks set out for me.

I shot out of bed, had a quick shower and dressed for the day. When I opened my front door, my breath stilled at the sight of Ethan already waiting at the bottom of the path, something told me he'd also had a sleepless night.

He turned his dark eyes towards me and said bluntly, "There are classes in the firing range all morning so we're back to combat training today."

I looked back at him. "So, we're just going to ignore what happened last night?"

"There are more important issues to–"

His eyes had found their way to my hip where my dagger sat in its usual place.

"I found it under my pillow." I shrugged. "It felt right in this spot."

His eyes made their way back up to mine and narrowed a fraction, but only for a second before he nodded and turned away. We spent yet another silent journey to The Dojo and took our positions in the private training room.

He'd barely had chance to put his stuff down and turn to face me before I was advancing on him. With enhanced speed, I struck him with a closed fist square in his jaw, and then directly under the ribs with the other. His breath huffed out of his lungs, but he only faltered for a second before his fist was swinging back towards my face. I blocked it with my arm and jabbed my elbow out aiming for his nose, but he too blocked me swiftly.

From there another day's training continued, we fought against each other as equals. As equal as we had been since my accident, neither of us hesitating or pausing for breath.

I realised then that he actually had been going easy on me, even my beatings had been lenient compared to the wrath I was facing now, yet still we were equals.

We fought all day, keeping up with each other while I waited for my moment. My neck was becoming stiff, our knuckles bloody, our faces bruised. We were not at our full strength, now was the time to strike.

I took a couple of steps back, as though I was letting myself take a few well needed breaths. He stepped towards me as I knew he would, he leant forwards on his strong leg to strike me. I ducked his swing and twisted sideways as I kicked my leg out with all my strength, directly on target.

Directly onto the weak spot on his back leg, above his knee.

He gritted his teeth in pain and his legs gave way, and before he had chance to push himself back up, I jumped onto his back with my knee pressed into his spine. From behind, I lifted his head and held my dagger to his neck. He tried to move but I pressed it further in until it drew blood and he had no choice.

He tapped out.

A Lotus in the Dark

I jumped up and couldn't help the grin that spread across my lips. It was the first time I had beaten him in a while.

He slowly stood and turned to face me, his face dark and serious. My smile faltered as his eyes turned suspicious and dropped once again to the dagger I'd placed back onto my hip.

"Good aim."

I swallowed. "You're a good teacher."

His jaw tensed. "Looks like we're done training in this field."

He moved forward to clean up his face and gather his things.

"That's it?" I asked. "I thought you'd be happy we don't have to train in here anymore."

"We still have a lot of work to do," he said seriously.

I nodded and ignored the hammering in my chest. "Fine, I'll see you at dinner."

Without another word I headed out and made my way back to my house. I slipped inside and turned on the shower and turned my back to the door.

And I waited.

It was a gamble, to assume he'd come here twice. He probably knew I'd be expecting him, but it was the only place we could speak freely and he was suspicious and desperate.

I waited, gripping my dagger tightly in my hand, until I heard the faintest sound. It was quieter than a pin drop, I'm sure I wouldn't have even heard had I not been on such high alert.

A faint footstep, followed by another.

I breathed as I waited for one more footstep, until he was directly behind me when I span around and swung my dagger with precision.

Ethan's eyes were wide with surprise as he lifted a hand to his neck. Blood covered his fingertips where I had slashed, not deep enough to do any real damage, but necessary.

"Aria, what the *fuck*?"

"You have to trust me," I breathed.

"You have your memories back," he said, his eyes flaming. "I knew it! Why didn't you tell me?"

I stepped forward with my dagger again, he didn't move.

"What are you *doing*?" he seethed.

I swung again but this time he dodged me, he swung a hand out to slap my knife away but I swiftly ducked under his arm and moved behind him. I jumped on his back and gripped my legs round his hips, he tried to pull them away but I gripped with all the strength I could muster.

"I'm really sorry about this," I whispered.

Then I sank my knife deep into his neck.

He yelled out in pain, but I didn't let go, I dug deep into the spot Dr Bowman had showed me, blood seeped down his neck.

The tip of my knife met the resistance I was expecting, and I yanked the chip out with the knife just in time as Ethan let out a grunt of pure anger and threw me to the floor. I landed painfully on the hard tile, water from the shower flowing around me.

He stepped over me and straddled my hips with his strong legs, his blood merged with the water, pouring from his neck all over his body and onto my face.

"What the hell are you doing? Who are you working for?" he yelled.

Pure fire blazed in his amber eyes, full of such betrayal that I fought the urge to shrink away from his gaze, but I kept my eyes on him.

It would work soon.

A Lotus in the Dark

"Ethan, you have to trust me!" I pleaded. I reached up to push him off me when his strong hands gripped my throat, and he leaned down until our noses were almost touching.

"Tell me!" he growled through his teeth.

I gasped for air. "Ethan, it's me! You know me!"

"I don't know why your knife was in my fucking neck!" he spat and squeezed my throat a little, although not too tight; just a warning.

"I was removing a chip in your neck; it was suppressing your memories, just like I had in mine!"

"Bullshit," he spat.

He opened his mouth to say something else but suddenly stopped still, his grip on my neck loosened.

He reached up to his head as he winced and then closed his eyes and swayed a little.

"Ethan?" I breathed.

He shook his head and looked down at me. His eyes searched mine and I searched his, for any sign of recognition, any sign of the Ethan I knew.

I saw his throat bob as he swallowed, and his eyes blazed again, but not with anger, with something else entirely and I finally felt like I could breathe again.

"Aria," he whispered.

Then, before I had time to react, his lips crashed down on mine, stealing the air from my lungs. For a second, I was too stunned to move, but only for a second before I deepened the kiss. I slid my arms around his neck and warmth flooded down my body and emptied my brain of all other thoughts but us in that moment.

His mouth devoured mine with a sense of urgency that began to make me dizzy. The water cascaded down over us, blending us together as one.

His hands moved into my hair, onto my back, down to my waist. We kissed frantically, almost desperately, like our time was running out.

Which it was.

Just as quickly as he was on me, he was shoving himself away until he was standing over me, leaving me in shock.

"I…" he paused and held a hand out to me which I gripped and let pull me up.

"Sorry, I… don't know why I did that," he said, rubbing a hand over his hair as he stepped out of the water and turned away.

"It was the chip," I said dismissively, heat reaching my cheeks as my lips tingled from our kiss.

He turned to face me, his hand going up to his neck which had now stopped bleeding.

"Fuck," he growled, realisation crossing his face. "Fuck! Those bastards."

There it was, he remembered everything.

-CHAPTER TWENTY-TWO-

I had convinced Ethan to sit down with me as the shower poured around us and explained everything that had happened since the moment I'd entered the labs all that time ago. What I had discovered, why we'd had our memories removed.

He had sat in silence the entire time, never interrupting, never asking any questions. Just listening.

When I finished, he let out a long breath as he stared down at his hands.

"Why?"

I knew what he was asking, why did he need an army so huge, with some of the deadliest and most ruthless human weapons, completely under his control. What could he possibly need it for?

I shrugged. "We haven't figured that out yet."

"We should have known they weren't letting anyone go free when they turned eighteen," he said, so quietly it was almost to himself, like I wasn't even there. "It would be far too risky. There must be hundreds of them at least, all trapped somewhere, under complete control of that psychopath."

I knew that not only was he thinking of the hundreds of operatives who had been taken before us, but also the ones we knew. The ones we'd worked with, the ones we'd had a part in training.

Raising them like cattle to join an army of human weapons.

I nodded and said quietly, "We are going to get them all out of there."

"We have to," he said and looked up at me finally, his expression grim. "Then I'm getting as far away from here as possible, no ties to this world, living as a free man for the first time."

I rolled my eyes.

"I'm serious," he said. "I'm sitting on a beach somewhere far away getting drunk and never looking back."

I swallowed and tried not to let his words sting as I could see the emotions flowing through him as he spoke.

Shock, disbelief, guilt.

"That's the point of it all," I replied. "We'll all be free."

He sighed. "Do we have a plan?"

"We need more people and more resources. We start here at Imperium before we even attempt to infiltrate Nightstone. We need to keep doing what we're doing but speed up the process, get as many people out as we can."

He nodded and stood up. I turned off the shower, we knew this place well enough now our memories were back. We knew where was safe to talk.

"The lotus is blooming tomorrow night," I said, my eyes meeting his as he smirked a little at the coded phrase.

His expression turned serious again as he let out a sigh and rubbed a hand roughly across his face. He looked down at his clothes, soaking wet and bloodied.

"Supposed I'd better go and freshen up. We're done anyway, it's not like you need any more training. Although it's in our best interest to keep up the pretence."

A Lotus in the Dark

I sighed. "*Obviously*, they nearly killed me once for knowing what we know. I doubt they'll let us off so lightly next time."

He nodded, but his eyes were distant and full of thought. They slipped up to meet mine for a second before he said simply, "See you in the morning then," and turned to leave me alone.

I swallowed hard and fought the shiver that ran down my body as my wet clothes clung to my body.

What a mess.

My alarm blared at 6am, but as usual I'd been awake well before. I pulled the blanket over my head and squeezed my eyes shut.

I missed Ivy. I had the urge to run to her and pour my heart out, but this wasn't the time. We had more pressing issues than my feelings towards Ethan, even if it was becoming increasingly difficult to deny they were there.

My body tensed as I felt the shift of the bed, as though someone had sat on the end. I subtly but swiftly slid my hand under my pillow and gripped my trusty dagger.

"You won't need that unless I need to yank another damn chip out of your neck."

I sat up at Ivy's voice and beamed at the sight of her sat on the edge of my bed. Of course, the lotus was blooming this evening and Ivy always arrived at Imperium in the morning of a drop day to ensure everything was prepared from the inside and out.

She smiled back at me, but I quickly looked away and sprung out of bed, mortified as I felt the burning sensation of tears start to fill my eyes.

"Hey," she said, I couldn't bear the softness of her voice. "What is it? Did it not go to plan with Ethan?"

"I thought I could hear the annoying shrill of your voice."

We both spun our heads towards Ethan who stood casually leaning in the doorway. He held a hand up to the scar on his neck. "All went according to plan I'd say. Thanks for that, by the way."

Ivy smirked, relief filled her eyes. She stood and walked over to him and looked at his neck. "Oh, don't be such a baby it's already healed. It was for your own sake anyway." She looked to the both of us. "How the hell two of our best operatives managed to both get themselves chipped with a bloody memory suppressant we won't even get into right now."

"You shouldn't be here." Ethan snapped. "The place is on high alert as it is now that they've realised more kids are going missing. They'll be expecting you, and they're already suspicious of the two of us."

Ivy looked at me and rolled her eyes. "I'm well aware of the risks, dummy. I covered all bases to get here ready for this evening."

"Well did you–"

"Yes." Her tone was final. "I did everything, because I'm bloody good at my job and we've been managing just fine without you, thank you very much."

Hurt flashed across his face for a second before it turned to anger and his jaw tensed. I looked pointedly at Ivy who rolled her eyes again.

"That's not to say we don't need you obviously, but I'm not here to stroke your ego. Now we've got work to do."

She pulled out a piece of paper from her pocket and handed it to me. We'd done this enough times now that I already knew what it was going to be.

It was a thoroughly researched list of operatives we were going to be rescuing this evening. Ten people who would

A Lotus in the Dark

have their lives changed in a few hours. Ten people who Ivy and the team were certain weren't as strongly affected by the implants and wouldn't give us away, and would also strengthen our team until we could start to rescue the rest of them.

I scanned through the list and relief flashed through me as I spotted Isaacs name.

"We saw you talking to him on the cameras so did a little recon, he'll be an asset to our side," Ivy said.

Of course, they'd managed to hack into all the camera's here at Imperium. My eyes flicked to hers as I wondered how much she'd seen, and a playful smile touched her lips. Heat flooded to my cheeks and I looked away.

I handed the list to Ethan, his eyes raked down the list and then seemed to pause on one name. His gaze flicked to Ivy and then back to the list, he nodded as he handed it back to her.

I frowned. "What is it?"

Ivy smirked but Ethan interrupted, "Nothing, it's a good list."

I narrowed my eyes but let it go.

We spent the next couple hours going over the movements of all the people on the list, ensuring they'd all be where we needed them to be. Essentially, they'd selected five operatives specialising in intelligence and five operatives who showed strength in combat and weaponry. It was a carefully considered and put together list. All of them were young, too young to be here as was everyone in this place, but half of the selected operatives were approaching their eighteenth birthday this month. We had to get them out before they were shipped off to Nightstone.

Now we knew about the effects of the Morallus, June could prep them throughout the day, attempting to break them out of the control of the implant so they were ready for us.

We formulated our plan before Ethan and I left Ivy in the safety of my house and headed towards the weaponry section to keep up the pretence of continuing my training.

I had always been a skilled marksman; it was an area I had excelled in right from the start of my training. Even without my memories I was a good shot. Give me any weapon and I'd hit my target. But I still favoured my dagger if the situation allowed.

We entered the weaponry section, I mentally surveyed the room as I did naturally with any room I walked into. Michael was overseeing target practice with the two Alvara Mentors, Arron and Rachel, and ten operatives, including Isaac. Three operatives in this room would be rescued this evening, as would the two Mentors Ivy and June had identified as hopeful allies. The other five were currently being monitored by June in the Dojo.

Those who noticed us step into the room stood up straighter and respectfully tipped their heads our direction. I had to remember I was not supposed to have my memories back, I was not the Valda Mentor they remembered, so I just looked away. Ethan led us to the two targets on the far side of the room where we spent the next hour or so target shooting with various weapons. Of course, my aim was spectacular, Ethan's wasn't far behind, but I couldn't help my gaze as it kept wandering back over to where Isaac was clearly struggling with his.

After a few more minutes of painful attempts at hitting his target, I sighed and put my weapon down and headed towards him.

"What are you doing?" Ethan asked.

A Lotus in the Dark

"My job, it's fine." I shot him a look and carried on towards Isaac.

I walked up and stood behind him and watched as he continued to practice, ignoring all the looks I received as I walked by. Isaac's bullets continuously landed around the edge of the target circle.

"Told you," Issac said quietly, without turning round. "I'm falling behind."

"You're standing wrong. Turn your body slightly and place your dominant foot forwards," I said as I leant forward to nudge his arms down. "And tuck your elbows in."

He aimed and pulled trigger, again and again. The bullets landed another few inches closer to the centre.

I took a step, so I was standing next to him, and I placed a gentle hand on his stomach.

"Breathe," I said quietly. "You're holding your breath and it's throwing off your aim. Breathe fully and naturally."

He fired a few more shots, again landing a few inches closer to the centre.

"Work with your skills, work with what's inside you. Breathe and let your body take over, let it do the work. You can do this," I said firmly.

He took a few seconds this time, inhaling deep breaths, before he pulled the trigger. Again, and again.

Bullseye. Each time.

"Thank you," he exhaled.

"God," I shook my head and couldn't help but smile. "I am just such a good mentor."

I saw Isaac's shoulders shake as he let out a silent chuckle, but he didn't dare turn around. So, I turned myself and my smile instantly dropped as I found myself looking up into Commander Michael's narrowed eyes.

"Impressive," he said, his voice so deep it was almost a growl.

I waved a hand dismissively. "He did the work himself."

I made to step around him when he placed his solid body in front of mine. I looked up into his dark eyes, I would not let him intimidate me. He stared down at me for a few long seconds before he tipped his head to the side and moved so I could pass.

I kept my head high as I walked back to Ethan, who glanced over my shoulder behind me and then focussed his attention back to his target practice.

I stood up beside him and without pausing he said, "Well that was fucking stupid. Are you trying to make everyone suspicious?"

His voice was muted by the noise of the ten weapons firing around us.

I rolled my eyes. "Yes of course that's what I'm doing, I thought it would really help."

His jaw tensed and I couldn't help but smirk.

"Calm down, you weren't always so uptight."

He rolled his shoulders and continued firing. I couldn't help but admire the shape of the muscles on his back and the protruding veins in his forearms as his strong hands gripped his weapon.

I blew out a breath.

Stop it.

I glanced at the clock on the wall.

Only a few more hours to kill.

-CHAPTER TWENTY-THREE-

June had successfully intercepted the ten operatives we were rescuing this evening undetected. It was a risk doing it this way around, in case they decided against joining the Rebellion and instead raised the alarm. But so far so good, they were all in their positions waiting for us, and it meant they were all fully prepared.

Jackson would hack into the camera feeds as usual. He'd have to drop in and out, as any unusual activity over a certain amount of time would raise their alarms. So, we would have to be in and out of view, in the correct spots at the correct times.

Ethan and Ivy stood behind me as we waited inside my front door for the beep of Ivy's watch alerting us it was time.

"Remember they are on high alert now, more than ever before," Ethan said, sternly. "We must remain unseen; they will show us no mercy if they find out we're behind this."

"Your whining is going to wake everyone up anyway," I muttered.

"I'm just saying–"

"You don't have to remind us what's at stake here," I snapped.

"Will you both shut up." Ivy stepped forwards as her watched beeped. "It's go time bitches."

We were in full black attire as usual, we pulled our hoods over our heads as we headed through the door. We shouldn't be spotted on the cameras thanks to Jackson, but it was better to be safe.

We split up, Ethan made his way to the door at the main entrance of the male dorms as Ivy headed to the females. I swiftly headed to the house a few doors over from mine. In sync we each gave three sharp raps on our allocated doors.

I pushed into the house and relieved to see Arron and Rachel, the two Alvara Mentors, smiling at me, their eyes laced with determination and a little apprehension.

I reached forward instinctively, and they both gripped my hands. We nodded to each other, communicating what we needed to without words.

I turned and pushed back through the door. Ethan was moving stealthily towards me with five operatives trailing close behind him. Their movements were so swift and smooth, it would have been hard for them to have been detected even if the cameras were enabled.

Ivy appeared around the corner followed by her three operatives. She gestured to us both and then tapped her watch twice with two fingers. The second beep.

We paused in our positions, hidden from any cameras for a few seconds while Jackson had to pull out of the camera feed to remain undetected. I steadied my breaths and counted, trying to level my heart rate as it thudded in my ears.

Ivy tapped her watched again twice and gestured forwards. Jackson was back in.

We all moved in sync again. We only had to make it to the trap door behind Commander Michaels' house. We were nearly there.

But nothing was ever that simple.

A Lotus in the Dark

Rachel let a small gasp loose as the lights flicked on in the house next to us.

Commander Kane.

We all paused. Horror struck my chest like a bolt of lightning as the lights beaming from his front windows lit up the whole darkened area, practically putting a spotlight on Ethan and his team.

They began to retreat backwards into the safety of the shadows when, to add to my absolute horror, the lights in the two houses at the end of the row also switched on.

That was Shane and Karl, the two Shamara Mentors. Which meant every house was now awake except for the last two Commanders.

This was not happening.

My heart stuttered at the recognisable noise of Kane's front door opening and closing.

We hid down behind the fence next to us as the others tried to do the same. I peered through a slight gap and watched Kane and the two Mentors meet in the middle.

I held my breath.

It was almost two in the morning. They were obviously doing something they didn't want anyone else knowing about. They spoke in hushed tones to each other for a few seconds before they began to walk away.

My shoulders dropped and I blew out my breath.

Then Ivy's watch beeped.

Quick as a flash, Kane had his head whipped in her direction and a torchlight shone over Ivy and her team.

Even from my position I could see recognition flash in Kane's eyes as he spotted Ivy and pieced together what was happening.

Before we had time to react his lips spread into a sinister, blood chilling smile.

"Code Black," he sneered.

Then all hell broke loose.

All the lights turned on and alarms blared over our heads. We were all up, running towards each other.

Kane pulled his weapon and aimed it at Ivy, she stepped protectively in front of the operatives behind her. I tried to reach Kane to disarm him when the two brothers stepped between us, their lips curled as they advanced towards me.

Ethan made to step towards us when flashes of scarlet appeared in my peripheral vision, I risked a glance around as about thirty of the President's team of guards were heading towards us, all dressed in their red uniforms. Their faces were covered by their usual red masks, only their obsidian eyes visible.

Shit.

We had no choice but to fight our way out of this. We were wildly outnumbered and we had chosen to rescue only half who excelled in combat and half intelligence. But still, we were all trained, we were all excellent.

We could do this.

Ethan and his five operatives, including Isaac, were already engaged in a head on battle with the guards who approached them first. Arron and Rachel spun around as they intercepted the guards coming up behind us.

Kane still had Ivy pinned under the aim of his weapon, I was unsure why he hadn't just pulled the trigger, but I didn't have time to worry about it.

The brothers stalked towards me together and I focused my attention back to them. I flashed them my best grin.

I was going to enjoy this.

Lightening quick I pulled the dagger from my hip and threw it. In less than a second it flew through the air and embedded itself deep into Karl's side, right under his ribs. He

A Lotus in the Dark

grunted in pain and snarled as I revealed the belt of knives I had around my waist.

With both hands I swiftly pulled them from their sheath, flinging the blades forwards as I stalked towards them, each one hitting its target. Their limbs looked like pin cushions, but it only slowed them down a fraction. I wasn't aiming to kill.

Before they reached me, I risked another glance around, relief flooded through me when I saw Ethan and his team fighting, heaps of red uniforms on the floor as they won their fights. Although it looked like Isaac was taking cover behind Ethan as they were inching closer to Kane and Ivy.

My eyes snapped back to the front as Karl's meaty fist swung towards my face. I dipped backwards, narrowly avoiding a broken nose, and in the same movement yanked my dagger out of his side and slashed it towards his face. He dodged swifty so I only scraped his cheek but still drew blood. My eyes flashed as I swung my knife again, he raised an arm to protect his face and he grunted in pain as I felt knife meet bone. Shane made to grab me from behind, but I threw my head backwards, wincing only a little as the back of my head broke his nose.

Kane tried to throw punches at me, but I dodged them all. I ducked and spun around, slashing my dagger through Shane's abdomen. My blade clanged to the ground as he also dropped to the floor, blood pooled around him. I cut a little deeper than I had intended to, but I was sure he'd recover.

Karl blanched at his brother on the floor, while he was distracted, I launched myself forward, grabbed his neck and swung myself around him until I was on his back. I gripped my forearms together around his neck with all my strength until he swayed on the spot, only letting go when I was sure he'd lost consciousness. He dropped on the floor next to his brother and I delivered a few kicks into his side just for good measure.

With no time to pause I grabbed my dagger and spun, I barely had time to register my target before the knife was flying through the air once again and landed straight into Kane's shoulder.

He lowered his gun as he raised his other hand to yank the knife out, but it was all the time Ivy needed. She leapt forwards, kicking her foot out and knocking the gun from his grip. He snarled and reached forwards and wrapped his hands around her neck with such strength he lifted her off the floor. Ethan and the others reached the scene just as another group of guards advanced on them. Arron and Rachel were now beside me as we joined the fight.

They all engaged each other, fists were thrown, knives were slashed. They all moved so quickly I could barely keep up with their movements, but my focus was on Kane.

Not only on the fact he was attempting to squeeze the life out of my best friend, but everything we had learned. All the evils he had committed.

He dropped Ivy as he saw me coming, she landed on the floor and held her throat as she gasped for air.

"I don't know how you ever thought you'd get away with this," he snarled.

He pulled another pistol from a holster on his other hip I hadn't seen and raised it to my forehead.

"Look around," I raised my hands. "We are getting away with it, and we have been for months. We know everything and there is no way *you* are getting away with it," I spat back.

He shook his head and let out a chilling, humourless laugh.

"There is so much you don't know. If you knew the whole truth, you'd be sick to your stomachs, and you certainly wouldn't be here fighting us," he sneered coldly.

A Lotus in the Dark

I ignored my stomach trying to drop out of my ass and threw a smirk towards him. Chaos still ensued around me as our operatives fought their hearts out. Over Kane's shoulder I saw Ethan as he worked his way through the guards towards us, they were dropping like flies around him.

My eyes snapped back to Kane as he stepped towards me, until the cold metal of the pistol pressed against my forehead, but I refused to break.

I stared with hard eyes into his. "We know all about your experiments. We know all about Nightstone."

No surprise crossed his expression, his cold, unflinching eyes still bore into mine.

"This is far bigger than Nightstone. It is a shame you'll never find out; I would have loved to see the look on your face as we tear apart the world as you know it."

He placed his finger over the trigger, but I kept my eyes on his and simply smiled at him.

"You sure about that?" Ethan growled as he stepped around Kane, his own gun pointed to Kane's temple.

Kanes lips tightened as fury blazed in his expression. Flashes of more and more red uniforms were flooding towards us as the alarms kept blaring above. We were running out of time.

The commotion had caused all the other operatives to flood out of their dormitories, I watched as they stood and observed the scene in front of them for a moment, as though conflicted and then my chest swelled as some began to join the fight. They were overcoming the implants on their own.

Ethan pulled his arm back and slammed his gun straight into the back of Kane's head with such strength he was forced to his knees. He dropped his weapon but looked up to me as the president's guards flocked towards us.

"You will regret this," Kane spat, his cold sneer sending ice through my bones. "I look forward to the day I will have you on your knees, begging me for mercy."

Ethan slammed his gun again into Kane's head, drawing blood from just above his eyebrow. He leant down and sneered into his face. "You don't speak to her, you don't even get to fucking look at her."

He pressed his gun to his temple once again when Ivy and the others ran over to us.

"We've got to go," she panted, blood was splattered across her face and down her front. "We're out of time, we're too outnumbered. We just have to get as many out as we can, Ben is waiting with more vehicles to get more out but we have to go. *Now.*"

She didn't wait for us to answer as she led a group of operatives through a clear path towards the trap door. She yanked it opened and hurried them down the ladder. Isaac met my eyes as he disappeared, sorrow filled his gaze as though he felt he should stay but I shook my head at him.

Ethan gave one last blow to the back of Kane's head, and he passed out, falling forwards. He held the gun over him when it was knocked out of his hands. The guards had reached us.

"Aria!" Ivy yelled.

I ducked the series of punches and kicks that were being thrown my way.

"Get them all out!" I yelled to her.

I sensed her hesitation for a second before she agreed and began rounding up all the willing operatives and apprentices, leading them towards the tunnels where Ben would be waiting for them. Arron, Rachel, Ethan and I held off the army of red as best as we could while they escaped but more and more kept flocking towards us.

A Lotus in the Dark

Ethan's amber eyes flared as he met my gaze. I raised my eyebrows to him, knowing we were thinking the same thing.

We grabbed Rachel and Arron and shoved them towards Ivy and the others.

"You all have to go. Now," I yelled. "Get them all out and do not wait for us."

"But-" Arron began to argue but Ethan interrupted.

"There's no time to argue," he growled. "Go."

They obeyed, rushing over to Ivy and shoving her down the ladder.

"NO!" I heard Ivy scream as the two mentors got the last of them down into the tunnels and pulled the trap door shut behind them, but my attention was back on the fight ahead of us.

I had a knife in each hand, flashes of silver glinting as I slashed and sliced down anyone who came too close. Ethan stood with his back to mine doing the same on his side.

We only had each other, trusting each other wholly. Our movements mirrored each other, turning and ducking in a synchronised partnership, as though we were one.

The rest of the students who had not joined the fight retreated into their dorms as the room filled with red. The President's team was far larger than we could have ever anticipated, although it worked in our favour that they didn't appear to be as well trained.

"There's too many of them," I breathed.

"We can do this. Together, we can do this," Ethan grunted as he kicked away the guard in front of him. I frowned as slight panic laced his tone.

My eyes flicked around the room as I knew Ethan's were too as we looked for an escape route.

"You absolute fuckwits."

Our heads snapped towards Commander Michael as his giant body bashed through the president's guards as he stalked towards us.

I raised my fists, and he shook his head.

Ethan and I flinched as explosions suddenly broke out all around us. Michael gave no reaction as he launched a series of stun grenades towards the guards and then practically hauled us towards the exit.

The grenades exploded, extinguishing my senses all at once, my vision was nothing but white and a high-pitched whistle almost pierced my ear drums. I shook my head at the horrendous disorientated feeling and when I came back to my senses, we were in the tunnels and Michael was pulling the trap door shut above our heads.

His eyes blazed as he looked down at us, both staring at him with wide eyes. He pulled two earplugs out of his ears.

"You always, always have a fucking Plan B."

-CHAPTER TWENTY-FOUR-

"You don't have much time, you have to go," Michael said, his knuckles turned white as he gripped the trap door as forces on the other side tried to pull it open.

"How did you know?" I gasped.

He shook his head, tensing as he used all his strength to keep the door shut.

"I didn't. I only hoped. Now go!" he growled.

"What about you?" I asked as Ethan gripped my arm and began to pull me away, anxiety flooded into my stomach.

"I'll be fine." His tone was final.

I hesitated for a second, but his voice boomed, "GO!" and then we were running.

We sprinted down the tunnels as fast as our legs would allow, plunged into darkness as we headed further and further towards the exit, trusting only our memory to lead us out.

We reached the lift at the end and Ethan yanked it open, a dim light illuminated his face from above.

"Get in."

I glanced behind him into the darkness but didn't argue. I hopped into the lift and yanked the lever.

I made the excruciatingly slow ascent back above the ground and just prayed it was safe on the other side. I prayed Ivy and the others had gotten away and back to Haven in time.

How many operatives did we gain?

More importantly, how many had we lost? I'd noticed a few black uniforms among the red on the floor that we were forced to leave behind.

Guilt weighed heavily on my chest and my stomach tightened painfully. How could it have gone so wrong?

I shifted and reached my hand down to my stomach as the pain began to feel deeper than guilt. When I held it back up, my fingers were coated in blood. I coughed lightly, a knife must have caught my side, unnoticed in my adrenaline fuelled state. I couldn't assess the damage in this light, but noticed my thighs were beginning to feel hot as the sensation of blood pooled down my body.

Okay, that wasn't good. We healed quickly, but we weren't invincible.

The lift finally clunked to a stop at the top and I tumbled out, swaying unsteadily on my feet. I blinked a few times as my vision began to fade around the edges. I glanced both ways down the alley, certain the coast was clear and with a grunt I yanked the lever to send the lift back down to Ethan.

I tried to steady my breathing as I listened to the low hum of the lift making its descent. I looked down as blood flooded from my stomach down my legs and into a pool around my feet.

I just had to wait to make sure Ethan was okay.

I swayed again, my vision fading faster.

I could wait on the ground.

I dropped to my knees and pressed my hand to my wound, blood seeped through my fingers.

Finally, the lift clunked to a stop.

Ethan stepped out, he looked unharmed.

"You're okay," I breathed, my head dropped forwards.

A Lotus in the Dark

His eyes widened in shock as he took in my state. He reached for me, and my injuries took over as my world descended into darkness to the sound of my name on his lips.

I sat up in a panic then winced in pain and laid back down. I looked around, my eyebrows pinching together as I realised that I didn't recognise the room I was in. I was in a bed, the sheets were dingy and outdated, as were the matching curtains. I heard the recognisable sound of a shower through the door to the other side of the room. I didn't need to be a detective to work out we were in a cheap inn.

The shower turned off in the bathroom and a few minutes later Ethan walked out drying his hair with a towel. He was wearing only his black joggers and his top half naked, muscular and glistening with water. The sight alone would have healed my wounds if I hadn't had my implant doing the job.

He lowered his towel as he noticed I was awake, and relief shone clear in his expression.

He smiled at me like he couldn't help himself. I gave him a soft smile in return.

"I thought we'd lay low for the night as you got yourself injured, again."

I shook my head. "You were worried about me."

His smile dropped, he swallowed and stepped towards the bed.

"You wish," he scoffed. "It was a deep wound; it's starting to heal now so you should be fine to travel in the morning."

I ignored the twisting in my stomach and tried to sit up higher again. He moved to help me, supporting me so I could sit in a comfortable position. He shoved a pillow behind my back and stepped away.

"Where are we?" I asked.

"Some dodgy inn on the outskirts of the city. It was the only place on our list that I thought would let me take you in in the state you were." He frowned and looked away. "I don't think we were tracked, but it won't be too long until they find us. They've got eyes everywhere."

I nodded. "I'm fine, we should go. We need to get to Haven, we need to check the others are okay."

I shifted to climb out of bed, but he spun and placed his hands firmly on my upper arms.

"Don't you dare," he growled, his eyes darkened. "You need to let yourself heal. We're fine here for a while and we don't want to lead them back to Haven anyway, just wait them out."

I swallowed and looked down at my hands, he was right. Ethan reached forwards and pushed a strand of hair out of my face that had dropped forward.

"They'll be fine," he said, his voice surprisingly soft. "They all got out before us."

I raised my eyes to meet his. "Not all of them."

He swallowed. "They all made a choice, they wanted to fight. We knew there was a chance we wouldn't all make it out, but we have to look at the bigger picture. All of the lives we are saving. All of the kids still at Nightstone."

I blinked a few times. "That doesn't make it okay."

He nodded and rubbed a hand over the back of his neck. "Nothing about this is okay."

There was a heavy silence for a couple of moments, both lost in our own thoughts.

"So," I said, my tone light. "Commander Michael?"

He shook his head and let out a slight chuckle. "I know, I'm not sure how many more surprises I can handle."

I chewed my lip. "We'd be lucky to have him on our side. We need to get him and the rest of them out of Imperium."

A Lotus in the Dark

He nodded in agreement. "We will, but we can't rush it. Look at what happened today."

Guilt filled my chest again. "We couldn't have predicted Kane and the brothers meeting in the middle of the night, it's never happened before."

He remained silent for a moment and then sighed. "You should get some sleep."

"You should too," I replied. Heat flooded to my cheeks when his eyes dropped to the bed.

The *only* bed.

"I need to keep watch," he said, gruffly.

"If they knew where we were, they would be here already. We have a few hours until morning, we may as well try to both get some sleep. We've been partners for ten years, we've been on countless field assignments together, we can share a bed without it meaning anything."

When he didn't reply I rolled my eyes.

"What are you afraid if we share a bed, you wont be able to resist me?" I teased.

But his head slowly turned, and his serious amber eyes met mine.

Oh.

His eyes dropped to my lips and heat flooded down my body.

We had been partners for years. We'd grown up together, spent our entire lives together. There wasn't anyone who knew me better. There wasn't anyone who I trusted as wholly or implicitly as him. Except perhaps Ivy. But I knew, in my heart, at some point the line was crossed from partnership to friendship to something *more*. Something far deeper than I could possibly explain and I couldn't deny my feelings any longer.

My eyes softened and I pulled back the duvet. He sighed as he accepted defeat and slipped into the bed next to me. He leant over to the switch by the bed and flicked the lights off, the room lightly illuminated by the silver moonlight shining through the curtains.

I shifted down onto my pillow, ignoring the pain shooting through my stomach, and rolled to face him. A few minutes of heavy silence passed. I closed my eyes to the sound of Ethan breathing softly and I realised how safe I felt with him by my side.

"I *was* worried about you," he breathed. I felt the mattress shift as he rolled onto his side, his nose only inches from mine. I fought not to squirm under the heat of his gaze as his fiery eyes bore into mine under the moonlight.

He lifted his hand and traced a finger lightly down my arm and I couldn't suppress the shiver it sent down my spine.

"In fact, I realised I'd never truly felt fear until that moment," he breathed.

His fingers continued to trace up and down my arm, then moved further down until he traced the curve of my waist and stopped at my hips. I struggled to control my breathing as the heat flooded further down my body.

"We have spent our entire lives training to be cold, ruthless killers. I've had a lifetime of... numbness, and you have ripped me back into the living and... I can't do this." He snapped his hand back and pushed himself out of the bed.

The heat in my body twisted into frustration. Ignoring the pain in my side, I pushed myself up so I was kneeling on the edge of the bed facing him.

"You are so scared of the way I make you feel because you don't want to feel anything," I snapped.

His head whirled to me, and he was standing in front of me in a heartbeat.

A Lotus in the Dark

God, I wanted him to touch me.

"Of course, I don't," he seethed. "We have been raised with no real love, for no real reason. All the things we've done, all the lives we've taken. You think I want to *feel* that? I don't want to feel anything and yet you make me feel *everything*, all the time."

"Ethan..." I breathed, I inched forwards on the bed and placed my hands on his strong chest. "I feel it all too. I feel the pain and the tragedy, it only makes us stronger, it's what fuels us to keep fighting. It is terrifying to let yourself feel so deeply, to let people in, because you've seen a lifetime of hurt. But it all must have been for something."

Before I could give him time to react, I tipped my head up and closed the space between us, placing a soft kiss on his lips.

His whole body tensed under my touch.

"Aria," he groaned against my lips and hesitated for only a second longer before he returned my kiss, soft at first and then more urgently. His hands began at my hips and slid their way up my waist, along my arms and then gripped my wrists.

He pushed me away and looked down at me, his heavy breathing matched my own.

"You don't want me?" I taunted.

"I want you." His eyes raked over me, and I felt naked under the intensity of his gaze. "*God*, I want you."

He shook his head, and I could already feel him pulling away. "But if I let you in, I won't ever be able to let you go."

"I'm not going anywhere."

He dropped my wrists and stepped back; I swallowed the hurt that tightened my chest as he paced towards the door.

"You aren't just the heartless murderer you were raised to be," I said, and he paused with his hand on the door handle.

"As soon as you realise that, the better, because I'm getting really fucking sick of this hot and cold routine."

He pulled the door open and walked out without looking back.

The longer it took for Ethan to get back the angrier I became, only sated momentarily by the sugary doughnuts I noticed he'd left on the bedside table for me.

I chewed my lip as I paced back and forth, the pain in my side had almost completely disappeared as the wound healed quickly due to our implants. One of the only positives.

I felt useless holed up in this room. I let out a frustrated groan as the night began to fade. What was he even doing? We needed to get out of here and back to Haven, time was not on our side.

Maybe he wasn't coming back at all.

My stomach clenched at the thought and I rubbed my hands on my thighs. Would he really leave? He had no reason to stay, he made that glaringly clear.

Or maybe he was hurt. What if they'd found him?

The thought alone was enough to make up my mind, I had to go after him.

I had just slipped my dagger into its place on my hip when there was a commotion outside. A crash, followed by a few bangs and then another louder crash. I shot to the window and peered through the edge of the curtain while trying to remain undetected. I paused for a few moments as my heart thundered in my chest. My head snapped to the door when Ethan rolled in.

Literally.

He looked up at me with a stupid grin on his stupid face, swayed forwards and then staggered towards me.

"What the hell?" I frowned and kicked the door shut. The relief I felt that he was okay, quickly replaced by rage. "Are you *drunk*?"

Once the door slammed behind him, he stood up straight and urgent. He reached for his belongings and started placing daggers into the belt around his waist.

"I'm not fucking stupid." His tone was cold. "I'm throwing them off."

"What are you talking about?"

His eyes slid to mine. "They've found us."

-CHAPTER TWENTY-FIVE-

"Shit."

"My thoughts exactly," Ethan replied. "There's four of them, that I could see, but there will be more. Two in a car outside, two likely approaching the room as we speak. They think I'm inebriated so may not be prepared for us."

We didn't have any belongings to pack up, only a few spare knives that I sheathed where I could easily reach them. Two on my waist, two on my thighs and my trusty dagger on my hip.

I turned my head towards the sound of Ethan reloading the pistol he held.

"Kane's." He shrugged.

At least we weren't completely unarmed. We could absolutely take on four of them. But now they had found us, evading them again would be more difficult.

We stood in the dark room and waited for a moment, Ethan waited by the door, and I positioned myself in the far corner.

When the door handle creaked as it slowly turned open, my gaze met Ethan's across the room, and he rolled his eyes.

Who trained these guys? It certainly wasn't us.

The door pushed open and two of the president's guards pushed through with their weapons raised. Their dark eyes above their masks quickly scanning the room.

A Lotus in the Dark

Simultaneously, I flung my knife through the air and smiled as it landed in the neck of the one nearest to me as Ethan snapped the neck of the one nearest to him. They both landed with a thud next to each other.

He frowned down at the bodies clearly thinking the same as me.

"They weren't trained at Imperium," he said quietly.

"That doesn't make any sense," I whispered back as I casually pulled my knife out of the guard's neck and returned it to its sheath. "Why would the President have hundreds of guards who weren't even trained at Imperium? Why would he not be using the highly skilled operatives, clearly trained better than these idiots? Where was he even recruiting them from anyway?"

"That," Ethan blinked. "Was a lot of questions in one breath, even for you."

"Shut up," I hissed. "I was just thinking out loud."

The edge of his lips tipped up into a smirk. "Come on, we need to go."

The front door was the only way out of this room, so we had little choice but to face the others head on. The sun was beginning to rise which I hoped would work in our favour, the president would have ordered his guards not to draw attention to any suspicious activity.

Ethan placed a hand on my lower back as we headed through the door, just that simple touch tingled through my body.

I needed to get a grip. We were in a potentially life-threatening situation and all I could think about was Ethan touching me.

I looked up at him with narrowed eyes and shifted forwards away from his touch. His heated eyes dropped down to my lips and his eyebrow twitched.

"Don't," I snapped. "Don't look at me like that."

"Like what?" His voice was thick.

"You know exactly like what. If you won't let me in, I won't let you in either."

His lips twisted into a wry smile and I felt the warmth in my cheeks.

"I didn't mean... stop it!"

I yanked the door open and crouched down as we surveyed the situation, our heightened senses on alert.

Ethan nodded towards the now empty car that was parked behind some trees ahead of us. They were around here somewhere, waiting for us.

"We're in the middle of nowhere," Ethan spoke softly in my ear, and I fought the shiver it sent down my spine. "It's surrounded by about 300km of forest, our best chance is to head North on foot, towards Haven, and go from there."

I nodded and began to move, then swiftly slammed my body to the floor as I heard the unmistakable whir of a knife flying through the air. It landed with a thud in the wall, right where my head would have been.

Ethan followed suit as two more flew towards us followed by two more thuds.

I jumped up, yanking the knives from the wall and flung them back in the direction they came. A low, satisfying, grunt told me I'd hit my target. One of them anyway.

We began to move down the side of the building, flashes of movement headed towards us through the trees in the distance. They'd swapped their red uniforms for a stealthier black, but we had no doubt who they were.

"How many of these fuckers does he have working for him?" Ethan hissed.

Knowing the President, it was likely an endless amount. They were merely dispensable weapons to him.

A Lotus in the Dark

We dashed around the corner, and I groaned internally. The expansive forest spread out in front of us, and Ethan was right, our best chance was to head North on foot, but I didn't like it. In the dark it would have been better, but heading through the forest in the morning light was a risk.

We both instinctively ducked our heads as a gunshot sounded from behind us and then we were hurtling towards the trees.

We sprinted, ducking and dodging our way through the forest. I doubted they could outrun us if they weren't trained at Imperium, they might not have the implants and so would only match half our speed. Still we ran until our legs couldn't take much more, even we needed to rest.

We slowed to a walk but pressed on further through the trees, then paused as the darkness of the forest started to fade as we reached the edge. Up ahead in the distance we could see a remote country lane.

"We'll follow the road, but we should stay under the cover of the forest," Ethan said.

"No shit," I muttered as I followed him.

His jaw tensed but he didn't respond.

"I thought you weren't coming back," I said quietly. I saw him stiffen and he turned his head towards me.

"I'm not a monster, Aria," he retorted. "I'm finishing the job; we're getting those kids out of there... and *then* I'm gone."

My chest tightened. "Getting drunk on a beach somewhere, not giving a shit about anyone." I mocked his voice.

"Exactly," he said. "You should do the same. There will be nothing left for us here."

He turned away from me and I hastened my pace to keep up with him.

This was going to be a long journey.

The sun was beginning to fade once again. We'd walked for hours through the forest and once we were certain they'd lost all sight of us we braved heading out to the country roads that led to a small village. From there we found a farm, hijacked an old tractor and, almost a day later, were finally approaching Haven.

The gates opened as we approached on foot, we'd ditched the tractor a few miles back. I waved up at the camera as we approached the doors. After taking the usual security measures, we both stepped through into the quiet hallway.

Seconds later Ivy was pushing through the double doors at the end of the hallway leading to the lounge area. Relief flooded through me so violently I almost buckled at the knees.

She ran over to us and launched her arms around me in an unrestrained embraced. I hugged her back tightly and stepped back as she cupped my cheeks.

"You're okay," she breathed and dropped her hands. "When you didn't show up for so long, we started to worry."

I lifted my top to show Ivy my almost healed wound, only because she'd go mad if she found out I hadn't told her.

"We hit a little road bump." I shrugged and she pursed her lips.

"I'm just glad you're both okay." She linked her arm through mine and led the way to the lounge area. "Come on, its dinner time. We got a lot more operatives out than we'd originally expected, and a few apprentices. Mum is still at Imperium, hopefully they believe she had no part in this." Worry laced her tone.

I nodded as I remembered the ones who chose to fight with us.

A Lotus in the Dark

"You need to tell us everything," she continued. "What happened? Where have you been?"

"You'll never guess how we got out," I smirked, and my eyes flicked to Ethan.

As we walked through the strangely quiet rooms towards the dining area, we told Ivy what happened, how Kane was still alive, how Commander Michael had gotten us out and how we escaped the guards at the inn.

She listened and gasped in the right places.

"What do you think Kane meant? Is there something bigger going on that we're missing?"

"He was just trying to fuck with our heads," Ethan said darkly from behind us.

"Ah he speaks," Ivy smirked. "I'd almost forgotten you were there, following behind us like our own personal thunder cloud."

He smiled sweetly down at her. "Would you prefer I was a ray of sunshine?"

"God no." She shuddered. "That would be way more terrifying."

I smirked as Ethan rolled his eyes but then Ivy stopped for a second and put a hand on his arm. "I'm glad you're okay too," she said, seriously. "Thank you for getting her out."

He swallowed and then nodded once and that was that.

Ivy smiled at me like that was exactly the response she'd expected and then pushed into the dining area.

The noise hit me straight away and I stopped still and looked around the room.

"I know," Ivy said quietly next to me. "It's going to take some getting used to."

The room was huge, set out into three long rows of wooden tables with benches either side, and it was full of life. Not just because of the added operatives, but actual *life*.

Groups of young men and women sat together eating their dinner, engaged in animated, friendly conversations. The sound of chatter and laughter floated towards us, and I hadn't realised how much I'd missed something we'd never had.

They were acting like excitable teenagers rather than stone cold robots, and my heart tugged.

I caught Isaac's gaze across the room, and he lifted a hand to waved at me. I smiled and waved back, and he turned his head to continue his conversation with the boy next to him.

Calling them "boys and girls" in my mind felt so juvenile for what they'd been through, what they knew; but they weren't quite men and women either.

"Mentor Ethan!"

A young operative called over as he joined us. I was sure his name was Jacob; he was one of Ethan's students selected for one-to-one classes.

I looked to Ethan as Jacob joined us, shocked to see relief flood into his eyes and a smile crack onto his lips.

"Hey kid," he said. "You did well back there."

Jacob's whole face lit up with pride. "I did just what you told me to."

Ethan shocked me further by placing a hand on his shoulder and giving it a light squeeze. "I know. We'll catch up later, okay?"

He nodded and raised a hand in a sheepish wave before he dashed back to his table. I raised an eyebrow at Ethan.

"I didn't know you had such a bond with your students," I said, sarcasm dripping from my tone.

"Because I'm a heartless robot," he shot back.

"If the shoe fits," I muttered.

Ivy nudged me in the ribs and my eyes snapped to hers. I suddenly remembered the way Ethan had reacted to the list of operatives she had selected for the rescue mission.

A Lotus in the Dark

Jacob was on there for Ethan for the same reason Isaac was for me. I let out a surprised huff and dropped the subject.

We followed Ivy to the middle of one of the wooden benches and sat down.

I smiled at Arron and Rachel across from me and then Jackson and Ben a few seats down from them.

I looked around the room for a few more moments in awe.

This was what it was all for.

Ivy nudged her arm gently into mine and I met her gaze, she nodded and smiled knowing exactly what I was thinking. We'd always been able to communicate without speaking.

I glanced up to where Ethan still stood.

"Aren't you going to sit? You must be hungry," I said.

He shook his head and looked around the room once, then rubbed one of his hands over the back of his neck. "I'm going to go and get cleaned up."

"Okay then." I glanced once at him and then made myself look back to the plate Ivy had placed in front of me.

I felt the shift in the air as he left the room and headed to his assigned bedroom.

I sighed and my stomach rumbled as I started piling food on to my plate.

"If you stare any harder, you're going to burn a hole in the side of my head," I muttered to Ivy as I buttered a roll.

She looked away. "Fine, that can be a story for later."

After a few hours or so of comfortable camaraderie, everyone gradually started drifting back to their rooms. I'd been itching to start planning our next steps, but it wasn't the right time. The morale was high, and we were celebrating a win, this was the start of a new life. It could wait until the morning.

"So," Ivy prompted as we walked down the corridor to our rooms. She glanced pointedly to Ethan's door next to mine. "Are you going to tell me about you and the thunder cloud?"

I snorted. "There's nothing to tell."

"Fine, you know where I am when you want to talk," she said as she slipped into her room opposite mine.

The top corridor had been converted into a huge row of bedrooms. I walked into mine for the first time in what felt like an eternity, it looked just how I'd left it. A typical dorm room; small single bed to the side with a simple desk, set of drawers and wardrobe. It was simple but it worked for us.

Of course, when we'd first taken over the mansion, we'd slept in the huge master bedrooms over the other side. When there were more of us it didn't feel right and we needed the space, so we'd had the bedrooms converted into large communal showers and moved to the dorm rooms with everyone else.

I changed into some comfier clothes I found in one of my drawers and slipped into the small but comfortable bed. I wrapped the duvet over my head and once again sleep consumed me quicker than expected.

I allowed myself to sleep in until 8am, we'd never had that luxury before on the strict Imperium schedule. I headed for the communal showers and washed and dressed quickly for the day – still all in black – and then headed down to the dining room for breakfast. We'd recruited a chef when we'd first moved in and had decided to put the operatives on a kitchen rotation when there was enough of us for the chef to need some extra pairs of hands.

There were a few sat down for breakfast, only about a quarter of the amount that were here for dinner. My heart gave a frustrating thud at the sight of Ethan.

A Lotus in the Dark

I poured myself a coffee with a bowl of porridge and sat opposite him.

"Morning," I said, trying to keep my tone casual. "Guess people are making the most of the relaxed sleep schedules."

He lifted his eyes from his breakfast to meet mine and then scoffed lightly. "Yeah right, you should see the training rooms. They've been full since about 6am."

I chuckled softly. "I should have guessed."

It didn't matter if they chose to be training, eating or sleeping. The point was they had a choice.

"We should lead a few classes in the next day or so," Ethan said thoughtfully. "It will be interesting to see their abilities now their humanity is free from the implant's control."

I tilted my head and took a sip of coffee. "Interesting, it hasn't affected us?"

He nodded. "I know, but we're different." Arrogant but right. "They've all been trained to fight without restraint, no feelings getting in the way. I'm interested to see how their humanity will affect their skills."

"You keep calling it their humanity," I said.

He shrugged. "That's what it is isn't it? Whatever part of us that makes us human, that's the part the implant shut off, with some it's obviously harder to get back."

"They have to want it back," I agreed.

He made a thoughtful sound as he took a sip of his own coffee, and I watched his throat bob.

His lips twitched as he noticed me watching him and his eyebrow raised slightly.

I sighed and feeling brave I reached forward and traced a finger down his other hand placed on the table. His gaze dropped to my lips and then back up to lock with mine as his eyes shone.

"This is getting tiring," I said.

He opened his mouth to reply when the door slammed open with a crash that made both of us jump and whip our heads to the door.

Ivy stood in the doorway with panic in her eyes as she searched for me.

We both shot up out of our seats and headed to the door.

"It's mum!" she called, before we reached her, she'd dashed back the way she came. Fear clenched at my stomach; June couldn't be hurt.

We followed Ivy to the hallway as the front door opened and June walked through, seemingly unharmed. Except for the fear swimming in her eyes and the fact that she wouldn't be here if everything was okay.

She gave Ivy a brief hug before stepping back.

"What is it?" Ivy asked.

Her hand clasped her chest as she took a breath. "We're out of time."

-CHAPTER TWENTY-SIX-

We were all sat around a large mahogany table in a side room we'd designated as a meeting room. We'd called in everyone we'd felt were necessary for this conversation and then waited for June to speak.

"As you can imagine they have descended into chaos at headquarters since the last rescue mission," June began. "The President himself even graced us with his presence."

There were a few light gasps from around the room. Everyone was thinking the same thing, the President ran the whole operation and yet none of us had ever seen him, only the Commanders and some of his guards.

"Obviously they now know your part in this and that there is a full Rebellion movement." Her eyes turned dark as she met each gaze around the room. "I've seen footage... from Nightstone."

I sat up straight and felt Ethan and Ivy both do the same either side of me.

She shook her head. "It can only be described as a war camp. The conditions are dire, they are being treated like prisoners... Some of them have lost all sense of humanity I'm not sure we will ever get them back." June swallowed. "We have no doubt about it, the President is raising an army."

"How did you see this footage?" Ethan asked. "Do we even know where Nightstone is?"

"I'm not at liberty to disclose how I came across the footage." I frowned at that. "And no, we are no closer to finding the location... And I don't think Nightstone is just Imperium operatives."

I raised my eyebrows. "What do you mean?"

She sighed and pulled a tablet out of the rucksack by her feet. "Again, I can't tell you who sent me this footage yet but..."

She slid the tablet over to us, Ivy and Ethan leaned closer, and I attempted to ignore Ethan's warm thigh pressed against mine as I clicked play.

It was drone footage; the first minute showed a landscape of beautiful snow-topped mountains, followed by an expansive, dense forest of what looked like giant sequoias. I shook my head. Where was this place?

The drone flew lower and showed a huge, enclosed area, the walls were a foot thick and almost as tall as the trees. Tents became visible through the trees, then there was a solid black movement around the area. My head tilted, confused at what I was seeing until the drone flew slightly lower again and the vision focused on the movement through the trees.

"Oh god," Ivy gasped next to me.

"What is it?" Rachel asked and we pushed the tablet over to her and Arron.

They watched the same footage and Rachel covered her mouth with her hand.

"Shit," Arron gulped.

Isaac swallowed hard. "There's... *thousands* of them."

Thousands upon thousands.

I blew out a breath. "We can't rush this, not after last time. We need to recuperate, retrain as a team unit and then formulate a solid plan."

A Lotus in the Dark

"That's the thing, we don't have the time, that's why I had to come back." June shook her head lightly. "They are shipping everyone left at Imperium off to Nightstone, regardless of age or training."

"What?" I gasped.

My heart thundered in my chest as voices raised around me.

"They can't do this!"

"That's barbaric!"

"What about the children?" Isaac asked.

"They're all children," I snapped and stood up, my eyes met Isaac's. "They are *all* children. So are most of you! None of us should be here, none of us should be in this position. We've all been forced here, raised to live a life we didn't have any choice to live and now we have to risk our lives to save the rest of them and we cannot assume everyone will want to."

Everyone nodded thoughtfully as I looked at each of them. Ethan, Ivy, June, Isaac, Ben, Jackson, Arron and Rachel, I knew they'd all fight for this.

"They will," Ivy said.

I said more softly, "I have no doubt every person in this room would risk their lives to shut down whatever the hell is going on at Nightstone. *No* doubt. But we must give the others the choice, else we're no different to Imperium."

Ivy placed a hand on mine. "Of course, we will, we're not forcing anyone to fight with us."

I looked around to see everyone nodding in agreement. Good.

"When are they moving?" I asked June.

She took a deep breath, her eyes glistened as they raised to meet mine. "In three days."

I squeezed my eyes shut and took a steadying breath as the others murmured their thoughts to each other.

June shifted and cleared her throat. "There's more."

I rubbed my temples. "Of course there is."

"They have Commander Michael in the President's chambers," June said, softly, ignoring my sarcasm.

My eyes snapped open. "What? He's being tortured?"

The President's chambers; a place I'd die before I ever unwillingly stepped foot inside. His personal torture chamber.

"They found out about his involvement in helping you escape," she said. "They're trying to torture more information out of him, the problem is he genuinely doesn't have any, except my involvement. I had to let him know we were going to get him out, I couldn't abandon him there with no hope after what he did to help you."

Ivy shifted. "You're not safe there then."

"He hasn't given me up yet," June countered but then sighed. "I'm probably of more use here now anyway."

Ethan pinched the bridge of his nose. "We'll add Michael to the plan."

We spent the next few hours formulating a solid plan, we had three days to prepare. Ivy, Jackson and Isaac were in charge of recon. Ben, Arron and Rachel were the exit plan. June, Ethan and I were going to spend the next couple of days training with the operatives we had at Haven and finalising the full operation plan.

We had three days.

Ethan and I met early the next morning, we'd called all operatives to the training room in the basement. It wasn't too dissimilar from the Dojo at Imperium.

We stood in front of the sixty-eight operatives looking back at us with alert eyes. We'd announced Imperium's motives last night after dinner, so that everyone was fully aware of what was being asked of them.

"First things first," I began. "I want to reiterate; you are under no obligation to be here. We know what we're asking of you, and we'd understand if you wanted no part in it."

I looked around the room and Isaac stepped forward. "You've given us our humanity. You've given us our lives back and you've given us the freedom to make a choice, that's why we're all here. I think I speak for everyone in this room when I say we want the same for the others out there who are still trapped in their mental prisons. We want to fight."

There were murmurs and nods around the room as everyone agreed. My chest swelled with pride.

Ethan stepped forwards. "We didn't give you anything, it was already in there, you all found your way out. If you didn't want to, you wouldn't have been able to. The problem is, that's what we're working against."

"They think our humanity makes us weak," I continued. "But they're wrong, its what makes us strong and it's why we're going to win."

"You've been trained to work on your own, possibly in pairs, but primarily you protect yourselves above all. That changes now," Ethan gestured around the room. "Look around, memorise the faces standing with you. They are your team. We are a unit, and we need to fight as one."

They spent the next few hours in groups of six, distinguished by coloured bands on their upper arms, altering their training techniques to work alongside each other. Ethan and I walked around the room observing.

We'd assigned one group with Arron and another with Rachel, first to force the other team into submission would win. Arron's Reds vs Rachel's Blacks. Simple.

Or it should have been.

Firstly, their humanity took over a little too much and they were afraid to hurt the other team, but they quickly got over the first hurdle and engaged in an impressive spar.

That was, until Arron swung for an operative on the Black team, who dodged swiftly, forcing Arron's fist into the face of a Red and subsequently resulting in a free-for-all.

Ethan blew out a breath as we watched all twelve operatives descend on each other, even if their techniques were exceptional, that was not the point of this training.

"Hey, morons!" I yelled, but my voice was lost in the chaos.

Ethan stormed over and yanked two of them off each other by the back of their tops and slammed their heads together. "Are you idiots colour blind?"

I followed suit, strolling over to Arron as he leaned over, beating hell into another member of his own team. I slammed my elbow down between his shoulder blades and then bashed my knee hard into his ribs, he fell to the side gasping for air and I shoved my foot down onto his chest.

"STOP."

This time they listened. The whole room stopped to listen.

"What are you *doing*?" I seethed. "If we go into it like this, you are going to get us all killed. What are you trying to prove? We have no doubt you can all fight, every person in this room has been trained to be ruthless killers, that makes you no better than the President and his heartless team of guards!"

I stepped off Arron's chest and offered him a hand. He took it and I pulled him up.

"When we can learn to work together rather than against each other, we'll be unstoppable. Go again." I demanded.

A Lotus in the Dark

To their credit they did just that; shook themselves off and took their positions beside each other and began again.

Ethan moved to stand beside me. I looked up at him as he watched over the training with dark eyes, his lips set in a hard line. His eyes flicked down to me and I smiled.

"What?"

"Thundercloud," I snorted. "Ivy was right on the mark."

He shook his head. "You and Ivy are two of the deadliest assassins I know and yet when you're together you're no better than two giggling teenage girls."

I put a hand on my chest and gave an exaggerated gasp. "Was that a compliment?"

I loved winding him up. The thrill of his eyes flashing, his jaw tensing, his fists clenching.

Heat flushed through me.

"How's that knee by the way?" I taunted.

"That knee is the only reason you won our last fight," he replied.

He loved the game we played, even if he wouldn't admit it.

I snorted. "You keep telling yourself that."

His arm whipped out to smack the back of my head, but I ducked and span towards him and punched him square in the abdomen.

He grabbed my shoulders and threw me onto the ground, my back hit the training mat with a thud. He crushed his body down on top of me and pressed his forearm into my throat, I wrapped my legs around his hips so he couldn't move.

His amber eyes flashed with the unmistakeable heat of desire and his gaze inevitably dropped to my lips and then back up to my eyes.

"That was far too easy," he breathed.

My eyes flicked downwards. "Was it?"

He followed my gaze to where my hand gripped my dagger and pressed it into his side, right above his kidney. It would be a fatal stab wound.

He looked back up at me and his lips tipped into a wry smile. He pressed himself into me and his desire pooled into mine.

"Admit it," I said, keeping my voice low. "You can barely keep your hands off me. You want me."

"I never said I didn't." His low voice was almost a growl, and it sent a shiver through my whole body.

I became suddenly aware of the operatives around us.

As though reading my mind Ethan tipped his head down to mine.

"They're not as easily distracted as you," he smirked.

His lips grazed mine lightly and I forgot how to think. He reached down and gripped my wrist, flinging my dagger to the side and then shoved my hands above my head.

I tipped my head up so my lips grazed his ear and squeezed my legs tighter around his waist, I fought a satisfied smile as his breaths deepened and he pressed his hips into me again.

"I'm not distracted," I breathed into his ear. "I'm the distraction."

I yanked my arms from his grip and slammed the heels of my hands upwards into his throat at the same time as I gripped his waist with my thighs and flipped him, so I was straddling him. I swiftly pulled the knife from the hidden sheath on my thigh and pressed it into his throat.

"And it was far too easy," I mocked his voice.

His eyes widened with surprise and then he chuckled darkly. "I'll get you back for this."

I looked down at him, aware my eyes were full of desire. "Is that a promise?"

A Lotus in the Dark

His large hands squeezed my thighs as I winked and pushed myself up and off him. I offered a hand down to him as I had done moments before with Arron.

Ethan reached for my hand, but in the split second before grabbing it he swung his leg out to knock mine completely out from under me. My back slammed down onto the floor again; my head fell back with a crack and the air rushed out of my lungs. Ethan pushed himself up and sauntered away chuckling.

I coughed and then yelled after him. "Nobody likes a sore loser!"

That evening we had all congregated in the common room after dinner. There was easy chatter flowing around the room although the air still felt thick with the tension of our upcoming mission.

Ethan sat on one of the red sofas talking to Arron who sat beside him. Ivy and I had sat on the floor in front of them, closer to the open fire that blazed next to us.

"So, you can *literally* seclude your eyesight to your target when you're aiming?" Arron asked Ethan, continuing their earlier conversation from target practice.

Ethan nodded. "It's the implant's affect I think, you just have to work with it. I can't explain it, I'd assumed everyone could do it." He shrugged and Arron's mouth dropped open as he looked towards us.

"Can you two do it?" he asked.

I smirked as Ivy said, "Of course we can."

Arron began to respond when Isaac and Rachel bounced over to us, their eyes sparkling.

"What have you done?" Ethan asked, his eyes narrowed.

Isaac sat on the opposite sofa as Rachel dropped next to him, they shared a look and then he said, "Don't be mad."

"Don't give me a reason to be," Ethan replied.

Isaac pulled out a gold topped glass bottle filled with shimmering liquid. "Imperium shots, anyone?"

"Isaac," I gasped but my lips had spread into a smile. "Where did you get that from?"

"I'd had a bottle hidden away for ages." He waved a hand dismissively. "I think now is the time to break it open."

Ivy chuckled. "I like you more everyday kid."

"Go on," I said to Ethan. "Say it."

"What?" He frowned.

"All the reasons why it's not a good idea."

His jaw tensed but then he shrugged, my eyebrows shot up as he reached for the bottle.

"I think," he said, taking it from Isaac and unscrewing the top. "We've dedicated our whole lives to train and work and behave with purpose. What would be the point in rebelling against that life if we weren't able to live a little."

He took a swig and then passed it to me with a wink.

Heat flooded to my core, a sensation I was becoming quite accustomed to around him.

He was right, we'd dedicated our whole lives to Imperium, following strict rules and training regimes. We deserved to have a little fun, especially knowing tomorrow we'd be back to training and planning our next steps.

I took the bottle from him, and we shared a small smile before I took my own gulp and handed it to Ivy. Immediately a warm, tingling sensation coursed through my body, as the alcohol mixed with the drugs flowed through my veins.

I giggled as Ivy proceeded to down a quarter of the bottle before Isaac tried to snatch it back.

She held the bottle out of his reach and smirked.

"You're underage."

A Lotus in the Dark

"Oh please, I've seen more shit than most fifteen-year-olds."

I gasped. "We missed your birthday."

"Well then, this can be my celebration." Isaac shoved Ivy's arm and she snorted and handed it over to him.

He lifted it to his lips and Ivy nudged the bottom of the bottle. We all fell back laughing as it jolted, fizzing up and spraying in his face. He spluttered before his own laughter followed and he passed the bottle to Rachel.

I looked to Ethan, his eyes bright as he chuckled softly, and my heart squeezed.

A few hours later, the empty bottle lay on the floor beside two empty bottles of tequila that Ivy had stashed away. Our group had grown, Ben and Jackson had joined us on the floor and other operatives had gathered around, laughing freely as they joked and drank.

At some point I'd shifted on the floor to lean against Ethan's legs as he sat on the sofa behind me. His fingers had made their way to my shoulder and had moved down, lightly tracing circles on my upper arm. I closed my eyes at the sensation.

The room spun around me and I knew my head would hurt in the morning but I didn't care. Not when I looked around to see my family, smiling like they didn't have a care in the world. This was what it was all for.

-CHAPTER TWENTY-SEVEN-

After three days of preparation, we were as ready as we could be. The operatives were working as an indestructible team unit. I'd been worried at first but after watching the last session, the way they blended together, their swift movements syncing together as one; they were a force to be reckoned with. It was surprising how quickly their protective bonds had snapped into place, but I knew it would give us the upper hand at Imperium.

The recon team had spent the last three days researching every possible scenario. The hacked camera feeds showed the President had unintentionally made our job a lot easier by providing *everyone* against the Rebellion with red uniforms to match his guards, although they did not bare the same red masks. It was likely for their own benefit so they could isolate the ones who dared to show a hint of humanity, regardless, it made our jobs easier.

The extraction team had found the best, if only, exit route for the number of operatives and children we'd accounted for. Best however, was by no means easiest and my heart had almost pounded through my chest when they'd told us the plan. Naturally, The President had created the easiest escape route straight from his headquarters; a tunnel large enough for vehicles to travel above ground straight into Imperium.

A Lotus in the Dark

"A tunnel, under full round the clock surveillance, leading straight to the President and his hundreds of killer minions?" Ethan had scoffed. "Sounds like a solid plan."

But after searching for any alternative, it was deemed the best strategy.

There would be no way to get in and out undetected, this would not be a stealth mission, but a full-blown attack.

Now all of us stood in the courtyard in front of the mansion, separated into teams each with our own objectives. We all wore matching black attire with as much protective equipment as we could find. I smiled as I noticed some operatives had painted black war stripes across their cheeks.

Ethan and Ivy stood either side of me at the front as June walked around the groups distributing all the weapons we had in our arsenal. There was a contagious anxious tension filling the air and I blew out a breath. I tensed as Ethan's fingers lightly grazed mine at my side and I looked up to him.

There was a chance we wouldn't all make it out of this alive, there was so much we had yet to say. I swallowed hard and turned away from him, I couldn't think about that now.

My eyes met Isaac's across the courtyard. He'd been assigned to the team in charge of rescuing the younger children. He flashed me a determined smile, the resoluteness in his gaze eased some of the tension weighing down on my chest.

"Every one of these operatives has chosen to be here," Ethan said, his voice low.

"I know."

"I know you." He shook his head. "If anything happens, you'll take all that guilt upon yourself, they've made a choice. The outcome is not on you."

I swallowed and nodded, not trusting my voice.

June stepped up beside us and I cleared my throat, every pair of eyes fell upon me adding further weight to my chest.

It was rousing speech time.

"You are all clear of your objectives," I said, loudly and clearly. "No matter what happens today, I am so proud of you all for standing up and fighting for something you believe in. Today we will be facing soldiers born to kill, they will fight with no humanity, no reservations, unwavering cruelty. But we will fight with a fire in our hearts that will obliterate their darkness." I stepped forwards slightly and traced a finger over the lotus flower tattooed behind my ear. "That being said, remember we have all risen out of that dark place ourselves. Some of them may have already broken out of the implant's control, some of them may be filled with a darkness so evil it cannot be fought, but some may simply be stuck in their mental prisons. If you have any doubt regarding their intentions, you do *not* go for the kill."

I paused as silence filled the space between us.

"Do I make myself clear?" I demanded. "We are not the callous weapons they intended for us to become."

The group nodded and murmured their agreements.

"Then let's move," I commanded.

They all made their way to the transport vehicles – local double decker buses. Not the most inconspicuous but also far less suspicious than the alternatives.

"Well," Ivy smirked. "At least we know if everything goes tits up you've got a career as a motivational speaker."

I snorted and jabbed my elbow into her ribs. "We're doing the right thing aren't we?"

"Of course, we are," she replied, seriously. "We always have done, even when we believed we were working as *vigilantes*." She laced the word with sarcasm. "We'd have never let a group of children under our assignment fall subject

A Lotus in the Dark

to trafficking. We have no idea what they're all being shipped off to Nightstone for, but we know it's not a life they'd want to live."

I took a deep breath and nodded.

This wasn't a life any of us would have chosen.

A couple of hours later, when our watches struck midnight, we were in position. Half of the team were positioned in the tunnels covered by Jackson, stationed in his surveillance van a good distance away. This half would attempt to infiltrate Imperium undetected and position themselves ready for our arrival, they'd oversee the rescue of the children, operatives and the lab technicians.

The other half of us would be entering the way we'd all leave – through the President's Headquarters. We'd be fighting our way in and out and would hopefully cause enough of a scene with the guards that the others would escape undetected. Ivy and I would then try to get Commander Michael out, hopefully alive.

I was struggling with not being able to help the other team, but I couldn't be everywhere at once. I had to trust and believe in them.

We'd found the entrance to the HQ down a side street barely wide enough for our vehicles and almost completely covered in darkness at this time of night. It was disguised as the back entrance of Aces Nightclub, designed purely for "stock deliveries".

Two security guards stood either side of a large grey garage door, in their attire they resembled standard nightclub bouncers with black suits and black earpieces that Jackson had already hacked into.

Ivy strutted over to them, her long tanned legs accentuated by her skimpy black shorts, all her curves visible in her tight black vest top and her blonde ponytail swaying behind her.

"Evening gentleman," she purred lightly as she pretended to stumble slightly. "I'm on the VIP list."

The two men swept their hungry eyes over Ivy's whole body.

"You've got the wrong entrance darlin'," said the one on the left with a feral smile and stepped towards her slightly.

Idiots. Ivy could have them both dead in seconds.

She pretended to drop her handbag in front of them and gasped as the contents spilled onto the floor.

"Gosh," she giggled. "I'm just such a clutz when I've been drinking."

They glanced at each other as a lipstick rolled towards them, not moving any further from their position by the door.

Ivy packed up the contents, turned and sauntered away back towards us, her eyes glistened, and her lips slowly spread into a wry smile.

"Miss!" One called as he bent to pick up her lipstick. "You dropped this."

She waved a hand dismissively without turning around.

"Keep it," she said.

And it exploded.

Only a small explosion, not enough to blow them to pieces but enough to have them both unconscious on their backs.

Ivy pressed a finger to her own earpiece as she spoke to Jackson and a second later the garage door began to slide open.

We all emerged from our positions in the darkness and moved as one to follow her through the open door, Ethan and June behind me, closely followed by the rest.

A Lotus in the Dark

The booming music from Aces flowed towards us, the club would be heaving at this time, and we couldn't move through unnoticed regardless of how much alcohol laced their systems.

We made our way past the two black doors that would open to the side of the dance floor and stopped by a small unassuming wooden door. One would assume the other side would lead to a simple cleaning cupboard, and not straight into the lion's den.

Right on schedule, as soon as we were in position, the door made a slight buzzing sound as Jackson hacked into the system. The sound increased in volume for few moments before there was a sharp snap as the circuit cut. Ivy touched her ear again as Jackson spoke to her, she nodded once and pushed open the door.

In less than a second, the two guards on the other side of the door were on the floor, one taken out by Ivy, one by Ethan.

In single file we marched through the short passageway that descended downwards and began to widen into larger tunnels. As we moved silently, Ivy stiffened as Jackson spoke in her ear and then relayed the information softly to the group. "The stealth team is in position; they've made it safely to the other tunnels waiting for our signal."

I nodded as relief washed over me. That was good, Isaac and his team would get as many of those more vulnerable out as they could.

As we headed down the tunnel, it began to widen then split in two. We continued a few meters when Ivy stopped on Jackson's orders and Ivy gestured with her hand down the right tunnel.

A few operatives headed past us; the right tunnel would lead to a large gate at the end that could only be opened from the inside. Ben would be waiting there with some others and the vehicles, ready for our extraction.

The rest of us followed Ivy's lead as she headed down the left tunnel and we descended straight into the President's Headquarters.

There was a simple underwhelming door that would lead to the foyer of the HQ. As soon as we opened this door, regardless of Jackson's many attempts at disabling the system, all alarms would be raised and we would be swamped with all the President's guards who resided here.

It was unlikely we would see the President. As soon as the alarms were raised the Ambassador and his inner circle would protect the President at all costs, getting him out of Imperium before anything else. We didn't care about that; we were not here for the President, even if I would be happy for him not to live another day. We were on a rescue mission and that was it.

I looked down the tunnel at the forty operatives, as June spoke, quietly telling them their orders, determination plastered across their faces.

I turned to Ethan and Ivy and held my hands out to them, neither of them hesitated as they took one of my hands each and then surprised me by grasping their other hands together. We looked between each other and took a deep breath; no words were needed.

As the three of us stood looking at each other, clasping each other's hands, a rush of ... *something* surged through me. Their eyes widened in synchronisation, and I was sure they felt it too.

Putting it down to adrenaline and anticipation, I gave both of their hands a squeeze then let go, unsheathing a dagger in each hand before turning towards the door.

A Lotus in the Dark

Ethan raised his pistol as Ivy raised her daggers. Jackson unlocked the door, Ivy nodded once and then swung the door open.

Once again, all hell broke loose.

The guards had obviously somehow been alerted to our arrival. We flinched and ducked the bullets that instantly whirred towards us from the mezzanine as we flooded through the door.

Ethan and I slipped behind the main desk in the centre, the receptionist was nowhere to be seen. I flung blade after blade towards any flash of red uniform in my vision, watching them drop one by one. I wasn't aiming for lethal hits, but was inflicting enough damage to take them down as some flipped over the banister, and some tumbled down the stairs.

I leapt out from behind the desk and headed up the large scarlet carpeted staircase in the middle leading to the rooms. Masked guards flocked towards me, either intercepted by other operatives or meeting my blades. I spotted my objective at the end of the corridor, a bulky wooden door with a black handle.

I made to move towards it when sudden pain spread across the back of my head, and I was knocked forwards. I stumbled but remained on my feet. I spun and swiped my dagger at the same time, slashing a guard's forearm as he attempted to bring his own dagger down upon me. I ducked and threw myself at him, taking him down rugby tackle style.

I almost smirked at the thought of Ethan shaking his head at the inelegance, but it did the job. His blade clattered to the side, and I grabbed fistfuls of his hair, slamming his head into the floor until he was rendered unconscious. I stood up and made to turn back towards the door, when I heard Ivy's voice in a scream that stopped me dead in my tracks.

"*No!*" Ivy screamed again.

I turned to her voice and then followed her panicked gaze and my heart almost jumped out of my mouth.

Time seemed to slow down as everyone all turned to witness the scene unfolding. We were up on the mezzanine area, but down on the ground floor one of the brothers, Karl, stood behind June. One hand gripped her hair, and the other pressed a silver blade to her throat.

"The President wants to speak with the three of you," he snarled. "You know who you are."

His gaze snapped up to mine and his lips spread into a sick grin.

My mouth dropped open. Me? The three of us?

"He has agreed to make a deal. He will let all the operatives you want walk out of here completely unharmed, if the three of you turn yourselves over to him."

Ivy stepped up beside me. "You let go of her you son of a bitch or I will ensure you do not walk out of here alive," she snarled.

"Ah," he glanced to Ivy and June gasped. She gritted her teeth as he pressed his knife deeper into her throat. "Two thirds of our beloved trio."

My eyebrows pinched together. Why did the President want us? And badly enough to make such a deal?

Stranger still, June was the picture of calm until I felt Ethan's presence next to me.

"Don't," June pleaded suddenly, her eyes filled with fear. "Whatever you do, do not trust him, do not–"

"Shut up," Karl hissed as he yanked her hair backwards into him.

I barely had time to think about the deal presented to us, barely had time to wonder why the President wanted the three

A Lotus in the Dark

of us and why June was so terrified, before my senses registered a high-pitched whistling sound.

It was only for a split second before an arrow suddenly pierced directly through Karl's jugular. June was shoved to the side as he fell forwards onto his knees, gargling as blood gushed around the arrow in his throat and up out of his mouth.

Ivy rushed down towards her mother, but my gaze followed the direction of the arrow.

I blinked rapidly as my brain failed to comprehend what I was witnessing.

The Ambassador, stood on the other side of the mezzanine, with an arrow nocked in his raised bow that pointed straight down at the guards.

-CHAPTER TWENTY-EIGHT-

I looked back down to where June was now looking up at him and... *relief* shone in her eyes. I shook my head, not understanding.

The Ambassador's lips turned into a snarl.

"Touch her again," he boomed, his deep voice emanating power. "And you too will get an arrow to the throat."

He released his arrow, and true to his word it struck straight through the throat of the guard who had made a step towards June. Ivy's gaze whipped up to the Ambassador, shock crossing her face.

As though his arrow had somehow resumed the fight, chaos ensued once more.

"What the fuck is that all about?" Ethan asked next to me as he casually shoved a guard over the railing who had attempted to stalk towards us. He looked towards the Ambassador as he shot arrow after arrow towards the guards, killing each of them instantly.

My mouth dropped open to answer, but I was rendered speechless as the Ambassador stalked over to June and... caressed her cheek.

"That is... seriously disturbing," Ethan whispered.

Ivy looked back and forth between them in utter shock, her gaze drifted up to me and Ethan at the top of the stairs and she mouthed, "What the *fuck*?"

A Lotus in the Dark

Guards flocked towards the three of them, followed by Imperium operatives in red uniforms arriving to join the fight. The only difference between the two groups were the red masks that covered the guards faces. June pushed Ivy towards us, clearly making the executive decision to discuss this later.

Ivy hesitated for only a second before she dashed back up the stairs towards me and Ethan, dodging or slashing down each guard who tried to intercept her. The three of us continued to fight off the few remaining guards around us, each of their fates ending the same way.

I registered the sound of Ethan's pistol firing and turned towards where he aimed at a group of guards heading towards us. His bullets landed in the exact same spot, straight through the chest just above their heart, downing each of them instantly but not necessarily lethal blows.

But then his pistol sounded once more, and I physically flinched as his bullet flew straight through the forehead of an unmasked operative in black uniform.

"Ethan," I gasped.

He just shrugged and gestured with his head towards the President's Chambers. Ivy's wide eyes looked away from Ethan to me and she shook her head, time was not on our side, so I added that to list conversations saved for later.

The last guard advanced on Ivy. He looked strong but she was fast. She ducked under his arm as he swung a dagger towards her head and she slammed her sharp elbow into his kidney, at the same time I approached from behind and slammed the butt end of my knife into his temple, and he dropped to the floor.

Her lips tipped up into a slight smirk. "Would it be completely sick if I said I'd missed this?"

I huffed a small laugh and shook my head, not sure I entirely disagreed with her.

I glanced to Ethan who nodded. "Go, I've got you both."

He turned to face the guards heading towards us from the other end of the corridor and my heart twisted. I had to fight every instinct telling me to stay and help him and the rest of the operatives still fighting down below, but Michael had risked his life to help us escape, we couldn't abandon him now.

The wooden door at the end of the corridor was blocked by several guards and operatives, black and red uniforms flashed as they engaged in their own battles. When our operatives saw us coming, they ensured our path was clear, fighting any guard who attempted to stand in our way. I took one last look at them, pride swelling my chest as they fought side by side, back-to-back. A strong, team unit taking down anyone who threatened their group.

I blew out a breath, threw the doors open and began to run down the spiral staircase, Ivy at my heels.

We moved quickly down the stone steps, and I shivered as the temperature began to drop. The lower we descended the darker it became; the scent of mould and blood filled my nostrils, and I fought a second shiver. We finally reached the bottom and I glanced at Ivy, her wrinkled nose and cold eyes mirrored mine.

We stepped into what could only be described as a small dungeon, iron barred cells lined the walls each with a thin bedroll and a bucket. Although they were all empty, their contents and blood-stained floors showed evidence of previous occupants.

We didn't linger, moving past the cells and to the faded wooden door at the end. I peered inside through the small black grate and gasped. Ivy stood on tip toes to peer in beside me and her gasp echoed mine.

A Lotus in the Dark

Michael was strung up in the middle of the room by his wrists that were bound together by rope, the only item of clothing on his body was a pair of dirty grey trousers. His bare toes scarcely grazed the floor and his shoulders looked warped as they bared most of his weight. His head was drooped forwards, his chin resting on his blood-soaked chest. He twisted slightly and nausea filled my stomach as his back came into view, lashes upon lashes covered his whole back in blood red.

I gripped the small black knob and shoved against the door, my heart sinking as it refused to budge. It was inevitably locked.

So, we paused, and we waited, hoping our prediction was correct. My heartbeat filled my ears as we waited and I glanced to Ivy.

"So, your mum and..."

"Don't," she snapped.

I clamped my lips together to prevent the smile threatening to form.

She let out an exaggerated shudder and then sighed. "I mean seriously, are they *together*? When could–"

Footsteps sounded behind us, faint but audible. Ivy and I glanced at each other again, her eyes flashed, and she swiftly moved into a darkened corner beside one of the first cells, hidden under shadows. I clenched my fists, my nails digging into my palms.

There was only one person we'd told the others to allow follow us down here.

Commander Kane took the last step down to the dungeon; his skin so pale it almost lit up the entire space.

"I knew you wouldn't be able to resist coming down here. Your *compassion*," he snarled, "making you weak, once again."

"Where are your faithful lackeys?" I taunted.

"They're where they are needed." His eyes glinted and my stomach flipped, but I ignored it.

He stalked towards me as he unsheathed a dagger. "I think I'm going to take my time with you," he grinned, sick excitement flashing in his eyes. "Tie you up next to the other pathetic traitor, another fool letting his feelings weaken him, and tear you apart, piece by piece." His lips turned up in disgust. "So foolish of you to come down here alone."

I raised my eyes to greet his.

"That's the difference between you and I." I let my lips slide into a sly smile. "I will never be alone."

At my words Ivy launched herself from her position behind Kane and dug her knife deep into his neck. He let out a deep growl and grabbed her by her hair, hurling her over his shoulder and onto the ground. She was up in less than a second, slashing her knife out again, grazing his cheek as she moved back beside me.

She flashed Kane her best smile as she jangled the keys that were now in her hand. One of Kane's hands went to his now empty belt, while the other raised to his neck, seeping with crimson. His eyes stared intently towards us as they turned almost completely black.

"Go," I urged, and Ivy wasted no time. She turned and unlocked the door and we rushed through together, shoving our shoulders against the solid wood as Kane barrelled after us.

"Bitch," Kane spat through the grate. He took a few steps back and then forced himself into the door again, I clenched my teeth as the force undoubtedly bruised my shoulder.

"I've got this," I gritted out, nodding towards Michael.

Ivy glanced between me and Michael for a moment before she nodded and hurried over to him. I turned and placed my

A Lotus in the Dark

back flat against the door, planting my feet on the floor as Kane attempted to force his way in from the other side. I wasn't going to be able to hold him off for much longer.

I watched as Ivy looked over Michael, his wounds much worse from up close. Additional to the weeping lash wounds on his back, blood leaked from the tight rope around his wrists and ran down his arms and dislocated shoulders and over his severely bruised torso.

Ivy hesitated for a brief second taking in his condition before she placed a hand softly on his cheek.

His head snapped up revealing his bruised face, his bloodshot eyes stared wildly at Ivy as he thrashed suddenly and kicked weakly out at her. His eyebrow was split, and his lip was swollen.

Considering the speed in which we healed with our implants and the extent of Michael's wounds... my stomach knotted at the thought of what he had endured in this room.

I gasped and shoved myself back against the door as Kane did the same from the other side.

"Ivy," I hurried.

She held her hands up to Michael in a defensive position.

"Hey, I'm not going to hurt you. You're okay, you're going to be okay," she said gently.

His head snapped towards her, and he stopped thrashing as his watery brown eyes raked over her face.

"My name's Ivy-"

"I know who you are," he replied coarsely, his voice rough like he hadn't had water in days.

She nodded and pulled a knife out of her belt, he flinched but looked up towards his wrists.

"I... I'm so sorry but this is going to hurt," she grimaced.

Another slam against my bruised back, my feet slipped out from under me, and my bottom slammed painfully to the floor. I shoved myself up, quickly pushing against the door again.

"There's no other way out of there," Kane sneered. "As soon as this door opens, you're dead."

"Ivy!"

Michael looked over to me and the doorway as if noticing us for the first time. He looked back to Ivy.

"Do what you have to," he said, gruffly.

She wasted no time and placed one foot on his hip and pulled herself up onto his back. He yelled out and gritted his teeth as her weight pulled down onto his already dislocated shoulders, but she was swift in cutting the rope from his wrists. He fell to the floor, and she landed gracefully onto her feet beside him, instantly putting her hands on his arms to help him up.

Knowing we had no other way out of this room, I spun sideways and sent Kane flying through the door as he shoved against it one last time. He was quicker than I had anticipated and before I had time to react, he spun gracefully and shoved me into the wall. His forearm pressed against my neck, and I swallowed as I glanced over his shoulder to see Ivy helping Michael out of the room and towards the stairs, relieved to see he was surprisingly steady on his legs, and they were moving quickly.

"Pathetic," Kane spat in my face, and I flinched. "It is shameful for people like you to be affiliated with our kind."

I frowned. "What are you talking about?"

I wasn't fighting back just yet as I kept him distracted long enough to ensure Ivy and Michael had made it to safety.

His lips spread into that cold sneer that turned my stomach. "You'll find out soon enough."

A Lotus in the Dark

"You just love to talk in riddles," I sneered. "I think it's because you don't actually know as much as you keep proclaiming."

His dark eyes turned obsidian, then he let out a cold humourless laugh that turned the blood in my veins to ice. My gut twisted at the look in his eyes.

"I know enough. I know we are always one step ahead of you."

He leaned forward until his cold lips grazed my ear, and he said slowly, "Where do you think we found Commander Michael in the first place?"

No.

The blood drained from my body.

No.

They knew about the tunnels.

-CHAPTER TWENTY-NINE-

I let out a scream as I shoved Kane away from me with a strength that I didn't know I had, and in the back of mind I noticed how the lights flickered around the room.

How could we have been so stupid to forget the one flaw in our plan. Of *course*, they found Michael in the tunnels, that's where we'd left him when he risked his life to allow us to escape.

The tunnels, where hundreds of people would be escaping; operatives, children, lab technicians, every soul in this place who wanted to leave, the chefs, the nurses... They'd all be in those tunnels.

Kane made to step towards me, but I could only think about those innocent lives.

I didn't have time to fight, I spun and hurtled through the doorway, Kane on my heel. As I sped back through the dungeon, I gripped one of the open doors to the iron barred cells and with full force I slammed it towards Kane. I heard the satisfying *twang* as it rebounded from him, but I had already turned and began to sprint back up the spiral staircase. Kane was close behind me, but I was considerably faster, I burst through the doors at the top where Ivy and Michael had just made it.

Surprise flashed across Ivy's expression as she noticed mine, but I didn't have time to stop. I ran as fast as I could

A Lotus in the Dark

down the steps and through the Headquarters foyer, so fast that I was almost a blur, no guards could notice me quickly enough to stop me. I barely registered Ethan calling my name, but I felt his presence as he followed me.

I panted as I made it to the door to the adjacent section, panic rising in my chest.

"Come *on*!" I yelled as I held up my palm and waited. The light flashed red, and I swore, slamming my hands on the door in anger. They'd denied my access.

"No, no, *no*." I banged my closed fists against the door again and again, until it flashed green. I blinked in surprise to see the Ambassador next to me, his palm raised to the silver panel.

I didn't have time to contemplate anything at that moment, so I simply offered him a grateful nod and then shoved through. I ignored the flashes of red and black uniforms as they engaged in combat as I dashed behind our mentor houses.

"Isaac!" I screamed, as I spotted him knelt, about to help a young child down the ladder. "*Isaac!*"

He turned, frowning at the clear panic in my voice.

"Get them out of there!" I waved my hands. "They know about the tunnels!"

I continued running towards him, ignoring Ethan screaming my name behind me.

Isaac's eyes widened in alarm, he hauled the child at the top of the ladder up into his arms and began to yell down into the tunnels.

But we were too late.

Huge explosions boomed from below us and the entirety of Imperium shuddered with the impact that knocked me to my knees. I shook my head at the ringing in my ears and coughed at the smoke beginning to fill my lungs.

No. Oh *god*, no.

I stumbled back to my feet and began to run again towards the tunnels, but I knew in my gut there would be nothing left to find.

Children cried around me as operatives in black began to help them up and gather them back together, thankfully they hadn't yet descended the ladder to the tunnels that were now reduced to piles of rubble. My heart jolted as I spotted little Zachary, his watery blue eyes wide as he took in the carnage around him. I began to step towards him as an operative scooped him up into her arms.

Satisfied that he was safe, I instead stumbled to Isaac who had been thrown backwards from the explosion. He was pushing himself up, his wide eyes mirrored my horror.

I put my hands on his cheeks as I quickly assessed the damage, blood seeped from a gash above his right eyebrow, but it would heal.

"They..." Tears brimmed in his wide eyes. "They killed them all."

I swallowed the lump in my throat as we both looked towards the tunnels. I was unsure how many had already made it to the other side, if any at all. I swayed on the spot, there must have been over a hundred of them still down there, all mercilessly killed whilst trying to escape. My eyes flicked to the flashes of red across the room as a group of guards, including the two brothers, stalked towards us.

My hands began to violently tremble as Karl's lips tipped into a sly smirk as he looked upon the carnage, his brother looked equally proud beside him.

Any restraint I'd had was obliterated.

Something came over me, a power that rippled under my skin and took control of my whole body. My vision blurred, my head pounded, and then I was moving.

A Lotus in the Dark

Faster than I'd ever moved before, faster than I'd thought was even humanely possible.

I moved to the guard in combat with one of our operatives and slashed my daggers out, slitting his throat. Blood sprayed across my unflinching face as he dropped to the floor.

I'd always aimed to disarm, render unconscious, but not now. No, now I was out for blood.

I'd always hoped to bring out the light in all that we could, but I was wrong. There was some whose darkness ran too deep, who would never see the light.

I moved again, it was as though time had slowed down around me as I shifted lightning fast and I slashed with my daggers, again... and again... and *again*. Blood sprayed until my vision was entirely crimson, bodies dropped around me and I couldn't stop.

I couldn't breathe.

Power rippled through me so intense I felt I'd explode if it wasn't released.

I let out a scream and gritted my teeth as three guards approached me, I barely registered my movements until seconds later the three of them were dead on the ground, blood pooling around them.

Strong hands gripped my wrists and I spun, yanking my arms from their grip with impossible strength and launched myself on top of them with my dagger pressed to their throat.

"Aria." Ethan looked me over with wide eyes. "It's okay, it's me."

I breathed erratically, my chest heaving up and down as I tried to control the rage inside of me.

I let Ethan flip me onto my back, leaving my daggers in my hands as he restrained me, breathing equally as hard.

My vision cleared slowly as the part of me I'd momentarily lost slowly returned.

I imagined myself from Ethan's eyes; my manic expression, splattered with the blood of the bodies I'd killed. He stood quickly, lifting me with him. I felt limp as though all my strength had been drained by a dark force that had taken over my body.

He pulled me back towards the Headquarters section. "Come on, we have to go *now*."

I glanced around as the remaining operatives, including Isaac, Rachel, and Aaron, rounded up all those vulnerable and unable to fight and formed an impenetrable circle around them as we moved as one.

Any remaining flashes of red uniform were either cut down as they stood in our way or began to back down.

Cowards.

I stumbled as my legs threatened to give way.

"I..." I tried to explain to Ethan I was unsure where my strength had gone when my vision blurred. He looked down at me, his eyebrows pinched together as he scooped me up into his arms. I didn't even have enough strength to protest, as I weakly wrapped my arms around his neck and my world completely faded into darkness.

-CHAPTER THIRTY-

I woke with a jolt and looked around the dark room in confusion, my mind took a second to register that I was in my small dorm room at Haven. No light flooded through the window, so I assumed it was the middle of the night.

My head turned to the hard body sat up in the bed beside me and I turned to look up. Through the shadows I could see Ethan, with his head leant back against the headboard, the soft rise and fall of his chest as he slept. I swallowed, unsure why he was in here with me when he had his own room across the hall.

The pressure in my chest suddenly weighed heavier as the memory of the events from Imperium washed over me and a million questions flew around my head. I wasn't even sure how long I'd slept.

How long had it been since all those people in the tunnels were killed? How many had got out? Was Michael alright? Were all our operatives alive? Ivy, Isaac, June... *God*, June and The Ambassador...

What... what had happened to me? What was the inexplicable surge of power... How many people had *I* killed?

The room swayed and I put a hand to my chest as my breathing became rapid. Ethan tilted his head towards me, as if my panic had jolted him awake, and he put a large hand over my own atop my chest.

"Breathe," he said softly into my ear. "It's okay, you're okay. Just *breathe*."

A lump formed in my throat at the softness of his voice. I took a deep breath in and slowly released it, heat rising to my cheeks at the thought of Ethan seeing the vulnerable side I liked to keep hidden. His thumb began to trace circles over my hand, and I breathed deeply, gradually my heartrate slowed to a normal pace.

"Is Ivy okay?" I asked, the question I needed answering before anything else.

He nodded. "She's fine, she got out with the rest of us, we... we lost a couple of operatives from the two original teams, but the rest are fine. Michael is fine... The Ambassador and June are fine."

My eyes shot to his as they flashed with a touch of humour, and he shrugged. "The story is still untold."

The corner of my mouth twitched but then fell as heaviness pressed on my chest once again.

"How many?" I forced out.

I wasn't sure what I was asking. How many were killed in the tunnels? How many of our operatives survived? How many had I killed?

He cleared his throat. "You should get some more rest, we can discuss everything in the morning."

I shifted as I turned my body towards him and studied his face.

"Tell me," I said.

He sighed, knowing I wasn't going to relent. "None of the children below apprentice age had yet entered the tunnels, and a majority of the lab techs made it to the other side before they collapsed."

Relief washed over me, marred by the inevitable bad news to follow.

A Lotus in the Dark

"The rest didn't make it," he said, softly. "About a quarter of the technicians and... all the rest." I swallowed and squeezed my eyes shut, calculating about seventy lives. All gone because of us.

"I know what you're thinking," he said, and I stood up moving away from him, unable to stand the softness in his voice any longer. I began to pace the room.

"This was *not* your fault," he continued, standing up from the bed. "Every person in those tunnels made a choice, they chose freedom. Freedom that *you* offered them, freedom taken away by the President. He is the only one to blame here and you know it."

I breathed and my eyes burned. "Then why does it feel like I sent all of those people to their execution."

He stepped in front of me and held my chin lightly as he tilted my face to look up to him.

"You wouldn't be you if you didn't take on every burden in the world as if it were your own." His thumb lightly brushed away a tear as it escaped down my cheek. "That's what started this whole thing, your ability to care does not make you weak Aria. Do you know how many people are currently residing at Haven? 467. We counted this morning. 467 lives saved from that prison because of us, because of *you*."

I wasn't sure if it was because of the swell of emotion threatening to burst from my chest or because of Ethan's words or the way he was looking down at me.

Either way I was not in control of my own actions as I stood on my tip toes and pressed my lips to his.

He stiffened for a moment before he groaned and began to kiss me back. His hands rested on my hips and then moved down to grip my thighs as he lifted me, my legs naturally wrapped around his waist. His lips devoured mine as he moved and lowered me down to the bed, pressing himself down on top of me.

I moaned lightly into his mouth as his hands explored every inch of my body, heat travelled downwards and settled between my legs to where his hardness pressed into me.

My stomach tightened as he kissed me and the entire world faded around us, in this moment it was just me and him and I realised this feeling was not purely lust.

Somehow, somewhere along the way, I had fallen in love with him and because of that, I could not give myself to him completely until he was willing to do the same.

Breathing hard I pulled away and looked up at him. His amber eyes flashed as his ragged breaths matched mine and he smirked. He dipped his head and pressed a softer, gentle kiss to my lips that caused my head to spin.

I almost ripped his clothes off right there, but I couldn't, and I think he knew why, so this time he pulled away.

"There is something more going on here," he breathed, and my chest tightened, but then he pushed himself away from me and sat on the edge of the bed.

"Something bigger than even we know about, bigger than Imperium and Nightstone, my gut is telling me there is more to this and we need to find out what is going on."

I knew he was right. Ignoring the way my lips tingled and my heart still beat hard against my chest, I sat up and cleared my throat.

"Something... happened," I said. "I lost control after the tunnels collapsed but, it was more than that... like I didn't lose control but rather something *took* control."

He nodded. "I know, I've felt it before too." My eyes snapped to his in surprise. "When you were wounded the first time we left Imperium, something took over until I knew you were safe."

A Lotus in the Dark

We stared at each other for a moment, neither of us understanding what any of that meant.

I lowered my voice to a whisper and dropped my gaze to my hands in my lap. "Sometimes I think I make the lights flicker."

It sounded crazy. I knew it did, and the only person in the world I would voice that theory to was him and perhaps Ivy.

"It only happens when I'm focussed or when my emotions are heightened, but... it *does* happen." I swallowed but continued, now I'd gone down this path there was no coming back. "And before, in the tunnels back at Imperium, when you and I held hands with Ivy I felt..."

"Power." My eyes snapped to his as he spoke and I nodded.

"Power," I replied softly. "Exactly."

I exhaled and rubbed my eyes.

"I think we should pause this discussion here before someone overhears and we both get sectioned," he said quietly.

My lips twitched into a smile before he stood up as though about to leave. "We have a lot to sort out in the morning, you should get some sleep."

"Will..." I paused but then swallowed and forced my voice to come out strong. "Will you stay here with me?" I asked and then frowned. "But no funny business."

He smirked. "I might not be able to resist the funny business."

"Try." I raised my eyebrows and pulled the blanket back.

He rolled his eyes but then slipped into the bed next to me and pulled me close, my head rested comfortably on his chest. His fingers gently stroked the top of my arms and I let out an involuntary shiver and then smacked his chest as he chuckled lightly.

I sighed, knowing tomorrow would be a heavy day I closed my eyes and I slowly drifted to sleep to the gentle rhythm of Ethan's heartbeat.

"Well, doesn't this look cozy?"

I groaned and pulled the blanket over my head at the sound of Ivy's voice. I lifted my head slightly up from Ethan's chest.

"Quick before she sees you," I whispered and tugged the blanket until it covered his head too.

The blanket was whipped away from the both of us, the cold air rushed over our warm entangled bodies.

"Bit late for that." Ivy grinned as she looked down at us both.

I swiped the blanket back from her hands and pulled it over myself.

"Do you two have any plans of getting up today?" She glanced at her fingernails and frowned as though she'd scuffed them. "I mean we've only got like 400 kids to look after, thousands of operatives to save, battles to fight... you know, all the mundane shit."

"What time is it?" I asked with a hint of a smile as I laid back down and rubbed my eyes.

"9am," she replied.

Ethan groaned and pulled the blanket over our heads again, wrapping an arm over my waist and tugging me into him. My silly little heart thudded against my chest, and I couldn't help but smile. A second later the blanket was ripped from us again.

"Seriously," Ivy looked at us. "Get up, we have a lot to talk about."

I rolled my eyes but gave Ethan a nudge. "Come on she's right."

A Lotus in the Dark

He let out another groan before standing up, I couldn't help but notice how good he looked with his hair slightly tussled from sleep. I glanced to Ivy who was staring at me with a raised eyebrow, watching me admire Ethan. I looked away, heat rising to my cheeks. He looked between us and shook his head, then completely took me by surprise as he bent down and placed a kiss on the top of my head before he headed for the door. As he walked past Ivy, he gave her a playful shove and she scowled at his back.

When the door slammed she spun towards me grinning and climbed onto the end of the bed.

"Things have certainly escalated," she said and I threw my pillow at her.

"Wipe that stupid grin off your face."

"Oh come on, give me some details."

I sighed. "There isn't a lot to tell."

She scoffed.

"Genuinely, there isn't. We've not spoken about what's going on, last night we kissed and that was it, he just spent the night here. We didn't... sleep together. I mean we did... but that was it, just sleeping, we didn't... you know." I fumbled over my words and her grin stretched even further.

"Say it like a woman Aria. Did you fuck?"

"*Ivy!*" I couldn't help the laugh that bubbled out of me. "No, he just slept here."

She wrinkled her nose. "You just... cuddled?"

I nodded and she rolled her eyes. "How disappointing."

"Shut up, we have more important things to talk about than my love life." Now was my turn to grin. "Like, I don't know... your mother's?"

Her smile dropped instantly.

"I know it's... unbelievable. They're just down there acting like–"

"*What?*" I interrupted.

"I know it's disgusting."

I stood up suddenly. "No I mean... he's here? At Haven?"

"Yes," she said hesitantly. "But my mother has assured us that he can be trusted."

"He most certainly cannot," I snapped as I started pulling clothes from my drawers. "Nobody can be trusted, isn't that what we're taught from the start? Foolish to bring him here, utterly foolish!"

I pulled on my clothes and shoved on my boots.

"Aria I think if you just speak to them both you'll–"

"I'll what?" I shoved on my boots, sheathed my dagger into its place on my hip and then spun to face her. "I'll understand? I'll understand how the man spent years helping the President abduct and drug hundreds of children and raise them as lifeless human weapons for his own personal gain? He was there, that day that I was in the labs and witnessed first-hand what they were doing to the operatives. Turning them into mindless killing machines to do whatever they will them to and–"

"And he let you go," she interrupted.

"What? He–" I paused.

He had. He'd let me go when he'd found me. It was Kane who had then caught me and erased my memories.

I shook my head. "Regardless, he has been a huge part of the operation that we are rebelling against! I don't care if June trusts him. I wouldn't be surprised if the President and his guards were on their way here right now. Does Ethan know about this?" I knew he'd agree with me.

Ivy shook her head. "He was with you the whole time; I only came in to give him food and update him on the basics."

I stormed out of my room across the hall to Ethan's and banged a fist against it. No answer.

A Lotus in the Dark

I turned but then the sound of raised voices escalating to screaming and yelling sounded from down the hall.

"He does now," I sighed.

-CHAPTER THIRTY-ONE-

Ivy and I followed the sound of raised voices into the canteen. I scanned the room when we entered and found Ethan stood in front of the Ambassador with his knife pointed at his throat, June yelling as she tried to wedge her way between the two men.

We hurried over to the scene unfolding.

"Just listen, Ethan," June pleaded. "I really do *not* want to have to hurt you."

Ethan's eyebrows furrowed but he didn't argue, knowing she probably could if she wanted to.

"We have to question him properly," Ethan growled, and I stood beside him as I glared at June.

"You trust me," she said firmly. "That should be enough."

"It's not," Ethan replied and hurt flashed across her face.

The Ambassador was studying all of us quietly, his eyes met mine for a second before he looked back to June.

He placed a hand on her arm. "They are right, my love. It is time."

June turned towards him with wide eyes that suddenly shone with *actual* tears. Ethan lowered his knife as he noticed the same.

We were not the emotionless robots Imperium had intended for us to be, but I had never seen any of the operatives shed a tear.

A Lotus in the Dark

"I'm not ready," she whispered.

"You are." He gently wiped her tear. Their eyes met, so full of love it felt like we were intruding on an incredibly intimate moment.

"Mum?" Ivy said quietly. "What's going on?"

June quickly wiped her cheeks dry then held her head high as she turned to look at us, back to the strong Commander June we knew.

"It is time you all learned the truth." She looked to Ivy for a moment before looking away and commanding loudly. "Gather all operatives to the common room, now."

Moments later we had assembled everyone into the common room, except for the children and the few down in the makeshift infirmary, including Michael.

The room was overfilled but we'd just about managed to fit everyone in. I stood at the front with Ivy and Ethan on either side of me. Arron and Rachel had sat off to the side with Jackson, Ben and Isaac and our loyal operatives all scattered behind us chatting, no doubt still high on the adrenaline of our recent mission. I was just relieved to see they were okay, to see so many of us were okay.

The Ambassador stepped up to the front of the room with June at his side and a silence swept over the room.

"We have gathered you here as you may have heard, as we believe it is time you all learned the truth behind Imperium." The power in his voice was undeniable and I swallowed hard. I felt Ethan's fingers tangle into mine and I gave them a squeeze.

The Ambassador waited a few beats, until everyone's full attention was on him, when he began.

"You all fought bravely yesterday, you protected your people and fought for what you believed in. My loyalty had always been spread between two alliances. I am ashamed of my past; of the things I have done. But I have chosen a side, the good side, the right side. And it is time to tell you all the truth."

I sat utterly still as my heart thudded in my chest.

My gut twisted, as if I could sense the enormity of what we were about to be told.

My eyes flicked to June who had stepped up beside him, her eyebrows pinched together. She placed a hand on his arm which he covered with one of his.

"It is a long, long story, beginning over a century ago, I will tell the whole story eventually, but for now, I must start here, where we are now." He breathed. "You all know at Imperium, at the age of twelve, the insertion of the implants is mandatory. You have all been brought up with the belief that these implants are enhancing your abilities, making you strong, better, powerful. This is not the truth."

June's hand slipped from his arm and he continued. "The implants aren't enhancing your abilities at all. They're suppressing them."

We all blinked back at him in utter confusion.

He let out a huff, a small humourless laugh.

He looked to June, she searched his face for a couple of heartbeats before she nodded sadly. She turned to Ivy and I and her throat bobbed as she swallowed hard.

"I am so, incredibly sorry," she breathed, her voice thick with emotion and I frowned.

The Ambassador waved his hand and suddenly the world shifted around them, as though they had been shielded from us this whole time and we were only just now seeing their true selves. I audibly gasped and involuntarily took a step back, as did those around me, a few even let out small screams, but I could not tear my eyes away from what I was witnessing in front of me.

Their features were strong and sharp, their eyes bright and searching, their ears had turned slightly pointed and their canines had extended. They even grew a few inches taller.

They radiated absolute power.

They were stunning, devasting and completely and utterly... inhuman.

Part Three

Amid Darkness Light Prevails

-CHAPTER THIRTY-TWO-

I stumbled a few steps backwards until I felt the comfort of Ethan's hard chest behind me, away from the beings that stood in front of us. Ivy had remained perfectly still, staring at her mother with wide eyes.

Hurt flashed in June's eyes and she looked away from her, around the room, to me.

I was going to throw up. I stared at this... being, looking back at me. No, definitely not human.

This could not be happening.

"What... what *are* you?" I willed my voice to come out strong.

"We are Fae, as are all of you."

"What the *fuck*?" Ethan growled. "This is some sort of sick joke, right? Some mind-game to get us back to Imperium?"

The Ambassador shook his head. "It's the truth and I swear to you I want nothing less than to go back to Imperium. I know it's a lot to take in. Please, let me explain."

Nobody argued, the air was thick with tension as nobody dared to move.

I was in shock, complete and utter disbelief; I didn't know who or what to trust.

I glanced at Ivy, all colour had drained from her face. For the first time in our entire lives, she looked utterly speechless.

"There are many worlds aside from this one, other realms, but one in particular is called Ankala."

The Ambassador's voice carried across the room; the entire audience silent and utterly captivated, as if they dared not move, not breathe. "That is where we originate, that is where the Fae reside and have done for thousands of years. The Fae existence extends far beyond that of mortals. It is where every one of you were born." His eyes landed on Ivy. "Aside from the exception."

Ethan scoffed. "I'm not listening to this bullshit."

He made to move but I grabbed his wrist. He turned to look at me.

"Just listen," I said.

Something was twisting deep in my stomach, even further inside. A feeling... an instinct. *Something* was telling me the Ambassador spoke the truth.

"The Fae, we possess powers... magic. In some there is just a slither, in others a mighty force. All have something, even all of you. The Fae of Ankala... it is difficult to explain without feeling it or experiencing it yourselves, but we are all connected spiritually to each other and to the earth. It is what harnesses our powers. Being separated from our world, with the added effect of the Implants, it would be easy to believe you were all mortal."

The world swayed beneath my feet and Ethan held my elbow.

We were not mortal... not human. How could this possibly be happening.

"Ankala is split into territories, similar to the countries and cities of Earth. Each is ruled by their separate councils, but the High Council rules from the Capitol over Ankala in its entirety. Many years ago, this was headed by King Vidon."

A Lotus in the Dark

The air felt thick as he spoke. Ethan tensed next to me, as though he felt it as well. The darkness that emanated just from speaking his name.

"King Vidon's reign was cruel, brutal and fortunately short-lived. Although the rightful monarch, he attempted to enforce a strict, unforgiving hierarchy of Fae which the council opposed. They staged a coup, they fought together with old magic and managed to strip him of his powers and banish him to the human lands." He scanned the crowd. "You all know him as the President."

Nausea swirled through my stomach and threatened to rise in my throat, but I swallowed it down.

"Why not just kill him?" I asked.

"There are... rules, in Ankala, restricted by Ancient Magic. If you kill a rightful reigning monarch, a terrible curse is released upon the lands. So instead, they banished him. Even in doing just that their own powers drained to a fraction of what they were, but together they rule as a High Council with no King or Queen. For almost a century, Ankala has been in peace, the council are kind enough and do not impose strict hierarchy. Everyone lives and works together almost as equals." He closed his eyes as if remembering. "It is a truly wonderful place."

"The Alvara, Shamara and Valda of Imperium?" I asked, although I knew the answer.

He nodded. "Fae classes the King attempted to bring with him to this realm, to Imperium, although he's been smart with it in this world, biding his time. The Valda in Ankala are the noble fae; officials or the rich, high society. The Shamara are powerful warriors or regular fae, what you'd call working class. The Alvara don't exist anymore, they were the poor, those with little powers; they were treated as slaves with no rights."

My head throbbed with the knowledge that I was struggling to even comprehend. I turned to look around, at the faces of all the operatives as their worlds were turned upside down. Some were staring wide eyed, some had their heads in their hands, some had tears streaming down their cheeks.

I turned back to the Ambassador. "And where do we all come into this?" I asked.

The Ambassador looked at June, who looked utterly defeated. She simply nodded to continue.

"Myself and all of the commanders of the four divisions of Imperium; that being June, Kane, Michael and Addison, we were all a part of the King's High council. It... is almost too difficult to explain, too much history to comprehend. But the Ancient Magic that was used against the King came with a price. All Ancient Magic comes with a price, and the requirements are long and complicated, but simply put, for each dark curse used against a rightful reigning monarch, we'd have to grant him one request that complied with the rules."

He sighed. "Thus, as we elected to banish him to another land, *and* strip him of his powers, we had to grant him two requests. He chose to commit the same fate to half of his ten council members... and Ankala were to sacrifice ten fae newborns to him, every year."

Ice washed over my whole body.

I startled as Arron stepped forwards and I looked to his face, his expression matching the horror I felt. "We... we thought we were all being rescued from broken homes or dangerous situations. You're telling us we were ripped away from our families and brought to a different world just because of a *request*."

"It is far more complicated than that."

A Lotus in the Dark

I closed my eyes and covered my face with my trembling hands.

Ethan put a solid hand on my shoulder. "What is it?"

I took a deep breath and let my hands drop. I ignored Ethan, looking directly between June and the Ambassador.

The answers to all our questions finally answered.

"This whole time." I seethed. "This whole time we've been asking why. *Why* spend our entire lives training? *Why* was the President creating an army with thousands of human weapons at Nightstone? This is what it has all been for. He's creating an army to take back his throne?"

Ethan's head snapped to the Ambassador for confirmation. He nodded.

"You knew?" Ivy said softly, but not weakly to her mother. "You were a part of this. You trained us!"

"Ivy," June breathed. "If I could have told you everything I would have, but it would have been too dangerous. It would have risked everything."

"So why now?" I asked.

They glanced between each other. "There are some things we still cannot explain. But you know now. This is a good start; we can finally put a stop to all of this and return home."

"*Home?*" Ethan spat. "We have no home."

The Ambassador rubbed a hand across his jaw. "The King has taken fifty years to build an army over here and he's nearly ready to take back Ankala, but he must be stopped. You may not think it is your home, but it is home to thousands of innocent people and children who will be slaughtered, his reign would be as cruel and terrible as before."

I swallowed and squeezed my eyes shut; this was too much.

I reached for Ethan as he again tried to walk out, this time he yanked his arm out of my grip, and I let him go as though it didn't feel like I'd been punched in the stomach.

He was followed by some others all muttering their disgust, I didn't blame them.

The Ambassador nodded. "Go, take the day to gather your thoughts. We will all reconvene in the morning."

I shook my head and looked to Ivy, she was still staring at her mother with tears sparkling on her cheeks.

"What are your real names?" I asked.

The Ambassador frowned down at me and I huffed. "King Vidon from the world of Ankala, calls himself the President, I'm sure your real name is not Ambassador *Jenkins* and yours is not June."

June flinched at my harsh tone, but I tried not to care, I was sick of all the lies.

"We have not spoken our birth names aloud in many years. King Vidon allocated us names he deemed appropriate to the world we were banished to, I suppose." He looked to June and then back to me. "My name is Romanoff Maru. Although a lifetime ago I was called Roman by acquaintances."

June looked to Ivy and said softly, "And mine is Alessandra Reighn. In our world, children take their mother's name."

"Does that make me Ivy Reighn?" Ivy asked, the snark in her tone was clear.

"Ivanna Reighn," she confirmed quietly. "Ivy, I am *so* sorry. If we could have told you sooner–" June, or *Alessandra*, stepped towards Ivy who held up her hands and stepped back.

I put a hand on Ivy's arm. "We just need time to process this."

A Lotus in the Dark

They both nodded their heads to us as I led Ivy out of the room before anyone but I could hear her release the sobs forcing their way out of her chest.

"I... I just need to be alone," she sniffed and hurried away before I could stop her.

I stepped back into the room, not yet ready to leave. I still had so many questions.

Noise filled the room as the remaining operatives began firing questions at June and the Ambassador, *Roman*.

"Why tell us now? Why wait?"

"We... we could not tell you before, due to the rules of the curse."

"What rules?"

"It is too complicated to explain."

"More lies!"

"We want to tell you the whole truth and we will tell you all that we can," Roman said, firmly.

"What was the point?" I asked quietly and June looked to me. "What was the point, in any of it? All of our training, all of our real world missions?"

June swallowed. "The King insisted you were all put into training, it was clear right from the start what he hoped to achieve, but we were stuck here with him, bound to him by the curse. He was, and still is, our only hope of ever returning to Ankala. So, we decided to at least put some good use to your training. While we were here under his command, some good had to come of it."

"We should have been told," I replied "Even if you couldn't tell us everything, there had to be a better way than this. Our whole lives have been a lie." Others nodded and murmured their agreements around me. "We've all been raised simply to fulfil his purpose in life, that's it!"

"What choice did we have?" Roman asked, his tone was firm but his eyes soft. "You were not the only one ripped away from your home, your family! I had two daughters." My breath caught at this. "I had a wife, who died during childbirth not long before the curse. I know absolutely nothing of what came of my children, if they were looked after, if they are happy or safe." I was shocked to hear his voice break slightly, but he swallowed and pushed on. "I would do anything to return to them, but we suddenly had the responsibility of ten fae newborns every year for *fifty* years. Trying to raise you all and navigate our way through this whole new world." He shook his head.

June continued. "You were not raised how we would have preferred, raised as weapons and starved of any parental affection, but I can promise you we did not have a choice. We did our very best to get to this point, and regardless of the King's attempts, look at you all. You have shown your true selves, the Fae inside you is stronger than any synthetic substance he can throw our way."

I breathed heavily, my hands rubbed anxiously up and down my thighs. I'd sat down at some point, or my legs had given way, I wasn't sure.

This was really happening.

"Where are our families?" I turned my head to the young female operative who voiced the question.

"They are still in Ankala," June replied softly.

I had a *family*. A real, biological family, that I had been stolen from, or rather, given away from. What were they like? Were they even still alive? I shook my head. I couldn't think of them, the chances of ever being reunited were non-existent.

"We have had no contact to our world since the day we left so we unfortunately cannot tell you more than that, but

A Lotus in the Dark

they are there. The Fae, we... we age slower than mortals. Far slower."

My heart seemed to still at this. Fifty years ago.

"How old are you?" I asked with wide eyes.

"I... we..." June looked to Roman. "We are well into our second century."

I thought my eyeballs were about to pop out of my head. Two hundred.

"We are not all gifted with immortality," she continued quickly. "The aging process slows around our 25th year and picks up again as we enter our fifth century."

Five hundred. I felt sick again.

I looked around, most of the operatives had horror plastered across their faces but some... some were smiling.

One of those with a faint smile on his lips stepped forwards. "And we have... powers?"

June nodded but hesitated for a moment, as though she was treading carefully. "Yes, but to which level we won't be sure until the implants are removed, and we are back in our homeland. As we said before, all Fae possess powers, some are stronger than others, most just possess low-level powers."

"Like what?" another operative asked excitedly.

I swallowed. I supposed, to some this would be exciting. We'd just found out we could live five hundred years and possess magic powers; it was any child's dream come true.

The corner of Roman's lip twitched up and he said, "We will go into the details later when the rest of the group is with us. As I said, take the day to gather your thoughts and we will reconvene in the morning."

And with that, we were dismissed.

-CHAPTER THIRTY-THREE-

I knocked and entered Ivy's room without waiting for a response. She sat at the top of the bed, her back pressed against the headboard, her knees pulled up to her chest with her arms wrapped around them. I sat cross legged on the bed facing her, neither of us spoke for a few moments.

My hands still shook from the enormity of what had been revealed. I squeezed my fingers into fists, my nails pressed against my palms, and I tried to level my breathing.

We were... not mortal. I could feel an entirely inappropriate laugh threatening to bubble out of me and I knew I was becoming hysterical. I wiped a palm over my face to stop the laugh, but it came anyway. I put my head in my hands, and I laughed and laughed until tears streamed down my face and then I wasn't sure if I was laughing or crying.

I looked up to Ivy who was looking at me as if I'd gone entirely insane.

"I'm sorry," I shook my head trying to compose myself. "It just... it's so ridiculous. It's so ridiculous and elaborate that it can't be true, and yet my whole body is telling me it is. As though we've known all along, deep inside, that something about us wasn't... *normal*. I'd always just associated it with the Implants."

I saw Ivy swallow hard, but she didn't say anything, simply lifted a delicate hand and wiped a stray tear away.

A Lotus in the Dark

I shuffled forwards on the bed and put my hands over hers. "I'm so sorry," I whispered.

This was a lot. It was a lot for me to take in and would be a lot for anyone, but Ivy had been lied to her whole life, by her own mother.

Her mother had a part in this, so much still didn't make sense. We needed answers, but nobody was in their right minds after this morning. We had needed some time to process the information and reconvene this evening.

"Our whole lives are a lie, everything we thought to be true... it's all been pointless. Our whole lives have been completely pointless."

"Perhaps," I agreed. "I know it sounds ridiculous but maybe we were meant to get to this moment, in order to stop... King Vidon."

Her eyes snapped to mine. "You're right... you sound ridiculous."

"Have you never... felt things? Felt a sort of power?" I asked and she shuffled uncomfortably.

"I suppose so. Isn't this every kids dream? To find out they have magic powers?" She huffed a sarcastic laugh. "So why does it feel so wrong?"

I stared down at my hands. Could it really be true? Could we really possess powers that were being subdued by the Implants in our arms?

I thought to the thousands of people being kept at Nightstone, if it were true, it would help us. We may have a chance of fighting against the President... or the *King*.

If what the Ambassador said was true, if the King did want to rage war against this world of Ankala to retake the throne... Thousands of innocent lives could be lost.

I said my thoughts out loud to Ivy who looked unsure.

"We formed the Rebellion to get all those kids out of Imperium, so that we could all have a chance at freedom. This... This is so much bigger than that," Ivy answered. "I'm not sure this is what I want to be a part of."

"It's not just a part of us," I said quietly. "This is who we are. You know it's true."

"I've barely had a chance to absorb any of this, how are you convinced so quickly?" she shook her head.

"I don't know," I said, honestly. "It's just a gut feeling."

"Well, there's a lot at stake over a gut feeling."

I sighed. "I know."

The room went silent again.

"Ivanna Reighn," she scoffed. "Stupidest fucking thing I've ever heard."

My stomach clenched and I voiced the thought that had been floating through my head since the moment we'd learned who we really were.

"I could have a family," I said, softly.

Ivy's eyes softened and she squeezed my hands that held hers. "We are your family."

I smiled back at her with watery eyes. "I know, you are my sister, and you know you mean the world to me."

It was true, Ivy was the person I could rely on the most in the world, the only person I could wholly be myself around, to love me for exactly who I was.

She made me the strongest version of myself, and I her, and I knew if we were together everything would be okay.

"But I could have a *biological* family out there somewhere," I continued. "And... the rest of them... the children, the babies here... they could have a chance at growing up with their real families, in a real, loving home if we could get them back to Ankala."

A Lotus in the Dark

She pondered that for a moment then sighed. "I hadn't thought of that. It's just... it just doesn't feel real. But, I suppose, we owe it to ourselves to explore this. Even if I tried to ignore it, what would I do, where would I go? I couldn't leave my mother, despite how angry I am at her right now... I can't imagine being apart."

"It wouldn't come to that, she would always choose you."

"I'd like to think that's true. I feel like I don't even know her."

I nodded in understanding. I couldn't imagine it.

She swallowed. "I just need some time to process this, but my goals haven't changed. I know what's right and I know we can't ignore what's happening at Nightstone so I'll come to the meeting tomorrow. I'll listen to what they have to say."

I let out a sigh of relief.

I wasn't sure why I was taking this so well. It was almost like my whole life I'd expected something... *more*. Something bigger. Like I'd never felt at home here.

There was a whole other world out there, we'd never truly be free in this world with the technology Imperium had. Perhaps this was finally our chance at freedom.

I squeezed her leg and gave her a small smile which she returned, although it didn't quite reach her eyes.

"I'd better go and check on the thunder cloud." I rolled my eyes.

She raised her eyebrows. "Make sure he doesn't rain all over you."

I frowned. "Was that supposed be a sex joke?"

She sighed and slumped back on her bed. "I know, I'm off my game. I'll have something better for you in the morning."

I snorted and shook my head. Half way out the door I turned to look at her.

"You know, you'll always be my sister no matter what happens, that will never change. You are my family."

"Stop it you soppy idiot," she said as she threw a pillow in my direction, but this time when she smiled back it shone in her eyes too.

I closed the door and headed across the hall to Ethan's.

I knocked softly and waited a moment.

"Ethan, I know you're in there. I know it's a lot to process but... you're not alone."

I waited a few more minutes, the pressure building in my chest the longer he ignored me.

"Don't shut me out," I said, quietly, but I knew he could hear me.

I heard movement from inside and waited, thinking he would answer but as the minutes ticked by my anger grew.

"Fine," I snapped banging my fist on the door once. "But we've all just had our world's turned upside down not just you, you know."

I turned and stormed into my room, slamming the door behind me.

Day turned to dusk, and I'd been left with my thoughts for hours. A thousand images had played out in my head and even more theories and worst-case scenarios about King Vidon and Nightstone.

Just as sleep was about to consume me, I was stirred awake by a soft commotion outside my door. I padded to my doorway as quietly as possible, the floor cold on my bare feet, and I pressed my ear to the door. I frowned as I recognised Ethan's low voice, his tone hushed as though he was trying to remain unheard.

I chewed my lip, even with our advanced hearing I couldn't hear enough. I slowly turned the handle and opened the door a crack.

Ethan stood a few doors down, speaking with Jacob, the younger operative who had approached us when we'd first returned to Haven.

I heard a light sniff and dared to peer around the corner to get a closer look. I blanched as I saw Ethan pulling him into a hug.

"Look I... I'm just not meant for a place like this."

My heart stilled.

"And... just so you know," Ethan said, his voice low. "*He* will never touch you or anyone else. Ever again. I made sure of it."

An icy chill washed over me.

"You mean that?" Jacob whispered.

"Without a doubt," Ethan said darkly.

His words held a deeper meaning and suddenly my mind flew back to Imperium, when he had mercilessly shot the operative in black straight through the forehead.

Oh. I swallowed.

"Go back to bed, I've got to go." Ethan pulled away and I retreated behind my door.

"Can't you stay? I-"

"No," Ethan said, his tone final. "You're safe now, kid. Stay at Haven, stay with the other's here, they'll keep you safe."

Jacob sniffed. "Okay... thank you."

He wrapped his small arms around Ethan's waist and sniffed again. Ethan cleared his throat, ruffled his hair and then lightly pushed him back into his room. He closed the door, and I saw his shoulders slump and his head hang forward. A second later he was turning towards me, and I pulled the door almost closed, breathing heavily.

Ethan was leaving? My chest felt like it was about to crack open.

I breathed heavily as he walked to his room, leaning inside to grab a small rucksack and then headed down the corridor.

With no hesitation.

He didn't pause for a second, even as he walked straight past my room.

Tears burned my eyes, and I couldn't help the emotion that burst out of me as I flung the door open and stepped out into the hall.

"No time for goodbyes?"

He stilled.

"After *everything* we've been through, with everything that's going on you're just going to leave, without a word to anyone. Without a word to me?" My voice cracked.

He turned slowly to face me, his expression hard.

"Everything is... it's too much. I just wanted a chance at a normal life. That's what all of this was supposed to be about, getting out of Imperium and helping as many people as we could along the way, and then getting the fuck out of here and enjoying some actual freedom." He shook his head. "This is not that."

"You're a coward," I hissed.

He sighed.

I stepped towards him, and his serious expression softened slightly, in the way it always did when he looked at me. His mask slipping.

"What are you more afraid of?" I asked. "Letting the light in, or letting the darkness out?"

A Lotus in the Dark

"There's enough darkness inside me to cast a shadow over this whole operation." His eyes turned black at his words. "I hurt people, it's all I'm good at, it's all I've ever known."

"We were all raised the same way, Ethan," I said, throwing my hands up. "We have all done terrible things. We are all terrified to let anyone in, because that's how you get hurt right? You can't get hurt if you're a stone-cold robot. Can't get hurt if you don't feel anything." I stared him down and his eyes dropped to the floor. "Is that what you want to go back to? The machines we've all fought so hard to destroy?"

"You don't understand." He kept his eyes on the floor as he spoke, his voice wavering slightly.

"I understand just fine." I forced my voice to come out strong. "You are so scared of being hurt that you are closing yourself off from being loved."

His molten amber eyes flew to mine, roaming over my face and I cringed at the vulnerability of my words.

"Come with me," he breathed.

"Ethan." I shook my head as a lump formed in my throat. "All of those people and children being kept at Nightstone... I couldn't live with myself if we didn't even try to help them and I don't believe you could either. And... and we owe it to ourselves, to find out who we are. I have never in my life felt at home in this world, and now we know why."

"I can't have all those people depending on me," he said.

I'll only let them down. The unspoken words hung between us.

I stepped towards him, but he backed up.

"I just... I can't."

And with that he stormed away, taking my shattered heart with him.

-CHAPTER THIRTY-FOUR-

After a sleepless night, at 5:45am I'd made my way to the makeshift training room downstairs and stood beating hell into a punching bag. I swung fist after fist, panting as I tried to shut out the world and all thoughts of Ethan.

With each jab the stinging in my knuckles grew sharper but I didn't care, it was a welcome distraction from the pain I felt in my chest. I wasn't sure how long I'd been down there until I felt a hand on my shoulder that I knew belonged to Ivy.

I stilled, knowing she instantly knew something was wrong. I hadn't needed to say anything, I hadn't even needed to look at her and she knew.

"He's gone."

I didn't need to say his name. Ivy placed her hands on my shoulders, twisting me round to face her and I couldn't stand the sympathy filling her blue eyes.

"He just needs to cool off. He'll come back."

I shook my head. "No, he won't."

Because I wasn't enough for him to stay.

I took a deep breath as the pain once again began to spread across my chest.

"Bastard," she muttered. "I can't believe he'd actually leave."

I turned and began punching the bag once again.

A Lotus in the Dark

"I thought his brooding was just a defensive mechanism, I thought deep down he was actually–"

I shot her a look to shut up and she held up her hands.

"I feel let down too."

I sighed.

"Come on," she said softly. "The others are gathering in the common room."

We had bigger things to worry about. Ethan was a selfish coward; he couldn't open his heart to let anyone in and I wasn't going to waste another second wallowing over it.

I knew I was lying to myself, but I'd at least try to mask my heartache with an unbothered pretence.

I turned to Ivy with my chin raised. I knew she instantly saw straight through me but thankfully didn't say anything.

"Have you seen June yet this morning?" I asked as we made our way to the common room.

"You mean *Alessandra*?" She shook her head and blew out a light breath. "No, not yet."

This was going to be interesting.

Isaac rounded a corner as we did and changed his direction to walk with us.

"I was just coming to find you both," he said, his eyes were bright and excitable. "I haven't spoken to you since... well you know! Can you believe it? It's just crazy isn't it and *god* your own mother." I shot him a look to shut up but he continued. "This whole time we had no idea what was going on. Do you think it's true? Do you think we have powers? And families? We could really have families... actual parents and–"

"Do you need us for this conversation?" Ivy interrupted him and this time I shot her a look.

Sometimes I forgot how young most of the operatives were, they'd had no choice but to act advanced in years when they were at Imperium. They were still far more mature than average, but Isaac was only *fifteen*. They were letting their juvenile excitedness rise to the surface and I certainly was not going to shut that down.

I nudged him lightly. "I suppose it is a bit exciting isn't it."

He nodded. "Terrifying... but exciting."

We entered the common room where most operatives had already gathered. There was a group of younger apprentices at the side of the room as well. The children were all being looked after by the ones who had volunteered for the job. It was not a permanent solution, but still better than Imperium.

Roman and June... or *Alessandra,* I was never going to get used to that, stood at the front. I was once again taken aback by their extraordinary Fae forms, the power and beauty that emanated from their direction was impossible to ignore.

The three of us joined some older operatives including Ben, Jackson, Arron and Rachel.

"I'll probably be able to read minds or something," Rachel was saying seriously. "I've always been quite intuitive like that."

"Nosey." Arron rolled his eyes but poked her light heartedly. "The word is nosey."

"Well, that too," she admitted with a light smile.

"What are you guys talking about?" Isaac asked as we sat down to wait for the rest of the group to arrive.

"What powers we think we might have," Rachel said, an excited gleam in her eyes. "Roman said all Fae have powers, even if it's just something small."

I swallowed. It still didn't seem real.

"We don't know how any of it works," I said. "I doubt he means powers like you're thinking, we aren't *superheroes*."

"Killjoy," Ben said. "I reckon I'll have super strength, enough to be able to lift a bus with one hand."

A Lotus in the Dark

"I don't think it's the type of world that will have buses," Jackson said as he shook his head and placed his hand on Ben's knee squeezing it affectionately.

I let out a slight laugh and when Ben looked at me, I explained, "When I didn't have any of my memories, I'd thought you and Ivy were together."

They both laughed at this. "Why would you think that?"

"I don't know, you just seemed protective." I shrugged.

He looked to Ivy and winked. "No, but I have heard she's been playing nurse to a certain Commander in the infirmary."

My head snapped towards her, her face remained a picture of cool, but her cheeks suddenly flushed with a hint of pink.

"Apparently she's not left his side," Isaac murmured to me.

"Michael? Commander Michael?" I asked, unable to keep the shock from my voice.

"I've simply been checking he's okay as I was the one who rescued his ass," Ivy snapped.

"His sexy ass," Ben said.

She snorted. "I can't argue with that."

He turned back to Jackson.

"Anyway, I reckon you'll be able to control technology with your mind or something," he said.

"Again, I don't think there will be any technology in this world," Jackson said, and I noticed the pile of books on the table beside him. "I've been doing some research, Fae are mostly folklore, written as powerful mythical creatures in our literature, but the legends may be laced with some truth. They all tend to hail from medieval, archaic worlds, no technology or modern inventions. Their power comes from the world they are living, the connections between them and the elements."

"Your research is relatively accurate," Roman's powerful voice spoke from behind us, causing us all to startle and turn towards him.

I looked around to the see Roman had captured the attention of the now almost full room. I instinctively looked around for Ethan, even though I knew in my heart he was gone. Ignoring the tightening in my chest I looked back to Roman.

"I hope you have all had enough time to think on what was revealed yesterday," he spoke to the room. "I can only apologise again for the extent to which you have all been lied to. The pretence under which you have been raised. I wish it could have been different, but here we are, no good will come from dwelling on the past."

Ivy scoffed. "Some apology."

"I can understand your anger," June looked to Ivy only. "If we could have done something sooner we would have, but we were limited to the restraints of the curse."

"So why now?" I asked again although I knew what they would answer.

"We cannot explain," said Roman and I fought the urge to roll my eyes. "But there is much we can."

Frustration built in my chest, but we had no option but to take their word as truth. I trusted my gut, whether we could fully trust Roman as a person was yet to be decided.

"Your distrust in me is valid," he said looking directly at me, as if reading my thoughts and my eyes widened. "It is true I spent my time in this world, and the last, getting close to the King, becoming one of his most faithful advisors. In doing so, I could learn his plans, although he would never fully divulge to me, I knew most of his plotting."

He took a breath and looked around the silent room.

A Lotus in the Dark

"As you all know, King Vidon is building his army at Nightstone. This number has reached its ten-thousanth. Not only has he been taking our operatives from Imperium, he has been gathering his soldiers from elsewhere, although where we are still unsure."

"As good as we are," Ivy said. "We cannot fight an army that large."

"Not alone we can't," Roman said. "Ankala have numbers, they have their own warriors, but they need to be prepared. If the King invades with no prior warning, with no preparation, he may very well win. And with the numbers he is gathering, the ruthlessness of his soldiers, it is clear he is not intending on taking back the Kingdom without obliterating it first."

My heart stilled and voices around the room began to murmur.

"If what you say is true," Isaac said. "Our families could be in danger?"

Roman nodded. "Thousands of lives will be lost, Fae, mortals, children, creatures, the King will show no mercy. He plans to start a new world, those he deems worthy will rule and others will perish."

"There are mortals in Ankala?" I asked, surprised.

Roman tilted his head. "Of course, there are mortal lands in Ankala. They tend to keep to themselves although there is no animosity between races. The King will not be so kind however and believes the mortals of Ankala to be no less than vermin and should be treated as such. Unprepared and with no defence, they will not stand a chance against the Nightstone Army."

"*Shit*," I breathed.

"Shit indeed," Roman's lips tilted up slightly and then he looked to June who nodded slightly. "We... We believe that The King has opened a Narthex to Ankala."

"A Narthex?"

"It is what we call a way between worlds... a door, a gateway... We think he has opened one to Ankala already. We have theories on how he regained some of his power, but we are unsure."

"What are your theories?" I asked and before he could answer I said, "Or let me guess, you can't tell us?"

"Not yet," he said quietly, his eyes glancing to June, as though he felt genuinely guilty.

I sighed.

"Why do you think he's opened a *Narthex*?" I asked. Every time I used their terminology, I felt ridiculous, like I was indulging in a child's fantasy, except that this was really happening.

"Do you remember when I showed you the footage from the Nightstone camps?" June asked.

We nodded.

"The trees," she continued. "The particular type of Giant Sequoias, they are the largest of their kind and are found only in the Mountains of Eriwald, in Ankala."

"You think Nightstone is in Akala? That he's already taken them to this other world?" I asked and they nodded their confirmations.

My head hurt.

We'd lived our lives contained to Imperium, none of us had even had the freedom or the chance to explore our own world and now there was the choice of another.

"Why Imperium?" I asked, suddenly. "Why there?"

Roman's eyes glistened as he looked to me. "Why do you think?"

"I'm not sure. It just seems like a strange place for such a classified institution. Under a club in the middle of a city, rather than in the middle of the wilderness somewhere out of sight. There must be a reason for that."

He smirked at me. "You're clever."

"We all are," I answered. We didn't have a choice in that matter. "So what does that mean?"

"What do you think?"

Frustration began to build in my chest and I gritted my teeth. "Why don't you just fill in the blanks?"

"Fine." He smirked again, and I wanted to punch his smug face but he continued, "In Ankala, power runs throughout the world, through natural connections, but there are certain locations where you may find a Pocket of power. We harness these Pockets, we build Temples or Healing Chambers upon them to harness the power. The same may be true for this world."

"There is no power in this world," Ivy answered.

"Do you really believe that?" He asked.

She opened her mouth to answer, and I was shocked to see nothing come out before she frowned and closed it again.

"You think Imperium has been built on a Pocket of power? That's how he's been able to achieve all these crazy experiments and get his power back?" I asked.

"That's part of it I believe, yes."

"And you think he's opened the Narthex to Ankala somewhere at Imperium?"

"I think it's the best place to start."

I chewed my lip. It was the start of a plan at least, we knew where to head next.

"Can I say something?" Isaac said, rising from his chair.

Roman nodded seriously. "Of course."

"How do we know we can trust you, after you've lied to us for this long?" Before either of them could answer he continued. "Because I want to believe you. I've been sat here listening thinking it should all sound *ludicrous*, when really, it feels like the answer to the questions I've had my whole life. I've never felt at home here, I thought it was being trapped at Imperium, but now it feels like it was something deeper." He placed his hand on his chest. "A sense of not belonging."

I'd felt it too, I looked to Ivy. We all had.

"And now you're telling us our real *home* is in danger, real lives and our families we haven't even had chance to meet, and I feel like our lives can finally have a purpose. To fight for our home and for what is right."

"The kid's right," Ben said. "We've all spoken about it in some way or another. How there has always been *something*, a part of us missing. We've never belonged here, but how can we trust you?"

"If you trust my answer to that question," Roman said. "Then you already do."

He looked to me and I swallowed.

"In Ankala we are incredibly spiritual, our power comes from our connections to the world and the nature within it, the elements, the life... each other." Roman continued. "Water revives and heals, the air refreshes and soothes our minds, fire is a burning reminder of our own power and strength and there is a deep connection between them all, and to each other." He placed his arm across his chest, his fist clenched upon his heart. "That ache for home, it lives inside us. We are not mortal, we are *more*, and we are not supposed to be apart from our world."

Home. All my life I had been homesick for a place I didn't even know existed.

I looked around the room at the operatives, all staring with awestruck, wide eyes at the hope in front of them. Hope of finally finding somewhere they belong.

A Lotus in the Dark

I thought of the children and babies upstairs, little Zachary. They were young enough that if we could reunite them with their real families soon, this world may not even leave its mark.

I stood up, looking around, looking to Ivy and then to June.

"The only thing worse than not knowing where we belong, is knowing where we don't."

Operatives nodded around me, the room filling with murmured agreement.

I wasn't sure why, but I crossed my arm over my chest, clenching my hand over my heart to mirror Roman's stance.

"I'm in," I nodded to him and something akin to pride shone in his eyes.

June too placed her arm on her chest, tears brimming in her eyes as Ivy beside me stood and did the same.

The lights in the room suddenly began to flicker and Roman straightened, his eyes flashed with surprise.

A familiar sensation began to build inside me, the same as I'd felt back in the tunnels when I'd held hands with Ethan and Ivy. The lights flickered again, and I was sure I was not imagining the light breeze that tickled our necks.

I looked around, my chest filling with such raw emotion I was sure it would well up any moment as others around me followed suit, eyes widening as the same sensation swelled inside them.

It was unmistakeably raw *power*, and we were stronger together.

One by one every single person in the room did the same. Until we all stood together, hands over our hearts and hope lighting the darkness in our chests.

I swallowed the lump in my throat.

"Let's get our people home."

-CHAPTER THIRTY-FIVE-

We'd sat in silence for a while longer.

There was no denying what had just happened, no denying the sense of power rooted deep inside us that we had all felt. In that moment everything had changed.

Movement from the side of the room broke the heavy stillness across the group, and gradually excitable conversation filled the air once more.

I looked to the door to see Michael stalking towards us, looking remarkably better than the last time I'd seen him. Others moved out of the way as his giant body waded through the crowd to our group.

"What are you doing out of bed?" I whipped my head towards Ivy as she spoke, surprise clear in my expression. "You needed at least one more day to heal."

"Worried about me, sweetheart?" He asked, his voice rough.

"I'm just trying to ensure you don't keel over old man, else rescuing you would have been a complete waste of my time," she shot back.

"I'm fine," he answered, amusement laced his tone.

I had no idea what was happening.

I almost shrank back from his gaze as he tore it away from Ivy and it landed on me.

A Lotus in the Dark

"I suppose I should thank you for your part as well." He nodded his head to me.

I gave him a small smile in return. "We would never have escaped the tunnels if it weren't for you in the first place."

"Well then, our debts are repaid," he said seriously, and turned to Roman and June.

Roman beamed towards him, a genuine, unrestrained smile that showed all his teeth. I noticed then that since the charm had dropped, his ridiculous white teeth had disappeared, an obvious camouflage for the fangs that now stood in their place. I ran my own tongue over my teeth, which felt relatively normal.

Roman reached his arm out.

"Malakai, my friend. Glad to see you up and well."

Michael or *Malakai* shook his head. "I haven't heard that name in a long time. I knew the darkness had not consumed you as they'd believed," he said, and reached his arm out towards Roman so they were gripping each other's forearms.

"It seems we were all playing a dangerous game," Roman replied and moved to place his hand on June's lower back. Michael's eyes followed the movement and his lips twitched. "I'm sorry we did not let you in on this sooner, we were unsure who to trust."

"I understand. Do we have a plan?"

We told him everything we had learned about the nanobot technology at Imperium, about the King and the army he was raising at Nightstone, about the Narthex and its possible location; others around the room joining in the discussion.

Michael simply nodded, listening intently, his gaze frequently landing on Ivy before quickly looking away.

Every time he looked at her, I felt her shift next to me and I tried to fight my smile.

June noticed too, looking between the pair with a slight frown creasing her forehead. She looked to me, and her eyes softened, I wasn't sure I'd fully forgiven her for her lies yet but I gave her a light smile anyway. Relief washed over her face, and she stepped towards me.

"He'll come around, it is a lot to take in and none of you handle emotion particularly well for obvious reasons," she said softly, and I knew she was talking about Ethan. "I'm sure he'll come down soon."

I swallowed and shook my head. "He's gone."

June stilled and her eyes snapped to mine.

"What do you mean he's *gone*?"

I frowned at the tone of panic that laced her voice.

"He left last night, this was all too much for him to handle apparently."

"But, it's not safe out there. *Roman*," she breathed as she looked to him in fear. He put his hands on her arms.

"We'll send someone out to find him."

Ivy shifted and I looked towards her, she was frowning at her mother. "Why do you care?"

"*Ivy*," I warned carefully.

"I care for *all* of you," June snapped. "You may be angry at me, you may be hurt by the deception, and I understand that. It *killed* me every single day having to lie to you all, to you especially," her voice wavered with emotion. "But I did not have a choice, I swear it and I care deeply about each and every one of you and it is not safe for *anyone* to be out there on their own."

Ivy began to respond when a high-pitched beeping alarmed from behind us. We turned to Jackson who frowned and pulled out his tablet, tapping the screen a couple of times.

All colour drained from his face as he looked up at us.

"They've found us."

-CHAPTER THIRTY SIX-

Jackson flipped through the camera feeds on the tablet, there were masked guards at every angle.

I whirled to Roman with narrowed eyes.

"Did you sell us out?"

"I did no such thing," he answered calmly. "The sooner you start believing that, the better we will all work together."

I nodded once. I believed him.

"It doesn't matter how they found us, they're here now," June said. "We need to follow our evacuation plan."

Of course, we'd put a plan in place, it was one of the first things we'd settled when we'd first arrived.

The mansion backed onto a *huge* amount of forested land, leading to a river. There was a bunker well hidden in the forest with an underground tunnel that led a few miles down the river, to a dock where we'd kept several river ferries for this exact reason.

I moved to Jackson and scanned the images as he swiped through the different camera angles. My stomach flipped at the huge number of guards surrounding the area, this was not a fight we could win without risking lives and that was not a risk I was willing to take.

I stood up and looked to one younger group of operatives. "We all know the procedure, get the children and the apprentices to the bunker immediately. The rest of us gear up, we may have to fight our way out, but any chance at escape you take it. You all head to the bunkers and down the tunnels to the docks as soon as possible."

In the next instant everyone was moving.

June and Roman took the task of ensuring our safety at the docks at other end and evacuating everyone in the process.

Roman headed towards the door with the rest of the group, some heading for the tunnels, some for the armoury. He paused when he realised June had not followed.

She moved to Ivy and placed her hands on her cheeks softly. "Regardless of who I am, or *what* we are, nothing has changed in here." She took one of Ivy's hands and placed it above her own heart. "I love you with all my heart, and I need you to promise me to get to those docks safely, as soon as you can."

Ivy pulled her hand back, but she nodded. "I will see you there."

June paused for a second before she too pulled away. She turned to me and placed a soft hand on my cheek. "The same goes for you, I want both of my daughters back safely, do you understand?"

I nodded, my chest filling with such emotion I didn't trust myself to speak. June smiled softly and then turned away, joining Roman as they made their way towards the bunkers.

I squeezed Ivy's arm as we headed towards the armoury located within the makeshift training rooms in the basement.

Michael and the others in tow, some drifted off as they saw other groups, either making their way to the bunkers or readying to fight. No matter what, we could not allow the President's guards into those tunnels.

Jackson caught up to us as we reached the main entrance hallway and shoved the tablet towards us.

"They're here, literally, they're going to blow–"

A Lotus in the Dark

He was cut off by a huge explosion as the front doors were quite literally blown off, taking half of the front wall with them. We rushed over to those closest to the explosion who were knocked to the ground, barely getting them onto their feet before masked guards in red flooded through the rubble towards us.

My heart sank as gunshots pierced the air.

It was completely foolish of us to all come into this meeting unarmed, we'd gotten too comfortable. All I had was my dagger, others had nothing at all.

We were exceptionally trained, but in this situation, we had no choice but to run.

I pulled Ivy towards the door closest to us, that happened to be towards the training rooms and armoury.

"We have to go!" I yelled. We glanced back to see others retreating, in the chaos we glimpsed Michael, Ben and Jackson pushing a group of unarmed operatives through the doors leading to the kitchens. They could get to the bunkers from there. My heart gave another painful thud as I prayed that they got out safely. June and Roman would be there helping the evacuation. Arron, Rachel and Isaac would hopefully be helping the others escape, or they may already be down at the armoury.

I shoved my palm against the door to unlock it and swung it open, Ivy rushed through along with a few other operatives before I slammed it shut. The guards couldn't get through our system unless they blew it open again, which they were very likely to do, so we quickly pushed on.

We sped down the corridor and to the stairwell leading down to the training rooms when, as expected, another explosion boomed behind us.

"Go, go, go!" I practically shoved our small group down the stairs.

In a matter of seconds, we had sprinted through the training rooms to the armoury and grabbed as many weapons as we could efficiently carry.

We spun and eliminated the entire group of guards as they made their way down the stairwell.

I frowned.

Why were the guards always so easy to down? It really was like they had no training at all. I'd have some sympathy if they weren't here to murder everyone inside this house.

I turned back towards the others who were piling weapons inside bags to distribute to the rest who needed them.

"You four go," I commanded. "Take these bags and head straight to the bunkers, we'll grab the rest."

They nodded and lifted their filled bags onto their shoulders before dashing out of the room.

"So," I breathed to Ivy as I shoved two pistols into holsters on my thighs. "Commander *Michael*?"

"Really? You want to do this now?" she answered as she holstered her own weapons before we both started to fill another bag.

"I need a distraction," I shrugged. "You know he's old? Like... five hundred years old *old*."

"What's your point?"

I stared pointedly at her, and she rolled her eyes, a slight amused smirk on her lips. "Look, we rescued him, I made sure he was okay while he recovered, there's nothing else to it." She sighed. "Is he one of the sexiest men I've ever seen? *Sure*. Is he so huge that sometimes I can't concentrate on anything but the sheer size of his arms? *Maybe*. Does that also make me wonder how large *other* parts of his body could be? *Definitely*."

I snorted at that as I zipped up the now full bag. "But there's nothing else to it?"

A Lotus in the Dark

"There is nothing–"

Her words turned into a yelp as we were both suddenly thrown to the ground as another huge explosion boomed, this time from above us.

My heart lurched as another blast rattled the entire room.

"Come on," Ivy said, moving to the doorway. "We are underneath the entire house here and I have no intention of becoming worm food."

I lifted the bag onto my shoulder and whirled to follow when *another* explosion boomed. This one hit its target.

A *huge* part of the ceiling came crashing down next to us, concrete and debris almost macerating us as the room began to cave in.

I coughed as smoke filled the room; I glanced up noticing orange flames roaring their way across the wooden beams above us from the explosives. I flinched as the wood cracked, threatening to completely collapse.

I turned to Ivy, expecting to see her waiting for me, when my heart froze in horror.

No.

"Ivy," I gasped and rushed over to her.

To where she laid on the floor, panting in pain, as that entire chunk of concrete ceiling had plummeted on top of her legs and torso, crushing them beneath.

"*Shit*," she grunted, trying to push the stone off her body. "I can't... it's too heavy. How bad is it?"

I quickly assessed the damage and nausea flooded up from my stomach.

"You'll be fine," I lied.

I turned sideways and shoved my shoulder into the concrete, pushing with all my strength, but it refused to budge. It was huge, heavy and had impacted itself into a crater in the ground, Ivy's lower half completely pulverised beneath.

I fought a sob as it tried to bubble its way out of my throat. "I'm going to get you out of here."

"No," she gasped for air. "You... have to leave me."

I whirled my head towards her as her eyes began to flutter shut.

"Ivy!" I cried and cradled her head. "No, *no*, stay with me. We go together."

Panic threatened to overwhelm my entire body.

"*HELP!*" I screamed as tears began to stream down my face. I shoved against the stone again, but it refused to budge. "*HELP!*"

"Aria, you have... to go," Ivy wheezed.

"I am *not* leaving you."

"You have to..." Ivy spoke between struggled breaths and my heart threatened to explode. "You have to tell my mother... that I forgive her.... else she will never know."

The sob did bubble out then.

"Don't," I said, I looked around as the room groaned again from above and realised I didn't have much choice. "Don't say your goodbyes. I... I have to go, but *only* to get help. I will come back for you."

I made to stand up when she grabbed my wrist.

"You... you came into my life and made me see light where... where I once saw only darkness."

"Ivy," I whispered, wiping my tears.

"You... believed in me, so much that... I started to believe in myself... believe in something bigger. You gave my life *meaning*." I stroked her cheek, wiping away a tear as it slipped down, sobs racking my own chest.

"I love you. I am coming back for you; do you hear me? Just hold on, *please* Ivy for me, just hold *on*."

A Lotus in the Dark

I pulled my arm from her weakened grip as she said, "You will always be my sister..."

With one last sob I turned from her completely.

I hurtled through the training rooms and up the stairs, looking for someone, *anyone.*

"Fuck," I cried as I ran through the empty house, barely seeing through my own tears.

The floor was a blur of red, uniforms and blood merged together but I didn't have time to process anything.

I pushed my way towards the back exit and through the trees until I reached the bunkers and then I was running, down through the tunnels.

I ran as fast as I could, I ran until the air burned my lungs and the thought of Ivy trapped in the fire threatened to burn a hole in my heart.

I flew as though the entire world depended on it, as fast as I possibly could.

Until I slammed full force into a solid body sprinting in the opposite direction.

The sudden collision against our speed caused us both to fly through the air and together we skidded along the cold, rough concrete before slowing to a stop. The air whipped from my lungs, and I tried to ignore the burning sensation down my legs and arms, knowing the cuts would be healed in minutes.

I groaned and gave myself only a second to recover before I tried to push myself up from the hard body that I knew all so well.

I stared down at Ethan, his wild eyes looking up at mine, silently saying more than words ever could. I let only the tiniest of sobs escape from my lips, before I pulled my hand back and slapped him. Hard.

He gritted his teeth, and I pulled my hand back to slap him again, my palm still stinging from the last, but he grabbed my wrist with a strong grip.

"I let you off the first one because I deserved it," he growled. "But slap me again and see what happens."

I opened my mouth to retort when a loud explosion sounded in the distance and both of our heads whipped towards the noise.

He stood up, pulling me with him and held tightly onto my upper arms as he studied my face.

"Aria I-"

"Not now." I shook my head, turning away from him.

"You have to listen to me, I-"

"*NOT NOW*!" I screamed at him and then began to head back in the direction of the house.

"You know you're running *towards* the explosion, right?" He yelled after me but paused for only a second before following and I heard him grumble, "How we are still alive I will never know."

My heart squeezed at the familiarity of his sarcasm, and I slowed so he could catch up with me. My eyes began to slide to his when sudden movement behind us had us both spinning with our weapons raised.

I lowered my dagger as Michael stormed towards us and I was surprised to feel relief wash over me. "Is she still in there?"

I nodded and without hesitation he dashed past me, as swiftly as a man of his size could.

"Who?" Ethan asked.

"Ivy," I breathed and upped my pace to a sprint.

With Ethan next to me and Michael a few paces ahead, we hurtled back towards the house. My heart hammered against my chest as another explosion sounded in the distance.

A Lotus in the Dark

Only a few metres later, as we rounded a corner, we practically collided with a group of about a dozen guards. Their dark eyes stared coldly at us over their red masks and fear began to creep in. Not because the three of us couldn't take them, we absolutely could. But we didn't have time for this, we *had* to get to Ivy.

Michael and Ethan didn't hesitate before throwing themselves into combat. The guards really didn't stand a chance.

I let out a frustrated groan as the guard directly in front of me raised his gun to my head. Before he had time to even *think* about pulling the trigger, I had sprung towards him, breaking his arm and sending the bullet flying straight through the skull of the guard beside us.

I kicked out into the chest of the guard to my right, sending him flying into Ethan's readied dagger that sliced directly through his kidney.

I ducked as another swung a strong fist towards me and I moved beneath his arm, positioning myself behind him as I sliced my dagger across this throat.

I didn't have time to be merciful, not when Ivy's life was on the line. That's all I could focus on.

In a matter of seconds, the entire group of guards were in a pile on the floor, and we sprinted once again towards the house. I could only pray to whatever gods may be, that it wasn't too late.

-CHAPTER THIRTY-SEVEN-

We'd made our way through the ground floor of the house, swiftly taking down the few guards that remained. This floor was still intact, somehow, they'd known exactly where the armoury was and had aimed straight for our weak spot. They either wanted our weapons or knew that's where most of our operatives would have headed, possibly both.

When we reached the stairwell to the basement the heat from below hit us instantly, the burning fumes stinging the back of my throat. At the bottom, the walls on either side had almost fully collapsed on top of each other, leaving nothing but a pile of rubble.

"*Shit*," I gasped. "She was down there; her legs were stuck and I... I couldn't get her out."

"We're getting her out," Michael growled as he pushed past me and began climbing down the stairs and over the pile of rubble.

Ethan and I followed suit, wincing as the smoke stung our eyes and burned our throats. Michael seemed completely unaffected as he pushed on through the training rooms, smashing through any obstacle in our way like a human excavator.

"*Ivy!*" I yelled. She had to be alive. "She was in the corner by the armoury."

I snapped my head up as a beam above us enveloped in flames gave a loud crack.

A Lotus in the Dark

"Move," Ethan growled, gripping my arm he yanked us out of the way just as the large beam came crashing down, he pulled me into his chest as smoke and burning embers flew our way.

"Get off me," I hissed, pulling myself out of his grip and pushing past him towards Michael.

"You're welcome," he murmured behind me.

I bit my tongue; this was not the time. He'd get a piece of my mind later.

As we pushed into the armoury, the smoke became thinner as it flooded out of the giant hole in the ceiling. My breathing became gradually easier until suddenly it stopped entirely as I spotted Ivy where I'd left her.

The giant chunk of concrete still crushed her legs, only now she was splayed unconscious at an awkward angle, blood seeping from her head.

"*Ivy*," I tried to yell but the word came out inaudible.

I rushed to her side, Michael and Ethan already trying to lift the concrete off her leg.

I stroked her head, trying not to whimper as I looked down at her too pale face.

"We're here, Ivy. We're getting you out. We're all going to be okay." I sniffed as a tear slipped down my cheek. "I'm not leaving here without you; do you hear me? You can't leave me."

She had to be okay. This would be a loss I would simply not survive.

"It... it's too heavy." Ethan stood back, horror on his face as he placed his hands on the back of his head.

We all looked up. The entire room groaned and cracked, cinders falling around us as though the room was about to crumble at any moment. We didn't have long.

Michael looked between us both for a moment, his eyes turned hard. "You know what we are. You're going to have to use your power."

Ethan's head whipped towards him. "We don't have any power."

"Your Fae abilities are *suppressed* by the Implants, but not diminished entirely," he shot back. "They are in there; you just have to find them."

"This is ridiculous," Ethan growled. "We are wasting time with this bullshit."

"Ethan," I breathed, the word barely came out of my lips as my voice cracked. "Please."

His eyes softened before they dropped to Ivy. His throat bobbed as he swallowed and when he looked back up to me, he nodded.

I sniffed and pushed myself up to stand between the two large males and I held both of their rough hands in mine. I felt Michael look down at me and I shrugged.

"Before, back at Imperium, I held hands with these two and I felt it... my power." I looked to Ethan. "And I know you did too."

Michael looked between us curiously and then nodded. "You know it's in there, you know it's a part of who you are, a part of your strength. Your mind is a temple," he said softly. "Your power is the deity; it needs to be worshipped. Find the heart of the temple, believe in your strength."

I had never experienced anything religious or spiritual, it was not a part of our upbringing, but this was for Ivy.

I closed my eyes and inhaled deeply, finding my centre, as I squeezed Ethan's hand encouraging him to do the same.

The room groaned around us again and I flinched as something crashed down near us. We were running out of time.

A Lotus in the Dark

I took another breath. My mind was a temple. My power was its deity. My strength comes from within.

I sucked in a breath. There it was.

In my mind's eye, a perfect picture of a temple evolved, with marble steps leading up to huge pillars surrounding an arched entrance. Atop of the entrance were mosaics depicting warriors in battle. I moved, unsure how, as I was not there in a physical sense, but my mind moved. Up the steps and through the arch, into the glorious temple. At the end stood a square altar and in front, a large ceramic basin on an iron mount.

I moved to stand before the basin and looked down at the blue flames that swirled at the bottom.

I felt it then, not just in my mind but something surged through my body. My power.

I wasn't sure what Michael saw as I kept my eyes closed, but he breathed, "That's it."

Was that it? I fought a frown as I looked down at the measly flames, they looked a second away from flickering out. I didn't know how strong my power was but *surely* it was better than that.

Tentatively, I reached out with my mind, as though extending a hand, and dipped it into the pool of power.

I gasped as it once again surged through me, and I realised this power had always been a part of me. Subdued by the implant, by Imperium, but it had been there.

I thought back to the tunnels, fighting side by side with Ethan and Ivy, knowing this was the power and strength fuelling me, and suddenly the blue flames began to grow, swirling higher, filling the basin.

I thought of the operatives at Imperium, their laughter and chatter once they'd been freed. I thought to all those lost in the tunnels.

The flames swirled higher, extending up my hand and wrapping around my arm.

I thought of Ethan, fighting by my side, his smirk as he teased me, his lips as they kissed mine. He came back for me, for us. I thought of Ivy, all the times we fought together, laughed together, soul sisters.

The flames entirely engulfed me, swirling around my whole body.

My eyes shot open, and I sucked in a breath, realising the flames were not just in my mind. I instinctively raised my hands as the blue flames flickered around my fingers, it was too much, the power needed a release.

Unable to contain it any longer, I let out a scream, a war cry, and flames exploded from my body.

The concrete flew from Ivy's body, finally releasing her but at the same time, the entire room came crashing down around us.

I yelled again and my flames cast a dome above the four of us, encasing us inside. Protecting us.

I breathed heavily gritting my teeth, I couldn't hold it much longer.

Ethan gripped my hand again; I was unsure when I'd let go. Michael took my other, and they reached their other hands towards each other. I looked up to see flames of orange and green swirling from them, until our powers mixed in a multicoloured spectrum. I could feel it within me, in my mind, in the temple, as our powers merged as one.

We stood together, Ivy in the middle, and the flames blasted from between us. The dome extended and pushed until there was nothing above us but blue skies.

With one final surge, everything else in our close radius was entirely obliterated.

A Lotus in the Dark

The three of us were thrown backwards, our powers separating and flickering out until the silence around us was almost deafening.

I put a hand to my chest, trying to catch my breath, when I heard a familiar voice.

"Holy shit," Ivy said, and I sat up quickly, looking towards her. Michael and Ethan too stared towards her with wide eyes.

She looked back at me, her skin pristine, her legs intact. She was completely healed, as though nothing had ever happened. Her eyes pulsed bright blue, the same colour as my flames, as her lips turned up into a sheepish smile.

I gaped back at her. "Holy *shit*."

-CHAPTER THIRTY-EIGHT-

"Are we going to talk about what happened?" Ivy asked, her eyes thankfully had returned to their normal colour.

"Not yet," Michael responded. "Let's get to safety first."

"So, what's the plan?" Ivy asked.

We'd brushed ourselves off and assessed the damage our combined powers had wreaked upon the area. The house had been reduced to ruins, the entire area completely decimated, including any remaining guards.

We'd managed to salvage a few weapons laying around and had begun to head through the trees towards the bunkers.

Ethan pinched the bridge of his nose. "At this point, all I'm trying to do is keep you two idiots alive."

Michael chuckled lightly but Ivy looked towards him. I kept my head down, my gaze pinned on the ground beneath my feet.

"You came back," she said.

"I never really left," Ethan sighed, and even though I refused to lift my gaze I could feel his shift towards me. "I thought the safest way out would be through the bunkers, so I headed towards the docks. I stayed on one of our boats for the rest of the night thinking about what a prick I'd been, and I was on my way back to you anyway when I found June and Roman–"

"They're safe?" Ivy interrupted.

A Lotus in the Dark

"Yeah, from what I could tell, the guards hadn't found the tunnels or the docks, they were boarding all the kids onto the boats when I headed back this way."

We both released a sigh of relief at that.

So, Ethan hadn't really left us. Hadn't left me at all. He'd received some monumental, life changing news and had needed some time to cool off and then had come back for us. I could forgive him for that, couldn't I?

So why couldn't I meet his gaze?

A branch snapped in the distance and simultaneously we whirled towards the sound with our weapons raised.

"Our ears were burning," Roman's voice purred as he stepped through the trees, June close behind.

She stepped around him and, in a few strides, had pulled Ivy into an embrace. She stood back, her eyes shining and then did the same to Ethan and me.

"I'm relieved to see you're all okay," she swallowed.

We seemed to silently agree not to disclose how close we came to very much *not* being okay.

"What happened? We thought we were meeting you at the docks." Ivy asked.

"We safely boarded everyone onto the river ferries when Imperium arrived with another hoard of guards," June shook her head. "I honestly don't know where he's recruiting them all from, it's like they're spawning from thin air... anyway, we managed to slip back into the warehouse undetected and set back down the tunnels hoping we'd find you here."

"So, it's just us?" I asked and they nodded in return. "At least they're all safe on the ferries for now. Are they heading to the safe house?" Another nod.

Of course, we'd had a second Haven prepared with the exact same precautions. Hopefully Jackson, Ben, Arron, Rachel and Isaac would take charge until we had a solid plan.

"Good," I said. "Because we need to get back to Imperium."

Ivy's head whirled to me. "What? Are you insane? We've just practically declared war against them."

Roman interjected. "I had fallen upon the same conclusion. We've already explained how we believe Imperium is built upon a pocket of power, and Nightstone is located in Ankala, meaning the King *must* have a way to our world. He must have opened a Narthex somewhere and our best bet is Imperium."

I nodded but then frowned and chewed my lip before saying, "There's something else bothering me. It's about the President's guards, I'm not sure why we haven't investigated them more."

"What do you mean?" Michael asked.

"Well, like June said, he has hundreds of them, not just here but in his Nightsone army. Where are they all coming from? Certainly not Imperium, their training is not at the same level as ours. They only ever manage to overpower us with weapons or numbers, not skill. And surely, we'd recognise them–"

"Would we?" Ethan interjected.

"I..." I thought back to whenever I'd found myself up close and personal with the guards, their cold obsidian eyes staring over their masks. A chill raised the hairs on my skin. "Their faces are always covered."

"I don't think I've ever seen a guards face," Ivy pondered. "Not that I can remember."

We were all silent for a moment as we considered this.

"It may be nothing, but it's worth looking into," I shrugged.

"No time like the present," Michael declared as he barged past us through the trees.

A Lotus in the Dark

Ivy rolled her eyes, but we all followed him to the bunkers and through the cold tunnels until we reached the pile of guards on the floor.

"Here's some we prepared earlier," Michael joked, resulting in another eye roll from Ivy, myself included this time.

We all peered down at the guards as he leant over the one closest to him, reached and pulled the red mask down under his chin.

His hand snapped back quickly as he retreated with a hiss. "What the *fuck*?"

What the fuck indeed.

I placed a hand over my mouth as my stomach churned with nausea. Roman and Ethan stepped forwards, yanking the rest of the masks down. I took a deep breath. I thought I was going to be sick and yet I couldn't look away.

Each face under the masks was identical. *Utterly* identical as though they'd simply been cloned.

Their faces were pale, cold and lifeless, and not just because they were dead. Their empty obsidian eyes stared at nothing; their cheek bones sucked inwards and thier mouths...

I gagged.

Where their mouths were supposed to be stood nothing but a rotten, gaping, black hole.

"What the fuck are they?" I was glad Ivy had asked the question, afraid if I opened my mouth I would vomit on the floor.

June brushed past me as she stepped forwards. "I... I recognise their face..."

I frowned. How could she possibly...

"Oh god," I gasped.

Then I really *did* vomit on the floor. Ethan stroked a hand over my back, and I was in too much shock to push him away.

"What is it?" he asked softly.

"Remember before, I explained what had happened in that room back at Imperium." I looked to Roman. "You were there. There was a room with operatives, they'd had some fucked up neurosurgery placing those nanobots in their brains, rendering them under their complete control. Kane set his *'alpha'* on that poor girl, under his command he slit her throat."

I swallowed bile as I remembered his lifeless eyes as they stood over her body, blood pooling around them.

Roman circled the bodies on the floor, his lips set in a hard line as his eyebrows pinched together.

"That's him." I swallowed. "Thats his face."

June sucked in a breath as Roman did the same. Their eyes met and my blood ran cold.

"What is it?"

"Aithris?" June whispered, barely audible.

Roman nodded.

"It's not possible," Michael frowned.

"Can someone tell us what the fuck is going on?" Ethan demanded.

Roman took a step back. "There is dark magic in our world, spoken of mostly in legends and folklore. One myth in particular spoke of these creatures created with dark magic strictly forbidden in Ankala."

"But what *are* they? Why do they all look the same? Why do they wear his face?" I asked, eyes still wide with horror.

"Aithris, a word from our old language translates literally to *imitation* from nature, from life." He swallowed. "I'm unsure on the facts, until now I had believed there was no truth to the myth, but the evidence lies before us."

He rubbed a hand over his face as he continued. "The myths speak of these creatures, born from the near death of a

A Lotus in the Dark

being, barely holding onto their last thread of life, they rise from bone, blood and flesh into these creatures, they are not mortal or Fae they are soulless, lifeless beings, they have no conscious or morality. They live to serve their creator."

I swallowed. "The creator being the one near death?"

He nodded. "Indeed."

"So, they are all imitations of their creators... their *Alphas*?"

The blood drained from Roman's face as his eyes lifted to mine.

"They are controlled by their Alphas who, thanks to this world's technology, are controlled by the King," Roman confirmed.

"So, let me get this straight," Ivy questioned. "The President, or the King, has been shipping off Imperium operatives to turn them into Alphas, from which he has created, and is likely *still* creating, a literal army of thousands of these creatures, all under his command, to take back his throne and pretty much slaughter an entire land in the process?"

Roman nodded. "That pretty much sums it up."

I crouched to the ground, my head in my hands.

We were royally fucked.

-CHAPTER THIRTY NINE-

We had decided to stay in the safety of the underground tunnels until morning. The King would not want to draw too much unwanted attention, so we would make our way to Imperium in broad day light, hidden in plain sight.

We'd walked down a little and sat down around the corner, where the disturbing creatures were out of sight. *Aithris,* as Roman had called them. I suppressed a shiver at the thought.

Ethan and Michael sat with their backs against the wall on one side, Ivy and I sat on the opposite side, our own backs resting against the cold, uneven walls. It was safe to say we would not be getting any rest.

June and Roman pulled out a couple bottles of water and energy bars from their rucksacks and handed them around the group. I gratefully wolfed down the bar and gulped half the water before handing it to Ivy. I couldn't even remember the last time I'd eaten.

Roman and June sat down next to the other two males, his hand rested comfortably on her knee.

Ivy shifted as though she too noticed the familiarity of the touch.

"So, how long have you two been together?" Ivy asked. It wasn't a confrontational question, just curious.

"A few years," June replied cautiously, as though afraid to start an argument. "It was towards the beginning of the

A Lotus in the Dark

Rebellion, I was on my way back from Haven one evening when I was caught by '*The Ambassador*'." Her lips twitched a little at this. "I guess I just... took a leap of faith, and I told him everything, remembering who he was before we were dragged into this world."

"I was so relieved," Roman cut in. "I'd been playing the King's faithful second for *so* long, gathering valuable information but with nobody to tell. I was unsure who I could trust or how long I could continue in this world, with no hope or reason to..." He paused and swallowed, then squeezed June's knee and his bright eyes looked down at her, shining with adoration. "Alessandra gave me hope, gave me a reason to continue. We decided it was best I stayed under the original pretence, passing along as much information as I could."

Ivy had flinched at her mother's real name and was silent for a few moments. "I always wondered how you knew everything," she said to her mother, her tone was light. "Thought you were just a damn good spy."

"I am," June replied with a slight smirk. "But having information straight from the source definitely helped."

"I wish you could have told us sooner about everything," Ivy said softly. "It feels like such a huge betrayal, being lied to our whole lives."

June opened her mouth to reply but Ivy held her hand up to stop her and continued, "But, if you say you couldn't tell us, *truly* could not tell us, then I believe you. I trust that you acted in our best interest."

"We did," June said quickly, her eyes shining. "We did all we could. There are complicated rules to the curse, we were unable to tell you until the right moment."

"And you can't tell us what that moment was?" I asked.

"Not yet," she replied. "But we will be able to... soon."

I nodded and Ivy did the same next to me, offering her mother a small smile.

June released a wobbly breath as she smiled back. Roman pressed a kiss into the top of her head and I couldn't help but look at Ethan then.

My heart stilled when I realised his eyes were already on me. I looked away; we would have a proper conversation in private.

Ivy nudged me and whispered softly. "We don't know what the next day may hold, this is not the time to hold grudges."

"You're just feeling all sentimental because you nearly died," I shot back, and she stiffened.

"Sorry," I said quickly. "The joke didn't land."

She snorted. "It's fine, you're right though. I realised how precious life is, how important the people we love are. What's the point in any of this if we don't have the people we love by our sides at the end of it all?"

I swallowed. She was right.

"I need to stretch my legs," I said, pushing myself up. I looked to Ethan. "Join me?"

His eyes shone as he nodded and stood up next to me. We walked down the tunnel a while until it curved, and we were away from Ivy's listening ears and June's watchful eyes.

"I'm sorry," Ethan said, his voice rough.

I carried on walking, but he stopped and reached out, lightly gripping my wrist and turning me towards him. I lifted my gaze to his and tried not to melt at the sight of his molten amber eyes on me.

"You left," I said. *You left me.*

"Barely," he replied. "I swear, I only made it to the docks, and I was already on my way back when shit kicked off. I guess I just needed to clear my mind."

A Lotus in the Dark

I sighed. "I suppose I can understand that, considering the whole, learning we're inhuman beings from another world thing."

His lips twitched. "It was a lot to take in, I know I didn't handle it well. We..." He sighed. "We've never been able to express any sort of emotion, we take everything in our stride, we've killed without so much as flinching and now I can feel *everything*."

"It takes a lot of getting used to," I replied softly.

"I don't know how you do it." He shook his head. "I don't know how you do what we do, and how you've learnt what we have, without crumbling under the pressure of it all. Knowing and *feeling* the horrors of it all; Ankala and Nightstone and those *creatures* without..."

"Packing my bags and running away?"

I'd meant it as a joke, but he lifted his serious eyes to mine and said, "I think you're one of the bravest people I've ever met."

I swallowed as my heart skipped a beat, but I didn't look away. "I need to know you're all in. I can't trust someone who turns their back on me the second shit gets tough."

"I didn't want to accept it, and I'm sorry I didn't see it straight away, but the way our... *powers,*" he winced at the word, "connected. I can't deny that."

He was right, hearing the words from Roman was no comparison to feeling the actual power coursing through my veins, experiencing it for myself.

Ethan swallowed and ran a hand through his hair as he took a step closer to me. I tilted my head up to meet his eyes as he towered over me.

"Before," he said, his voice low. "You said you had never in your life felt at home in this world, and I didn't get it. I've always felt a sense of home here... it wasn't until I left that I realised, that feeling of home it wasn't anything to do with this world. It was you."

I swallowed again as my breath caught. He lifted his strong hands and softly placed them either side of my face, his thumb grazed across my cheek.

"You have been by my side every step of the way, every chapter of this insane story." He leant down, his face unbearably close to mine, his breath teasing my lips. "I'm with you Aria. My home is with *you*, wherever that may be."

I sucked in a breath, unable to find the words to express the way I felt. So instead, I closed the distance between us, and I kissed him.

The kiss was soft at first, but then deepened as my hands slid up his hard chest and around his neck. His own made their way to my waist. He swiftly moved us until my back pressed against the wall, his large hands roamed over my body until they made their way up to my breasts.

I let out a breathy moan into his lips that seemed to trigger his own. His hands moved to either side of my head on the wall, his hardness pressing into me. He broke our kiss to slide his lips down the sensitive skin of my neck and I squirmed as liquid heat flooded down my body.

Caught up in the moment, my senses entirely overwhelmed, I spoke before I could think.

"I love you," I breathed.

His entire body stilled.

Shit.

He pulled back slowly, his amber eyes turned dark as they looked into mine.

It was too much too soon.

I opened my mouth, intending to tell him I was a bumbling idiot and he didn't have to return the sentiment, but he beat me to it.

A Lotus in the Dark

His throat bobbed as he looked down at me, his eyes shining as he breathed, "I love you too."

-CHAPTER FORTY-

We walked back towards the group, hand in hand, a stupid smile on my face that could not be wiped away no matter how hard I tried.

Ivy glanced our way and then down to our hands, her eyes sparkled, and her lips twitched but thankfully she only muttered a soft, *"Finally,"* before turning back to her conversation with the others.

I slid down the wall next to Ivy again, only this time Ethan sat down beside me, his warm hand settling on my thigh.

"So, you can literally command fire?" Ivy said.

Michael's jaw ticked. "Most Fae possess some level of Elementalism, but yes I am a Pyromantic."

"Elementalism?" I asked.

"It's in the name," he replied. "Elemental manipulation. Like I said, most Fae dabble in Elementalism of some kind, most have simple low-level magic, but some powerful Fae may wield a stronger version. Some may wield two... or even more, although that is rare."

"And you?" Ivy asked her mother quietly.

June rubbed her hands across her thighs. "I'm an Aeromantic predominantly, but also possess low-level Hydromantic abilities. Air and Water."

We looked to Roman expectantly. "Similarly, Aeromantic predominantly. Elementals tend to be drawn to each other,"

A Lotus in the Dark

he said as he winked down at June, and she *actually* blushed. "But also, Terramancy... Earth."

I swallowed and Ethan squeezed my thigh. It was a lot to take in, I was half afraid he would run in the opposite direction at any moment, but I had to trust him.

"What was that magic... before," I asked, thinking of the coloured fire that had whirled around us, healing Ivy. "Was that Pyromancy?"

Michael shifted and cleared his throat. "No, it wasn't."

Roman turned his head in his direction with a frown.

"Malakai, what is it?"

Michael's eyes looked towards me as though I shouldn't have said anything.

"It... it was a magic I'd not felt before," Michael answered.

I turned towards him. "Really?" I asked quietly. "I'd just assumed that was normal..."

We all shifted awkwardly, we had yet to tell June about Ivy's near-death experience.

Sensing the tension, she looked between us.

"What aren't you telling us?"

Ivy sighed and began to tell her everything, June's hand covered her mouth as she listened. I filled in the parts Ivy missed.

Roman pondered for a moment, but his hard eyes didn't move from me. I shifted under the weight of his gaze.

"Her magic," Michael continued. "It drew our own out of us, seemed to blend them and use them together."

"I couldn't reach mine..." Ethan said. "It was like I knew it was there, but there was something blocking it, perhaps the implant. Until I felt yours, it pulled mine out from under the surface."

"And then healed Ivy from near death?" Roman asked.

We all nodded.

"That is… very rare magic indeed," Roman said.

I swallowed, unsure how to feel about that.

"Why are you looking at me like that?" I snapped.

"You just… you remind me of someone."

I stiffened, there it was again, a memory flooded to the surface that I couldn't quite place. "Of who?"

"Just someone back in our world."

"Right…" I was unsure what else to say.

I frowned, chewing my thumbnail.

"We should all have our implants removed," Ivy changed the subject as though sensing my discomfort. I leant into her gratefully, although my mind was elsewhere.

Roman nodded in agreement. "In time. The Fae children in Ankala spend their entire lives being taught how to harness their powers, even before they manifest at twelve years of age, they learn to connect with them, control them."

"So, you're saying we shouldn't allow a bunch of kids to run around with uncontrolled magical powers?"

He shook his head with a slight chuckle. "There are only so many worlds we can be at war with."

Ivy nodded. "We'll have to research it properly; I'll speak to Dr Boman when we're back."

Roman and I shared a look then. *If* we made it back.

"Only a few hours until daylight," Michael cut in. "Do we have a plan?"

"I… I think I have one," I answered and looked to each of them carefully. "And I'm not sure you're going to like it."

After formulating our plan, I'd laid my head on Ethan's shoulder and closed my eyes, hoping for a couple hours rest at least, but sleep refused to come.

A Lotus in the Dark

The plan was risky. It depended on a lot of factors that may not even come into play, but my gut instinct was usually right, and it was time I started listening. The others had not been particularly fond of the plan, but they'd come around.

We'd decided, most importantly, we needed to get back to Imperium. Firstly, we needed to get hold of the King's technology that allowed him to turn Operatives into Alphas under his control, and subsequently creating an army of Aithris.

Secondly, Roman and June were certain Imperium was built on a pocket of power and believed the King had built Imperium there for that exact reason and had somehow managed to open a Narthex back to Ankala.

We needed to get back, all of us.

We all needed to get back to our world and then we would go from there. The children would be reunited with their families, we'd all be returned to our home world and then we could face the bigger issue.

We'd packed up our few belongings and headed on foot through the woods and into the town by the docks. We were safer in broad daylight with the public swarming around us, out of the reach of the King and his guards.

We walked to a phone box, I was relieved to find it still in use. It was covered in graffiti and stank of piss, but it worked. I dialled the number I'd memorised and set the first step of the plan in motion.

We made our way to our destination on foot and a couple of hours later I was in position and waiting where we'd agreed.

I bounced back and forth between my feet, rubbing my sweaty palms on the backs of my thighs as I looked around. It was an old, abandoned building on the edge of the forest, it looked like it was used to store equipment of some sort but clearly hadn't been used for a long time, as evidenced by the cobwebs and moss climbing up the walls.

I blew out a breath, unable to stand still.

What if I'd been wrong about this?

Before I had time to dwell on that too much a voice came from behind the building.

"There you are," James beamed at me, his piercing eyes as bright blue as I'd remembered. "I was starting to think I'd never hear from you again."

I forced a smile. "I know, I'm sorry. I can't even begin to explain the madness that has consumed my life over the last few months."

"That's alright, I understand," he nodded. "I assume you still cannot tell me the details?"

I shook my head. "I'm afraid not. I'm sorry to jump straight in but time is not on my side."

He gestured at me to continue, so I took a deep breath.

"I was hoping your offer was still open? There's a group of us, we could really use a place to gather ourselves and form a plan."

He studied my face for a few moments too long and my palms began to sweat again.

His lips turned into a small smile. "I said I'd be on hand if you needed me, the offer is of course still open. Where have you been staying?"

"Thank you," I breathed, ignoring his question. He took a step towards me, and I forced myself to stay rooted in my spot.

"How big is your group?" he asked.

"I'll tell you everything I can when we're in safety," I answered looking around. "There are ears everywhere."

"I'm only trying to protect you, Aria."

My heart thudded in my chest.

A Lotus in the Dark

Now I did take a slow step back. My eyes slowly lifted to his.

"I never told you my real name."

His eyes darkened and his lips twisted into a cold smile.

"I tire of this game."

He flicked his hand, and in the same way it had for June and Roman, the enchantment dropped to reveal his true form.

He was clearly Fae, his ears turned slightly pointed as did his canines, his blue eyes swirled with power. The power that emanated from him was almost overwhelming and I took another step backwards.

"King Vidon," I breathed, my voice barely audible.

His eyes flashed with surprise for barely a second.

"You know everything then. I shouldn't be surprised that weasel turned on me, I never fully trusted him," he sneered. "Always questioning my methods, worrying about the welfare of the children." His lips turned up in disgust.

"Why?" I asked, I tried to take another step back when he raised an eyebrow and flicked his hand again and his power shot towards me.

Green vines burst from the ground and wrapped their way around my ankles, weaving their way up my body until they pinned my arms to my sides. I wriggled but the vines only squeezed tighter as the King's Earth magic held me in place.

"You'd learned too much," the King explained. "I knew you'd be useful to us, you'd make the perfect Alpha, but then that idiot gave you the wrong dose and erased all of your memories so, I took the opportunity. It was easy to infiltrate the police, with powers like mine the mortal brain is easily manipulated, as was yours. I managed to fabricate some memories, so you'd believe you genuinely recognised me. I thought I'd try to get close to you, in hope you'd lead me straight to the rebels or at least divulge some useful information. You went silent on me all these months after returning, I was beginning to think my attempt had failed, but here we are."

He waved his hand again and branches crunched behind me. I spun my head to see a group of his masked guards surrounding us. Not guards... Aithris.

"Why do any of this? Why build an army in Ankala?" I asked. "You are already powerful in this world."

He sneered and stepped towards me. "You think I want to rule in a world of *mortals*?" He spat the word as if it disgusted him. "I deserve to take my place in my world, to rule over those who deserve to be ruled by *me*."

He stepped towards me again and towered over me. I instinctively tried to back away, but his magic tightened.

"How do you have your powers back?" I asked, attempting to distract him.

He tipped his head sideways. "So, they have not told you everything then."

I cringed as he leaned forward until his face was only an inch from mine and then he... *sniffed*. He closed his eyes and inhaled a long deep breath.

"Could you take your perversions elsewhere, you creep," I snapped.

His eyes shot open.

"I can feel it inside you, you know. Raw magic." He smirked. "You could rule beside me with such power."

My lips curled up in disgust. "I would die before serving you."

"We'll call that Plan B," he said. His tongue traced his bottom lip and nausea swirled inside my belly as he inhaled again. "Yes, I underestimated you it seems."

Enough.

"I'd hoped you would," I smiled.

A Lotus in the Dark

And with that, solid thuds sounded around us as arrows and knives simultaneously flew through the air and pierced the throats of the Aithris around us. They dropped to the ground and rage simmered in the King's eyes as Roman stepped through the trees with June and Michael at his side, Ethan and Ivy close behind.

There had been something niggling in the back of my brain for a while, something bothering me. The feeling only worsened in the tunnels, the way Roman had spoken of the King.

"Pure curiosity, Vidon," I smirked.

I quickly reached into my temple of power. It came far easier than last time; my blue flames swirled around me and snapped his vines in seconds. I stepped forwards this time towards him, freed from his grip as the others around me raised their weapons.

King Vidon simply tipped his head back and laughed.

"You fools."

He swiftly lifted both hands and before we could react, shadows swirled around us, enveloping us into complete darkness. I instinctively reached for Ethan and Ivy as the world seemed to shift beneath our feet. My head swirled with the sensation as my body was thrown backwards.

A second later the darkness lifted and my mouth dropped open.

Shit.

It would seem we had entirely underestimated the King.

-CHAPTER FORTY-ONE-

We had somehow been transported back to Imperium.

King Vidon stood before us, with Commanders Kane and Addison at his side. Shane stood to the side of the room with a group of Aithris at his side. I cringed at the creatures as I realised they did not wear masks, and yet all wore the same face. One I couldn't place.

We were down in his chambers, although we were in a room I didn't recognise, I knew from the smell of stale blood that's where we were.

I looked down to see my hands and ankles restrained by fire similar to my own power, only the flames that licked my wrists were onyx black. They didn't burn, only held me in place as they swirled up my arms.

My heart dropped as I looked around to find the others in the same position, struggling against their own restraints. I reached into my mind for my power only to find it completely out of reach. Panic built in my chest as I found the entrance to the temple blocked by a raging wall of black flames.

I met Vidon's eyes and lifted my chin, refusing to show even a hint of fear. I realised the three of them stood in front of a ceramic basin, exactly like the one that held the power inside my mind temple.

A Lotus in the Dark

Behind the basin, two thick golden sceptres protruded from the ground, each with a ruby atop and between the two the air seemed to... *shift*.

June sucked in a sharp breath.

Vidon smirked. "Yes, as I had no doubt you would figure out, I have managed to open a Narthex to Ankala, and here it is, in all its glory." He gestured behind him. "Although it cannot remain open for long periods of time, but that will not be an issue."

"How?" I gasped.

Vidon turned back towards us; his blue eyes darkened.

"While my loyal council members have turned their backs on me, it seems they have not been entirely truthful with you either."

Roman hung his head forwards as June breathed, "Please, don't do this."

Vidon turned his lips up in disgust at June's plea.

"My council staged a coup, unjustly stripped me of my crown and banished me to this world with Ancient Magic. They knew some of the rules, Ancient Magic comes with a price thus per each curse they would have to grant me one request."

"We know this already," I said, sweat forming on my brow. "You committed the same fate to half of your council members and the people of Ankala were forced to sacrifice ten Fae newborns to you each year."

The King looked to me, and I swallowed. "If you would like to know the whole story, I have to start from the beginning, or perhaps I should just kill you all now and get it over with."

I kept my mouth shut.

"Indeed, of my council I kept two of my most faithful and three of the most powerful." He took a couple of steps forwards until he stood before June. "There was one considerably important stipulation the council were blissfully unaware of, although I believe you've figured it out?"

She didn't say a word, so he continued. "Ancient Magic stipulates, any curse cast against a reigning monarch, will be broken when their rightful heir comes of age, which in our world is twenty-five."

June raised her eyes to Vidon, swallowing hard.

Then, she pulled back and spat in his face.

I blinked in utter shock, gasping as he pulled his hand back and slapped her hard across her cheek.

"Get away from her!" Ivy seethed.

"Oh yes," Vidon gripped her chin, leaning into her face. "You've been keeping one dirty little secret from me, haven't you?"

"Mum?" Ivy's voice was pleading. "What is going on?"

The King turned to Ivy now. His dark features roamed over her face. "I suppose it's time we were formally introduced, since your mother has kept you from me all of these years."

The blood drained from my body as his icy gaze washed over Ivy. Her eyes narrowed and she began to struggle against the restraints.

"Hello," he purred. "Daughter."

My heart stopped.

Ivy's knees buckled but Vidon's power whipped around her legs and locked her upright.

"You're lying," Ivy spat.

Vidon could *not* be Ivy's father.

He shook his head, his eyes flicked back to June. "I must admit, I lost control of my own desire, and I took something that was not offered to me." His lips spread into a sickening smile. "Although that's not to say it wasn't enjoyable."

A Lotus in the Dark

June looked as though she was about to throw up.

"I will kill you for that alone," Roman growled but Vidon ignored him.

He once again looked back to Ivy. "Of course, I knew your mother was with child, but as soon as I scented a female, quite frankly I couldn't care less. You see, in our world only a male can become reigning Monarch. Only a *male* could be classed as a rightful heir to the throne."

The Narthex behind him suddenly sputtered, the spectres shook slightly, and the lights around the room flickered.

I swallowed, sharing a look with Ethan.

Vidon stepped back a few paces, addressing the group.

"So, imagine my surprise, when on our daughters 25th birthday, my powers suddenly flickered back into their rightful place."

"Please," June breathed.

"I did always wonder why your stomach swelled so largely; I admit I never paid close enough attention once I caught trace of the female scent. It would seem it was far stronger than that of her brother's."

June let out a small sob and Roman reached for her, but black flames held him back.

The rest of us stared with wide eyes.

"Aha, we're all catching on," King Vidon laughed. "*Twins*! A glorious rarity in our world but possible, of course, with blood as strong as mine."

And then, he stepped in front of Ethan.

My hands began to shake as the colour drained from Ethan's face.

"A shame, for you to have been in the dark this whole time, as I was. It could have all been so different." Vidon shook his head. "Nevertheless, now we stand in the presence of a future king."

He placed his hand on Ethan's shoulder. "My son. The Crown Prince of Ankala."

-CHAPTER FORTY-TWO-

Ethan backed away from his father as much as his restraints would allow, fury blazed in his amber eyes.

"Fuck you," he growled.

My head was spinning.

Not only from the insane revelations, from learning my best friend and my partner were *twins* and heirs of the evil King standing before us.

No, my head spun as I worked to strike while the King had been talking, distracted by his divulgence.

This whole Rebellion started because the King could not understand one thing.

Our light was stronger than any darkness he tried to control us with. Our love for each other, our connection to each other, was something he would never comprehend.

I thought back to what Ethan and Michael had said back in the tunnels. My magic had merged with theirs; it had brought Ethan's out when even he could not reach his own.

So, I imagined that power temple in my mind and carefully moved towards the steps. I approached the blazing wall of onyx flames, but I didn't try to fight them.

I stepped right into them, and I consumed them.

Taking them as my own.

I was unsure how I did it, perhaps my magic was different, but the black flames merged with mine the way my powers had merged with Michael and Ethan's.

In my temple, flames of black and blue swirled around me as the King had kept talking.

I had no idea if it would work, but slowly, I mentally reached my magic out towards Ethan's, as though extending a hand and knocking on his front door.

I felt it, a moment of shock, before he let me in.

His own green flames merged with mine and together, we reached out to Michael as he had already experienced this before.

Again, a moment of shock before he too let us in, and his orange flames joined ours in a multicoloured spectrum.

Carefully, the three of us reached out to Roman.

I saw him stiffen and his nostrils flared as his gaze shot towards me.

I looked back into his eyes.

Trust me.

He swallowed, and then easily his own red flames joined the spectrum in my mind.

My entire body shook with power, as it did back at Haven.

The Narthex shuddered and the lights flickered.

I had to release it; I couldn't take any more. I couldn't bear to reach out to June and Ivy, although they may have been too distraught at this point anyway.

I barely even registered the King's words.

"My son. The Crown Prince of Ankala."

I exploded.

Power exploded out of me, my own mixed with the others. Our multicoloured flames whirled around the room, slicing into the restraints and somehow downing the few Aithris around us.

A Lotus in the Dark

I heaved deep breaths as the power threatened to consume me, it wouldn't stop. *I* couldn't stop.

My power surged as it reached the Narthex, it merged with the strange power between the two spectres and the entire room shuddered.

"*Stop!*" Vidon's voice boomed.

But I couldn't, the flames continued to flow out from every pore of my body. The room shuddered again, this time so violently we were all knocked from our feet.

Then I heard Ethan's voice.

"Aria," he said urgently. "Aria, that's enough."

He'd only had to say my name, the power in me subsided and the others jumped into action as Ethan steadied me. Kane and Addison launched themselves towards June and Roman. Shane approached Michael.

My chest threatened to burst as I noticed Ivy stood in shock, unmoving.

King Vidon had retreated towards the Narthex as it flickered.

The floor beneath us continued to vibrate, booming as a large fissure suddenly opened directly beneath the Narthex and split towards us. We jumped backwards and I gawked down into the gaping crevice that seemed to lead to nowhere but *exuded* raw power.

This was the pocket of power.

"You *fool*, do you realise what you have done!?" Vidon seethed. "There is only one pocket in this world! Only one way back to Ankala, I will not let you destroy it. I *will* take my place at King."

He retreated again towards the Narthex, towards the giant fissure in the floor where the air seemed to shift.

"We can't let him get back to Ankala, knowing what he will do to all those people," I gasped to Ethan. "I couldn't live with myself."

"We won't let him," he said.

Certain I was not going to fall, he let go of me and began to stride towards Vidon.

I rallied my strength and made to follow him when he lifted his hands, the ground shuddered once more as if his magic targeted the weakest spots.

I turned my head towards June's scream.

Kane held her above the crevice in the floor, his hand wrapped around her throat.

I reached for my power to find Vidon's black flames overpowering mine once again.

I did not have the strength or the element of surprise on my side this time as I failed to reach my powers.

"You gave him his heir," Kane snarled down at her. "He has no use for you anymore."

And he let go.

Time appeared to slow down as June fell and I ran and launched myself towards her. I heard Ethan scream my name as my hand grasped around June's wrist as my other hand somehow managed to grip onto the edge of the crevice. My shoulder screamed in pain as it bore June's weight with my own as we slammed into the side of the earth.

I risked a glance downwards, into the black endless abyss below. My eyes shot back to June's.

"Don't let go," I gritted my teeth as I tried to pull her upwards towards me. Her feet scrambled to find a grip on the loose earth as it crumbled around us, but finally she managed to wedge herself into place and throw a hand up towards the surface.

A Lotus in the Dark

I released a breath as her weight was lifted from mine and we let go of each other's slick hands and attempted to lift ourselves up. Kane's hard eyes suddenly appeared over us.

I yelled as he stomped down on my fingers, but I couldn't let go. I reached for my power but again found nothing but dark flames as Vidon's power overwhelmed mine.

Kane smirked as he lifted his other foot, prepared to slam it down into my other hand, when Ivy threw herself at him. He went down with a thud as they rolled unnervingly close to Vidon and the Narthex.

I managed to heave myself upwards, glancing around to see Roman engaged in combat with Addison, Michael with Shane.

Ethan was still approaching Vidon, but his eyes were on me, wide with panic.

"I'm okay!" I yelled, pulling myself fully up and onto my stomach. I began to reach down to pull June up when the ground began to shudder again.

I lifted my head to see Vidon, his dark eyes leered towards us as his lips turned into a snarl. "He's right, I have no use for *any* of you."

His hands lifted again, and the ground began to shudder once more. My grip on June slipped as the fissure began to open, the ground crumbled beneath us, threatening to swallow us whole. I grappled for something to cling on to, the rough ground tore my palms to shreds as I skidded to a halt.

I lifted my eyes to Ethan's, expecting to see fear but all I saw was sheer determination.

That terrified me even more.

"I've said it once, and I should have said it sooner Aria, but I love you," he yelled towards us. I began to slip as the ground shuddered violently. "There is nothing more important to me in this world than you."

"Ethan, stop," I called back. "Whatever you are about to do—"

"I said it before," he cut me off. "You are my home. No matter what world we are in, no matter where we are, my home is with you, and we *will* find home again."

He turned towards the King, and he ran.

"*NO!*" I screamed as Ethan hurtled towards Vidon.

My heart shattered as he collided with him at full force, throwing them both straight through the Narthex.

The second they vanished the ground stood still, and I scrambled to my feet just in time to see Kane turn towards us with a sickening smug grin on his face.

My already broken heart snapped completely into two as his eyes flicked to Ivy and I foresaw his plan.

He leapt backwards, following his King through the Narthex, but not before wrapping his hand around Ivy's wrist and dragging him with her.

I ran forwards, but I was out of time.

The Narthex shuttered closed, and I fell to my knees as it disappeared into nothing, the four of them with it.

-CHAPTER FORTY-THREE-

A shocked silence washed over the entire space before June's piercing screams erupted.

She fell to her knees beside me and wept after her children. Tears streamed down my own face.

I was unsure what had happened to Addison and Shane, I couldn't bring myself to move to check, but I felt Roman wrap June up into his arms beside me.

Michael's hands rested upon my shoulders as he looked numbly towards the space where they had vanished.

"You should have told us everything," I breathed.

I whirled towards June and Roman. "We *never* would have risked coming here if we had known the truth!"

Roman let go of June and turned towards me. "We couldn't tell you–" he began but rage consumed me.

"I don't give a *fuck*," I yelled, I shoved my hands against his chest, forcing him backwards. "This is on you *both*!"

Michael grabbed my arm, I spun towards him to shove him away, but his hard eyes were looking towards Roman.

"She's right," he said, his jaw tensing. "If we had known the whole truth, we would have approached the situation differently."

June sniffed but I couldn't find the sympathy to care.

"What now?" I croaked.

"Jackson sent a message not long ago," Michael answered. "Imperium has been cleared out, not a soul remains apart from us."

"So, he beat us to it." Roman shook his head. "He bested us in every sense. He managed to take the whole of Imperium with him to join his army in Ankala, along with his powers and his two heirs." He ran a hand down his face. "It won't be long until he makes his move."

I wouldn't accept that.

"Not the whole of Imperium," I raised my eyes to his and then turned to Michael. "Call Jackson, tell them to turn around and make their way back here."

He looked at me for a second before he nodded.

Without Vidon and his guards, Imperium was the best place for us all to be. Not only was it fully equipped and prepared for the ranged calibre of people in our group, but it was our best shot at returning to Ankala.

"Some power may remain here; we might be able to open a Narthex again," I said. "The labs are here too, all Vidon's technology, his experiments. He may have left something behind that could help us."

The three of them nodded. June's shoulders still shook as she looked towards the space where she last saw her children.

My eyes burned, and I swallowed as my throat tightened. Ethan had been raised at Imperium with the intention of becoming nothing but a remorseless human weapon.

Yet, without a second thought, he had opened himself up to the very thing that had terrified him.

He had sacrificed himself to save all of us.

Granted, he took Ivy with him, but that had not been his intention and I would not stop until I found them both again.

I took a trembling breath. The light inside me, the power swirling through me, it was still there. I'd expected it to extinguish the second Ethan and Ivy were lost to me, instead it burned even brighter, fuelled with grief and rage and... *hope*.

"Then what?" Michael asked.

My eyes slipped to his.

"Then we prepare for war."

Epilogue

Ethan

I awoke in a dungeon of some kind. It was cold and stank of sweat and piss. I shifted uncomfortably, the shackles around my wrists and ankles dug painfully into my skin.

I exhaled harshly. The last thing I remembered before I woke was Aria's face.

The fear in her eyes.

I didn't have a choice; I didn't have time to think before I acted. All I cared about was her in that moment, not just her, all of them. I'd had to do something, *anything* to give them a chance at survival so they could end this.

I didn't regret my actions.

Until my gaze drifted across the room.

"Suppose we shared a womb entering life," Ivy muttered dryly. "It's only fitting we share a cell as we leave it."

"What the *fuck*?" I demanded. "Is everyone here?"

"Nope, Kane felt the need to grab just me." Ivy's jaw ticked.

My... my sister's jaw ticked.

I wanted to believe it was some twisted story Vidon had concocted, but I knew deep down it was all true. He was our father and I... oh *god*.

Crown Prince. Heir to the throne.

Ivy tipped her head sideways as though following my train of thought.

"I would bow, but ya know." She jangled her shackles.

A Lotus in the Dark

I shook my head.

"I'm sorry," I muttered. "I only tried to–"

"I know." My twin looked to me. "You're a fucking idiot but I get it, and I forgive you since you likely saved my best friend and my mother."

Her words hung between us.

"Our mother," she said quietly.

"Isn't this nice?" Vidon's voice sent a chill down my spine as he stepped down into the dungeon. "Sorry we couldn't find you better accommodation on such short notice, although I suppose it won't be needed anyway."

"What's that supposed to mean?" Ivy sneered, although I noticed her throat bob as she swallowed.

"We cannot allow you to take your place as King in this world," he said, his dark eyes shifted toward me. "Unfortunately, if I stand any chance at reclaiming my crown, it all has to be done officially." He waved a hand as though it was all nonsense.

He stepped forwards, stopping beside my shackled feet and looked down at me with irreverence. Nothing in his eyes reflected the fact he was looking down at his own son.

"Thus," The King continued with a sneer. "As the Crown Prince, Ethan Reighn, has committed a list of treasons the length of my arm, he has hereby been sentenced to death."

Katie Masterman

Afterword

Firstly, I would just like to thank you for reading, as I said in the acknowledgments in the beginning, the fact that even one person has read my book does not feel real, and is a dream come true.

I read a lot of fantasy and the idea behind this book is that it is an introduction to those who may not have yet dipped their toes into the fantasy genre. You, as readers, are learning alongside the main character as she too discovers this whole new world. I hope that you enjoyed reading it as much as I have loved every moment of writing it.

This is the first part in a series, so sorry about the cliffhanger, but hopefully you will not have to wait too long for the next one, where we will delve deeper into the world of Ankala.

If you did enjoy A Lotus in the Dark, if you could please take a moment to leave a review it would be hugely appreciated, as it really helps indie authors in this extremely competitive market.

Thanks again, and on to the next one!

Printed in Great Britain
by Amazon